MEET JAKE TANNER

Born: 28.03.1985

Height: 6′1″

Weight: 190lbs/86kg/13.5 stone

Physical Description: Brown hair, close shaven beard, brown eyes, slim athletic build

Education: Upper Second Class Honours in Psychology from the University College London (UCL)

Interests: When Jake isn't protecting lives and finding those responsible for taking them, Jake enjoys motorsports — particularly F1

Family: Mother, older sister, younger brother. His father died in a car accident when Jake was fifteen

Relationship Status: Currently in a relationship with Elizabeth Tanner, and he doesn't see that changing, ever

By The Same Author

The CID Case Series

The Conspiracy

The Community

The Confession

The Cadre

The Company

The Cabal

The SO15 Files Series

The Wolf (coming 2021)

Dark Christmas (coming 2021)

The Eye (coming 2021)

St Paul's (coming 2021)

Power Station (coming soon)

School Attack (coming 2021)

Mile 17 (coming 2021)

The Wedding (coming 2021)

Arena (coming 2021)

The Terror Thriller Series

Standstill

Floor 68

The Jake Tanner Terror Thriller Series Boxset 1

(Contains Standstill & Floor 68)

THE CONFESSION

JACK **PROBYN**

CLIFF EDGE PRESS

 Published by: Cliff Edge Press, Essex.

ISBN: 978-1-912628-51-3

eBook ISBN: 978-1-912628-21-6

First Edition

Visit Jack Probyn's website at www.jackprobynbooks.com.

| PART 1 |

CHAPTER 1

POCKETS

ONE YEAR AGO

Elliot Bridger didn't think of himself as a bad man, but he was sure that others did. Almost certain of it, in fact. And what he was about to do – no, what he was being *forced* to do – would do nothing to change that perception.

Through a dense mist that had settled on the cul-de-sac, a single street lamp illuminated the one place he wanted it to: the home of the person whom he would begin to rely upon for so much.

Danika Oblak.

She'd left her house less than half an hour earlier, wearing that large, green River Island jacket she frequently chose when the weather was neither too hot nor too cold – like Goldilocks – clutching her bag close to her body as if she was afraid someone was about to leap from behind the bushes and steal it. On the balance of things, she had a greater chance of being struck by lightning than being robbed.

Bridger knew exactly where she was going and what she would do when she got there. The past few days of surveillance had taught him everything he needed to know about her movements and habits. Now all he needed to do was wait for her return. Impatiently. He had some news he wanted to share.

The wait wasn't long.

Still clutching her bag, Danika emerged from the fog and scurried across the street, twisting her neck left and right. At the sight of her, Bridger clambered out of the car, closed the door and glided across the road. Pounced on her, using the darkness to his advantage, cutting her off just as she was about to turn into her driveway.

'E-Elliot,' she said, letting out a little gasp, her eyes wide. Her pale face was tinged a slight shade of orange, making her look more ill than she probably was. 'What are – what are you doing here?'

'I've come to see you.' He smiled insidiously. Something inside him had switched. Without realising it, he'd turned into the bad man everyone perceived him to be. If he was going to go through with this, he needed to tap into the darker side of his psyche.

'What do you want?'

'A chat.' With his hand wrapped around her arm, he ushered her closer to the door. She offered no resistance.

As they reached the house, Danika plunged her hand into her bag and found her keys. The house was a mess, unlike anything he'd had the pleasure of seeing – and he'd stepped into crack dens and some other ropey establishments.

The first thing Bridger noticed was the rancid stench. As though a dog had lived there, died there, and was now a permanent member of the furniture, left to rot and decay into the floorboards. The smell clung to Bridger's throat and made him gag. Shoes were strewn across the floor carelessly. Coffee and soft drink stains soiled the wallpaper, which was beginning to peel by the ceiling and skirting. A skyscraper of post, magazines, flyers and leaflets was pushed against the wall, remnants scattered across the floor. As for the carpet, dirty. And as Bridger glanced down at it, he saw a woodlouse crawling amongst the fibres, probably running towards a cleaner hiding place. The sight of it made the skin on the back of his neck crawl.

'Bet this place is cheap,' he said, staring at the insect.

'It's a former student let,' Danika said with defiance in her voice. 'I live here because it's cheap, guv.'

Bridger came to the sudden realisation that he was still holding her and let go.

'We're outside office hours,' he said. 'You know the rule: off duty, it's Elliot. My mother gave me the name so we might as well use it. Just like she gave my brothers theirs, and your mother gave you yours.'

Danika set her bag on the floor and then kicked it behind her legs, shielding it from view. 'What do you want, Elliot? Last time was a mistake. It can never happen again.'

Bridger moved forward. It was only minuscule – a slight shift in his stance – but it was enough to intimidate Danika. She retreated closer to the front door.

'Relax. Please. I don't want to hurt you.'

'Then what do you want?'

'I told you. A chat.'

Bridger's eyes flickered to the bag on the floor, then he swooped down and reached for it. Danika attempted to defend it with her arms, but it was no use. Too deft, too strong, she was no match for him.

Once it was firmly in his grip, he hurried into the living room, ignoring Danika's protestations.

'Give it back! Elliot! Give it—'

He held his hand inches from her face. 'Quiet. Please.'

If she didn't stop shouting, the migraine would come back with a vengeance. Keeping his eyes locked on Danika's, he lowered his hand into the bag. *Time for some fishing*. At the top, he found two small bottles of vodka. Russian Standard. Thirty-eight per cent solution. Enough to put her to sleep for the rest of the night, despite her Eastern European heritage. Then he sifted through the rest of Danika's belongings. A purse. Lipstick. Pack of tissues. Pen. A bag of make-up. Until—

There you are.

He removed what he was looking for and held it aloft.

'How did you...?' Danika said, her voice clipped.

'Interesting,' Bridger said as he inspected the small bag of marijuana in his hand. 'Elijah's a good kid, but he shouldn't be giving out quantities like this. From what I hear, he's spicing this shit up with loads of other stuff as well. Probably helps the value of it go down, am I right?'

Danika rubbed her forearms. 'What are you talking about?'

'Is it just the weed you bought today or is there a bit of MDMA in there too? Or is that only for Wednesdays?'

Danika's face turned pale and she looked faint.

'Bit of a risky thing to be doing, what with these random drug checks in place,' he jabbed.

'Elliot, please. You can't tell any—'

'I won't. You know why?'

Danika shook her head.

'Because I've got you in my pocket. And when I've got you in my pocket, it's very difficult for you to get out again. Understand?'

Danika dipped her head. Tormenting her, teasing her, making her regret the last two months of drug abuse gave him some sort of bizarre kick. He could only imagine how much sweeter it would have felt if he were a straight copper, getting rid of the dirty brass from the force and burning it down to the ground.

'I need you to do something for me. Reckon you can handle it?'

'It depends… It… It depends what it is.'

Bridger held a finger in the air, silencing Danika immediately. 'Maybe you didn't understand properly. When you're in my pocket, you will do *anything* I tell you to. It was a rhetorical question. And now that I know how much you rely on these little goodies, I know it's going to be very easy for you to follow orders. Think of your children, your husband.'

'Please,' Danika said, 'I said that night was a mistake.'

Shaking his head, Bridger replied, 'I'm not talking about that night. I'm talking about something else.'

'What?'

Bridger dropped the handbag to the floor and pocketed the weed. 'I need you to help me. I need you to get Michael and Danny Cipriano out of remand and into the witness protection scheme.'

CHAPTER 2

PLANS

PRESENT DAY

'Coffee?'

Jake looked up from his desk to find DCI Liam Greene, the man in charge of the Major Investigation Team here in Bow Green, Stratford, standing over his shoulder. Behind him were DS Drew Richmond and DC Pete Garrison, trying to find support for the black bags dangling under their eyes.

'No, ta,' Jake replied. 'Not today.'

'Sure?'

Jake nodded and returned his attention to work. As soon as Liam, Drew and Garrison exited the office, the room fell silent, save for the therapeutic and soothing sounds of the other members of the team tapping away on their keyboards. Jake enjoyed indulging himself in ambient noise. It helped him relax, focus. And it soothed him, like the world was in constant motion, and any pause or blockage was cataclysmic. Throughout his life, people had judged him wrongly for it, but he didn't care. He wanted the world to continue moving.

He leant back in his chair and drummed his fingers on the table. In the past few days their workload had been sparse – they'd just cracked a minor case involving an attempted rape – and now they were filling in the mandatory paperwork. The part of the job that Jake despised the most. The number of forms he needed to fill out were unnecessarily long, laborious and repetitive. It often made him want to return to his life as a bobby on the beat, back when he'd been actively doing things on the streets rather than behind a desk. But then he thought how there had been more aspects of it that he'd hated than he'd enjoyed, and how he wanted to move into the big leagues with the MIT and Liam. This was a career – *his* career – and he was willing to do anything to further it.

After less than five minutes of brief peace, Liam, Drew and Garrison returned. In each of Liam's hands, he held a cup of coffee.

'Here,' he called across to Jake. 'This one's for you. Americano's your poison, right?'

'What?'

'Americano. I got you one.'

'Why?' Jake said, getting his back up. 'But I didn't… You didn't have to.'

Liam set the cup on Jake's desk. 'But today's a special day. Y'know why? We've got some celebrating to do!'

'Celebrating for what?'

Before Liam was able to respond, a chorus of cheers and a round of applause erupted in the office. Everyone in the team – the civilian staff, the detective constables, the detective sergeants – was standing on their feet with party poppers in their hands. To Jake's left, coming from the kitchen, was Lindsay Gray, the civilian facilities manager for Bow Green station, who spent the majority of her waking hours in the building making sure that everything was working as it should. In her hands, she held a chocolate cake iced with the word congratulations.

Jake's mind raced. What was happening? Practical joke or something a lot nicer?

'Well done, buddy.' Liam slapped Jake on the back jovially, breaking him from his reverie. 'Still haven't worked it out?'

Jake shook his head as he stared at the cake nearing him, the candles and sparkler atop it burning furiously.

Liam bent down by his side and shouted in his ear amidst the noise of the room: 'I pulled in a couple of favours and put in a few good words about you. You're officially a detective!'

Another chorus of cheers echoed around the room. And then, as soon as Lindsay set the cake on the table, Jake was assaulted by playful slaps and digs in his ribs and back. Mostly coming from Drew and Garrison, but with a few rogue hits from the remaining members of the team.

After a few long, hard, challenging – yet equally rewarding and exciting – years, Jake had done it. He'd become a detective, clearing the first hurdle in his career. From his early days with the team in Croydon to his brief stint with Surrey Police – where he'd apprehended one of the country's most organised crime groups and sent them to prison – to his new home in Bow Green, it had been an exciting time. And, for a while, Jake was speechless. His body was surging with pride, an emotion he'd last experienced when Ellie had been born six months before – though it was beginning to feel like six years.

'Wow,' he said after the commotion had died down and everyone had returned to their seats. 'I… I… I don't know what to say.'

'So long as you don't use the fucking J word, you'll be all right,' Garrison yelled, cupping his hands over his mouth.

Jake flashed a smile.

'It helps when you have friends in high places,' Liam said, giving Jake a wink.

'I'm grateful, guv.'

'Now we can actually call you a detective!' Drew said from his desk, which was situated beside Jake's on the other side of a narrow aisle.

'But you did anyway.'

Sniggering, sniffing hard, then wiping his nose with the back of his hand, Drew replied, 'We also called you a lot of other things when you weren't around.'

The room burst into laughter. Drew was regularly responsible for the majority of the laughs in the office. He saw himself as a bit of an office clown, though many people found that to be true about him in a more general sense too, Jake included. Whereas Garrison was the complete opposite. Silent, reserved, methodical. Though when it came to ripping into Drew, he was always the first on the scene.

'Ignore him,' Liam said, silencing Drew – and the laughter – with a wave of his hand. 'He's just being a dick.'

He placed a hand on Jake's shoulder and squeezed. 'We're proud of you, kid. All of us. When I took you under my wing, I knew you were going to be a good egg. And what did you turn out to be?'

'A good egg?'

‘Precisely. What’re you doing this evening?’ Liam asked, but he gave Jake no time to respond. ‘Cancel your plans – the rest of us have – because we’re going to the pub to celebrate. All of us.’ He pointed at Garrison. ‘Even old soppy bollocks McVitie’s over there. Assuming his pacemaker holds out.’

CHAPTER 3

HOPES AND DREAMS

The Head of the House was busy for a Tuesday night. Knots of drunk punters occupied the chairs and booths that ran along the longest wall to Jake's left, while smaller groups stood swaying from side to side as alcohol raced through their bloodstreams, craning their necks towards the television screens that hung from the wall. Football. As ever. UEFA Champions League – Tottenham versus Inter Milan, apparently. Jake hadn't watched nor been to a football match in years. His father had been a physiotherapist for Chelsea FC, and after his tragic passing in a car accident when Jake was fifteen, Jake couldn't bring himself to go.

As soon as Jake and everyone from MIT and a few of the guys from Missing Persons on the floor below set foot in the pub, the atmosphere dropped until there was nothing, save for the sounds of the stadium bellowing from the TV sets. All heads turned to face them. Even though they were dressed in plain clothes – consisting of suits and ties and blazers and waistcoats – everyone in there knew who they were and what they represented.

'Don't worry, guys,' Liam called, raising his hands in the air as he advanced to the bar. 'We're not here to arrest anyone. Not unless you give us a reason to. We just wanna enjoy our pints like the rest of you.'

The bartender didn't waste any time in serving him.

'Evenin', Liam,' she said with a thick East End accent. 'What'll it be?'

'The usual for me please, Maggie. What you having, Jake?'

'Foster's please, guv.'

Liam grimaced. 'Forgot you drank that. Pint of piss for him, and I'll let the rest of these fuckwits order what they want. They don't need me holding their hands. Put it on the tab when you're done. I'll pick up the bill later. Come on, kid. Let's find ourselves a seat.'

They waited until Maggie poured their drinks and then moved around the bar into the back room. The bar was in the centre of the building, and it curved round 270 degrees, while the other ninety was occupied by a kitchen. Jake climbed a small step and found himself a seat in the most secluded part of the bar: the furthest right-hand corner. There were no television screens here, and so there were no angry and pissed punters screaming at the wall, yelling at the players, chiding them for being shit and profusely telling the screen that they could do a better job. Ten times out ten, it was evident they couldn't; otherwise they already would have.

'Sit,' Liam ordered, pulling a chair out from the table.

Jake eased himself into the one closest to him.

'Now, quickly, before all the others get here, there's something I wanted to tell you…' Liam hesitated, and then as he opened his mouth to speak again, Garrison arrived, holding a beer in his hand. The DC's stance and demeanour suggested that he'd already downed several.

'Nice little mother's meeting?' Garrison asked, slipping himself down on the seat beside Jake. Garrison was a big man – taller than he was wide – and, in the cramped confines of the booth, Jake fought for shoulder space.

'Should have brought yours along,' Liam jibed.

Garrison ignored the comment, lifted his hand, hovered and then lowered it. Jake knew them well enough to know that Garrison was contemplating giving Liam the finger. And Jake supposed it was warranted; when it wasn't Drew, Garrison was usually the next target in line for all the jokes in the office. Outside duty hours, there was no professional divide between them – they could do and say whatever they pleased.

Garrison swallowed a third of his beer in one go and set it down hard on the table. Wiping the leftovers from his mouth, he said, 'Congrats, pal. I'm proud of you. *We're* proud of you. You've really proved yourself these past couple of months. Want me to give you some advice? How old're you?'

'Twenty-five. Same age as last time you asked.'

Garrison nodded with his mouth open, his tongue searching for a piece of food in his teeth. 'Good age. Not too young, not too old. Y'see, when you get to my age, you'll start thinking about things differently—'

'How old are you?' Jake asked, realising that he'd never asked the question before.

'Fifty-eight.'

'Fifty-eight?'

'Fifty-eight. Soon I'll be at retirement age, then I'll be out of here.'

'He's already started preparing,' Liam interjected, nudging Jake's shoulder.

'Oh?'

Garrison removed his phone from his pocket and loaded a picture of a car on the screen. 'This, *soon,* will be my new baby. My *only* baby. My retirement toy. A Jaguar XKR Coupe. I'm picking her up in a coupla days' time.'

'Hope you requested that as holiday,' Jake said.

'No need. I'm going down there before work. They're opening early just for me.'

'How much did that set you back?'

'Seventy big ones.'

Jake eyed him suspiciously. 'How'd you get the money to pay for that?'

Garrison tapped the side of his nose. 'I've got a few investments in a few places. Fingers in pies and all that.'

All that.

'I'm sure it'll be a nice retirement treat for you,' Jake added.

Garrison smirked. 'I can't wait to piss off out of here. Don't get me wrong… the job has been the love of my life, but eventually, that can run out of steam at some point – and you have to find something young and exciting that's going to keep you on your toes and stop you from killing yourself. Shame I never listened to my own advice. But you… you've got your whole life ahead of you – is this what you wanna do for the rest of it?'

'Yes,' Jake replied almost instantly; it didn't require much thought. 'For as long as I physically can. We make a difference to people's lives, and nothing's gonna stop me wanting to do that.'

'I like your spirit, pal. But I'm counting the days. Just… keep your options open. I wanted to become an F1 driver back in the day. Even started training as an engineer and working my way through Mercedes. That was, until I got kicked out for sleeping with the boss's wife – the woman I now share a bed with… reluctantly. So then I joined this place instead. Every day I miss what could have been, my passion. Don't let this place make you forget about your dreams.'

The small table fell silent as Jake contemplated Garrison's words of advice. It hit him that he didn't have any big dreams or aspirations like that. He didn't even want to win the lottery or own the flashiest car. He didn't want to live in a mansion or climb a mountain. Sure, those things would have been nice, but they were materialistic, fake. He was a simple guy with simple requirements. He was happy with his job, and so long as he could continue to provide for and support his family, and give them everything they wanted – and needed – then he was content.

They were his dream.

They were his aspiration.

CHAPTER 4

PIT

They called him The Farmer. Real name, Georgiy. To colleagues, he was George. To friends… well, he didn't have them. He made it his business not to. The moniker was a homage to the meaning of his name in his native Russian, and, more figuratively, he was known for ploughing through everyone that got in his way. It was never personal; it was just his job.

Georgiy pulled the black Transit van into the London Olympic Stadium. The vast structure and surrounding area were still under construction, and looked almost complete – the sheer size of it dwarfed the van and everything in the vicinity. They were well into the early hours of the morning, and they were enveloped in darkness. A light persistent drizzle – the kind that was barely visible to the naked eye yet managed to render everything in sight soaked – descended on the city.

Georgiy killed the engine, stopping the wiper blades mid-swing and turned to his side. 'Where is she?'

Vitaly, the youngest member of the crew, and also the most inexperienced, shrugged. With a body that was almost twice the size of Georgiy's, it was difficult to understand how they were related. Distant cousins from an uncle Georgiy had never heard of, yes, but they were family nonetheless. Vitaly was a hard worker, a listener and a learner, with a lot of promise. His only shortcoming was his choice in nickname; he insisted on being called The Lion. Under no circumstances was Georgiy prepared to call him that. It was a ridiculous name, and if Vitaly wanted people to respect him, then he should let other people choose his name for him. That was the way it worked. All he needed was a stern mentor and a guiding hand to make that possible.

Georgiy twisted his body and looked into the back of the van. The backboard had been cut out, revealing the entire cabin. Situated inside were two men – one friend; one foe. The friendly's name was Nigel Clayton, dressed in a black hoodie and balaclava that bore a silhouette of a skull on the front by the mouth, standing beside sacks of gravel, sand and cement that lined the walls of the van. Meanwhile, at the back, was the foe – a figure lying on its side with its hands behind its back, face covered, wriggling and groaning.

Georgiy nodded at the figure. 'Any issue?'

'Nah, none yet,' Nigel replied in a quintessential British accent.

'Good. Where the spot?'

'Just over there.' Vitaly pointed out of the window to a large stretch of tarmac that ran around the stadium.

As Georgiy turned round to look where Vitaly had pointed, his eyes refocused. A woman, tall, slender and slight, prowled towards them like a jaguar in the night. She walked with speed and vigour – purpose. *Tatiana,* he thought wistfully.

Georgiy opened the door and hopped the short distance to the ground. 'Where you been?'

'Making sure you lot weren't followed,' Tatiana replied in almost impeccable English despite her thick Ukrainian accent. She was a polyglot, one of those intelligent people who had the enviable ability of adopting and speaking several languages. It was her biggest skillset – among many.

'Everything clear?'

'I wouldn't be here if it wasn't,' she snapped. 'And neither would you.' In the low light, her dark eyes sparkled, but he knew that, behind them, a fire of determination burnt.

Tatiana strode towards the back of the van, and he struggled to catch her. She came to an abrupt halt by the handle, unlocked the rear doors and pulled them open. The man on the floor recoiled and retreated, gasped and panted heavily, groaning excessively with fear and confusion. Tatiana pointed at the bag on his head.

'Seriously?'

Georgiy ignored the remark and grabbed the man under the arm. Heaving the body out of the van, he replied, 'Don't tell me how to do job.'

The man was heavy, like a dead weight in his arms – a dead weight that was very much alive and kicking.

But not for much longer.

Georgiy dragged the man to his feet and scanned his surroundings, studying the pockets of holes in the earth that ran around the perimeter of the stadium where work was still incomplete.

'This way,' Tatiana said, and by the time Georgiy paid attention to her, she was already heading in the opposite direction.

Vitaly and Nigel disembarked the van and were in the process of lugging the cement mixture out as Georgiy followed her, dragging the man in his arms with him. A hundred yards later, they came to a stop by a large ditch. Six feet deep, three feet wide. Beside the hole was a large concrete mixer. A long metal tube protruded from the top of the machine and was pointed at the ground beside Tatiana's feet.

Georgiy's eyes fell on the hole. 'What this supposed to be, swimming pool?'

'A garden patch. Somewhere for trees to grow. They were supposed to fill it in a couple of days ago, but the plan was scrapped, so now nobody knows what's going on with it.'

'Is it big enough?'

She turned to him. Shrugged. 'Find out for yourself.'

Georgiy tightened his grip on the man's body and ripped the piece of cloth away from his head.

As clean oxygen flooded his lungs, the man gasped and choked on his breath. It was a wheezy, raspy noise that sounded like it caused physical pain. He opened his mouth to speak, but doing so only made it worse.

'Shut it,' Georgiy said.

'Pl-Pl-Pleas—'

Georgiy shoved the body into the ditch and watched as the man tumbled in, his face catching on large rocks and pieces of dirt and gravel. He let out a little yelp, his voice carrying across the stadium walls, and for a moment Georgiy panicked – loud and abrupt noises were unsavoury dealings in this business – but then he realised there was nothing to worry about. The site was uninhabited. Nobody would be there for the next couple of hours. Which meant they had plenty of time to finish what they were there for.

Georgiy disregarded the man in the ditch and turned his attention to Vitaly and Nigel standing beside him. He gave them the nod, and they instantly began funnelling the bags of sand, gravel and cement into the mixer. Vitaly grabbed the tube and moved it closer to the edge of the hole. Behind him, the machine started, producing a low, rhythmic hum as the barrel rotated and mixed the contents together.

Georgiy jumped into the pit and grabbed the man by the neck. All hope had left his eyes.

'You have three minute until concrete mixture ready,' he said, tightening his grip. 'Which mean you have three minute to tell me all information I need hear. After that, we bury you alive. Understand?'

'Pl-Pl—' the man babbled. Tears formed in his eyes, saliva foamed at his mouth and a lump swelled in his throat.

Georgiy couldn't believe it. One of the country's most prolific and notoriously violent armed robbers – or 'blaggers', as they were called in the criminal world – was crying like a baby. It was embarrassing. Pathetic.

Georgiy punched the man across the face. 'Less than three minute now, and you want spend time *fucking* beg? Use time wisely, otherwise, you have no left.'

The man spat out a globule of blood. 'What do you want from me?'

'Who have you been talking to?'

'Nobody, I swear.'

Georgiy cracked a smile. 'Funny. My employer say otherwise.'

'I have money.'

'So do my employers.'

'Who are your employers?'

'Two minute.'

'I don't know what you're talking about – honestly.'

Georgiy shrugged. 'If that the case, we bury you anyway.'

'No!' the man's eyes widened. 'No!'

Georgiy punched him around the face again. This time his fist landed hard on a cheekbone, sending a flash of pain up and down his wrist. He ignored it.

'Who was you talking to? What was reporter's name? Simple question. Name. Tell me what you told them. That information is worth your life, no?'

Another globule of blood, this time bigger than the last, lined with pieces of gravel and dirt. The corners of the man's lips rose and he smiled, baring blood-stained teeth. 'They'll find you, you know.'

'Who?'

'My employers.'

Georgiy's skin prickled. 'What you talk about?'

'They'll find out you paid to get me out. They'll find out you brought me here. They'll find out everything. And then they'll get rid of you. Just like you're tryna do to me. We're all pawns in this fucking game. You're dispensable. Like the rest of us. And by the time you realise it, it'll be too late.'

'Who else you tell information?' Georgiy continued.

'Someone who's gonna do something about it.'

Georgiy raised his fist again. As he prepared himself to swing it down on the man's face, Vitaly called from behind.

'It's ready.'

A thin trickle of concrete dribbled from the end of the tube. Georgiy reached his arm out and grabbed it. He kneed the man in the stomach, grabbed the back of his head and then shoved the tube into his victim's mouth.

Within seconds, the stodgy mixture filled his mouth and spilled out the sides. The man choked and gagged, spitting some of the contents onto the floor and Georgiy's arm.

'That's enough!' a voice came, but he paid no attention to whomever it belonged to.

'I'll decide when is enough!'

He was the voice of authority, and he didn't mind reminding people of it. They all had a job to do, information to extract. And there was only one way they were going to get it.

Georgiy smacked the man on the back, forcing him to choke the concrete mixture onto the floor.

'Give me name!'

'Wa… Way…'

'Name! Now!'

'Wa… Wanker…'

Georgiy lost it. Gritting his teeth, he poured the concrete over the man's face, smothering him in it. The dense, coarse contents wetted his hair and quickly filled his eyes. Screams erupted from him as the salt and grit burnt them before it crept down his throat.

'Name!' Georgiy screamed.

The man shook his head violently, flinging flecks of cement onto the ground and Georgiy's legs and hands. He continued to gag. Coughing. Choking. Spitting. Spluttering. Drowning. Rapidly cutting off the circulation to his brain.

Georgiy glanced at the floor. A small pile of cement had landed beside him and was lined with blood. The mixture was destroying his victim's insides. It wouldn't be long until he was dead.

Georgiy decided to speed up the process.

He grabbed the back of the man's head and pulled down until his airways were straight. Then he held the tube over the mouth and watched as the mixture poured in as if he were filling a hot water bottle. At first, the man gagged and shook violently, but it was no use. The cement was working its way down his body and the flow was too much for him to overcome.

After a few seconds, his latest victim had drowned in cement and his own blood. His body became rigid.

For a while, the atmosphere around them froze. The only thing Georgiy could hear was the sound of his breath. Even the hubbub of London in the distance became muted and silent.

'*Eto pizdets*,' Tatiana said, her voice suspended in disbelief.

'What?' Georgiy retorted. 'We had instruction. You knew it going to happen. You knew he going to die this way.'

'Yeah, but... we didn't even get any information.'

'You saw smile on his face. He never going to give to us.'

'You don't know th—'

Georgiy turned his back on her, cutting her off. She knew better than to speak to him like that, and he was going to have to make sure she understood what her position was.

He let the body fall naturally to the bottom of the pit. It landed with a dull thud that seemed to echo around the stadium's entrance.

The London Olympic games were set to be the biggest and best ones yet. Or so the news kept reminding them. With thousands of athletes and their respective camps coming into the country, and with the whole world watching them, it was set to be a spectacle. One that they'd never forget. Soon, in just over two years, hundreds of thousands of people would be walking across this very stretch of tarmac, trampling over something they had no idea existed. It was the perfect hiding spot.

'Fill it in,' he instructed.

At once, Nigel climbed in and moved the body until he lay flat on his back, before pouring the rest of the churning cement into the pit.

'What about his clothes and his ID?' Tatiana asked.

'We took them from pocket when we picked him. They're in van.' Georgiy wiped his nose with the back of his hand.

'Do you need me anymore?'

'No. Go home. Prepare for tomorrow.'

Georgiy watched the woman wander away, the lights casting a stretched shadow across the pavements that moved in harmony with her body. He stood still until she entered a black van, similar to their own, and drove away in the opposite direction.

The sound of cement pouring into the hole distracted him.

'How long until done?'

'Five minutes,' Nigel replied.

'How long to set?' Georgiy gazed at the moisture in the air. The rain had slowed but showed no signs of stopping. 'Is cooling agent in?'

'Yes. Should set in 'bout four hours.'

Perfect timing.

'You sure?'

Nigel paused as he replied, ‘I’m an accountant, not a scientist.’

CHAPTER 5

PLAYING CATCH-UP

Jake struggled to find the keyhole. He poked and prodded at the door, hoping the weak light from the street would illuminate the hole just enough so that he knew where to guide it.

He was drunk. And it was the first time he had been in a long time. He'd only intended to stay for a few. One of those old adages, a lie that unhappy people told their partners as soon as the relationship had started to sour and stagnate. One turned into two, two into three, and then things had escalated. Everyone else in the team had bought a round. At first, he'd tried to protest – which they didn't listen to – and then, by the fourth round, he'd given up trying. Or was he too drunk? After all, they were celebrating, and if they wanted to treat him then that was exactly what they were going to do.

Somehow, without him even touching it, the door swung open, and light from the hallway fell out of the house and blinded him.

'What the fuck're you doing?' Elizabeth asked, her arms folded across her chest. A welcoming response from a loving wife. 'You'll wake the kids up.'

She stepped aside, grabbed Jake by the sleeve and hefted him over the finish line.

'How much've you had?' she whispered sternly as Jake tried to shake his shoes off… unsuccessfully.

'Only a few,' he lied. 'Ev'ry'ne kept boying r-rounds in… I din't know whatta do.'

'Say no.'

'We were cele'rating. I'm officiawwy a dete'tive.' Jake hoped the smile on his face would placate Elizabeth slightly. It didn't.

'You missed dinner. The kids were looking for you, and I even had a nice little treat prepared for you later.' Elizabeth wrapped the sides of her dressing gown tighter across her body. 'There's something you need to see as well.'

Before he could respond, Elizabeth stormed down to the other end of the hallway and into the kitchen. He wondered how she managed to walk in a straight line – and so quickly too. He'd tried it from the cab to the front door and found it a struggle, almost hugging the wet pavement outside. The walls around him spun and he felt a headache coming on; the onset of a nasty hangover rolling in, knocking on the door.

Jake slid his shoes off and shuffled down the hallway, holding onto the wall for support.

In the kitchen, Elizabeth was standing beside the centre island holding a piece of paper.

'Whassat?' Jake asked. The harsh kitchen light prompted a flare of nausea in him.

Elizabeth slammed the paper down on the worktop. 'Read it for yourself.'

As she folded her arms again, Jake caught a glimpse of the black lace bra she was wearing underneath her dressing gown. He didn't recognise it, which meant it was new. Which meant she really *had* had a surprise for him. Jake tried to approach her and wrap his arm around her small waist, but she held him at arm's length and pointed at the letter instead.

Jake glanced down at the white paper and attempted to read. The words swam on the page and merged into one block of text. Two, however, stuck out to him. important and notice. Stained in red.

'I thought you said you'd sorted it!' Elizabeth said.

Jake held a finger in the air as he tried to read, swaying as he did so.

'I… I… It shoulda bin sorted. Issa work in progress. I spoke to 'em th'other day, but—'

Elizabeth snatched the document and waved it in the air.

'We can't afford this. On top of everything else that we have going on here. Rent. Food. Tax. Internet. Water. Electricity. Nursery. The kids. It's insane, and it's stressing me out. I can't believe they ever let you do it.' Tears swelled in her eyes, puffing her cheeks.

Jake rushed over and embraced her tightly. Stroked her arms.

'Iss going t'be all right, Liz, OK? We'll sort it. I'll sort it. When have I ever let youuu d-down?'

Sniffling, she said, 'I'm worried, Jake. About the kids. About what might happen to us if we can't fix this.'

'You've got nothing to worry about, Liz, trusss me. Get yourself to bed. I'm g-going to stay up for a bit.'

Elizabeth pulled herself away from him, nodded, then air-kissed his cheek before leaving the kitchen. He waited until he heard the soft sounds of her feet on the floorboards overhead, then he poured himself a glass of water, downed it and moved over to the chair nearest the sink.

The previous year, in Jake's attempt to catch Lester Bain, a serial killer who had brutally murdered and dismembered six women he'd met through an online community, Jake had entered his debit card details onto the Dark Web. It hadn't taken long for them to be cloned and a significant amount of money to disappear from his and Elizabeth's joint account – the home of their entire savings. After some convincing, and a lot of back and forth between the banks and the Met, he'd rescued some of the money, closed the account and set up a new one. But in the time it had taken to do all that, he'd defaulted on several payments for his car insurance, rent, gas and water.

Now they were playing catch-up.

And the interest rate was rising, while the money in the Tanner bank account was constantly dwindling.

CHAPTER 6

BAD FEELINGS

A few hours later, Jake was awoken by a call from Liam, summoning him to the Olympic Stadium construction site. It was still dark outside. Feeling hungover, and without a car to drive in, he'd called Drew, who'd ventured across the city to pick him up. Much to Jake's surprise, they were the first to arrive.

They pulled up to the stadium's entrance, flashed their warrant cards to the uniformed officer stationed on the outer cordon, dressed in forensic suits and then strolled towards the stadium. Jake admired the structure in front of him. It reminded him of visiting Stamford Bridge with his brother and sister when they were younger, watching the games, searching for their father in the dugout with his medic pack by his side, ready and waiting to run on to the pitch to attend injured players. Those were the days.

It wasn't often that Jake thought about his dad, because even the tiniest image or reflection always depressed him; his father had been taken from them too soon, and there was nothing that was going to bring him back.

Jake wandered up to the inner cordon of the crime scene. There, he signed in on the attendance log, dipped beneath the tape and started towards the knot of uniformed officers standing outside a white forensic tent.

A few seconds later, they were greeted by Poojah, the forensic pathologist. She was dressed from head to toe in a white and blue oversuit. Staring at them from behind a face mask was a set of piercing jet-black eyes. Jake had always admired them; he felt like you could get lost in them forever.

'Drew…' she began. 'Jake… Congratulations, by the way. I bet you're pleased.'

'Thrilled,' Jake said, trying as hard as possible not to sound sarcastic and rude. It was the alcohol talking, making him take longer to think cohesively.

'I remember when I graduated from training. All those years ago. I was a lot slimmer—'

'So what are we dealing with, Poojah?' Drew interrupted as he started towards the tent in a concerted attempt to hurry her along.

Inside was a large perimeter about ten feet square. Within that was the beginning of a hole. The top layer of concrete had been excavated and was loaded into a pile in the corner of the tent. On the outskirts of the pit, Jake saw the remains of an outstretched left hand. The skin had been lightened by the chemicals in the cement and it looked like a giant piece of chalk.

'Site worker found it early this morning,' Poojah said, coming to a stop beside Jake.

'When?' he asked.

'About seven o'clock, I think.'

'Any idea how long it's been here?'

'Recent. It wasn't there last night apparently.'

Drew hovered around the perimeter of the hole, leant forward and peered inside.

'Cause of death?'

Out the corner of his eye, Jake saw Poojah's eyes crease as she smirked. 'Wasp sting. Allergies. Shark bite. Maybe someone hit him round the head with a kettle...'

Drew stared at her, deadpan. Clearly not in the mood for jokes. Jake had noticed that recently his morale and energy had been deteriorating. He was snapping a lot more at the smallest of things. Jake supposed he'd fallen out of love with the job. He'd heard of it happening, but he'd never imagined it would happen to another member of his team. Correction: he didn't *want* it to happen to anyone in his team. They were like a family, all of them – a dysfunctional one, to be fair – and Jake felt partly responsible for the well-being of his friends and colleagues as though they were his brothers and sisters. It was the paternal instinct in him.

'Asphyxiation would be my first guess,' Poojah continued. 'But I won't know for certain until I do the post-mortem. I'll have to examine the trachea and lungs for signs of inhalation.'

'Buried alive.' Drew shook his head in disgust. 'What a way to go. Where's the witness?'

'Witnesses. Two of them. They're talking to uniform now.'

Jake turned his head towards the tent's entrance. Over a hundred yards away in the distance was a small group of construction workers clad in their high-visibility jackets and helmets. They were laughing and cajoling one another, waiting to be spoken to by the law enforcement officers who were currently occupied with two other individuals.

As he and Drew bounded towards them, Jake removed his pocketbook and flipped to a new page. He scribbled the date and location on the top of the page and underlined it several times.

When they reached the two individuals, Drew was the first to introduce himself.

'And this is DC Tanner,' he finished. 'I understand you two were the ones who found the body. Is that right?'

Standing before them were a man and a woman. They both nodded, though at the mention of Drew's name and title, the woman's eyes had bulged, the colour rushing from her cheeks.

'Do you mind if we take you down to the station?' Drew asked, his head dancing between them rapidly. 'Somewhere more comfortable. There's a lot we'll have to get through.'

'Yeah, sure,' the man said. 'No problem.'

As the man spoke, Drew observed him, as if sizing him up for a fight.

'And you?' he asked the woman, who retreated. 'Do you have any problems with going down to the station? You're just being treated as a witness.'

'No, no, I don't have a problem. But I'd like to be questioned by this gentleman if that's all right with you?' She pointed at Jake.

For a moment, Jake felt himself blush. He didn't know why the woman had chosen him specifically, but he wasn't going to argue.

Just as the four of them headed out of the crime scene and back to the car, they crossed paths with Liam.

'All right, guv,' Drew called. 'Where's DC Garrison?'

'Delayed,' Liam replied. 'He's on his way. I'll meet you back at the station. I've got a bad feeling about this one.'

CHAPTER 7

TOMMY

This was one of the very few parts of the job that Drew truly enjoyed. The interrogation round, the interview, going toe to toe with a potential suspect with the full force of the law behind him. It made him feel powerful, and he knew that in his position of authority he had autonomy over anyone who set foot in the room with him. It didn't matter whether they were a stranger, witness, relative, friend – Drew had the ability to turn anybody. Garrison had taught him that a long time ago.

Opposite him, with his wrists resting on the arm of the chair, was Richard Maddison. Early-thirties but somehow looked ten years older. He'd removed his high-visibility jacket and was sitting in a grey T-shirt with slight dark moons hanging beneath his armpits. His hair was sun-kissed red and was showing signs of receding at the top and sides. A sandy beard had started to grow on the bottom of his face but looked as though it'd given up and he'd been too lazy to do anything about it. His skin was dirty and messy and there were scars in the crook of his arm – tiny puncture marks.

There were two plastic cups on the table. Drew grabbed one. Beads of condensation abseiled down the side of the plastic as he took a sip and exhaled deeply, letting the cool water descend his throat.

Setting the cup back on the table, he began.

'How're you doing today, Richard?'

'A little shaken up. But… other than that… good.'

'Most people would be having nightmares if they'd just seen what you saw. Must've been terrifying, seeing the hand in the ground. Run me through what happened.'

Richard took a moment to respond, licking his lips. His eyes danced between Drew and the MG11 witness statement form on the desk.

'I got to work at… it must have been about seven. I was the only one. I had some stuff I needed to do before everyone else arrived.'

Like hide a dead body, Drew thought.

Richard licked his lips again. 'I should have done it last night but I had a dinner appointment.'

'An appointment?'

'Well, no. Not an appointment. It was… like a date.'

'*Like* a date?'

'Yeah… you know.'

'How'd it go?'

Richard's brows creased. 'Fine… I don't think I'll be seeing her again though.'

Drew tutted. 'Sorry to hear that. Where was the date – what time?'

'Alinka's coffee house on Roman Road. About sevenish.'

Ah, yes. Drew knew it well. Very well. One of his favourites. His and Liam's regular haunt whenever they needed to discuss their next operation for The Cabal, or whenever they needed to discuss anything they didn't want anyone else at Bow Green hearing about. It was also the place where serial killer Lester Bain – dubbed the Stratford Ripper by the media – had found and haunted his second victim, Jessica Mann.

'What time did your date finish?' he continued.

Richard scratched the back of his head. 'About nineish, I think. Then I went home and watched TV all night.'

'All night? From nine-oh-one to six-fifty-nine the following morning?'

'Well, no, right. I was asleep for most of the night.'

'When?'

Richard shrugged. 'Same time as I usually do. 'Bout eleven, half eleven.'

Drew nodded like he had a vested interest in everything Richard Maddison was saying, but the reality of it was he couldn't give a shit. There were more important things on his mind – bigger, grander things – although he was able to derive some enjoyment and satisfaction from making the man sweat and squirm because that was an answer in itself. If Richard Maddison was innocent, he wouldn't behave that way. And it was only a matter of time until he dug himself a little deeper.

'What happened after you got to work?' Drew asked to move the conversation along.

Richard let out a long breath of air. 'The usual. Did the rounds. Same as we're told when we're first to arrive – make sure everything's in its place, machinery wise – and make sure nothing's been stolen by some yobbos down the street.'

'Does that happen often?'

'More than you'd think.'

'How did you find the hole?'

'I trod on it.'

'Did you fall in at all?'

Richard shook his head.

'So we won't find any forensic evidence on your clothes?'

Richard shook his head again, this time a little less confidently.

'What was going through your mind when you found it?'

'At first, I thought it was a hand. You know, one of those prosthetic ones—'

'The Paralympics doesn't start for a long time.'

'What? No. I… I thought it was a prop. Something out of a fancy-dress shop.'

'Halloween *was* a few weeks ago.'

'That's not what I mean,' Richard said. He was getting his back up now. Becoming defensive. His mind wouldn't be thinking clearly. He would be acting rashly, saying whatever came into his mind without thinking twice about it. And that was what interrogators like Drew aimed for. 'I thought it was a joke.'

There it was. Hook. Line. Sinker.

'You think murder's a joke?'

'That's not what I'm saying!'

'Sounds like you think someone being buried alive is a joke. Is that funny to you, Richard? Do you find that funny?'

'No, I—'

'Then what do you find funny?'

'Nothing, I—'

'Did it all get a little out of hand?'

Richard's eyes widened. 'Did what get a little out of hand?'

Drew leant forward and placed his palms face down on the table.

'Here's what I think happened. You were out with a friend, playing, chilling, catching up, maybe sucking each other off – whatever you're into. You took them to where you work and showed them the hole. Maybe you'd been drinking or getting high. One thing led to another and the other person fell in. You thought it would be funny to cover them in cement. Another thing led to another, and then, next thing you know, they've drowned in it. And then this morning, when you find the body, you become the hero, the innocent party in all this. That's what I think happened.'

Silence encompassed the room. For a long while neither of them spoke. Gradually, Drew eased himself back into his chair, studying Richard's reaction. The man looked shocked –

worse, taken aback. His skin had turned pale and his lips parted.

'You can't be… You've got to be joking? Where'd you get that from?'

'Are you saying it's true?'

'Fuck no! I just want to know where you're making this stuff up from.'

'I'm just telling you what I think happened.'

'You're wrong.'

'Then tell me what *really* happened.'

'So you can put words in my mouth again?'

'Nobody's said anything about putting words in your mouth. I'm just speculating…' Drew snapped his fingers. 'What's that saying? Speculate to… speculate to… accumulate! That's the one! Speculate to accumulate. That's what I'm doing. I'm not putting any words in anyone's mouth. So please indulge me – what happened?'

Richard sighed heavily. For a moment, Drew thought he was about to answer, about to reveal all his deadliest and darkest secrets. But when he remained silent, Drew realised he'd lost his opportunity.

That was, until, a new one arose.

Drew's eyes fell on Richard's forearms. 'You ever take any drugs, Richard?'

Richard's body tensed. 'Drugs. What? I…'

'Of the illegal variety. You ever take any?'

'No. I… Sure, I've had some in my time, but that was just to clear my head when I was going through a difficult period.'

'Needed to get rid of the demons?'

Richard looked into his eyes. 'We've all got them, haven't we?'

You bet, mate.

'What about a drink?' Drew asked. 'You like a drink?'

'Not excessively, no. But I don't understand what relevance this—'

'So you're no stranger to a pint or two, here or there?'

'What's this got to do with what I saw?' Richard shifted uncomfortably on his seat. 'I thought I was just giving you a witness statement?'

For now.

'I'll be the one asking questions, thank you.'

'You know, you're not scaring me or anything. I've been in this situation before. I know what type of things you guys do. I'm not stupid.'

'Nobody's saying you are.'

'But you're treating me as though I am. I had nothing to do with this – I'm telling you. All I know is that when I left for home yesterday, it wasn't there, and when I came in this morning, it was. Simple as that.'

Drew looked down at the witness statement in front of him. He scribbled on the page and read aloud as he wrote. 'It's as simple as that. Nothing more to it. Just that: you go home one night and there's no body buried beneath cement, and then when you come to work, there is. Nothing more to it. All a bit of a joke.' Drew shrugged. 'So… what were you doing last night? Where were you when this mystery took place?'

'At home,' Richard said. '*Asleep*.'

'Oh yeah? And no one's able to confirm that? Not even your hot date?'

Richard lowered his head.

'Nobody?' pressed Drew.

Richard remained silent.

'Nobody can corroborate your whereabouts last night? Tough living on your own, eh, for situations like this? I imagine it can be quite a nuisance.' Drew paused to take a sip of water. 'What were you doing after your date? That's a big window of opportunity unaccounted for? Enlighten me.'

At first, Richard didn't respond. He bit his lower lip, rubbed his forearm and looked around the room, avoiding Drew's gaze. Then his eyes fell on the trickle of water running down the side of his cup.

'I… I…'

'Take your time. This is a safe place. I'm here all day. I get paid for this regardless.'

'I…' Richard pulled his eyes from the cup and looked into his lap again. 'I was having… you know… a Tommy.'

Drew smirked. He made no effort to hide the smile from his lips, although he struggled to stifle the laugh that followed it.

'Of course you were,' he said, eventually having to take his mind away from it. 'How many times? One? Two? Three? So many you began to lose count?'

'No, it was just the one.'

'Well it can't have been if it lasted the whole night.'

Richard gave a long, unending sigh. 'What do you want from me? I told you I had nothing to do with it. I had my date, it didn't work out, we called it a night, so I went home. Then I watched some TV and went to bed. You're not charging me with anything, are you? So… so can I go?'

Drew paused a beat. He knew there was nothing he could do except let Richard go. It wasn't worth the hassle of unlawfully arresting him either. He'd made that mistake before and only just lived to tell the tale.

'You can go, but don't go too far,' Drew said eventually. 'We might need you at some point.

Although… be careful what you get up to when you're alone – we don't want to walk in on you having a wank.'

CHAPTER 8

GREY AREAS

Liam had a bad feeling about this. A dark premonition. Perhaps it was something in the dust-filled air, because a dead body had turned up in the middle of the Olympic Stadium, right in the centre of construction, and it wouldn't be long until the whole world found out. Or perhaps it was because the murder – and the circumstances surrounding the death – screamed of The Farmer.

Liam had only ever seen The Farmer's handiwork on two previous occasions. And both carried the same resemblance, but there had been a certain precision to them. This was different. This seemed rushed, clumsy, messy, out of character. And that was intolerable.

According to Poojah, it was going to take at least a couple of hours to excavate the body from the concrete, which meant Liam had two hours to try and allay the shitstorm that was going to come their way.

He wandered back to his car, his mind awash with thoughts, concerns and apprehensions on how best to weather the storm.

Before he could do any of that, he needed answers.

He slumped into his Volvo C30, the suspension bouncing and screeching in agony under his weight. He removed his burner phone from his pocket and spun it in his fingers, staring out at the chaos in front of him. Within a few minutes, he'd coordinated the arrival of over twenty scene of crime officers and thirty uniformed police officers, who were busy questioning witnesses and anyone in the vicinity. The day's construction had ground to a halt, and it was only a matter of time until the bloodhounds in the press and media caught a whiff of the scent of murder.

Liam scrolled through his address book and dialled. As he waited for The Cabal to answer, he prepared himself.

'Yes?' The Cabal answered.

'It's Liam.'

'Yes…'

'The Olympic Stadium. That your doing?'

'I did what needed to be done.'

'Who is it?'

'You'll find out soon enough.'

'Why won't you tell me? I'm the one who has to deal with this shit now.'

'Remember your place, Liam.'

Before he was able to respond, Liam coughed violently. He spluttered and spat into his arm. And as he pulled away, he saw his sleeve was covered in mucus and blood. The lung cancer was eating away at him more aggressively as the days passed. And the pain and nausea and tiredness that came with it were unrelenting. But, on the bright side – if it could be called that – his treatment was showing signs of fighting the disease.

'Are you up to the challenge?' The Cabal asked.

'Is that what this is?'

'I can find someone else, if necessary. Plenty of people willing to step into your position.'

'No,' Liam snapped. 'I can do it. But I should've been the first to know.'

'You know how I like throwing curveballs your way.'

'And I don't have enough to deal with at the moment?'

'I'm sure you'll prioritise correctly.'

Liam hesitated before responding. He was afraid he knew what The Cabal really meant.

'Now's the time to really test Jake Tanner's loyalty,' The Cabal said. 'It's your responsibility to get him onside. You know the consequences if not. Last chance saloon, Liam.'

The line went dead. Liam's body turned cold.

It was what he'd expected to hear. The time had finally come. For too long now he'd been protecting Jake, pussyfooting around him whenever he spoke to The Cabal, trying to do his best to ensure that no harm came to the young detective. But that wasn't possible anymore. Those days were gone. And the fact that The Cabal hadn't told him who the victim was worried Liam. It had to be a big name, someone prominent. And to be able to put a lid on it quickly, he was going to need *everyone* in agreement with one another.

Jake included.

Without allowing his mind to think on it for too long, Liam scrolled through his address book again and dialled another number.

This time it went through to voicemail. Liam remembered to follow the pattern.

After the tone, he left a message: 'Hi, I was wondering what your floral arrangements are for funerals. If you could please call me back I'd love to discuss some business with you.'

He hung up.

Within twenty seconds, the device in his hand vibrated and the screen illuminated.

'This is Floral Beauty,' came The Farmer's monotonous, heavily accented voice.

'I was wondering what flowers you do for funerals,' Liam replied. 'I'm looking for some lilies.'

There was a long pause as The Farmer absorbed his coded message. Eventually, after a long time, he spoke. 'Why you call?'

'I need to know what happened. Who the fuck did you bury, and who gave you the order?'

'Our mutual employer.'

'Why?'

'The Cabal need them disposed of. They talk too much.'

'Who?'

'Danny Cipriano.'

The words caught in Liam's throat and made the hairs on the back of his neck stand on end. In the past six months, he hadn't heard that name once, and he'd foolishly thought he could put that saga behind him – they all did, every single one of them. How wrong he'd been.

For a brief moment, he tried to process the information, understand the wider situation, evaluate the ramifications. But his mind was warped by one question, and one question alone. Why?

'He talk too much,' The Farmer replied after Liam asked him. 'He talk to someone. I don't know what about. He did not say.'

Liam opened his mouth but only air escaped.

'But we have problem,' The Farmer continued.

'What?'

'He said he have employer too. He said his employer come after us.'

Liam pinched the bridge of his nose. 'No, you idiot. It's the same one.'

'What?'

'The Cabal is both yours and Danny's employer. It's the same person. But let it be a lesson to you,' Liam explained. 'If you do anything to piss The Cabal off, or step out of line at any point, the same thing'll happen to you.'

The Farmer chuckled. 'They can try.'

Liam sighed. This was worse than he'd originally thought. And he couldn't shake the uncontrollable questions racing through his mind. How was he going to cover this one up? Why did Danny have to die? Who was he talking to? How much had he shared about his time as The Crimsons' leader? Had Liam's name been mentioned at all?

He closed his eyes, leant back against the headrest and thought.

His trance was broken by the sound of a commotion coming from outside the forensic tent. In the distance, two men in suits charged towards the crime scene, leaving several uniformed officers in their wake.

'Ahh, shit,' Liam said as he recognised one of the suited individuals.

Before he hung up on The Farmer, he told him to lay low, stay hidden and that he'd be in touch soon.

As Liam bound across the site, the sound of shouts and disgruntled arguments grew.

'Hey!' he called just as one of the individuals tried to enter the tent. 'What's going on here?'

The man causing the altercation reached into his blazer pocket, removed a lanyard with a plastic ID card, and waved it in Liam's face.

'Oliver Penrose,' Liam said, reading the name. '*Lord* Oliver Penrose… from the London Organising Committee for the Olympic Games.' His suspicions were correct. 'It was only a matter of time till you guys got here. But I can't have you barging onto my crime scene like this. Otherwise, I'll have you arrest—'

'I demand to know what is going on here,' Oliver said, stepping closer to Liam. The man was six-five and looked like a stick insect, he was that thin. *Gangly* was the word that sprang to mind.

'My name's DCI Liam Greene. This is an active crime scene. We're trying to conduct our investigations. Could you—'

'What's happened?'

'That information is—'

'You'll tell me right now, or I'll find out myself. I can speak to your senior office if that helps? I'm good friends with Assistant Commissioner Candy and Commander Field. The three of us play a lot of golf on the weekends. Field's mentioned your name a couple of times, come to think of it. I'm sure he'd love to hear how you're behaving.'

Liam didn't like that. Not one bit.

'I don't know who you think you are, Oliver, nor what type of credentials you hold, but this is an active crime scene. If you don't refrain and do as I say, then I'm going to have to arrest you.'

'I demand to know what's going on.'

And I want to sleep with Kelly Brook, but you don't hear me complaining it isn't going to happen any time soon.

'We all want things we can't have,' Liam replied, stifling a smug smile. 'Regardless of what you do for a living and how big your wallet is.'

'Please?'

Better – that was better. Manners hurt no one. For a second, Liam wondered whether that was the first time the man in front of him had ever used the word – and judging from the strained expression on his face, it looked like it pained him to say it. In the end, Liam ceded, sighed quietly and looked to the ground. The short of it was, what Oliver had said about being close with Candy and Field scared him. His reputation with both of them was important, and he didn't want some snobby bastard ruining it for him.

He pulled Oliver to the side, out of earshot of the small crowd of officers that had surrounded them, and ordered them to stand down and resume their work.

'This morning a construction worker found a hand in one of the holes on the promenade here. Forensics are in there now, but we've been unable to identify the body.'

'Holy Mother of God,' Oliver said, inhaling sharply. He turned to his colleague and gave him a look that only the two of them understood. Then he turned back to Liam. 'How many people know about this?'

Liam looked around him. 'Everyone you see in front of you.'

'The media?'

'Not yet.'

'Good. I'd like to make sure this doesn't get out.'

'I can't see a way we can keep this out of the press.'

'Be creative,' Oliver said. 'You're good at that. How long is it going to take to excavate the body entirely and clean up?'

Liam shrugged defiantly. 'As long as it takes. This is an intricate case, and we'll take our due care and duty in making sure we do our jobs properly. I'm sorry, but if that's everything, my team and I have got work to do.'

Oliver held Liam back from walking away. 'Lunchtime. I'd like it done by lunchtime. That should give you a couple of hours. Our construction is currently on track for the opening ceremony. But we're close to the edge. One little hiccup can send this entire project up the fucking spout. We can't afford that. Too many people have invested too much time and money for this to be a problem. The entire world is watching us to make sure we perform and deliver on time. Sooner rather than later we'll be ordering the workers to fill in this hole and pretend it never happened. We're going to pour water down this little problem's neck, exactly the same way you'd fix a hiccup. Do you understand what I'm saying, Detective?'

Liam hesitated before answering. 'I understand you completely. But what you're asking me to do is illegal and, not only that, fundamentally immoral.'

'All of our morals lie somewhere in a grey area. You of all people should know that.' Oliver slapped Liam's shoulder and walked away.

CHAPTER 9

MAKING PROMISES

The air conditioning was on full blast inside the interview room, chilling Jake's arms and the back of his neck, desiccating his throat. Opposite him, on the other side of the table, was Hannah Bryant, the second witness. They each had a glass of water, courtesy of one of the DCs in the team. Jake took a long sip of his before pressing the record button on the tape machine beside him. A buzzer sounded. It was a deep monotonous sound that lasted five seconds – although it felt considerably longer.

As soon as it finished, Jake completed the formalities and began.

'Wait,' Hannah said. She looked down at her lap and played with her hands. 'I… There's something I…'

'Go on,' Jake said as politely as he could.

'I didn't have nothing to do with this murder. Richard was tha one who called me over soon as he found it. I told him to call you guys, but when he din't, I was the one who made tha call.'

Hannah hesitated. Her face told him there was more she wanted to say, so Jake remained quiet and let her continue. 'But… but there's summin' else too.'

Jake's ears perked up. Maybe he could add this case to the growing list in his portfolio that he'd been responsible for solving.

'I… I…' Hannah continued to struggle.

'Please take your time. Perhaps a sip of water will help?'

Hannah did as Jake advised, and as she set the cup on the table, she lifted her head. Her eyes were filled with the onset of tears, and lines like whiskers crawled out from the sides of them.

'Your name's Detective Constable Jake Tanner, in't it?'

Jake's eyebrow rose. 'It is…'

'And your colleague – the one who was with you at the construction site – is called Detective Sergeant Drew Richmond, in't he?'

Jake nodded.

'Well, I… erm… I'd like to…' She swallowed before she delivered the final blow. 'I'd like ta make a complaint 'bout DS Richmond.'

Jake waited for the tension and the initial shock of the statement to dissipate – both in the room and in his mind. His pulse had risen, and he was beginning to sweat himself. Now he was grateful for the air conditioning.

'May I understand why?' he said, trying hard to keep his composure in front her.

'He raped me.'

Jake blinked several times as he repeated the words in his head.

'He what?'

She stammered as she spoke. 'It was a long time ago, when I was seven'een. It was… it was fifteen years ago, I guess… I think he was just a constable then. And he looked different, but as soon as he said his name I reco'nised him.'

Jake's mind was blank. He only knew to ask the first question that came into his mind while the rest of it processed what Hannah was telling him.

'Did you report it at the time?'

Hannah hung her head low. 'Not at first. I wanted ta, but I couldn't. I mean, who'd believe me? Who was gonna listen to me? I didn't have no evidence. I cleaned myself as soon as I got 'ome. And then I cried tha 'ole night. My mum found me in the morning and she made me tell her what'd 'appened.'

'She convinced you to go to the police?'

Hannah nodded.

'What happened then?'

'I spoke to someone 'bout it—'

'Who?' Jake asked, cutting her off.

'I can't remember his name that well. I think it was… I think it was DC Harrison. Or… no, Garrison! Garrison. It was DC Garrison – I reported it to 'im.'

Jake's body went cold. Comprehension escaped him. He'd known there was something suspicious between Drew and Pete. They were separated by twenty-five years yet were always with one another, joined at the hip. And then there was the banter. The jokes they shared with one another. As if it were a disguise to mask their secret. There was a bond – a mutual experience – that bound them together.

'What action did DC Garrison take?' Jake asked after a long moment of silence.

'Nothin'. He did nothin'. He put the case on the pile on his desk and left it there. When we tried ta follow up, he came back and said there was no evidence, or that it had been misplaced, and that the case wouldn't stand up in court anyway because I was a untrustworthy little girl. It was Richmond's word against mine.'

Hannah sniffled away the tears and spoke vehemently; Jake admired her courage. 'We even got a different solicitor involved who said there was no evidence to support the claim, and that I was just supposed to let him go.'

'Can you remember the solicitor's name?'

'Haversham. Rupert Haversham. I'll never forget 'im. He was a sweaty old man. Overweight and he stank of grease. Gave me the fucking creeps.'

Jake nodded understandingly, logging a mental note of the name. He couldn't begin to comprehend what Hannah had been through. It was inhuman, abominable and unjust.

'Would you mind...?' There was no easy way for him to approach the subject. 'Would you mind explaining to me what happened?'

Hannah rubbed the underside of her eyes with the back of her sleeve. 'What do you wanna know first?'

'Everything. What were the circumstances? And... what he did?'

Hannah took a sip of water before beginning. 'I was seven'een. I'd just left school. I din't know whatta do with myself, so I went ta college. I hated it. So I started to mess 'bout a bit. I had a few minor ASBO-related offences, but nothing major. Petty stuff like nicking sweets from a shop, or keying someone's car. I even got caught with a bag of weed on me. I got warnings a couple of times, but nothing serious. DS Richmond made sure of that.'

'Made sure of it how?'

Another sip. 'He told me he'd be able to keep the criminal record away if I did what he wanted me to. At first it was little things, like buying 'im alcohol and drugs and stuff like that – stuff he couldn't be bothered to buy himself, or knew he couldn't be seen with. But then the demands grew, until… until…'

'It's OK,' Jake said. 'Take your time. If you don't want to do this here, then I can organise for it to take place somewhere else.'

Hannah shook her head again. 'The night it 'appened, he told me to come over to his place. I din't think a lot would 'appen… I just thought he'd wanna chill.'

She sucked in cold air through her teeth. 'When I got there, he invited me in and led me to the kitchen. He had a coupla glasses of wine on the table. He gave me one and we sat down on the sofa. We got talking for a bit and then he made a move on me.

'When I tried to push him away, he grabbed me and held me down. I tried to shove him off and get out of his house, but he wouldn't let me. He held me down harder and undressed me.' Tears formed in her eyes. 'He pulled my trousers down and then he raped me until I bled. I passed out from the pain and embarrassment of it afterwards, and he just left me there. After I woke up, I grabbed my things and got out. I went home, showered, and well… you know the rest.'

Jake licked his lips. His mouth was so dry it pained him to swallow, but it was insignificant compared to the pain and torture that Hannah had suffered.

'I… I don't know what to say,' Jake said slowly, struggling to meet her eyes.

'Promise me that you'll do something about it.'

Jake nodded. 'You have my word. I can't promise it'll be a quick investigation, but it will be carried out, I can assure you. There are also leaflets about making complaints against the police in the entrance to the station. Take those and call the numbers – speak to someone. I'll escalate the situation through my channels, and together we can get this sorted, OK?'

Hannah smiled.

Jake was used to making promises – mostly to Elizabeth and the girls about silly, childish things like never forgetting about them, never letting anyone hurt them, or never loving one of them over the other.

But this was one promise he'd never thought he'd have to make.

CHAPTER 10

LOYALTY

An hour later, and Drew was in the middle of setting up the Major Investigation Room – the hub of their investigation – when Jake stormed in and slammed the door behind him.

'I think you need to sit down,' Jake said, his mind still struggling to process what he'd been told. He'd spent the past thirty minutes running it over and over in his head in disbelief. Thinking of all the reasons why she might be making it up, why she might be throwing him off the scent. At the end of it all, there were none.

'You all right, fella?' Drew asked, spinning to face him.

Jake nodded to the chair nearest to Drew. 'We need to talk.'

Drew did as he was told. Jake pulled out a chair on the other side of the table for himself. He exhaled deeply, thinking of the right words to say and the best way to say them.

He drew blanks on all accounts.

'What's this all about, Jake?' Drew asked, scratching the back of his head. 'What did that Hannah woman want?'

'She made a worrying accusation, Drew.'

'Go on…'

'I shouldn't be telling you this, not in the slightest, but I can't get my head around it.' Jake paused, and his eyes fell on the desk – on the mountain of paperwork and folders sitting in front of him. 'She says she knows you from somewhere. Long time ago. You and her go way back.'

'Right…'

His mind was set. He needed to tell Drew.

Jake swallowed and licked his lips, but his mouth, devoid of saliva, gave no relief. 'She's accusing you of raping her.'

'What? How? When? Where? Jesus!'

Drew leapt out of the chair and threw it across the room. It bounced on the floor and ricocheted against the whiteboard. Jake glanced at the rest of the office behind the glass partitions; members of the team were up on their feet, peering round the door and pillars, attempting to catch a better look at the commotion.

Jake dismissed them with a wave of his hand and returned his focus to Drew.

'I don't believe this. I don't fucking believe this.' Droplets of phlegm propelled from his mouth like the spray from a bottle of bleach; his words were almost as good as poisonous. He paced from side to side, one hand massaging the back of his neck while the other rubbed the underside of his nose. 'I don't… Wait. What did *you* say? D'you believe her? D'you believe *it*?'

Jake hesitated before answering. The situation's development – and Drew's temper – was dependent on his response.

'I don't know what to believe,' Jake lied. 'But what I do know is that I can't ignore it.'

'Of course you fucking can. It's simple. There're ways around this sort of thing. There always have been, always will be—' Drew stopped suddenly, his chest heaving, his eyes wild.

'What are you saying?' Jake asked.

Drew froze a moment longer, and then he raced across the room and pounced on Jake. Inches separated their faces. Drew's thick, steamy, coffee-stained breath assaulted Jake's senses, sending his hangover into minor disarray.

'You still don't get it, do you?' Drew began, spittle colliding with Jake's cheek and chin. 'About *us*. About how we work. About how we *do things* here? There's a loyalty between all of us. *Loyalty*. We've got each other's backs, no matter what – no matter what sort of shit comes our way,' Drew snarled. 'If you wanna have an affair with some bint from the office, nobody's gonna say anything to your wife. If you wanna take some drugs, nobody's gonna find out – and we'll make sure there's a way around the random testing too. Why? 'Cause we look out for each other. We can pay her off. But if it's money *you* want, then I can sort that out. Ten grand? I can give you ten grand. I don't have it now but I can give it to you. No problem. You just have to give me some time. As soon as I have it, I can show you where the rest of it comes from – where it comes from for the rest of us as well. Once you see that, you ain't ever gonna change your mind.'

Ten thousand pounds was a lot of money. Life-changing, in his instance. Enough to settle all his bills and outstanding debts, and leave some remaining. Perhaps he could use it to buy something nice for the girls. A new television. Some toys. New car. Holiday—

Wait, what was he thinking? Taking the money was wrong, illegal. It would cross the line into territory he'd sworn never to get into. Drew had broken the law and ruined someone's life. There was no amount of money that could make up for that.

Unless… unless… An idea popped into his head. A good one. One of his best yet. It just needed fleshing out.

'Jake? Jake?' Drew insisted.

Before he could respond, Drew placed his hands on Jake's chest, scrunching his tie and collar. 'You'll help me with this, won't you, Jake? You'll help me get out of this, yeah? Remember what I said, yeah? *Loyalty*. We rate loyalty pretty fucking highly in this team, and it is *always* rewarded, like I said.' Drew prodded Jake's chest. 'Listen, you can pay off all your debts with that ten grand. In this team, one person's problem becomes everyone's problem. So this is yours as much as it is mine. Remember that. Because if I go down, then I'm taking you with me. Remember *that*.'

Drew patted Jake on the shoulder, ironing out a crease on the seam, and then left.

Jake grunted to himself then paced, collecting his thoughts. There wasn't much to think about. Drew had backed him into a corner. He didn't know how his colleague knew about his financial struggles, but he did. And Jake was going to have to make sure that it didn't spread to the rest of the team.

By the time he left the MIR a few minutes later, he'd made his decision.

And it went against everything he believed in.

CHAPTER 11

KINGDOM OF EMPIRES

The game was called Kingdom of Empires. It was an online game where users were tasked with building a settlement and, through means of agriculture, civilisation, industrialisation and development of arms, were responsible for turning it into an empire.

Garrison had spent too many hours indulging himself in the mechanics and algorithms the game offered – sometimes losing a good chunk of sleep his aged body lambasted him for the following morning. But the biggest kick he got from the game was raiding other people's settlements and watching their hard work crumble to rubble in front of his eyes. It was a lesson for those who tried to take him on – and, by his own estimations, it was a lesson in life too.

Being ill-prepared is ill-advised, read his empire's motto.

His username was *McVitreason*.

He thought it was apt.

In the past few weeks, Garrison had found that his motives for using the game had changed. And that was all down to one person.

The Cabal.

Randomly, one day while he was at home pretending to watch a repeat of *The Great British Bake Off* with his wife – when, in reality, neither of them had been watching it; it had been a source of background noise – Garrison had received a message from the username *LG540* introducing themselves as The Cabal. Up until that point, Garrison's only interaction with the mysterious employer had been through Liam.

Now that was all about to change.

Garrison was sitting in his car with the window rolled down in the middle of Bow Green car park. He'd been instructed to head straight to the station with news of Liam's imminent return. But he couldn't bring himself to go in. He couldn't be bothered to do anything. With the scourge of a few added years on Liam, Drew, Jake and the rest of the youngsters in the office, he was the one who suffered the most whenever they went out on the lash. It was always his own fault for drinking too much – no one else to blame – but that didn't make it hurt any less.

Old habits really did die hard.

His phone chimed as a gentle breeze whistled through his ears.

A message from *LG540*.

Garrison knew from experience that he had a thirty-second window to respond before The Cabal signed off – and then there was no knowing when he might get a response.

LG540: *L called.*

McVitreason: *And?*

LG540: *Pissed. Talk with Farmer – body discovered too soon.*

McVitreason: *OK.*

LG540: *LOCOG aware. Applying pressure. TTT.*

Garrison considered the last part of the message. He was well aware of what it meant, but its intentions confused him. He replied.

McVitreason: *Consider it done.*

LG540: *Once complete, move on to phase two.*

CHAPTER 12

IDENTIFICATION

The team were in the briefing room, waiting for Liam to return. He was a few minutes away, with a major update. It could have been that the case was solved and closed, or that the DCI's cancer had disappeared, or that there was another body down there and that they hadn't even scratched the surface. But all Jake was able to think about was the impact Drew had made on Hannah Bryant's life. How he'd committed a heinous crime and evaded justice for it. And how he had been blackmailed into keeping a vindictive and malevolent secret from the very people who trusted him to pursue it.

Patience, he told himself. Patience. The time would come.

Before he was able to dedicate any more thought to it, the briefing room doors opened.

Liam burst into the room and smashed the door into the adjacent wall, shuddering the blinds on the windows that looked out onto the rest of the office.

'Everything all right, guv?' Drew asked, considerably chirpy despite everything that had happened in the past half an hour. He kept his focus on Liam, who moved to the front of the room.

'Far from it,' Liam replied with his hands on his hips. His breathing was heavy and he looked as though he'd just sprinted back from the Olympic Stadium. 'But it's nothing we can't handle. By some miracle, in the past two hours, forensics have expedited the exhumation process against all instruction and procedure, and now our Nominal One is lying on the pathologist's table, whiter than the sheet that's covering him.'

'How come, guv?' Garrison asked, twiddling a pen in his hands, the customary pack of digestive biscuits lying on his knee, half opened.

'Lord Oliver Penrose. Snobby prick from the London Olympic Games Official Committee who thinks that, because he's got a title and a lot of this' – Liam rubbed his thumb over his index and middle finger; the international symbol for money – 'he thinks he can get what he wants.'

'What'd you tell him, boss?' Garrison asked. 'You tell him where to shove it?'

'If only. I had the assistant commissioner on the phone to me a few minutes later. My hands were tied.'

'I'm sure you did what you had to do,' Garrison added as he reached inside the packet for another biscuit.

'Penrose and the LOCOG want to keep the lid on this as much as possible,' Liam added.

'Not asking for a lot, are they?' Garrison scoffed. 'I can't wait till the day I'm gone so I don't have to deal with this bullshit anymore.'

Everyone's head turned to Garrison.

'You retiring soon, Pete? You should've said. We had no idea,' Drew remarked.

Garrison gave him the middle finger.

Liam continued. 'Poojah's had the body for about an hour now. I've been informed the victim had all his teeth, nails, blood, hair – everything. The only concern would be the amount of concrete inside the body having a detrimental effect on the speed of the results coming back.'

'Did you see the body, guv?' Jake piped up.

Liam shook his head. 'They kept that one well hidden. What about your witnesses – tell me about them.'

'I spoke with Richard Maddison,' Drew replied. 'One of the workers. Bloke found the body. Didn't really go anywhere. Worth doing a background check on him nonetheless to rule him out though.'

Liam turned to the whiteboard, grabbed a dry-wipe pen and started to scribble.

'What about CCTV?' he asked after a prolonged silence. 'Jake – can I leave that one with you?'

Jake dipped his head. 'Already on it, sir.'

'That's what I like to hear. I think after today we—'

The briefing room door opened, cutting him off. Standing in the doorway was DC Sheridan, one of the team members who'd been instructed to stay in the MIR and pick up the phone if any calls came in.

'Alex,' Liam said, a hint of worry and surprise tinging his voice. The DC entered the room and shut the door behind him. 'Everything all right?'

In his hand, he held a Post-it note.

'We got the results back. DNA—'

'Already?'

Alex nodded. 'Yes. The victim's DNA and fingerprints were already on the database.'

'Whose?'

'We've managed to identify the victim as Danny Cipriano.'

CHAPTER 13

TWO LITTLE WORDS

Those two little words reverberated in Jake's head like an air-raid siren. They turned his body cold, the same way they had when he'd first heard them. The same words that had been in the media for months following the last heist in Guildford. Jake repeated them in his mind over and over again.

Danny Cipriano.

Danny Cipriano.

Danny Cipriano, member of the organised crime group called The Crimsons, was dead. Buried alive. In concrete, no less. But why? Why Danny? And why now?

Jake's mind was awash with thoughts and he was struggling to stay afloat. He needed to get out of there. He needed to take his mind off it.

He needed a drink.

Racing out of the briefing room, Jake stormed towards the kitchen and then switched on the kettle. He placed his palms on the table and leant forward, opening his lungs. He inhaled sharply through his nose and exhaled gradually from his mouth.

Six months earlier, Jake thought he'd put The Crimsons saga behind him the moment he'd stepped away from their corrupt investigation and let them enter the witness protection scheme. But he was wrong, and now the man was back to haunt him.

How? Who? Why?

The kettle started to boil, but he paid it no attention. Flashbacks of when he'd jumped into the frozen waters of the Itchen after Danny entered his mind. He'd dived two hundred feet from the top of a cruise liner in an attempt to save Danny's life, but it had been Danny who'd saved his. Without meaning to, Jake had suffered an anxiety attack under ten feet of water and nearly drowned, but by some miracle, Danny had found him amidst the murky blackness and pulled him to safety. For that, Jake felt as though he was indebted to the man forever. And, in his death, he'd failed.

A knock came at the kitchen door. It was Liam.

'You all right, kid?'

Jake shot into action. He grabbed himself a spoon, heaped instant coffee into his mug and then poured the water. 'Just a bit of a shock, that's all.'

'It's a shock for all of us.' Liam moved closer towards him, rested his backside against the surface's edge and then folded his arms across his chest. 'Nobody expected it to be him, you know. But I'm sure there's a reason behind it. The man had a lot of enemies.' Liam paused. 'There anything else going on?'

Your detective sergeant is a bent cop and a rapist.

Jake shook his head. 'Nothing that I can think of.'

Liam patted Jake on the back and gave him a thumbs up. 'Good man,' he said. 'I need you on your A game for this. The press backlash is going to be huge. Especially considering how high-profile he is. Doesn't help that Danny was in the WPS. Someone in there's going to be partly to blame. But that's why I need your A game, mate. There's a shitstorm about to come our way, and we need to trust each other for us to be able to weather it. A team of good eggs. Understand?'

Liam hesitated and stared into Jake's eyes. Jake already knew what he needed to say; Drew had given him the answer earlier.

'Don't worry, guv,' Jake replied, feigning a smile. 'You'll have my A game. You have my trust. And you have my loyalty.' Jake gave a slight dip of the head as if to further highlight the point.

A small grin – just enough for Jake to notice – flashed on Liam's face and then disappeared again.

Liam gave him another slap on the back. 'You never fail to impress me, Tanner.'

With that, he left, leaving Jake feeling slightly more stunned than when he'd entered the kitchen. Liam had just confirmed a minor suspicion that had entered his mind: Liam was in on it all as well. They were all corrupt. One against three. And he had no one else to turn to. No one else he could discuss it with.

Lindsay, he thought. Yes, she'd be able to help. But how much could she do? She was just a facilities manager – she had no power of authority over anyone. But what if he was wrong and he was just being paranoid? What if it had all been a test like when Liam and the team had given him the Regulation 13 notice?

No. He couldn't tell Lindsay just yet. Not until he knew for certain what he was dealing with.

He'd have to give it some more time.

But for now, there was a job to do.

Sipping from his mug, he headed back to his desk and opened his inbox. In the past few minutes, he'd received complete access to the CCTV files from the construction site. Perfect. If whoever was responsible for the murder had made any mistake, it would be the fact they forgot there was CCTV on the site. All Jake needed to do was sift through the playback and wait for a hit.

It didn't take long.

After twenty minutes of watching the video at double speed, a small black van appeared on the screen. It pulled into the construction site and then rounded a corner before disappearing. To catch up with it, Jake tried different angles but was unsuccessful. The van – and Danny's murder scene – was in a black spot.

As Jake watched the playback, he made a note of the vehicle registration number and checked it through the ANPR and CCTV in the surrounding area, as well as the PNC.

The vehicle was last registered to an owner seven years ago and 150 miles away in Birmingham. A dead end.

Within an hour, however, after trawling through the CCTV footage, he'd found the van's last known location.

The place where Jake was headed next.

Tyred Out Mechanics.

CHAPTER 14

USUAL

Liam finished typing the message on the secret Gmail inbox. It was the only form of covert messaging between the three of them. Simple, yet effective. A random Gmail account which all of them had access to. Whenever any of them needed to say something without the prying eyes and ears of the office watching them, they created a draft email in their account, wrote the message, and then deleted it after a few minutes, hoping that everyone had had the chance to read it. That way there was no trace of it, no messages that needed to be permanently erased. It was quick. It was efficient. It was perfect.

The message read:

Brief Room. 30 seconds.

As soon as he'd typed the message, Liam lifted himself out of his chair, exited his office and made his way towards the briefing room. As he moved across the floor, he met eyes with Garrison. His colleague knew better than to follow immediately after him, but as Liam passed, Garrison leapt out of his chair and chased behind.

'What a way to make it discreet,' Liam said as he closed the door.

Garrison rolled his eyes. 'Oh, come on, Liam. Nobody's paying that much attention.'

'*Someone* might have been watching.'

'You're getting paranoid.'

Before Liam was able to respond, Drew entered the room. He froze, his hand on the door handle, mouth agape, as if he'd just walked in on the two of them having sex.

'Interrupting, am I?'

'You wish,' Garrison replied.

Drew threw him the finger and Garrison responded in kind.

Liam sighed and moved towards the window. He closed the blinds and submerged them in their submarine of secrecy.

'Right, both of you. This is big,' Liam began, making a point to not waste any more time than was necessary. 'I got a call from The Cabal. They organised the hit on Danny Cipriano. I don't know why, and I don't know how. But now it's our job to deal with it as quickly and as quietly as we can.'

'Who did it?' Drew asked as he folded his arms across his chest.

'The Farmer.'

'Jesus fucking Christ.' Drew ran his fingers through his hair and rubbed his nose. 'Do you know what that means for the rest of us? It'll be us next, won't it? Jesus, Jesus, Jesus, fuck.'

Liam stepped to the side and glared at Garrison. 'Now who's being paranoid?'

A smirk grew at the sides of Garrison's mouth. He slapped Drew on the shoulder with the back of his hand and lambasted him. 'What you talking about, you daft sod? Why would we be next?'

'It's obvious, isn't it? Danny opened his mouth. He told someone about us, about who we are, about what we do. The Cabal found out and now look what's happened to him.'

'Be quiet,' Liam snapped. He had half a mind to slap Drew across the face to calm him down but thought better of it. 'Danny didn't say anything about us, and—'

'How d'you know?' Drew interrupted.

'I don't for definite, but The Cabal would have said if Danny did. We'd have been given a heads-up.'

'And you think that's the sort of thing The Cabal'd admit to you? Give you a chance to run away before The Farmer comes after you?'

Liam sighed again. This was going nowhere. He paused a moment to observe his friend. His eyes were wild. His nose was running, and he kept rubbing it. He was jittery. A thin sheen of sweat covered his forehead. And, to top it off, he was getting paranoid.

He'd seen the signs before, but he'd never thought he'd see them again.

'Listen,' Liam said through gritted teeth, 'I called The Farmer as well. He confirmed it all for me. The Farmer has no loyalties to anyone, so he has no reason to lie to protect us.'

As soon as he finished, Drew calmed down – his breathing steadied, his nose stopped, and his attitude became placid.

'What we doing about it now then?' Garrison asked, distracting Liam from Drew.

'Tonight. Usual spot. Usual time. And, as usual, come alone. The three of us have got to figure something out by the end of the day. I want you to come prepared.'

'Four of us…' Drew said slowly. A grin grew on his face and his eyes twitched, except this time Liam didn't think it was any effect from substance abuse.

'You what?' Liam replied.

'Four of us. Jake… bring Jake along.'

'Eh?' Garrison retorted. 'Nuh-uh. No way. Not happening. He's too much of a liability.'

'Trust me,' Drew said, licking his lips. 'He's onside. Trust me. I spoke with him earlier. Showed him what the wonders of our real job can do. Especially when he's going through a spot of financial difficulty.'

Liam relaxed a little. His earlier conversation in the kitchen with the young DC had intrigued him. Jake had mentioned loyalty – a word that, up until that point, had never come out of Jake's mouth. But it wasn't the word he'd said; it was the *way* he'd said it. The same way he and Drew and Garrison used it. Like he *meant* it. Like he was finally on the turn, finally beginning to realise the true possibilities of the darker side of policing – something that Liam should have been ecstatic, overjoyed, about. But wasn't, couldn't be. Jake was a good detective, with a family, a bright future ahead of him, and Liam didn't know whether he wanted to corrupt and destroy that for him.

But, on the flip side, now it was Jake's chance to finally prove himself. And if Jake didn't like what he saw and it came down to it, then Liam would have to do what he needed to: silence Jake and remove him from the force. The methods were simple, but he hoped that was a last resort. But if Jake did like what he saw, then he could join their ranks, earn some real money, work his way up like the rest of them.

Liam cleared his throat. 'You sure about this, Drew?'

'Haven't let you down to date, fella.'

'Then you better be right. Usual place. Usual time. I'll let Tanner know.'

CHAPTER 15

CONVEYOR BELT

Tyred Out Mechanics was a business that was exactly as the name suggested. The building was a mess, decrepit. Tyres and tools and old bags of dirt were strewn across the courtyard, while plants and overgrown weeds hugged the foot of the building, some of them climbing their way to the top. And inside, the employee behind the reception desk looked bored.

'You a'right, love?' the woman holding an oversized mug of tea in her hand asked. 'You lost?'

Jake wasn't sure whether he looked it, or whether it was just in her nature to approach prospective clients in that manner. Either way, his impression of her was the same.

'That depends if you can help me,' Jake said, leaning on the desk with one arm.

'You got a motor that needs fixing?'

'Not quite. I was wondering if you had a motor that you were currently fixing.' Jake was being deliberately vague. By the time she opened her mouth to respond, he'd already pulled out his warrant card. 'Do you mind if I take a look around?'

The woman held her hands in the air. 'Hey, I don't want no trouble. I don't know what Benny's been up to again, but it ain't nothing to do with me.' She leapt out of her chair. 'Boy, when I find out what he's up to, I'm gonna smack him into next week.'

She stormed off to the workshop on Jake's right, screaming Benny's name. As soon as she'd crossed the threshold, the noise of drills and heavy machinery stopped.

Jake chased after her.

About thirty feet away, standing next to the rear of a Ford Mondeo was Benny, dressed in coveralls, holding a blowtorch in both hands with a protective visor pulled over his face.

'Mam, wha's goin' on?' he asked as he lifted the visor from his face. 'Ev'ryfin' alrigh'?'

'What have you been doing, Benny? What have you got yourself up to now? I'm done protecting you.'

While the duo argued, Jake took a moment to survey his surroundings. The workshop was empty, save for the car that Benny was currently working on. There was enough space in there for at least three cars to be worked on at any one time, and the inside was just as decrepit as the outside. Tools and machines and protective clothing and old pieces of dishcloth were left in sporadic piles about the place. Skid marks and oil stains dotted the concrete flooring like a discount version of a Jackson Pollock painting. And the smell of grease and old leather lingered in the air, clinging to the walls and furniture.

'Mam, I ain't done nowt this time,' Benny replied. 'Wha' you sayin'?'

A sharp whistle pierced the air, making Jake flinch. It came from Mama Benny. She beckoned him over with a wave of her hand.

'Speak to him,' she said, prodding Benny in the chest.

Jake hurried across and whipped out his pocketbook. He opened it onto the latest page. In the top-right corner was the number plate of the black van he'd followed on the CCTV.

'Benny,' he began as he came to a stop a few feet away from the young man. A pungent smell of body odour rose through his nostrils and overpowered the rest of his senses. 'I was wondering if you'd be able to tell me what you were doing last night?'

'Workin'.'

'And what time did you finish?'

'I ain't bin 'ome yet.'

Jake scribbled in his pocketbook as he spoke.

'You've been working the whole night?'

Benny nodded.

'So you were aware of the black van that came in at twelve minutes past four this morning?'

Benny nodded.

'Could you tell me what happened, please?'

Benny set the drill down on the floor, pulled his face mask off his head and placed it on the boot of the Ford.

'I got this importan' deadline 'n' that, and I was workin' 'ard on it. Gotta get me this car fixed by tomorra. But when I was workin', I 'ear this bang-bang-bang on the shutta, right. I go up to it and this van just pulls in. Fuckin' fing nearly knocked me off me feet! I tried ta tell 'em to fuck off 'n' that, but she weren't 'avin' none of it.'

'What happened after that?' Jake asked, trying to decipher Benny's vernacular.

'She done put a gun to me 'ead and told me to change her numba plates.'

'And did you?'

'Yeah, she already 'ad the numba plate ready 'n' that. She just wanted me to put it on.'

Jake turned his attention to the four corners of the workshop. 'Did you catch any of this on CCTV?'

'Nah,' stepped in Benny's mum. 'We don't have none of that. Costs too much to run. We hardly get any business as it is – ain't nobody gonna wanna steal anythin' from us anyway.'

That was a lackadaisical view to have on security, Jake thought, but if there was no footage, then he was going to struggle to find the vehicle with its new number plate.

'Can you describe her for me?'

Benny shook his head. 'Nah, sorry, pal. She was wearing a balaclava 'n' that. Din't fink some broad comin' in wiv a gun was gonna let me see her face, did ya?'

'Nothing at all? What was she wearing? How tall was she? What did she sound like? Any accents?'

Benny considered for a moment. 'She was 'bout your 'ight. Maybe a little taller, I dunno. She was wearing black, and a pair of boots. Fink she might 'ave bin Eastern European as well. Fuckin' foreigners – scum the lotta them.'

Jake scribbled down the description, ignoring the blatant racism.

'Anything else?'

'Nah. Sorry.'

'Which way did she go after she drove off?'

Back at Bow Green, he'd watched the roadside footage of the workshop for two hours after the van had originally pulled in, but he'd found nothing. Almost as if it had just vanished.

'She went down the uvva end of the shop, pal. Runnin' the shop like a conveyor belt, kna' what I mean? Lost her after I lowered them shuttas.'

Shit. Dead end. He had a blacked-out van, a blacked-out woman and a blacked-out set of number plates.

Just as he was about to open his mouth to thank them both for their time, his phone vibrated. It was an instinctive reaction for him to check it, just in case it was an emergency. Elizabeth. The girls. Everything else.

In that order.

Instead, it was from Liam. It read:

Drop what you're doing and get to Stratford Flyover. 6 pm. Come alone. Important.

CHAPTER 16

HOMEWORK

Jake was running late. He hadn't known what to make of the message. What if it was about Drew? And the two of them were going to work against him and Garrison to get them both locked up?

Jake romanticised the idea before dismissing it.

As he pulled into the car park beneath the flyover, all his questions were answered. And it wasn't the answer he'd been hoping for. Liam, Drew and Garrison were standing in front of Liam's car. Did this make him one of the team? Was he now officially 'in'? Had they inducted him into their secret group?

He prepared himself.

The deafening sound of cars whizzing past a small bump in the tarmac above his head created a din and swallowed the noise of his engine. All three men stood with their hands in their pockets, still in plain clothes.

'Good to have you join us, Jake,' Liam said. He was wearing a beige overcoat, but despite his seniority in a professional capacity, it was Garrison who seemed in charge. He was the older and more experienced member of the group – the one who had started from the bottom of the corrupt pile and made his way to the top, and now it was time for the new recruit to come in and do the same dirty work he'd once done.

'Thanks… I guess,' Jake replied, not knowing how to respond. Everything about this situation was new to him. 'Is something wrong?'

'You could say that. But there are some things you'll need to pick up fast. We don't have time to explain a lot.' Liam turned to both Drew and Garrison. 'Did you prepare what I asked?'

Both men simply nodded, further raising questions in Jake's mind. For a split second, he thought his colleagues were about to pull out an arsenal of knives and guns and throw him into the back of their car and drive him out to a remote part of the country.

The reality of it was much worse.

'Jake,' Liam said, snapping him from his thoughts. 'Remember when I told you about your A game?'

Jake nodded.

'Now's the time to show us what you're made of, buddy. Danny Cipriano was murdered by a close associate of ours called The Farmer and his team. They like to keep their identities hidden. None of us knows who he is. But he works for the same employer as we do. The Cabal. A few days before Danny was murdered, he attempted to reveal intelligence and secrets to someone. His death is the result of what happens if you betray The Cabal – and, by extension, us. Understand?'

Liam didn't leave enough time for Jake to respond; instead, he continued immediately. 'Now it's our job, in the positions that we're in, to pin the murder on someone so we can get it all brushed under the carpet – like Danny was under the cement – before it leaks to the press and the general public.'

Get it all brushed under the carpet – like Danny was under the cement.

Jake stared at Liam in disbelief. He couldn't believe what he was hearing. He was being asked to turn a blind eye to a murder, to pin it on an innocent person, to become the very thing he'd sworn to destroy, to work for the person who'd threatened his life and his career. He wanted to run away, but his legs weren't working. He wanted to shout at them and scream at them for ruining someone's life, but his mouth was sealed shut. He wanted to call the police and grass on them and get them locked away, but his arms wouldn't work.

Liam's face contorted and turned into a chuckle. 'I suppose you've got a lot of questions, haven't you?'

Jake nodded. He did. A lot.

'It's probably best if you don't ask them,' Liam said. 'It's need-to-know. The less you ask, the less you know. And the less you know, the better it is for everyone. Until we know how much we can trust you. For now, we're gonna need your help with this. And at the end of it, there's the potential to make an absolute killing. You'd never have to worry about your financials ever again. I know Drew's already hammered home about how we deal with loyalty in this unit. I don't think you need to hear any more about it.' Liam hesitated as he turned his focus to Drew and Garrison. 'Gentlemen, what've we got...?'

'I've got a name,' Drew said. He puffed his shoulders and chest out, giving him the arrogant air of looking more important than he was. 'And I reckon it'll be an easy one too.'

'Who?'

'Richard Maddison. The bloke I spoke with earlier. Easiest scapegoat possible. I'm sure we can find a link between him and Danny Cipriano as well. Or make one.'

'Perfect,' Liam said, removing his hands from his pockets and rubbing his palms together. There was a bitter wind chill in the air that ripped from one side of the flyover to the other and they were caught in the middle. 'Garrison. Anything?'

Garrison shook his head. 'Nothing from me. I haven't spoken to anyone yet.'

Liam cleared his throat. 'And, Jake – what about you? Anyone you reckon would be a good person to take the fall. What was the name of that woman you were speaking with this morning? Hannah Bryant, wasn't it?'

Jake watched Drew's head snap towards him out the corner of his vision. But there was something else that caught his eye. Drew's reaction was obvious, given what Jake knew about him. But Garrison's reaction was more interesting: he gave a side-eyed look towards Drew, which suggested to Jake that he remembered the name well, and confirmed that they were both in on it – and that they were going to have to keep a close eye on him if they were going to keep it a secret any longer.

'She's not got it in her,' Jake said. 'I can't think of any link that we could manipulate to implicate her with Danny. I think Richard's a better shout.'

He hated himself for saying it. He was going against everything he'd ever believed in, and he was being complicit in a crime. He was part of the team who were about to frame an innocent man for murder. It made him sick to the pit of his stomach. But he needed to look on the bright side, the positives. He could use this information against them, to roll over and blow the whistle on his colleagues. But, in order to do that, he'd need hard, solid evidence. And for him to have that, he was going to have to do this longer than he wanted to.

'Perfect,' Liam announced. 'Seems like we've got our man. Now, all we need to do is work out how we're gonna do it. I want you to spend the night thinking about it. Come back to me tomorrow with an idea.'

That was it. Meeting adjourned. Time for them all to go back to their normal lives for the evening. And the last thing Jake expected from the meeting was to be leaving with homework.

CHAPTER 17

WITHOUT A PADDLE

Liam wanted to hear the sound of her voice – yearned for it. It had only been a few days and he was already longing for her. The stresses of the past few hours had got to him. Danny. The Farmer. The Cabal. Garrison. Drew. Jake. Lord Oliver fucking Penrose from the London fucking Olympics Committee. His mind was frazzled from trying to work out what they were going to do next. How much he could trust Jake. How much Drew had told him. How the consequences would be catastrophic if he didn't cover up the murder as soon as possible. Both Drew and Garrison were liabilities at the best of times – and that was when they weren't dealing with high-profile crimes like this.

Fuck! He slammed his hand on the steering wheel. He could really do with some Charlie right now. Or Molly. Anything. Something that would take the edge off and make him forget for a short while.

No. No, no, no, no, no. He shook his head. *Don't do it, you silly fucker. Don't do it. You know what happens when you do.*

Instead, as he sat there in the parking space outside his flat, he made a call.

'Hello, stranger,' the other person said in his ear.

'Hello, you. You been missing me?'

'Don't flatter yourself too much,' she said, shooting him down in her usual way.

'Where are you? You busy?'

'I might be available for a few hours or an evening. Who wants to know?'

'I do. I've got a big one for you as well. I'm sure you'd love to hear it.'

'You really know how to turn a girl on, Liam.'

He rolled his eyes in delight. He loved the way she said his name. There was something so raw in it, so sexy – an inflection in her voice that made him want to rip her clothes off. Or perhaps it was because, in his mind, she was already half naked.

'I'm coming over now. I'll bring the champagne. Hope you're feeling naughty.'

It took him fifteen minutes to get to Tanya Smile's house – four minutes less than it should have done.

As Liam sauntered towards the front door, he banished all thought of The Farmer and The Cabal and Danny Cipriano and Jake Tanner from his mind, slicked back his hair with his fingers, and cleaned his ears.

'Somebody doesn't hang around,' Tanya said as she opened the door to her house in North London. She was dressed in a thin black-and-white-striped T-shirt with a pair of blue denim shorts. Her hair was pulled off her face and tied in a ponytail. She'd even gone to the extent of putting on lipstick for him.

Liam held the bottle in the air like he was a warrior returning with an enemy's severed head. 'I'm thirsty,' he said, winking at her as he wandered past.

Tanya's house was like a second home to him. He'd spent a lot of time there in the few months they'd been seeing each other. Their relationship was a secret, and they both had to keep it that way. The success of their jobs relied upon one another. Tanya was a reporter for BBC News, and he always tried to give her exclusive breaking news wherever possible. At first, it had been in exchange for a chunk of her bonus, but then, as their relationship developed, it stopped being about the money and started being about their feelings for one another. They'd been in business together for a few years – ever since they'd met at a television awards ceremony, and she'd been receptive to entertaining the idea of forming a partnership.

'So what's this story you've got for me?'

'Business… already?'

She grabbed two wine glasses from a cupboard and set them on the counter. 'You know I don't like to mix business and pleasure. It makes things messy.'

'You weren't saying that the other week.'

She eyed him playfully and then returned her attention to the conversation. 'What's it like, on the scale of things?'

Liam moved across the kitchen, found a bag of peanuts in the cupboard and set them in a bowl. 'It's the Danny Cipriano scale of things,' he said. 'The highest scale there is.'

'Now you have my attention.'

'Nice and easy, really. He's dead. Buried alive in concrete. London Olympic Stadium.'

Tanya froze and held her hand to her mouth. 'Oh my God.'

'I know, right. But it's a tricky one.'

'They always are when you're involved.'

'What can I say? Danger has a way of finding me.'

'So... what's the plan then?'

'We're in the middle of finding someone, but we'll have to see how it goes. But there's another problem...'

'What?'

'The LOCOG don't want any wind of this getting out. Some flash billionaire prick called Oliver Penrose wants to keep it under the lid.'

Tanya sighed and folded her arms. 'Then why are you telling me about it?'

'Because I wanted you to be the first to know. But you can't say anything until I confirm it's good to go.'

'You're such a tease,' she said, smirking at him, flashing a set of bright white teeth.

'Otherwise, we'll be up shit creek. Without a paddle. Upside down.'

'Doesn't sound like a place I'd want to be.'

'It doesn't sound like a place you'd want me to be either,' he said. 'So you best keep your mouth shut for the time being.'

He moved across the room and kissed her. 'And I can think of a few extra ways we can make that happen.'

CHAPTER 18

SITTING PRETTY

On the hour-long drive home, Jake had come to an easy conclusion. What Liam, Drew and Garrison were doing was wrong. That much was simple. What they were doing needed to be stopped. Also simple. But what they were doing was of vital importance. Without them realising it, they were contributing to their own demise. For the time being, he just needed to stick with them, gain their trust, make them believe that he was on their side and then use the evidence to his advantage. Like a Trojan Horse, attacking them from the inside. So far, he'd convinced himself that keeping Drew and Garrison's secret about what they did to Hannah Bryant was a good idea. He just needed to see more of it through. But how far? And for how long?

Those two questions raised an important point.

If he was going to go through with this – betray his friends and... his *family* – then he couldn't do it alone. He needed external help, just in case they caught wind of what he was doing and decided to finish him off like they had Danny Cipriano. These people were dangerous, and he was almost certain of the fact that they wouldn't show him any leniency.

Jake pulled onto his driveway and wandered inside to the kitchen.

'Sorry I'm late,' he said to Elizabeth after kissing her on the cheek. 'Where are my girls?'

'I've just put them down.'

'Let me go and say goodnight to them quickly.'

He gave Elizabeth another kiss before hurrying up the stairs. He dashed into his bedroom quickly, retrieved the cordless phone they kept by Elizabeth's side of the bed and skipped into the girls' bedroom. As the thin slither of light split the room in two, he tiptoed across the floorboards, taking extra care to avoid the ones that made a noise – the same ones that were on his to-do list to fix.

Maisie and Ellie were sound asleep, their breathing gentle, soothing, rhythmic. Peaceful.

He leant over them, stroked their hair and then gave them each a kiss.

In the corner of the room was a wooden chair that Elizabeth's grandma had given them before they'd moved into the house. She'd died a week later. It was now considered one of their only family heirlooms, and it was one of the most comfortable chairs Jake had ever had the luxury of sitting on.

He pulled out the landline from his pocket and his mobile from the other. Using his mobile to search for the number of the DPS – the Directorate of Professional Standards – he typed in the digits on the landline then stared at the numbers on the small screen, contemplating. If he did this, there was no turning back. He would commit himself to ratting out the team. By doing this, he was not only putting his life in danger but also his family's. Elizabeth's. Maisie's. Ellie's.

But he believed in himself to do it unnoticed. Because if he didn't, then he might as well hand himself over to them now.

Jake stared at the phone a little while longer.

After a few more seconds, he clenched his jaw, dialled the number and waited, the ringing tone sounding in his ears.

'Good evening, this is the DPS. How can I help you?'

Jake swallowed before responding.

'Hi… yes… this is Detective Constable Jake Tanner. I'd, er, I'd like to make a complaint.'

CHAPTER 19

COME DOWN

Richard Maddison wandered the streets aimlessly, his mind devoid of any thought. He didn't know how long it had been since he'd been escorted out of the police station; time just seemed to stand still while his legs continued moving. Although he knew that it must have been the entire day. It was now dark outside, and the workers and students who had prowled the streets a few hours ago had clocked out and swapped shifts with teenagers and drinkers and partygoers. He was still in shock. Understandable, really, all things considered. He thought about that arsehole detective. How he'd behaved. How he'd pulled him up on the drugs and the drink. Did he already know? Or was he just playing with him? It didn't matter. It wouldn't be long until they found out everything. And then where would he be? Town Fucked, that was where.

One check. That was it. That was all it would take. One check and his whole life would be over. He didn't want that. Worse, he didn't want to think about it right now. He wanted a distraction – *needed* a distraction.

Richard rubbed his forearm and came to a stop. In the distance, above the row of shops in front of him, distorted by the traffic lights and street lamps, was a high-rise tower block. He recognised it instantly.

He came to a slow halt, pulled out his phone and scrolled through his address book until he found the only number that didn't have a name registered to it. He dialled.

'Hello?' the voice finally answered.

Richard relaxed. The voice was familiar, friendly, oddly comforting.

'Jermaine?' Richard asked.

'Who wants to know?'

'It's good to hear your voice, bro,' Richard began. 'It's me, Richard, from Whitemoor. Prisoner alpha-sierra-seven-nine-three-two. We were on the ones together.'

There was a slight moment of hesitation, followed by deep laughter. 'Richard, my guy. I ain't forgotten about you that easily. What you saying, bro? You good?'

Richard was standing beside the telephone box outside a Sainsbury's Local supermarket. 'You remember that offer you made me when we were inside? I might have to take you up on it.'

'Course, bro. Whatever you need. No matter the time. You know I got you,' Jermaine said, his voice deep.

'What about now?'

'Yeah, bro. Come over.'

Richard smiled. 'Perfect. I'll be there in about ten minutes. Just got to get some provisions on the way down.'

'Safe,' Jermaine said, closing the conversation.

Richard hung up, made a right turn into the Sainsbury's Local and purchased a bottle of Russian Standard vodka. He was set for a heavy night. It had been a long time since he'd last drunk. And he couldn't wait to feel the burning sensation consume his throat and body again. He couldn't wait to relive the mind-altering feeling that helped block out all the shit in the world. He was in desperate need of it. The antidepressants weren't doing anything, so maybe this would help.

Richard left the shop, hailed a cab and then ordered the driver to stop a hundred yards from Jermaine's estate – the Huntingdon Estate. Then he made the rest of the journey on foot, with the neck of the bottle clutched tightly in his grip. When he arrived at the estate, he climbed a set of concrete stairs and headed towards the thirteenth floor. Jermaine Gordon's domain.

While they were in prison together, Jermaine had boasted to him about having the top half of the estate as his bachelor pad and then owning everyone else inside the building. In one way or another. They were all either working for him – running copious amounts of drugs and weapons to junkies in the surrounding area – or had worked for him, and were now settled in some sort of early retirement – that was, until a rival gang member stabbed them or mowed them down in a drive-by shooting. Nonetheless, all their hard work had helped him become the second-largest drug dealer in the East End of London. Second to Henry Matheson.

Richard stopped outside Jermaine's flat and knocked on the door. The heavy din of music inside stopped, and a few seconds later, Jermaine appeared. Even inside, he was wearing a thick black jumper with a hood pulled over his face and the drawstrings knotted across his collarbone. Jermaine was an intimidating guy – a hard bastard – and Richard had seen first-hand that he wasn't to be messed with; he doubted the other prisoner's face had ever healed from the beating he'd received after pissing off Jermaine over something minor. So insignificant, in fact, that Richard couldn't even remember what it was.

'Safe, bro,' Jermaine said, flashing a set of white teeth. 'It's good to see you, fam.'

They shook hands with a familiar greeting they'd practised and perfected in prison and then they both stepped inside. There was a handful of people Richard didn't recognise seated on the sofa playing video games, each slouched, their eyes glazed over.

'Drink?' Jermaine asked, calling Richard back.

Richard raised the vodka. 'I came prepared.'

'Knew I could rely on you, bro.' Jermaine gave Richard a slap on the back, took the bottle from him and headed to the kitchen. A few moments later he returned with two glasses in his hand, filled nearly to the brim.

'You expecting it to be a heavy night?' Richard asked.

'I know you are. Who brings a bottle of vodka with no mixer? It's calm, bro. We can get fucked together.'

Richard took the glass from Jermaine and scratched the back of his head with his free hand. 'I was kind of hoping you had some stronger stuff.'

Jermaine froze. 'Things that bad already?'

'You could say that.'

'I got you, bro. I got you. All in good time though, my friend. All in good time. What you after?'

'All of it.'

'Well, shit. Things must be tough. Come – let's go.'

As they entered the living room, Jermaine introduced him to the others. They mentioned their names, but he paid them no heed; he wasn't expecting to remember any of them in the morning. In the next thirty seconds, Richard went around the room and shook everybody's hand and eventually found himself a seat on the sofa beside Jermaine.

'Nice place you got. I heard you chat so much about it inside, for a long time I thought you were just chatting shit,' Richard said.

'I'm a man of my word. Like I told you. I got your back if you ever need it.'

Richard took a large gulp of the vodka. The alcohol rushed down his throat and burnt his insides. He grimaced, swallowing the taste, feeling his body warm and tingle.

'Easy, fam,' Jermaine said. 'Still a long night ahead of us. So, you gonna tell me what's up or am I gonna have to force it out of you?'

Richard exhaled deeply. Then he took another sip of the vodka.

'You hear about that body they found by the Olympic Stadium?' Richard asked.

'Yeah, I got my contacts down that way. I heard of it.' Jermaine paused, as if the cogs in his brain had begun to rotate.

'I found the body. It was buried in concrete. I found it and called the brass. I've been in an interview room all day.'

'Fucking pigs. They got anything on you?'

'Nah.'

'What you stressing about then, bro?'

'It was Danny Cipriano.'

'You shitting me?' Jermaine said. 'How you know that?'

'I recognised his hand, fam. The tattoos. The scar. The wart on his thumb.'

'You messing?'

Richard shook his head. 'Wish I was. And as soon as the feds start looking into me, they gonna find out everything there is to know.'

'You need me to sort it for you?' Jermaine pointed at one of the guys on the sofa. 'You know we're strapped.'

'No,' Richard said hastily.

'You want protection for yourself? You know I can give you anything you need.'

'Fuck that, J. I can't do that. I'm not getting involved with that. I'm not going back to prison again, man. I can't do time again. Do you know how hard it was for me to find work after getting out? It took me eighteen months, and I've only been in this job for a couple. Nah, I can't fuck it up like that.'

'You could work for me?'

Richard glanced at Jermaine, dumbfounded. The sincerity in Jermaine's voice was apparent.

'All due respect, I'll pass.'

'So what d'you want?'

'Right now, I just wanna forget. Forget any of this shit happened today.'

'You sure?' Jermaine said, placing his hand in the air. 'You ready for prison coke? Thought that shit was too much for you to handle?'

'The way I'm feeling, ain't nothing too heavy.'

Jermaine kissed his teeth, set the glass down on the table and lifted himself out of the chair. Richard hadn't realised, but in the short space of time they'd been talking, he'd already finished off three-quarters of his drink and the contents were beginning to take effect. In the corner of the room was a small chest of drawers. Jermaine pulled open the top one and removed a syringe and a few bags of white powder.

'You sure you wanna do this?'

'For the next few hours, I don't give a fuck what I do. So long as it gets me out of here.' Richard prodded his temple.

Jermaine shrugged. 'Your call, bro. But be careful with that one.' Jermaine pointed to the heroin in one of the plastic bags. 'That shit will give you the best high, but the nastiest comedown.'

Richard smirked and leant forward. 'What if I don't want to come down?'

| PART 2 |

CHAPTER 20

AN IRRESISTIBLE OFFER

The skin on Jake's arms and chest prickled as a gentle breeze rolled in through the window. Sleep evaded him like a star in the sky. In fact, his eyes hadn't closed since he'd climbed into bed, his mind warped with thought. The woman from the DPS had been helpful, but the investigator who would be looking after the case was even more so. His name was Craig, and he'd listened attentively as Jake had explained everything. About Drew's rape. About Garrison covering it up. And about how the three of them had tricked him into agreeing to fabricate evidence against an innocent man. He'd left no detail unexplained, no piece of evidence unaccounted for, no matter how small and insignificant he thought it was. He'd got it all out, like word vomit. But he felt better for it.

'I appreciate everything you've told me, Jake,' Craig had said. 'I'll be making this a priority for one of our investigation teams. We should have someone working with you on this case very soon.'

Jake hoped so. He didn't know how long he could maintain the façade of being a bent cop. It was important he didn't get in too deep. He had a family to protect, even though he knew he'd already endangered their lives by making the call.

As he stared up at the ceiling, images of Danny Cipriano buried alive in cement flashed in his mind, and in one of the stills, Danny's face was replaced with Elizabeth and the girls. Visceral, vivid. A layer of sweat formed on his body at the thought of what might happen to them if Liam, Drew or Garrison found out that he'd betrayed them.

He wondered whether he'd made the right decision. His colleagues were his closest friends – he didn't really have anyone outside of work that he considered close. He spent every day with Liam, Drew, and Garrison. He knew them better than he knew anyone else. At least he thought he did. What he'd done to them all was a betrayal of their trust and the friendship that he'd spent so long trying to make work.

But they also betrayed me when they involved me in this.

He'd had enough of thinking about it. Time to take his mind off it.

Jake rolled himself out of bed and checked the time – 3:46 a.m. Rubbing his eyes, he shuffled his way towards the kitchen. There, resting on the countertop, was the letter Elizabeth had shown him the other day. The one that was covered in the same red as his credit score. That was still very much a pertinent problem, one that was still outstanding.

One down, one to go. An idea sparked within him. He moved around to the other side of the kitchen and opened his laptop, logged in and began searching for quick, legitimate ways to make money. A few spam websites popped up, inviting him to take part in medical trials and sell products that would make him several hundred thousand pounds in the space of a few days. Pyramid schemes and all that. Jake knew it was bullshit – complete bullshit – and he ignored the first few hits on the top of Google. The search page was littered with exclamation marks and capital letters, offering him the next best-kept secret that was going to make him a millionaire. But there was one that stood out from the rest.

An article listing several ways to make money.

Investing. Loans. Gambling. They were all there. And they were screaming out to him.

He did some brief research around investing in stocks and shares and dismissed it as soon as he realised it was a long-term investment rather than a short-term gain. They couldn't afford to waste what little money they had and not see an immediate return. In twenty years maybe, but not now.

Loans, he learnt, were also a complete waste of time. The interest rates were astronomical and he knew the risks weren't worth it.

But gambling? That was something he was interested in. He didn't know a lot about sports – ever since his father died, he'd stayed as far away from football as possible. But he knew enough about Formula 1 and motor racing to be able to make educated guesses. Start off small, reinvest the winnings. Easy.

Interest piqued, Jake read through the article again and scanned the text for the best gambling website he could use. He found one and signed up. The company was promoting an offer. Bet £10, get an extra £10 to gamble on a free bet. Perfect.

Jake started entering his debit card details into the submission page. As soon as he hit enter and his dashboard loaded, the kitchen door opened. It was Maisie, rubbing sleep from her eyes. Her hair was a mess and she held a blanket in her hand.

Jake leapt out of his chair. 'Maisie! What are you doing out of bed?' He bent down by her side and held her in his arms.

'Why you up, Daddy?' she asked.

Jake chuckled. 'Daddy can't sleep. He's got lots of things to do that are keeping him awake.'

'What things?'

'Adult things. Why aren't you in bed?'

'You woke me up,' she said. Her eyes were bloodshot.

'I'm sorry, sweetie. Let's get you to bed.' Jake started towards the door.

'You come too?'

'Daddy's going to stay awake for a little bit longer. He's got to finish off those important things.'

'Please.' Her eyes widened and the sleep behind them seemed to disappear in an instant.

'OK.'

He looked at the computer, closed the lid and then headed upstairs. When he finally awoke in Maisie's bed two hours later, it was time to go to work.

CHAPTER 21

APLENTY

The streets were dead. It was just after six when Jake left the house, and Liam, Drew and Garrison were already there when he arrived at Bow Green minutes before seven. The three of them were in the kitchen, making a round of coffee.

'Morning,' Jake said groggily. He yawned. His eyes were heavy. It felt like a pair of weights had been strapped to them, keeping them permanently closed.

'What time do you call this?' Liam said to Jake as he entered, sounding more excitable than was normal for 7 a.m.

'Too fucking early,' Drew said, without realising that Liam was talking to Jake.

‘Not even the birds are awake yet,’ Garrison added as he dipped a chocolate digestive in his tea.

‘I know you’d rather be asleep, but we’ve got important work to get on with. Just send me a list of your overtime hours at the end of the week and I’ll get them all approved.’

Liam snatched a biscuit from Garrison and then left the kitchen with the detective constable following behind him.

As Jake moved about the kitchen, preparing his toast and coffee, he felt Drew’s stare boring into him. If he could help it, he’d avoid the man as much as possible. But he knew it was impossible.

‘Hey, pal,’ Drew said as he moved closer to Jake. ‘How you feeling?’

‘Fine.’

‘I’ve, erm… I’ve got something for you.’ Resting on the floor between Drew’s legs was his backpack. He bent down, reached inside it and pulled out a brown paper bag, and placed it next to Jake’s mug. ‘Ten grand. As promised.’

Jake stared at the bag in disbelief.

‘Put it away!’ he said, sliding it across the counter.

‘It’s yours.’ Drew slid it back.

Tentatively, Jake took the bag and looked at its contents. There, buried deep inside, was a thick wad of notes. The most money Jake had ever held in his life, and he was in awe of it. The unmistakable smell of cash wafted through the air, defeated the smell of burning toast and claimed victory in his nostrils. He didn't know for certain, but he was sure his mouth had fallen open.

'Plenty more where that came from as well.'

Yeah, Jake thought, course there is. For a while he hesitated, contemplating whether to take the money or not. And then he remembered he *needed* to. If he was going to maintain the façade that he was on their side – in *every* aspect of their operation – then he was going to have to take it, regardless of whether or not he truly wanted to keep it.

Jake wrapped the money in the bag, held it underneath his plate and moved into the office with his coffee in his other hand.

As they returned to their desks, Drew whispered in his ear. 'Like I said, plenty more where that came from. *Plenty*.'

Jake nodded in acknowledgement and feigned an impressed smile.

Drew whispered again. 'Remember what can happen if you don't keep up your end of the bargain.'

CHAPTER 22

H

Drew Richmond had never been a man for superstition. Or was it intuition? Either way, he was a good judge of character, and he knew when something wasn't right. And there was certainly something wrong with Jake's reaction just then. Specifically, he didn't know what, but it was off – the voices in his head were telling him so. And it worried him.

He'd known that getting Jake on board was going to take a while, but the way it had just played out wasn't what he'd been expecting. Jake was ready to accept the money. To accept the bribe. As though it were only a fiver or a tenner, and not ten grand – a complete contrast to the way he'd behaved yesterday. Was it possible that Jake had completely changed overnight? Or was he just being paranoid?

Yes, he thought. Yes, I am.

The voices of doubt had been coming in thick and fast recently, trampling the voices of reason. There was one simple explanation. And that same explanation was the same method of silencing the voices of doubt. A double-edged sword. But, like with most things, you had to take the good with the bad. For Drew, he took a lot of the good, with a lot of the bad.

Whistling 'Elephant Walk' as he exited the office, he made his way to the men's bathroom on the third floor. Inside, the urinals were empty, and he made a quick recce of the cubicles before jumping into the one furthest from the bathroom door.

Once inside, Drew lowered the toilet seat and sat on it, pulled out his burner phone from his pocket and switched it on. It was for emergency use only. The small screen of the Nokia 3110 illuminated and displayed the home page. He scrolled to the address book, found the number ending 783 – Liam's – and sent him a message.

Jake = confirmed.

He hit send and waited, twirling the device in his fingers.

Twenty seconds later, he had a response.

How?

Drew typed out his next response.

Drew: *10G sitting in his drawer. Buying silence. Trust me.*

Liam: *I hope I can.*

Drew: *Have you spoken to H?*

Liam: *Give me time. I have to deal with DC first.*

Drew's eyes fell over the message several times, incredulous, with a bit of rage sparking in the pit of his stomach. Liam had promised he'd speak to Henry a week ago, and he still hadn't. Danny Cipriano had only died two days ago, so what was his excuse?

Just as Drew started to type another response, Liam beat him to it.

Relax. H said Charlie and Mandy were coming to town. Maybe HU Archie Arnold ;)

That told Drew everything he needed to know. It wasn't what he wanted, but there was nothing he could do about it. A certain hierarchy was in motion when it came to bringing drugs into the country and distributing them through the city with the help of Henry Matheson, and if he was going to make any headway into it, he needed to abide by the rules. For now.

Sighing heavily, Drew switched off the device, eased his back against the cistern, and rested his head on the concrete wall uncomfortably. Now it was time for him to relax a little more, clear the noise and distraction in his head, silence the voices of doubt to stop them making him go crazy. The good with the bad.

Drew reached inside his blazer pocket, pulled out a small bag of white powder, dipped his finger in and rubbed the substance into his gums. The hit was almost instant, a numbing sensation swelling inside his mouth and the rest of his body. His pulse climbed, and a thin layer of sweat coated his body, slick, like the plans he had for the future. It wouldn't be long until the full high hit him.

All he had to do now was play it cool and make it look like there weren't Class A drugs surging through his system.

On his way out, Drew sealed the bag and placed it back in his pocket, flushed the toilet and then washed the sin away from his skin.

CHAPTER 23

SCOUT'S HONOUR

The money was by his leg, hidden in the depths of his drawer, resting beneath four lever-arch folders and a fresh packet of Post-it notes. But, despite hiding it under all those layers, Jake couldn't shake the feeling that it was on his person, that it was wrapped around him, plastered over his skin and clothes and face. A fancy-dress costume that declared to the world he was the victim of police bribery. He closed his eyes and tried to banish all thought of the money from his mind, but it was pointless. It lingered and followed him around like a ball and chain, weighing his conscience down.

Liam's office door opened.

'Jake,' he called. 'A word?'

Jake looked at his desk, then his drawer, and then the rest of the office before climbing out of his chair and moving across the floor. He shut Liam's door behind him. The hubbub of the office played quietly in the background.

Liam was swinging from side to side in his chair, drinking from his coffee cup. It was nearly filled to the brim.

'Another one already, guv?' Jake asked, attempting to lighten the mood and soften the blow of what was about to come.

'There's more coffee in my body than blood right now,' Liam replied.

They both chuckled, but it was over as quickly as it had started. An awkward silence descended and an ominous air followed. Mercifully, it was ended by Liam telling Jake to sit.

'There's something I wanted to discuss with you, Jake…'

'Oh…?'

Liam cleared his throat. 'Last night. I know it was a bit of a shock and may take a while to process, but I wanted to check in, see how you were doing.'

Jake swallowed, preparing himself for the torrent of bullshit and lies that was about to come out of his mouth. Whichever way he played it, he needed to be careful; Liam was a highly trained officer, and there was no doubt in Jake's mind that he would be scrutinising Jake's actions for any sign that he was lying: dilated pupils, sweat forming on his skin, constantly averting his gaze, rapid speaking, over-explaining – all of them telltale signs of deceit which he needed to be careful not to display.

'I mean… it was a bit of a shock, to begin with. But…' He paused. 'It made a lot more sense when I thought about it. I mean, I worked out why you guys were so interested in Archie Arnold during the Stratford Killer case. You needed someone to pin the murder on, just like you do now.'

'Good man. I always knew you were a good egg, Jake. But I trust we have you fully on board with this?'

'You do, sir.'

'And, not that I hope it ever comes to this, but you're aware of what will happen if you turn into a bad egg?'

Jake nodded. 'Very much so.'

'Even better.' Liam took another sip of his coffee. As he set the cup down, he burped, sending a dense cloud of alcoholic spirit towards Jake. There certainly wasn't any hint of coffee inside that mug. 'From what I understand,' Liam continued, 'Drew's already shown you how loyalty works in this team?'

Jake lifted his head, his eyes locked with Liam's. 'He's made it very clear.'

'You can always rely on Drew to do that.'

He hesitated again, this time leaning closer towards Jake with his arms on the desk. His dark, unassuming gaze bore into Jake's, ruffling the hairs on his arms. 'You know you can trust me, right?'

'Of course, guv.'

'Is there… is there anything you wanna tell me?'

Jake considered for a moment and then settled on telling the truth. At least, part of it.

'I'm just tired,' Jake said. 'Didn't get much sleep last night. Maisie was up and it was my turn to look after her.'

'I know how it is. I was fifteen when my little sister was born. Fucking nightmare. Had to look after her and make sure she was all right. So I know what you're going through. But you sure there isn't something else? You look like you've got the weight of the world on your shoulders.'

That ain't the half of it.

Jake glanced down at his lap. A lump swelled in his throat.

'Please keep it between us,' he said, making sure to get the caveat in as soon as possible.

'You have my word.' Liam raised his fingers in a salute. 'Scout's honour.'

'We're having issues… financially.'

'Still?'

Jake nodded. 'I feel embarrassed even telling you. It's an accumulation of a lot of things. The Dark Web cloning my details didn't help. But, basically, a long time ago I crashed into a car and the driver's insurance turned out to be fraudulent. So now my insurances have gone up, the premiums are through the roof and I've got legal fees I'm struggling to pay. No matter what car I look at changing to, the prices are astronomical – and I need a car to get to work. And, to top it all off, our energy and water bills have gone up. They've said we underpaid in the past year so they've "adjusted the bill to reflect this".' He used air quotes for the final few words.

It took Liam a long time to respond. For a moment, Jake wondered if his boss had been listening at all.

'I don't know what to say, mate. Has it been tough?'

Jake nodded.

'And you and Elizabeth...?'

'For now. We both know it's an issue. I've told her I'll fix it, but it won't be long until things get really bad.'

'Sure. Sure.' Liam trailed off again. 'Do you have a solution? A way to fix it?'

Jake smirked. 'Well, Drew's reward was a nice, welcome gift, I can assure you. That'll help cover some of it. Without that, I mean… I even looked up gambling and loans last night. You don't know how close I was to making a mistake.'

'A big mistake,' Liam replied. 'You never wanna resort to that type of thing. Trust me. I've been there and have got the scars to prove it. Everything'll sort itself out, kid. I s'pose our new work together can help pay some of it?'

'I reckon so.'

'And I'm sure we can keep this out of the Directorate of Professional Standards' noses. They don't need to know just yet.'

'I… I… thank you, sir.'

'Now, stop flattering me and get back to work. I've got a call to make.'

CHAPTER 24

TENACIOUS TANNER

The cold air bit Liam's fingers and nose as he pulled his car door open and hopped inside. He placed his hands on the steering wheel, then paused to look around. Everything was as it should be. The empty coffee cup he'd left there this morning. The pair of sunglasses hiding in the glove compartment. The Jo Nesbo book that he hadn't read for weeks lying on the back seat. The air freshener hanging from the rear-view mirror.

But there was something different. Something wrong. Out of place. There was a funny smell, strange. As though someone who sweated profusely – or just permanently stank of body odour – had been inside.

At once his thoughts turned to The Cabal. Was this their doing? Had The Farmer been sent to give him a warning – and at his own place of work? Staying inside the car wasn't worth the risk. Better to get somewhere that hadn't been compromised.

Liam jumped out and locked the car repeatedly, just for good measure, then made his way out of the grounds and found an isolated bench next to a tree by the main road. Cars paraded past, paying him little attention, and pedestrians scurried across the pavement with their headphones in and heads down, looking into their black mirrors. Nobody looked his way, almost as if he wasn't even there. Perfect location for a conversation. He removed a small burner phone from his pocket – different to the one he'd used to speak with Drew – and dialled the only contact in it.

'Yes?' the voice on the other end asked.

'Can you talk?'

'Wouldn't have answered otherwise. What do you want?' There was that usual hostility in Elliot Bridger's voice.

'How's retirement?' Liam asked. 'Treating you well?'

'I know you didn't call for a chat, Liam. You and I are busy people.'

'Retirement's busy? Well, I don't like the sound of it if that's the case.'

'Get on with it, Liam.'

'I thought I'd call to tell you the news.'

'What news?'

'Danny Cipriano. He's dead.'

Silence.

'Bridger… You there?'

'How?' Bridger asked.

'Taken from witness protection. The Farmer. Drowned in cement and then buried in it.'

'Fucking… what?' Bridger choked. 'Where?'

'Olympic Stadium construction site.'

'You're shitting me?'

'Wish I was.'

Another brief silence as Bridger controlled his breathing.

'Hold on a minute…' he began. 'Why's he dead?'

'Because apparently Danny thought that freedom of speech applied to him, and that he could talk to someone about us.'

'Did he mention any names?'

'None. That I'm aware of.'

The last time they'd met, Liam had been pointing a gun at Bridger's head, forcing the man to lie to Jake down the phone. Since then, they'd become acquaintances, dangling on the precipice of becoming friends. They were allies, united in their common goal of climbing the ladder of The Cabal's ranks, and both men knew first-hand what The Cabal was capable of.

Sometimes in this business it was better to make friends than enemies. Especially if you wanted to survive.

There was a heavy sigh on the phone. 'Of all the places to do it as well,' Bridger said. 'They've left you with a mess to clean up.'

'Unless The Cabal's got a plan I don't know about.'

'What are you saying?' Bridger's tone dropped.

'The Cabal wouldn't tell me who the body was, and I only found out it was Danny from the pathologist report. I had no warning that it was going to happen either. No preamble. It just happened. Now *I've* got to deal with it. And something doesn't seem right. It's making me think maybe Danny did mention names. Maybe Danny did implicate either me or you or the rest of us. And I'm being kept in the dark as a precursor for what's about to come.'

Bridger started to speak – babbling incoherently – but eventually trailed off.

'I'm just saying you need to be cautious. Put all the bad blood behind us and listen to me. You just need to be sure you've got an alibi at all times and that your whereabouts are well documented.'

'You and I both know that counts for nothing when it comes to this. You could have all the evidence in the world and all it would take is one administrative error, and *poof* – all gone.' Bridger hesitated. 'Fucking hell, Liam. I said I was done with this shit. We agreed that this shit would be over as soon as I got Danny and Michael out of remand.'

'I'm just telling you to be careful, that's all. Nothing's happened yet. And we don't know if anything will either. You just need to be prepared to take the necessary actions.'

'This is bullshit.'

Liam rolled his eyes. 'I don't like it any more than you do. But this is something we've got to deal with. We both knew this day was coming.'

'Not this soon though,' Bridger added.

'There's something else as well.'

'What?'

'Tanner.'

Silence. Liam knew the name sent palpitations through Bridger's body.

'He's on the case. We're investigating Danny's death. But this time it's different. He's onside. Drew managed to work some magic on him.'

'Magic doesn't exist.'

'It's true.'

'Drew's even more of a loose cannon than Jake. I've seen it. And I've warned you about him in the past.'

Liam rolled his eyes. 'I don't need reminding. My point is, you know that Jake's going to want to speak to you. It's inevitable. Wherever Danny appears, you appear.'

'Looks like you need to watch out for yourself as well then, Liam. Tanner's tenacious.'

'You look after yourself, and I'll look after myself. If Tanner does anything he shouldn't, you can leave him to me. I know his weaknesses.'

CHAPTER 25

UNEXPECTED DISCOVERY

Uncovering shocking and unhelpful information was becoming a somewhat recurring theme throughout the investigation for Jake. First it was Drew and what he'd done to Hannah Bryant. Then the identification of Danny Cipriano as the dead body in the cement. Then uncovering the corrupt organisation Drew, Liam and Garrison were running.

And now it was this. To top it all off.

In the last half hour, Jake had been tasked with investigating the life and times of their number one suspect, Richard Maddison. After running his name through the PNC, Jake had unearthed a wealth of information on Richard Maddison that would undoubtedly seal the man's fate. He had a past, a history that he probably didn't want people to know about – least of all the bent cops who were trying to pin a murder on him.

In 2005, he had been convicted of sexual activity with a child, after sleeping with an underage girl he'd met in a nightclub in Newcastle. He'd found out about her age the following day, and was later sentenced to sixteen months in prison and put on the Sex Offenders Register.

But that wasn't the most interesting thing Jake had discovered.

Imprisonment for the sexual assault wasn't the only time Richard had ended up behind bars. In fact, when he was younger, in his early twenties, he'd been arrested a couple of times for robbing shops and convenience stores on an estate in Newcastle. The same estate that Danny, Michael and Luke Cipriano – The Crimsons – had grown up on. Following his arrest, he'd been served with an ASBO and given far more warnings than he deserved. But then something went wrong: Richard had broken into a car and tried to pilfer the contents, but was arrested and charged with the help of some keen eyewitnesses – who later turned out to be Danny and Michael Cipriano.

After Richard's conviction for sexual assault, he and Danny's paths had crossed for the first time in years. Danny had been sentenced to six months for domestic violence at the time – which, with the wonders of hindsight, should have been the other way round, given that it was later found out he was the one being abused by his girlfriend Louise. During their time together, Danny had come clean about being a witness and helping put Richard in jail the first time round.

Their relationship was complex and that was what scared Jake the most.

There was a history between the two of them, a vendetta, a justice owed. And it meant there was now a credible motive for Richard to have killed Danny. They were now one step closer to slamming the final nail in his coffin.

Jake was torn.

If he'd made this discovery without knowing that they were trying to pin the murder on Richard, then he would have told Liam – or whoever cared most – immediately. But now that he knew an innocent man's life balanced on this piece of evidence, a part of him didn't want to turn it in. *Couldn't* turn it in. But then he remembered he had colleagues working towards the same outcome. What if Drew or Garrison found the information when it was his job to find it? They'd realise he wasn't all-in like he'd convinced them he was. No… it was the right thing to do. For the good of the investigation. For the good of his fight against Liam and Drew and Garrison. He needed to do it this way.

It was the only way.

Reluctantly, Jake pushed himself away from his desk and wandered over to Liam's door. He knocked and then entered before giving Liam a chance to respond.

'Guv, I've got an update for you. I think you're going to like it.'

CHAPTER 26

FAVOURITES

Nigel Clayton was a man of many talents. First and foremost, he was a businessman, an entrepreneur. Good with people; even better with numbers. Which, as the only British member in the group, helped. If they needed a solicitor's hand to smooth things over with their money laundering businesses, or even another accountant, Nigel knew just the people. Nigel was also very creative, and he was good at coming up with ideas on how to launder money – the reason he was here. As a group, they had a surplus of it, and they needed to siphon it through the system and turn it into clean cash somehow. That was where Nigel stepped into a league of his own.

'Send it abroad.'

'No. Keep in country.' Georgiy wagged his finger in Nigel's face.

They were sitting in their nightclub, just on the outskirts of West Ham. Coalesce. A shitty name they'd pulled from the dictionary. It was the first of three properties they used for money laundering. The process had been foreign to Georgiy when he'd first started out but after years of experience and learning on the job, it was beginning to make sense. But it made even more sense to entrust it to someone who was an expert.

'Hear me out,' Nigel said, pointing his finger at Georgiy. 'How much are we set to get from the Danny hit?'

'Two-fifty.'

'Two hundred and fifty grand? I thought it was five hundred.'

Georgiy leant forward, closer to Nigel's face. 'Your fuck-up lost us half money.'

'Fuck-up? What fuck-up?'

'The cement. It not set in time. You said cooling agent would cool down. For that, we lose fifty per cent.'

Nigel gesticulated wildly. From appearances, he came across as an inferior, an insubordinate; he was physically small, and he looked as though he couldn't carry himself in a fight. But he was the complete opposite. He wasn't afraid to stand up for himself; nor was he afraid to argue and defend his point.

'Bullshit!' Nigel exclaimed. 'I told you – I'm a fucking accountant, not a fucking scientist. How was I supposed to know it wasn't going to cool down in time? Blame Vitaly just as much as me.'

'Don't worry,' Georgiy said, raising a hand and quickly silencing Nigel. 'Vitaly on my list already.'

But you already have an extra black mark against your name, he thought.

'Enough, all right, fine,' Nigel said, resting back in his chair. 'As I was saying, we need to launder a quarter million outta the country. We've already got enough businesses as it is. If we send it abroad, we can make back our investment… and then some.'

'How?'

'Gold.'

Georgiy rolled his eyes and scoffed.

'It's simple.' Nigel leapt out of his chair, grabbed a pen and notepad, and returned to the desk. 'Ship the money to France. Get someone to transfer it further afield – Belgium, Germany, the Netherlands. Find a contact who can supply gold, cheap. Buy it with the laundered money, and then take the gold down to Dubai or the Middle East. There, sell it – for either the same amount that we paid for it, or more – and then send the money to our offshore accounts.'

'Does not sound simple,' Georgiy said, trying to deny the fact that his interest was piqued.

'It's not easy when you don't know how. But that's why you've got me involved.'

Georgiy rubbed the side of his face as he considered. 'Who we use as mule?'

'Tatiana. She's a woman, and she's got several passports. They shouldn't suspect her. Or anyone you want… a stranger on the street… anyone, so long as you pay enough for their silence.'

It was a lot to think about, and it was a lot of money to be laundering – their biggest haul yet. Up until this point, they'd only ever received low levels of money for carrying out hits on targets. Twenty grand. Thirty. Fifty. Even a hundred grand one time. But nothing as substantial as this. And then there were the other branches of the business that he was currently looking after on behalf of The Cabal. The bootlegging. The arms deals. The small-scale drug dealing with the Albanians and Romanians that was kept out of Henry Matheson and Jermaine Gordon's noses. There were already too many facets to their businesses. Perhaps it was time to change it up.

'Arrange everything,' he told Nigel. 'Plan it for couple days' time. Wait for dust to settle on Cipriano hit. But tell me before you agree. I will tell Tatiana.'

Nigel bowed his head, grabbed his things and then left.

Just as Nigel shut the door behind him, the telephone in Georgiy's office rang. He eyed the number and waited a moment before answering it, reaching for the television remote and switching on the news.

'Hello?' he said tentatively as he held the phone to his ear.

'It's me.'

'What is it now?'

'I have another hit for you.'

'Has it been approved?'

'Yes.'

'What is the name?'

'Richard Maddison. But this is different.'

'Yes…'

'You have to make it look like a suicide. Russian suicide. Your favourite.'

'Same pay?' Georgiy asked.

'Same pay.'

Georgiy turned his attention to the television. Something caught his eye.

'Fine,' he said. 'Send me details.'

Just as he was about to end the call, the images on the BBC News screen changed. Staring at him was a live image of the London Olympic Stadium.

'Fuck,' he whispered.

'What?'

'Danny Cipriano. He's on the news.'

'Oh, I know. I told the news reporter to put him there.'

CHAPTER 27

COMING CLEAN

Liam lowered the lid of his laptop slowly, as if that would delay the inevitable. The shit was about to hit the proverbial, they were swimming up the creek, and they were wildly unprepared.

Tanya. She'd betrayed him by releasing the news story too early. He'd told her explicitly to wait for his instruction. And now she'd placed pressure on Liam and his team to solve the case quickly – with the eyes of the whole world watching. It was too late to regret giving her it in the first place, but it was the only emotion in him right now. That and rage. How could he have been so stupid as to trust her with information this big? The answer was simple. Hormones. Ego. Thinking with his penis. Again.

Liam groaned heavily and pinched the bridge of his nose.

He needed a drink. A strong one. Bottle of bourbon maybe? Or perhaps something a little stronger – like absinth? He had a bottle stashed away for when times were really tough.

As Liam scooted himself over to the filing cabinet behind him, a knock came at the door.

Drew.

'What do you want?' Liam said as he kicked himself back to his desk.

'I… I…' Drew rubbed his nose and sniffed profusely. 'I… I just wanted a chat.'

Liam climbed out of his chair, took a step forward and paused a foot away from Drew. The man's pupils were like disks. His pores were open, his lips parted, his chest bouncing up and down ferociously.

The symptoms were the same. Always the same.

'Empty out your pockets,' Liam ordered.

Drew's eyes widened even further. 'You what?'

'Don't "you what?" me, *fella*. I said empty your pockets.'

Tentatively, Drew placed his hands in his front and back trouser pockets, removing his phone, wallet and a loose business card that had his contact information on it.

'What's this about, Liam?'

'*All* your pockets.'

Drew's face dropped. Busted, and he knew it. Slowly, his hand moved inside his blazer pocket.

As soon as he pulled out the small bag of powder, Liam yanked it from Drew's hand and threw it to the ground. Then he grabbed Drew's collar and shoved him against the wall, using his body weight to pin Drew in place, leaning into him with one arm pressed against the man's collarbone.

'Guv! Relax! What are you—'

'Don't you dare!' Liam growled in Drew's face, baring his teeth, keeping them pressed together so his voice didn't travel through the walls. 'What the fuck are you playing at? You're using again? I thought you'd stopped.'

Drew babbled like a baby, struggling to cogently place his words in a sentence.

'You said you'd stopped,' Liam grunted.

'I had!'

'The evidence suggests otherwise. So don't lie to me, Drew. Don't fucking lie to me!' He was seething with anger. 'Is this why you keep hassling me to speak with Henry? So you can get your next fucking fix?'

Drew nodded sheepishly.

'I don't believe it. I…' Liam released his grip on Drew and shoved him onto the ground before stepping over him. 'I've told you to get away from it, Drew. That stuff will fuck you up.' Liam pointed at the packet of powder on the floor. 'And, trust me, you don't want to go down that route. It's very difficult to get back from.'

'I'll… I'll…' Drew choked as he clambered back to his feet. 'I'll try, Liam.'

Liam clenched his fist. He was ready to punch Drew in the face repeatedly – to use him as a boxing bag to vent his frustrations with Tanya – but he didn't want to give her the satisfaction of staying in his head rent-free any longer than she deserved.

'You need to stop,' Liam ordered. 'Otherwise, it won't be able to continue.'

'What won't?'

'I've been doing some thinking. About the possibilities of a partnership. You. Me. Henry.'

'We already have a partnership…' Drew brushed himself down and cleared his throat.

'It's small-time. Minor. Nothing in comparison to what it could be. Think about it, that shitty estate – with Archie and the rest of them – it's little league. We want big leagues. Like Milner moving to City. Nobody saw that coming – now look at him. Considering we're the ones letting Matheson bring the stuff into the country, we should be taking a bigger hit. We just have to find out how. Any suggestions?'

Drew shook his head.

'Maybe when you've sobered up,' Liam said.

Drew didn't respond, and for a while neither of them said anything. Even though he'd cleared the air about Drew's drug habit, there was still an elephant in the room. Now seemed like the perfect opportunity to air it out. Liam swallowed. Hard. 'There's something else as well.'

'Oh?'

'I need you to be honest with me. I won't get mad if you tell me the truth.'

'What is it, guv?'

'Only you know what it is you need to tell me. Hannah Bryant.'

At the mention of Hannah's name, Drew remained still, placid; the rapid rise and fall of his chest was the only visible part of his body that moved, his entire face glazed over with fear.

'How do you know about that?'

'It's my job to know. And I'm assuming Jake does as well. Is that why you gave him the money?'

Drew sighed. His gaze fell to the floor and he kept it there as he spoke. 'He found out about it when he took her witness statement. I had no idea she was going to be there. I haven't seen her since then. Hardly recognised her either. It was fifteen years ago.'

'What happened?'

'I was just… I was just starting out – with Pete. She was a little shitbag, causing aggro on the streets. ASBO-related stuff. Minor. Not worth the hassle of dealing with it properly. But she was pretty – *really* pretty. So I stuck with it. Promised her that if she did a couple of things for me, I'd be able to do a couple of things for her and make the charges go away.'

'Sexual things?'

'No! Never any of that. I got her to buy me alcohol and food and cigarettes and drugs and stuff. She's the one who introduced me to Embassy cigs! I wanted her to think I was a good one, and that I wasn't just using her for things. One night I invited her over. I'd done a bit of coke beforehand – you know, settle some of the nerves, take the edge off. But when she came over she was jumpy. Nervy. So I offered her some.'

'She accepted?'

'Yeah. But not much. Not as much as me. And then we started talking. Getting to know one another. We ordered a takeaway, had a few drinks, and then before either of us knew it, we were in my bedroom, having sex.'

'Was she conscious?'

'I… I…'

'Drew?'

'I don't know. I can't remember. It was all a bit of a blur. I was off my nut.'

'So you kept doing it anyway?'

'It felt good. It had been so long since I'd last… you know.'

Liam exhaled deeply, keeping his stress levels as low as he could. He'd promised he wouldn't get angry, and he was going to honour that.

'OK… OK…' Liam said, his mind starting to consider next steps. 'Who else knows about this? Garrison?'

'Yeah. He was the one investigating. We managed to dot the Is and cross the Ts on that one so nobody knew we were in the same department. He pretended to be from the Police Complaints Authority. Back then everything was so lax, nobody gave it a second glance.'

'And what about any evidence?'

Drew sniffed and wiped his nose with the back of his sleeve.

'Forensics found some on her body. But he managed to get rid of it.'

'Are you sure?'

'Yes. He promised me. Why? You afraid Jake might do something with it?'

'I don't think it's Jake you have to be worried about this time.'

CHAPTER 28

FLYTRAP

Garrison returned to his desk after taking what felt like the longest shit of his life. It was almost as if it had taken on a life of its own, like that worm inside the copper from the book *Filth*. But there was one silver lining though: on his way back to the office he'd caught sight of Drew and Liam having a go at one another in Liam's office. It was difficult not to smile; his plan to split them up was working. They had no idea what he was doing, and they never would either. Confidence could be a cruel mistress, but not this time.

So long as Drew didn't come running to him expecting him to pick up the pieces. The soppy little shit always looked up to him for guidance and approval, like some stray mutt seeking attention, companionship, someone to look after him. Always had, always would. It was draining, and it was one of the biggest things he was looking forward to during his retirement.

No. More. Drew.

Garrison removed his phone from his pocket, unlocked it and loaded Kingdom of Empires. There was a notification informing him that his clan was under attack. His castles and barracks were rapidly losing men and weapons; he was being ransacked by another clan. All those hours – and the considerable amount of money too – that he'd invested in it, all gone to waste. But right now, there was nothing he could do about it – there was something more important going on.

He had a message he needed to send.

He opened his chat with LG540 and typed out a message.

BBC gone live. D and L arguing already.

Garrison hit send. Waited. And waited. When an immediate response didn't come, he tapped his foot on the floor, bouncing his knee up and down. He exited the chat and then re-entered, hoping that would force a notification through. The Cabal usually responded quickly. When a response didn't come, he compiled another message.

Think L will hold press conference. Advise phase 2.

The moment Garrison hit 'Send', Drew exited Liam's office, hurried over and placed his hand on Garrison's computer monitor. Panicked, Garrison exited the chat and returned to the home screen where his village was being pilfered.

'Are you playing a game?'

'Good spot, genius. And what?' Garrison hoped Drew hadn't seen anything that would give him away.

'We've got shit to do. Important shit. And not a lot of time to do it. Yet, here you are playing poxy video games...'

Garrison shrugged and gave him a steely, unperturbed look. 'Practising for when I retire.'

'I suppose people need hobbies, don't they?' Drew rubbed his nose and snorted.

'Yes, and what's yours?' Garrison raised his eyebrows and glanced at Drew's nose. It looked a little redder than usual. Was that a nostril caving in?

'Wouldn't you like to know,' Drew replied. 'Jake's found a link between Maddison and Cipriano. Now it's *our* turn to do what we're good at.'

Perfect. Come to Daddy, Garrison thought. He was like a Venus flytrap, lying dormant, waiting for its prey to fly straight into its mouth. And Drew had done just that.

Garrison smirked. 'I've got the perfect idea. Listen up, and listen good. Here's what I want you to do…'

CHAPTER 29

THC–27

Drew was grateful for the little kick of ecstasy he'd taken in the bathroom – his second of the day – before leaving the office. It was much needed. It had given him a gentle boost right in the sweet spot.

Skipping down the stairs two at a time, he felt the blood surge through his body. At the foot of the building, he exited Bow Green and made a left turn. The station was positioned on the corner of a main road, and opposite was a row of small, independent businesses. One of them, an off-licence called Prime Time News, was a place he frequented on lunch and coffee breaks. The owner always gave them a discount on fizzy drinks and snacks. Drew had joked that it was because he was an illegal and he was afraid they'd use their contacts in the Home Office to get him deported. But there was no substance to it. Drew saw it as a fair trade-off; they were keeping him safe out there in the big wide world, and he was returning the favour in kind by making sure they were well fed and hydrated enough to do it.

'Afternoon, mate,' Drew said as he approached the cash register.

'Ah, Detective! It is good to see you! You are looking very well. What can I get you today?'

'Nothing from here, mate. I need something else. You still having that extension put in out back?'

'Yes, why?'

'You got any bags of cement, or any large blocks of concrete I could take? I need it for an investigation.'

The proprietor hesitated before responding. 'Erm… I will have to just check. I will only be a moment. Please wait there.'

'Perfect, mate. Nice one. Anything you've got'll help!'

The shop owner disappeared through a door, travelled along a narrow corridor and then out of the shop. As he waited, Drew tapped his finger on the cash desk. His head darted from left to right, admiring the variety of sweets in front of him. And then his eyes fell on the wall of tobacco and alcohol. His mouth became dry and he licked his lips. He needed a smoke, but —

The shop owner returned, distracting Drew from his thoughts. In his hand, he held a small chunk of concrete, four inches long and two inches wide in the shape of a dagger. Drew's face lit up at the sight of it. He placed his hand in his pocket, pulled out an evidence bag and ordered the shop owner to place the concrete inside the bag.

'My hero,' Drew said, sealing the bag shut. 'Don't you go changing.'

He left, raced across the road and skipped up the steps into Bow Green. One piece of the puzzle down, one to go. At the back of the station, in a separate annexe, was the evidence building, where the SOCOs and crime scene managers were tasked with collating and submitting evidence for forensic analysis. The place was a fortress that required key card access.

It was times like this that he was grateful for the second hit.

Standing before him was a set of revolving doors. Bloody things always invoked fear inside him. Ever since he was a child. What if they stopped midway through and he got trapped inside one? Irrational fears – no matter how crazy and absurd – were always heightened by drugs.

Eventually, and what felt like a thousand steps later, he fell out of the revolving doors and into the main lobby. In front of him was a set of double doors, and to his right was a reception desk.

'Can I help you?' a balding man asked. He was perched all high and mighty on his office chair, peering over the top of his computer monitor.

'How's it going?' Drew asked, feeling slightly gutted it wasn't a woman working behind there.

Each to their own.

'How can I help you?'

'I've got a meeting with Sandy.'

The crime scene manager.

'You want me to tell her you're here?'

'It's cool. Just buzz me through and I'll find her. I know where she is.'

The man's brow furrowed in a look that he'd obviously mastered through years of shooting it at untrustworthy-looking people.

'You got your warrant card?'

Drew nodded and flashed it at him, keeping his index finger over his name as much as possible.

The desk jockey seemed content. 'Sign in as well, if you wouldn't mind.'

A wry smile grew on Drew's face. He took the pen from the surface and scribbled Jake's name, forging his signature along with it. Then he made his way through the double doors, thanking the man as he left.

The corridor he entered was a world away from the ones he was used to in Bow Green. Modern, contemporary. Everything about the wall fixtures, flooring and ceiling told him that the department had a much bigger budget than MIT, that much he was certain of. It reminded him of the science labs from his school years – white, sterile, bright lights overhead, large worktops visible through windows, row upon row of evidence shelves and a storage unit at the back of the room.

Feeling like a defiant adolescent, Drew wandered to the end of the corridor. He soon spotted the room he needed.

The only problem now was how to get into it. Beside every door handle in the corridor was a key card scanner. Find the key card, find the evidence, make the switch. But whose? The building was empty. In the minute that he'd been standing there, he'd heard nothing – not even the sound of movement, chatter, laughter, or someone dropping a mug in the kitchen somewhere. It was eerily silent.

And then he had an idea.

Sandy. The crime scene manager. The reason he was supposedly here.

Her office was on the second floor, on the other side of the building. He strode across the linoleum floor, feigning confidence, attempting to make it look like he had every right to be there, while in his mind he formulated a cover story, hoping he wouldn't need to use it.

Sandy's door was made from wood; a small, rectangular hole, filled with glass, allowed Drew to peer through. His cheek hovered millimetres from the glass, his eyes scanning what he could see of the room. On the right-hand side was a chair, on the left was a shelf with filing cabinets beneath it and immediately in front of him was Sandy, sitting at her desk with her back to him, working on a laptop with a set of files beside her. A coffee cup rested on them, stains running down the side of the mug. She was plugged into a set of headphones, the sound echoing to Drew on the other side of the door. Heavy. Lots of thrashing. Drums. Symbols. Screaming. Metal.

As his eyes moved about the room, he found her lanyard resting on the corner of her desk.

Bingo.

Drew tried the door carefully, holding his breath. Much to his surprise, it opened.

He was in.

Keeping one foot on the door to hold it open, he reached across the room and lifted her lanyard. He clutched it tightly in his hands, beads of sweat forming in the small of his back and on his forehead, then pulled the door to gently. As soon as it was closed, he hurried down the corridor, into the stairwell and down the steps, the adrenaline levels in his blood reaching new highs. At the bottom of the stairs, he snapped his head left and right. Empty still. He paused for a second, and then made his way towards the evidence room.

Before him, in the centre of the room, was a row of shelving units, like the ones he'd seen in Costco. Evidence bags from the various cases that the SOCO team were working on dangled from thick metal poles which ran across the length of the units. At the end of each one was the case number.

Drew wandered the length of the shelves, searching for Danny's.

HC/08921/D.

He found it and began to forage for a piece of evidence that had been lifted from the scene. A piece of cement. A piece of concrete. Anything that he would be able to switch with the sample he'd taken from the shop.

He thumbed through the evidence bags until he stumbled across what he was looking for.

Evidence number THC-27. The letters were the initials of the staff member who'd bagged it up, while the number corresponded to the number in the evidence list. This small piece of concrete that had been extracted from the crime scene was the twenty-seventh exhibit. In the top corner of the bag was a label that signified the evidence had been examined.

Lovely.

He placed the bag on the shelving unit, removed the one he had in his pocket and switched the stickers over. Returning the fake sample to the shelf, he pocketed the original and rearranged everything so that it was back to the way he'd found it. Breathing a sigh of relief, he made his way out of the evidence room, past the desk jockey and out of the lab.

Mission complete.

Now all he needed to do was plant the evidence.

But, as he headed back towards MIT, he realised that wasn't enough. It wouldn't do. He wanted another piece of evidence. Something that would incriminate Richard Maddison for something else and make sure he went down for a *really* long time.

Before he headed to his car, Drew made a detour to his computer, grabbed his USB flash drive and started transferring files onto it.

Richard Maddison had no idea what he would be coming home to.

CHAPTER 30

FOR THE BUSINESS

'Where are you?' Garrison asked into the phone. He was sitting inside his car, with the keys still in the ignition.

'I'm walking up to it now.'

'Where? I don't see—'

Garrison swallowed his words. A figure came into view in the distance, with one hand pressed against his head and the other in the pocket of his gilet. Dressed in jeans and a forest-green jumper, the man looked like he'd just stepped off a farm. He strode with purpose and Garrison watched him wander up to the café they'd agreed to meet at.

'I'll be there in a minute. Find a table. I'll have a coffee. You're buying.'

Garrison brushed himself down and pulled the collar of his trench coat above his ears. With his hands in his pockets, he started towards the café. By the time he entered, there was a coffee already on the table for him. There was one other couple sitting in the far corner of the café. After a quick – and in his experience accurate – assessment, he didn't deem them as a risk.

'All right, Phil,' Garrison gestured to the man behind the counter with a nod.

'All right, Pete, how's it going,' the owner replied.

Garrison didn't respond. Instead, he focused his attention on the man at the table. He was small and well built, with short, jet-black hair and a shaggy beard. A set of stitches graced his chin, and another graze decorated his cheek. But what surprised Garrison the most was that he wore the countenance of a man who had nothing to worry about, when, in actual fact, Garrison knew he should be more worried than he was letting on. The man's name was Isaac, and he'd been chosen very early on in the process.

'Pete!' Isaac said, rising out of his chair and shaking Garrison's hand. The man's handshake was how Garrison remembered it: firm, like he'd been wanking too much.

'Good to see you.'

They both sat, and Garrison took a sip of his coffee.

'It's good to see you,' Isaac repeated, shuffling forward on his seat. He sat hunched, and his shoulders looked like separate heads growing from his back. 'I'm glad you called. I've been shitting myself after the other night.'

'You don't look it,' Garrison remarked and glanced down at the man's Rolex, which sparkled in the light. 'You been treating yourself with the money already?'

Isaac looked at his wrist. 'Hey, you know what they say: if you've got nothing to hide, then act like it.'

Nobody's ever said that. Now he remembered why he didn't like Isaac. The man was full of shit. But to save face and lure Isaac into a false sense of security, Garrison chuckled, while the other part of him didn't want to dignify Isaac's comment with a response.

'This is the first time someone's made contact with me,' Isaac continued.

'What did you think was going to happen? We were going to come round to your house, make sure you were OK, give you a cuddle? What did I say when I briefed you?'

Isaac hesitated as he searched his memory. 'That I had to sit tight?'

'Yes. And what else?'

'That… that…'

Now and then the whooshing sound of a car passing the front of the café could be heard.

Garrison sighed. 'I told you if I needed to speak with you, then there was an issue.'

Isaac's eyes narrowed. 'What's wrong? I did everything you told me. I told my bosses nothing. I told them I was ambushed in the middle of the street by a group of thugs. I've had the IPCC hounding me about this ever since. Naturally, I've told them nothing.' He pointed to the stitches on his chin. 'I even told them that Danny's abductors did this to me.'

'You sure they don't suspect you of anything?'

Isaac nodded.

'Good. But that's not the issue I'm talking about.'

'Then what?'

'We might need to use you for something.' Garrison was deadpan as he spoke. He supposed that, in another life, he could have been a successful businessman sitting in the boardroom dishing out P45s. Perhaps even a politician.

'You what?'

'We're going to use you for evidence.'

'What evidence?'

'We need you to take the fall. There's this guy we're pinning the murder on. So far we've got some evidence stacked against him. But he's supposed to be a one-man team.'

'Right…'

'So it begs the question: how did a one-man band manage to break Danny Cipriano out of his high-security detail on the same night that he was being transported to a new location?'

'He… he…'

'Don't stumble, Isaac. I'll give you some time to work it out.' Garrison was enjoying this. He finished his coffee and set the mug on the table.

Isaac's face contorted as he considered what Garrison had told him. Garrison lost his patience.

'I'll put it simply for you, Isaac. It would be incredibly difficult – but not impossible – for one person to stop your security van in the middle of transit, break in, and then make off with Danny Cipriano, exactly the same way that The Farmer and his team actually did. He would have needed inside help.'

'He could have done it on his own…'

Garrison shook his head. 'I said it was incredibly difficult but not impossible. And that's cutting it too fine for us. In our business, we don't like those kind of margins.'

Garrison leant forward. 'So what I want to happen is: you and Richard were working together, he propositioned you with a large sum of money – the same sum of money we gave you to let The Farmer take Danny – which *you* accepted. And now you're going to take the other large sum of money we're going to give you for agreeing to this.'

Isaac slammed his fist on the table, startling nobody.

'I could go to prison… I could lose my job…'

'How's your love life, Isaac? Going well? From a quick check of your social media accounts, it looks like your missus just left you. I haven't seen her face appear in any photos recently.'

'You don't even know how to use social media.'

'I know enough,' Garrison snapped. He didn't take kindly to being offended. 'And when was the last time you spoke to your mum?'

'She's…' Isaac swallowed, turned his head away. 'She's in hospital.'

'Tragic,' Garrison replied. 'Didn't you say that's what you were going to use the money for?'

'Yeah.'

'Except the watch, of course. But at least now she'll have double the charitable donation. Is she going to live?'

Isaac bounced his leg up and down, shaking the rest of his body. 'Maybe. Doctors don't know for certain.'

'Well, I hope she does. But you might want to consider using the money for yourself then, when you get out.'

'You—'

Garrison shot him down with a wave of his hand. 'I haven't finished yet. As I was saying, would you say it's fair that you've not really got anyone? Under these circumstances, your mum doesn't count.'

Isaac didn't respond. A tear formed in his left eye and he wiped it away with his thumb. Garrison watched the man's movements, remorseless.

'No? Nobody that relies on you? Well then. Makes perfect sense. Y'see, this is a business, Isaac. And you're a product of that business. And sometimes products go bad, so we have to get rid of them for the good of the company – for the good of the *business*. Otherwise, the rest of the company suffers as a result. It's nothing personal; I hope you understand that. But you knew the risks when you signed up to this. What happens next is on you.'

'You can't!' Isaac protested. 'You said nothing would happen to me.'

'And I wasn't lying. Nothing's happened *yet*. I just need to know you're aware of what *might* happen to you next.'

'I don't want to.'

Garrison chuckled. 'Funny. Because I don't remember mentioning you had any say in the matter. There's nothing you can do about it. You just need to prepare yourself. You've got us working on the case, so chances are we might not even need you. And if you can prove worthwhile in the meantime, then that can only add to your case.'

Garrison hesitated for a moment while an idea blossomed in his head, like a flower in spring. He wasn't finished playing with Isaac's emotions just yet.

'Unless...' Garrison began. 'I might be able to work something out.'

'Go on,' Isaac said eagerly.

'I can't make any promises but it'll put you in good stead.'

'What is it?'

'Tell me the name of the person that Danny Cipriano was talking to. Who's the reporter?'

Isaac didn't even hesitate; as if he were answering a quick-fire round in a game show.

'Tanya Smile. BBC News woman. She's the reporter that met with Danny.'

Interesting.

'And who's the contact that put her in touch with him?'

'Danika. DC Danika Oblak. Surrey Police. She's the only one who knew about Danny's location who could have leaked it.'

At that point, the coffee-shop owner approached them and placed a metallic tray with a receipt on it on the table. The conversation had reached its conclusion, and Phil was aware of that. Garrison enjoyed not having to signal to him. After years of experience, he was finally getting the hang of things.

'Here you are, boys.'

Garrison looked at it, then at Isaac.

'You didn't even pay?'

'I… I…'

Garrison lifted himself out of his chair. He had everything he needed. And more.

'Thanks for the coffee, Isaac. I'm glad we had this chat. Oh, and if you want my advice, don't do anything stupid. Remember what I said. We know where you are, and where those closest to you are as well. Either myself or one of my guys will be in touch.'

CHAPTER 31

MEMORY

Richard Maddison lived in a small terraced house, as tall as it was wide and constructed mainly of brick that was beginning to fall apart. Can't be a very good builder if he can't fix his own house, Drew thought as he approached the front door. The door was constructed from wood, and there was a thin gap that ran along the top and bottom, too small to fit in the frame. As he stood in front of it, Drew felt a draft flutter around his feet.

To his right was a small bay window. The curtains were drawn and there was an old ashtray resting against the windowsill. Either side of Richard Maddison's house was the exact same building, built in the exact same style – except his neighbours looked as though they exercised better care of their properties than he did.

By Drew's foot was a plant pot. He bent down and tilted it to the side, hoping Richard wouldn't have been so stupid as to leave a spare key underneath it.

He was right. It was empty, save for a few disturbed woodlice scurrying back towards the darkness.

Drew stretched his legs and let the plant pot fall back into place. It swayed from side to side and then began to spin. Eventually, it stopped. It wasn't in the exact same position, but it would do.

Slinging the backpack off his shoulder, Drew unzipped the top of the bag and plunged his hand in. There, tucked away in a small compartment, he found his lock-picking tools. Before picking the lock, he did a small recce of the neighbours and the street, made sure he wasn't being watched or spied on by anyone, and then set to work.

Within seconds, he was in. The door swung open and Drew flung his hand out to stop it from knocking into the adjacent wall. Once inside, he checked his watch – 3:57 p.m. There was no knowing when Richard would be back, but he knew it could be soon. He gave himself three minutes to get in and out.

Without wasting any more time, Drew headed upstairs and moved straight for the second door on the right – the bedroom. The room was small and cramped. The bed was on the right-hand side, so close to the door that he almost bumped his knee on it as he entered. To his left was a desk with a laptop on it. Clothes hung from the wardrobe door, and there was a fan standing beneath the window in front of him.

Drew approached the wardrobe, reaching inside his backpack for the piece of cement. The clothes hanging from the wardrobe looked fresh, clean, like they were part of an outfit Richard had already prepared to change into when he got home. Unhelpful. Drew needed dirty clothes – clothes Richard would have worn on the night Danny died.

Drew opened the wardrobe and found a washing basket inside.

'Perfect,' he whispered.

Crouching, Drew placed the bagged cement on the floor and stamped on it, crushing it into smaller fragments and dust. Ten stamps later, he opened the evidence bag, dug his finger in, swept up some of the dust and placed it on a T-shirt that was at the top of the pile. Within seconds, that part of his operation was done. He sealed the bag shut, closed the wardrobe and moved towards Richard's laptop. Keeping the gloves on, Drew opened the lid. The screen illuminated, a stock image of a mountain behind a lake appearing in front of him.

Drew hit enter and, to his surprise, the laptop unlocked and took him to Richard's desktop. He reached inside his pocket and inserted the USB memory stick. On it were thousands of images of child pornography he'd stolen from the online archives back at the station. Deeply rooted in the hardware of the device was a piece of software that encrypted the source of the files so that it was imperceptible to computer forensics, untraceable. Signs of his involvement were non-existent, and now it was Richard's problem.

Not only would they arrest him for the murder of Danny Cipriano, but they'd also send him down for being a prolific paedophile.

CHAPTER 32

OVERRULED

Liam massaged his hands anxiously. The fallout from the BBC News report was immense. And it hadn't taken long for the press to come thrashing at the door, howling for answers and tearing anything he said to shreds – like the wolves they were. To combat the shitstorm, Liam decided to host a press conference. It was moments from being underway, and nearly all the city's news outlets had gathered in the largest conference room Bow Green had to offer. The room heaved with bodies: news reporters, people holding cameras, people holding microphones on the end of long sticks, and also an army of civilian support staff who were manning the perimeter of the room, filtering everyone into the space in an organised and civilised manner.

As he sat there, waiting for the conference to begin, Liam hoped that Drew and Garrison had finished what they were doing. It would make him look comfortable in the eyes of The Cabal if he could end the conference with news of an arrest. That would surely give him some of the extra credibility he'd been campaigning for. Whether The Cabal was watching or not, he didn't know, but given the pressure he was being put under, it seemed likely.

Four spotlights switched on and blinded him. Assistant Commissioner Richard Candy, the man who Liam had aspired to become for so long, arrived from a door on the right and sat beside Liam. He was dressed in his uniform, with his police cap under his arm. His epaulettes shone in the artificial light, and he carried an air of authority about him. partly due to his rank, partly due to his very demeanour. The man was easy-going when he wanted to be, but his temperament often had the tendency to snap, Liam had learnt. The hard way.

'Ladies and gentlemen,' Candy started. 'Thank you for coming here this afternoon. Your attendance is greatly appreciated. As I'm sure you're aware, we are all here regarding the mysterious circumstances surrounding the death of Danny Cipriano. His death is tragic, and we are doing everything in our power to resolve the case and find the person or persons responsible as soon as possible.'

Candy stopped speaking suddenly, and Liam took that as his cue to begin.

He cleared his throat. 'In the very early hours of the morning of the twenty-fifth, Danny Cipriano was murdered at the London Olympic Stadium. His body was filled with cement before he was later buried in it. The current construction work that is taking place on the site has ground to a halt while our investigations continue. In this short space of time, we are pursuing several lines of enquiry, and we are hopeful of an arrest imminently. For reasons of confidentiality I cannot disclose any information pertaining to the suspects in this ongoing investigation.'

He paused to clear his throat again. 'While we are conducting our investigations, we would also like to point out that, if anyone does have any information regarding this incident, please call Crimestoppers on their usual number. I have been in touch with them and they are offering a reward of five thousand pounds in exchange for accurate and relevant information.'

The room illuminated with flashes and furore. Hunger stepped in the way and hands rose and waved at him, asking a torrent of questions.

Liam craned his neck at the crowd and then immediately wished he hadn't. In the distance, shuffling past the reporters, advancing towards him and the panel, was Lord Penrose and his associate.

Oliver stopped and glared at Liam, his arms folded across his chest. Liam's eyes snapped left and right, trying to focus on the reporters who were eagerly awaiting his approval. But he couldn't focus, not with the lord staring him down like that, shooting bullets at him with his eyes.

For a moment, Liam searched for Tanya, hoping that she'd be there; she had the ability to distract him at a single glance. He found her, sitting down with her hand resting on a notepad on her knee.

Just as he opened his mouth to select her – despite what she'd done in the past few hours – Assistant Commissioner Candy held his hand in the air and concluded the interview. 'Unfortunately, we won't be able to take questions right now. Please, if you have any information regarding this incident then do get in touch with Crimestoppers.'

The assistant commissioner stepped out of his chair and glided out of the room to Liam's right. Meanwhile, Penrose turned his back on Liam and exited the way he'd come, leaving Liam to deal with the fallout. After the cameras' lights were switched off, the reporters and journalists hurried towards him, holding microphones under his chin.

'No questions please!' he yelled as he hurried after the assistant commissioner. 'We have nothing further to add, guys – come on.'

He waded his way through the barrage of people and breathed a heavy sigh of relief as soon as he slipped through the door and into the corridor. His brief moment of respite didn't last long; what he saw in front of him increased his heart rate tenfold.

Oliver and Candy. Talking quietly.

Oliver was the first to notice Liam, then Candy, who was holding his police cap under his armpit and letting his free arm dangle by his side. At the sight of him, Oliver hurried over.

'I thought we told you to keep this out of the media. We're already dealing with the leak earlier. We don't need more information getting out about this.'

'With all due respect, sir,' Liam replied, 'this is an active operation. We can't just pick and choose who we tell when it suits us. Or rather, when it suits *you*. Have you ever worked in the police service, sir?'

Oliver remained tight-lipped.

'Then perhaps you'll appreciate that you have no fucking idea what you're talking about.'

'Chief Inspector!' AC Candy bellowed, his voice filling the hallway. 'How dare you speak to Lord Penrose like that.'

Candy turned to Penrose. 'Oliver, please forgive my colleague. As I'm sure you can imagine, he's feeling a little pressured right now. Not only is there pressure coming externally, but also internally – from me.'

Candy shot Liam a final glare.

'It's understandable but inexcusable. I hope I've made myself very clear, Inspector.' Oliver's expression was stern. His brows were furrowed, revealing thick, deep lines on his forehead.

Reluctantly, Liam dipped his head. He knew when to pick his battles, and this one wasn't worth the aggro. 'Understood, sir.'

'This isn't over yet. I want more bodies on the investigation working to solve this as quickly as possible,' Oliver retorted.

'I'll see what I can do,' AC Candy said.

'Good. Now, DCI Greene, if you'll excuse me, I have a job to get back to, as I'm sure you do too. And, if you don't mind, I need to have a further word with your boss.'

CHAPTER 33

WE

One name. That was all it took to strike fear into Jake's heart. He had avoided talking about it, *thinking* about it, for so long, but now things were the way they were, there was no hiding from it. And now, while he was in the office alone – Liam, Drew and Garrison had all disappeared without mention or forethought – was the best time to do it.

To face his fear. To face an old enemy.

DS Elliot Bridger.

If there was anyone who would know anything about what had happened to Danny and would be able to provide any evidence against Liam, Drew and Garrison, it would be him. Ever since the beginning, way back when Jake had started out at Surrey Police – briefly – the man had proven that he knew all the intricate little details when it came to The Cabal and The Crimsons. During their final heist in Guildford, on Jake's first day, Bridger had been the bent cop lurking in the background, trying to help them get out of the country. Their relationship with one another had been up and down like a cruise liner bobbing on the surface of the Channel.

They'd agreed to meet at Farnham Golf Club, West Surrey, over an hour and a half away from Bow Green. In the car park, he recognised Bridger's Jaguar – number plated: BR1D G3R – and parked beside it. As he killed the engine, Jake scanned the surrounding area. Nobody had taken it upon themselves to follow him; nor were there any suspicious silhouettes lurking in the background. Just because Liam, Drew and Garrison were all preoccupied didn't mean they hadn't sent anyone after him.

Jake entered the brick reception building where he was greeted by a small gift shop. Luminous shirts and jumpers glared at him, boasting fifty per cent off for a limited time only, and to his left was a rack of golf clubs. He'd never been a fan of the game, but he did like the way a club felt to the touch. Light at one end, heavy at the other end. Great for breaking into things and smashing a man's skull. If the time ever came.

At the back of the building was the reception desk, and Jake recognised the man behind it from their previous encounter a few years earlier, when he and Bridger had been trying to locate a set of keys that unlocked a deadly spiked collar device. The owner, James, had been useless then and Jake wondered whether he was about to find out if lightning ever struck twice.

'Afternoon, sir,' James said as Jake approached him.

'Afternoon.'

The man pointed to a door that led into a restaurant and bar area.

'He's waiting for you,' James said.

'Excuse me?' Jake replied, more out of reflex than anything else.

'He's waiting for you. Our mutual friend.'

Point proven. Lightning, twice? Never.

Jake creased his brow but said nothing before walking away and disappearing round the corner. The inside of the restaurant was clean and empty, save for one man sitting at a table with a glass of water in his hand. There were twenty circular tables, of varying sizes and widths, dotted around the restaurant, glasses overturned, napkins missing. To the right of the space was a bar, beads of condensation abseiling down the neck of the taps. Music played in the background. Soft jazz.

Bridger looked up, then lifted his glass, beckoning Jake to join him.

'Have you got your finger in this little pie?' Jake asked, pulling a chair from the table.

'James is an old friend of mine.' Bridger nodded over to the bar. Jake turned and saw the owner was now there, cleaning a beer glass with a towel.

'It didn't seem that way when we were here last? From what I remember, he told us one thing and you believed him. You couldn't get us out of here fast enough.'

'That was the old me. I needed a favour and he owed me one. He was just doing what I told him.'

'And is this another favour he owes you?'

'This is where I spend a lot of my time now. For the membership prices he's charging, it's probably fair to say he does.'

Jake looked around the restaurant. The tables and chairs were made from a dark, glossy oak that reflected the light from the mini chandeliers overhead. Floor-to-ceiling windows ran along the length of the building, showcasing the greens of the golf course beyond. The building screamed luxury, and bled wealth and arrogance.

Sitting there, Jake noticed how desolate and quiet it was.

'Why do I feel like I'm in a nineties gangster movie, waiting for a couple of thugs with nothing but their bare fists and a couple of knuckledusters to jump out of the shadows and beat me until I shit myself?'

'Because you have an overactive imagination. One of your flaws and strengths. But there's nobody else here. Just us. I thought this would be a good place to meet you because nobody else knows about it. Nobody would think to look here.'

'Our little secret,' Jake said, noticing the tone of their conversation was already more docile and calmer than their previous encounters had been. There was no animosity between them now, nothing. Just two coppers. One trying to right the wrongs in the world, the other trying to wrong the rights.

'I hear you decided to get out early – while you still could?'

Bridger took a sip of his drink and slid the empty glass across to the centre of the table. 'I got out as soon as I realised it was all fucked. I knew they were never going to let Danny and Michael live. So I got out before it happened. I'm done with it all. Clean slate.'

'How's that working for you?'

'So far so good. But, before you ask, I had nothing to do with Danny Cipriano's death, you know that, right?'

From the first time they'd met, Jake had never taken anything Elliot Bridger said to be gospel. There was always some layer of deceit, always something that he was declaring. Ninety per cent, missing ten per cent. But, in that moment, that all changed.

'I believe you. But I know who did.'

'Oh?'

Jake sighed. The dynamic of their relationship had changed in the past few months. During the Stratford killings, and before Danny and Michael Cipriano had been let out of remand and entered into the witness protection scheme, Bridger had given him one single piece of advice, which had stayed with him for a long time. Get out. That was it. Stay out of The Cabal's way and stop messing with things he didn't understand. And, for that, Jake admired him, trusted him even. But now he was beginning to understand the things he hadn't before, it was time to heed that advice.

'They're all in on it,' he said. 'They're all bent. Liam, Drew, Garrison – my entire team. Danny Cipriano opened his mouth when he shouldn't have and now he's paid the price for it, and someone called The Farmer finished him off.'

Bridger pursed his lips and nodded like he wasn't surprised to hear it, like he'd known all along. Like Jake had thought he would. 'I never thought I'd see the day that you joined the dark side…'

'I'm not. Well… I am, but…' Jake paused and scratched the side of his face. 'Now they're going to pin it on one of the construction workers who found Danny's body. Bloke called Richard Maddison.'

'I told you,' Bridger said, making no effort to hide the smugness in his voice. 'If they want you, they'll have you. There's no escaping The Cabal's clutches.'

Bridger poured himself another full glass of water from the jug on the table. His hands shook as he drank.

'But what about you?' Jake asked, leaning forward, bringing his voice close to a whisper. 'What if the same happens to you?'

'It won't. I'll be fine.'

'How can you be sure?'

'I've managed to work myself into immunity.'

'What immunity? You were shitting yourself a few months ago.'

Bridger tapped the side of his nose. 'I wish I could tell you. I really do, but you'd be gambling with your own life rather than mine, unlike last time.'

Jake sighed, folded the corners of the napkin in front of him and controlled his breathing. 'Work with me, Elliot, and we can end this. How many times have I said this? We can help you. We can put The Cabal behind bars, once and for all.'

'We?' Bridger asked, tucking his chin into his neck. 'What do you mean, *we*? Before it was always "I"… "I can help you"…' Bridger hesitated. 'What have you done, Jake?'

'I went to the DPS. They're helping me investigate Liam, Pete and Drew.'

Bridger swept his arms sideways across the table, knocking most of the knives and forks onto the floor. He didn't bother picking them up.

'You're playing with fierce fucking fire, my friend,' he said, his face filling with blood. 'You've made a big mistake. Perhaps the biggest mistake of your career. Of your life. I told you once before but you didn't listen. These people have the power to end it for you. And nobody can stop them.'

'That's because nobody's tried.'

Bridger exhaled deeply, leant back in his chair and picked up the knife that remained on the table. He began tapping the bottom incessantly on his napkin.

'You're an idiot, Tanner.'

'And you're a coward. You know that, don't you? Covering your own arse so they don't come for you. And what about Michael? His life's in jeopardy too.'

'Michael doesn't know anything. He never did. It was always Danny's job to be in control of the information.'

'Do you know where he is?'

No response.

'What about the person who helped you get them out of remand? They know just as much as you do. Do they have immunity too? Or is it just your selfish arse?'

Still no reply.

'Tell me who it is, Elliot. If you're not worried about your own safety, then let me help protect *them*.'

Bridger's stare remained focused on Jake. 'You're not going to like it, Tanner.'

'Try me,' Jake hissed.

Bridger leant across the table. 'Danika.'

CHAPTER 34

CHOO-CHOO!

Richard Maddison was exhausted. Physically. Mentally. Emotionally. The great waves of depression had rolled in with the early morning tide and had been battering him all day. He'd spent hours staring blankly out of Jermaine Gordon's window, only distracted by the news from the television set. It had been confirmed. The Concrete Cadaver, they were calling it – Danny Cipriano, abducted from witness protection and buried alive in a merciless killing. Gangs? Organised crime? Drugs?

None of that. The reality had been much more damning. The police officer in charge of the investigation had told the media – and the entire country – that they had a suspect in mind. It didn't take a genius to work out that suspect went by the name of Richard Maddison, the thirty-three-year-old builder who'd found the body. They hadn't needed to say his name explicitly, but he knew that they were talking about him. And he was even more certain that they'd find the link between him and Danny, if they hadn't already; how, years ago, they'd once been friends. How they'd robbed convenience stores and clothing outlets, taken drugs with one another. How Danny and his brothers, Michael and Luke, had grassed him up to the police after a car-jacking had gone wrong.

The police would undoubtedly say that he had motive to kill them. And they'd probably lie and come up with some other bullshit evidence to plant the murder on him. Christ, he could do their job for them and just hand himself in now, knowing there was no escape – no way he could get himself out of this one. If the coppers working on the case were anything like that cunt DS Richmond, then they'd all be as bent as him. He imagined them bending each other over in the office, forming an orderly queue with their pants down, making train noises, with DS Richmond as the conductor. But it did little to lighten his mood.

Richard stepped off the bus and wandered up to his porch, pausing by the front door. His eyes fell on the plant pot. He was sure it looked out of place – jolted to the side slightly. It was only a minor movement, but he was certain it *had* moved. He told himself it could have been anyone. The postman. The neighbour coming to check on him. Someone from work asking why he hadn't shown up for his shift. Even himself as he hurried out of the house yesterday morning. But what was the likelihood of that?

Choo-choo. All aboard!

Richard sauntered into the house and shuffled up to his bedroom. He needed a lie-down, some form of respite to recover from the comedown his body was going through. Something that would make reality disappear again, no matter how briefly.

As he closed the bedroom door behind him, he kicked off his shoes, bent down to pick them up and placed them directly beside his small desk. Something in his bedroom caught his attention, but he didn't know what. Something wasn't sitting right. Something had been changed, altered. Something he hadn't touched in over twenty-four hours.

His laptop.

The lid was half closed. He never left it half closed, always completely open or sealed shut. There was no in between.

The wheels on the bent train grew nearer.

Richard opened the lid fully, prodded a key and waited for the screen to illuminate. His desktop appeared, and in the top-right corner of the screen was a new folder icon. Beneath it, the word photos.

Chugga-chugga-chugga-chugga…

He clicked on the folder. Thousands of files flashed in thumbnail view, too small for his eyes to discern them. With his mind running on autopilot – fear and intrigue working together to run the show – he opened the first file and immediately regretted it. Wanted to throw up.

It was an image of a child being subjected to sexual abuse.

'Oh my God,' Richard whispered to himself, closing the photo and shutting the application down.

He slammed the lid shut and froze on the chair, his chest heaving. He wanted to scream, to run away, to destroy the laptop, but he knew it wouldn't change anything. Someone had deliberately placed the files on his laptop, and disposing of the device would only incriminate him further if it was ever found.

As he sat there, struggling to move, a panic attack kicked in. Shortness of breath. Tunnelled vision. Blurred vision.

Chugga-chugga-chugga-chugga… All aboard!

Richard pushed himself away from the desk and raced into the bathroom, switched on the tap in his bath and started to undress himself.

Baths were his only coping mechanism for his panic attacks. They helped soothe him and instil calm back into his mind. Right now that was what he needed. That or an opportunity to close his eyes forever.

The hot water gushed over his right shoulder, massaging his muscles, and it wasn't long till the tub was half full. As the water reached his stomach, he slowed the flow until it was nothing more than a slight dribble, tickling his skin as it landed on him.

His chest continued to heave and he struggled for breath. He closed his eyes in an attempt to fend off the four walls closing in on him, but all he saw was the image of the child being molested. Stained in indelible ink.

And then the little boy morphed into a man, and then a hand – Danny Cipriano's, buried, covered in grey. The starling tattoo. The wart. Richard already had one person's blood on his hands – the underage girl he'd slept with had taken her own life shortly after the case went public – and he wasn't prepared to have another's. He'd done his time for that, been in and out of the judiciary system. Never again.

For a moment, he considered how she must have felt. Alone. Isolated. Nobody to talk to, nobody to share her experience with, nobody to help heal her. Feeling like the world was closing in around her…

She'd taken a route out. Some might argue it was the easy one, the coward's way, but what right did they have to question it? They weren't living inside her head; they didn't know her struggles. Just like they weren't living inside his right now.

Choo-choo!

Richard's eyes fell over his razor blade on the side of the tub. He fumbled for it, then held the handle in his palm, ran his finger over the blades.

It could all be over before it had even begun. He could make it stop, make it all go away, silence the debilitating voices and thoughts in his head. If the police didn't have him, then they couldn't ruin his life any more than it already had been.

Richard moved the razor closer to his face, so he could see what he was doing. In the low light, and the panic of the situation, he fumbled and cut himself as he tried to pry the blade free from the handle.

Eventually, he did, as the sound of the bent train gradually weakened.

Thick droplets of blood dribbled into the water and swirled about like a pinwheel, staining it a thick shade of crimson. Richard ignored the pain; soon it would stop.

Richard lowered himself into the bath, allowing the water to trickle over his face. He stared at the ceiling as he brushed the blade up and down his arm, grazing it gently against his skin, teasing the nerves, making sure his brain was aware of what was to come.

Then his right hand stopped where the blue rivers were most prominent. He pressed the blade firmly into his skin and held it there. This was it. Now or never. He couldn't back out. Once it was done, it was done.

And then the train would disappear forever.

Richard buried the blade deep into his skin, cutting through the layers and breaking into the vein. He groaned in agony but chomped down on the pain, forcing it from his mind. His breathing increased tenfold and his chest heaved more so, rapidly increasing the blood flow around and out of his body.

He made another incision, this time on his other wrist, numbed by the adrenaline and euphoria that surged through him. That gradually made him weaker and weaker. That echoed the squeaking beat of his heart as it struggled to pump more blood through his body. Richard continued staring at the ceiling, ignoring the metallic taste that flooded his mouth as he slowly sank deeper into the bathtub.

But before he was completely submerged, the door to the bathroom burst open and, hovering over him, were four individuals dressed in balaclavas.

The great bent train had arrived – a little too late. Before he was able to do anything, the world went black.

CHAPTER 35

NO ANSWER

Jake drove the journey from Farnham Golf Club to Mount Browne – Surrey Police's HQ – in shock, his mind trying to process the myriad thoughts that were spinning their way around his brain. One of his closest friends in the police force had betrayed him and turned bent; another added to the growing list that was slowly growing out of control. He and Danika Oblak had been together from the start. Back when they'd been bobbies on the beat in Croydon, started their training together, even helped convict The Crimsons together. In that time, Jake had felt like he knew Danika better than most people. But that had all been a lie.

On the drive, Jake considered her motives, the possible reasons for doing what she'd done – trying to justify it for her when he wasn't even sure she deserved that. But he couldn't think of any.

He needed to hear it direct from the horse's mouth before she galloped away.

Jake pulled up outside Mount Browne and sprinted towards the building. He'd only spent a few weeks there during his tenure with Surrey Police, yet he was familiar with his surroundings. As soon as he'd realised that nobody in MIT would pay any heed to his allegations that Elliot Bridger and DS Murphy, another detective working with The Crimsons, were corrupt, he'd handed in a transfer request. But the funny thing – if it could be called funny – was that Danika had also pointed the finger at Bridger and Murphy. Hypocrisy had reached new heights.

Jake paced towards the reception. The civilian member of staff seated behind the desk was the same one Jake had encountered on his first day with the Major Investigation Team. Judging from the look on the man's face, he recognised Jake, and hadn't quite forgiven him for leaving the polystyrene cup on the table after being explicitly told not to.

But right now, none of that mattered. What mattered was finding Danika.

'Do you know where I might find her?' Jake asked. 'She's not answering her phone.'

Just as the staff member was about to respond, the double doors in the corner of the room opened, and out stepped DCI Nicki Pemberton, the SIO in charge of MIT. Jake hadn't seen, nor spoken to her, since his final day with Surrey Police.

'Jake…' she said, shocked to see him. She still looked as pretty and proper as he remembered her to be. 'What're you doing here?'

'Danika. Have you seen her?'

'You haven't heard…'

A pang of fear struck him.

'She's handed in her notice?'

Jake opened his mouth but couldn't bring himself to say anything.

'I thought you would have known. Sorry, I—'

'When?'

'Her final day's in a week.'

'No, when did she give it to you?'

'A couple of days ago. She requested immediate effect, but we couldn't give it to her. She's using up the rest of her leave to make up for it.'

'Do you know if she's still in the country?'

Pemberton shrugged. If she was confused by his line of questioning, then she showed no signs of it. 'I would imagine so. I've not heard anything to suggest otherwise. Think she might have gone back up north to see her family, but with the way things are going with that, I can't imagine… you know…'

Jake did know. He'd been helping Danika through her marital issues since they'd started working together. Her and her husband's relationship had been on the rocks ever since the incident that rendered him disabled, and Jake was acutely aware that she'd had a dependency on alcohol before then. Somehow that information had slipped through the net in the application process, and she'd managed to keep it hidden from everyone. It wasn't until Jake had found a bottle in her handbag by mistake that he'd realised something was seriously wrong. He'd kept that secret for her, risked his job in the process, and this was how she repaid him?

Jake thanked Pemberton, hurried back to his car and then raced to Danika's address in Guildford. Since separating from her husband, she'd decided to leave that life in Croydon behind and move there permanently. Jake had visited her house once before. It hadn't been all that exciting, but it was enough for one person. It had a bed, bathroom and a kitchen, and that was all she needed.

Five minutes later, Jake skidded to a halt outside her house. He left the car parked awkwardly on the side of the road and hurried to Danika's front door.

He knocked. And knocked. And knocked.

Nothing.

He considered why Danika had handed in her resignation. Maybe the job was getting too much. Maybe she'd heard about what had happened to Danny. Maybe she thought she was next…

Jake knocked again.

Still nothing.

Just as he was about to knock again, his phone rang.

He answered it without checking the caller ID.

'Jake? You there? It's Drew. Where are you? I tried calling everyone else but nobody's picking up.'

'What's wrong?'

'I didn't know who else to call.'

'Where are you?'

'I'm outside Richard Maddison's flat waiting for him to come home, but I think The Farmer and his group have just broken into his house. Can you get here ASAP?'

Jake took a moment to think. Drew pulled him out of the present and made him realise that he had another job to do.

'I'll be there as soon as I can.'

CHAPTER 36

FEELING THE PRESSURE

His instructions were simple: plant the evidence, wait for Richard Maddison to return and under no circumstances do anything fucking stupid. That was it. Garrison had been clear on it. Crystal. So far so good. He'd planted the evidence – check. And he'd waited for Richard to return – check.

But now there was a problem – one he hadn't accounted for.

There was no doubt in his mind that the group of individuals who'd followed Richard into his house were the same people who instilled fear in him every time he thought about them. Every time their names were uttered in conversation with Liam or Garrison. As soon as he saw the black-clad figures, Drew quickly realised he needed to tell someone. To cover his own arse.

Was he on the hit list?

Like any good criminal, he needed to make sure he had an alibi at all times. And the last person he'd ever expected to be his was Jake. After they'd finished their call, The Farmer and his crew had bolted out of the house and raced back to their unmarked black van.

Odd.

Something didn't seem right. They'd been in and out too quick – too quick to kill a man at least. No screaming, no ear-shattering sound of bullets. Not even enough time to kill a man and dress it up to make it look like suicide – as they were wont to do.

Drew needed to inspect. Needed to know what they would be dealing with.

He opened the car door and slipped out, recced the area for any signs that he was being followed and then headed towards the house. Keeping his head low, he skipped across the road and up onto the pavement, jogged towards the front door and then donned a pair of forensic gloves.

The door had been left ajar.

Drew hesitated as he crossed the threshold into Richard's house. He listened and waited for any sign of life, any sign of movement, any sign of someone – or something – being there that he didn't want.

There was nothing. Just his paranoia playing tricks on him again. And, by now, the drugs in his system had worn off and he was running on pure paranoia, rather than the drug-induced type that he'd been accustomed to since he'd started using again. It wasn't his fault he was slowly becoming addicted. It was the pressures of the job. The stresses of his home life. The non-existent relationship he had with his wife. He hadn't even seen her in six weeks. For all he knew she could be halfway across the world and he wouldn't even know. She was probably being fucked by someone right now. Wouldn't be the first time. The stupid little bitch.

Before he knew it, the stairs stopped and he was standing in the mouth of Richard's bedroom, where he'd been less than an hour before. He poked his head through but saw nothing, and then moved down the hallway into the bathroom.

He paused as soon as he noticed the puddle of water by the door, and swallowed. Gently, already afraid of what was on the other side, he pushed.

Richard Maddison was lying there in the bathtub, his body submerged under the water, his arms resting atop the surface. There were two incisions on his wrists, and blood was flooding out of them like they were holes in a dam, staining the water a dark crimson colour.

Drew took a step back to observe the room. The taps were turned off and there was water overflowing the lip of the tub. Rivers of red dribbled down the side of the plastic to be absorbed by the bath mat. On the walls, fingerprints and smears stained the white tiles. Richard's wet and matted hair floated as his body lay perfectly still.

Drew tried to process what had taken place, but no immediate answers presented themselves. Had The Farmer and his associates slit Richard's wrists and then run out? Had he bled out in the time it had taken Drew to enter the house and find his body? Or had he already killed himself, and The Farmer had simply stumbled upon him? Was there a tussle? Had Richard tried to defend himself?

The thoughts were deafening, screaming in his ears. A tremendous pressure pushed down on his head and he clutched the sides of his skull, squeezing the pain away. But he soon realised it was there to stay, like the wedding ring stuck round his finger because he was too much of a pussy to confront his own wife about her adultery.

Soon after, the pain gave way and opened the avenue for a torrent of paranoia to flush through his mind. Richard Maddison was dead. And he was next. No doubt about it. He didn't know how, nor why, nor when. He just knew that he was next.

He turned on the spot, keeping his arms down. The last thing he wanted was to incriminate himself by planting his own DNA all over the scene. There was no amount of procedure that would protect him from that – especially if The Cabal became involved somehow.

Just as he was about to turn his back on the bathroom, a figure appeared out the corner of his eye.

'Jesus fucking shit!' Drew yelled.

'Easy, mate,' said Garrison who was standing at the top of the steps with his hands in his pockets, looking like Drew was the one in the wrong. 'Only me.'

'The fuck you doing here?'

'Making sure everything's all right.'

'Well, it ain't,' Drew replied. 'Richard Maddison's fucking dead, Pete. And I don't know if he killed himself or if he was killed. But, either way, you and I need to start looking out for each other. We're in this together, right?'

'Of course mate,' Garrison said. 'Of course we are. Which is why I'm going to need you to do exactly as I tell you.'

CHAPTER 37

ARRIVAL

By the time Jake arrived at Richard Maddison's property, the emergency responders who'd been called to the scene were just beginning to set up their forward control point at the inner and outer cordons. A small portion of the street had been cordoned off, and the neighbours were beginning to gather like blowflies, buzzing for the latest in street gossip. At the foot of the porch was a forensic van. Jake hurried over to it, grabbed a full forensic bodysuit and donned it. Just as he was about to slip through the cordon and into the house, one of the uniformed officers called him back.

'Have you signed in?'

Jake replied sheepishly that he hadn't and quickly scribbled his details on the page before entering the house.

The building was swarming with scene of crime officers. Each SOCO was wearing the same oversuit, and it quickly became difficult to discern anyone from anyone. He relied on his knowledge and intuition of Drew's height, build and stance to find his colleague. Fortunately, he was a small man, which narrowed down the field somewhat.

Jake moved through the house, stepping on the footpads that the SOCOs had already laid down, and climbed the stairs.

He found Drew at the top, hovering by the bedroom door frame. Jake tapped him on the shoulder. His colleague spun around and his body jolted as he recognised Jake before him.

'Scared the shit outta me,' Drew said.

Jake chuckled. 'Sorry, mate. What's happened?'

'Richard Maddison's dead. Suicide. Slit his wrists in the bathtub. Bled out in the tub and onto the floor.'

'Jesus…' Jake felt at a loss for words, but then he realised where he was and who he was in the company of. 'How does this… how does this affect *us*?' He kept his voice low as he spoke, lest any of the SOCOs overhear.

Drew pulled him into the bedroom. There was a SOCO rummaging through the contents of the wardrobes, taking dozens of photographs of the clothes in situ and documenting the evidence. Drew ordered him to leave.

'It's fine,' he said as soon as the scene of crime officer was gone. 'If anything, it's perfect. Pukka. Sorts us out nicely. Him killing himself makes it look like his guilt was too much.'

'Did you get a chance to plant the evidence?' Jake kicked himself as he realised he'd made the same mistake again and forgotten to record the conversation. His mind was in a whirlwind – still reeling from the news about Danika – and it was difficult for him to think clearly.

'Kiddie porn on his laptop and cement dust on his clothes.'

Drew pointed to the laptop and the washing basket that had been removed from the wardrobe. Jake noticed a piece of paper with scribbles on it on the floor beside the desk chair. He said nothing.

'My guess is he found the evidence and then realised there was no way out. Now we make it look like his guilt compelled him into committing suicide. You said yourself he's got a history of depression, and we've got a link between him and Danny. Everything's pukka.' He gave Jake a slap on the back. 'I knew you'd come true. I should have always had faith.'

Drew winked at him and then left the room, leaving Jake alone.

He was in shock. His body turned cold and a fat knot formed in his stomach, crippling him. His worst fear had just come true. The thing he didn't want to happen just had. And Drew had confirmed it. He'd helped murder Richard Maddison and helped Liam, Drew and Garrison get away with it.

All thought escaped him. His mind turned blank and he stared at the clock on the wall, wishing he could roll back the hours, days, months, years and change everything.

A knock on the door distracted him.

It was Garrison. He was squinting, and the lines around his eyes looked like dark ravines.

'You all right, pal?' Garrison asked.

'Stellar,' Jake replied.

'You wanna see the body?'

Jake shrugged. 'Might as well,' he said, getting back into character again.

Garrison stepped out of the way and allowed Jake through. He made a left turn into the bathroom next door, the sound of his overshoe protectors squelching on the floor and bath mat. Richard Maddison's head was surrounded by bloody water, resting beside the tap. The colour had drained from his skin, and his arms were resting on the side of the tub. The incisions he'd made to kill himself were two inches across and at least half an inch wide. The knot tightened and made Jake gag. That he'd been partly responsible for pushing this man to the edge made him want to vomit.

He swallowed it down.

Jake surveyed the room, searching for any abnormalities, anomalies. And then he remembered what Drew had told him: that a group had stormed into Richard's house moments after Richard himself. Maybe there was more to this than he thought. Maybe it was a cover-up. Maybe The Farmer and his associates had slaughtered Richard and made it look like a suicide. Maybe they'd made a mess and left signs of their presence without realising it.

Jake searched the walls and scrutinised everything he saw. To his left was a towel rack. Beside it, facing him, was the toilet. And that was it. Nothing untoward about any of it.

But then he saw it. How wrong he was.

A footprint, muddy, on the floor, on the corner of the bath mat. And it looked as though it hadn't been spotted by any of the SOCOs. But there was another problem – Garrison. The man was standing directly behind him. If he was going to secure it as evidence and overturn their suicide theory, then he couldn't do it with Garrison there.

'Must've been a horrible way to go,' Jake said as he spun on the spot to face Garrison.

'There's no easy way…' Garrison replied.

As Jake moved closer to the door, something in the corner of his eye struck him. It was a blood smear, and the indentations of the fingerprint were thick and clear. He couldn't believe it. He had a muddy footprint and a bloody fingerprint where it shouldn't have been.

He was onto—

'Jake! Garrison!' a voice called from the stairwell.

'What do you want, Drew?'

'We gotta go,' Drew said as he came into view halfway up the stairs. 'Guv's called a meeting.'

Fuck.

'All right, we'll be done in a sec,' Garrison replied and started towards the landing.

Double fuck.

There was no opportunity to photograph or examine the fingerprint closely. But he had an idea: the SOCO working in the bathroom. Yes. She could do it.

Jake snapped his fingers, caught the SOCO's attention and then pointed at the mud on the floor and the smear on the door.

'Jake!' It was Garrison. 'You coming or what?'

Jake snapped his head towards his colleague. 'Yeah… Yeah… I'm coming… Yeah.'

He gave one last look at Richard Maddison, as if to offer penance for being responsible for his death, and then left the bathroom, hoping the scene of crime officer had understood what he was talking about.

'Guv's called us back to the office,' Garrison told him as they stepped out of their forensic suits.

'Any idea what it's about?'

'He's probably gonna have a little bitch fit. His press conference didn't go so well.'

'Oh?'

'Apparently that Oliver Penrose bloke turned up unannounced so they shut the whole thing down.'

'Oh dear…'

Jake was grateful that he had his own car to go back to where he could collect his thoughts on the drive back to Bow Green, though that was easier said than done. There was so much going on that he didn't know what to focus on first. And before he'd finally settled on something, he was back at the station.

As the three of them entered MIT, nerves began wracking Jake's body. They were amplified by what he saw in front of him.

Seated in the vacant desk opposite his was a woman that he didn't recognise. She was dressed smartly in a suit with the sleeves rolled up. Beneath the suit, she wore a blouse with navy-blue anchors on it. She had wavy blonde hair and wore thickly rimmed white glasses and had a complexion to match.

'Hey!' she said, smiling ebulliently. She advanced towards them, holding her hand out.

'Who might you be?' Garrison asked as he and Drew stood either side of Jake.

'My name's Charlotte. I'm from Croydon. Part of the Major Investigation Team there.'

All three of them stared at her blankly.

'Has nobody told you?' she asked.

'Told us what?' Drew took his turn to speak.

'I'm the new DI. I've been seconded to help with your investigation. I start tomorrow, but I just wanted to introduce myself today while all the paperwork's being finalised.'

Jake's mouth fell open. It was as if the stars had aligned and a weight had lifted from his shoulders. For once he didn't feel like he was alone anymore. He knew exactly who Charlotte was and the reason she was there.

She was going to help him convict Liam, Drew and Garrison.

| PART 3 |

CHAPTER 38

INTERFERENCE

Jake's mouth was wide open – caught in the middle of a yawn – as he attempted to spoon a mountain of cornflakes into his mouth. On a normal day, he would save himself for when he arrived at the office and ransack the canteen on the ground floor – where he'd pick up his favourite of scrambled eggs on toast with a strawberry yoghurt for dessert. But today wasn't any normal day. Nor was there any time for him to fit that in.

Charlotte was joining the team. And he wanted to be ready for her arrival.

Since seeing her standing there, in the station, looking happy and excited to be there, he'd been unable to focus on anything else. It was like he was a child at Christmas, only focused on the presents. What surprised him most though was just how fast the DPS had managed to deploy a fully operable undercover officer. Less than twenty-four hours. Some sort of record, he thought.

Jake just hoped she was well prepared and had been briefed with as much detail as possible. That she had her legend in place. He knew what Liam, Drew and Garrison were like when it came to newcomers. Tenacious. Hell-bent on breaking apart every facet of whatever backstory her handler had created for her.

Charlotte's presence created a minefield of potential pitfalls for him too. With the rest of the team watching her every movement suspiciously, how would he make initial contact? Outside of work or in? What if he risked blowing her cover and got her taken off the case – or, worse, killed – just like he'd been responsible for what had happened to Richard Maddison?

It was a lot to think about.

Fortunately, he was greeted with a welcome distraction in the form of Elizabeth. She was dressed in the purple gown that hugged the contours of her body, her hair flowing down to the small of her back, and as she wandered into the kitchen, she rubbed her eyes and attempted to stifle a yawn with her hand.

'What're you doing up?' he asked as she moved towards the kettle. 'Why aren't you sleeping with the kids?'

'Good morning to you too.'

'You know that's not what I meant.' Jake set the spoon down in the bowl.

'Sounds like you're trying to get rid of me. And when it feels like the morning is the only time I get to see you, I don't know how to take that. I hardly ever catch you now, Jake.' She grabbed a mug and put three heaped spoonfuls of instant coffee into it, followed by two spoonfuls of sugar. After she finished, she faced him, resting her back against the kitchen surface. 'I'm worried about us.'

'Why?' Jake pushed the bowl into the middle of the table. He didn't feel like eating anymore.

'You're never here, and when you are, I'm always too tired, and so are you. These hours you're working are unforgiving. I'm exhausted from looking after the kids all day. I don't have any time to unwind and relax and focus on my photography like I want to. And then we've got all of these bills that just seem to be mounting and mounting and mounting. And I don't know when it's just going to—' She paused, looked down at the ground and inhaled sharply, like she was preparing herself to deliver the final powerful blow. 'It's just… it's happening all at once, and I feel like it's beginning to put a strain on our marriage.'

Jake opened his mouth to respond, but nothing came out. He wanted to run over to her and hug her, embrace her, hold her, comfort her, support her – do anything that would allay her fears and put her mind at ease. They'd never argued like this, and he'd hoped they never would.

But there was something she'd said that had annoyed him.

'Funny you should say that…' he began.

'What're you talking about?'

He pointed to one of the letters on the island in the centre of the kitchen.

'When were you going to tell me about this one?'

It was the car insurance bill that had come through a couple of weeks before, telling him that he owed over a thousand pounds. The letter beside it was from the same company, thanking him for the recent payment.

'I don't remember paying that off,' he said sternly. 'So who did?'

Elizabeth fell silent; even the sound of her breath was muted.

'Who paid it, Liz?'

She glanced up at him. 'My… m-my mum.'

Jake rolled his eyes. *Typical. Fucking typical.*

'Were you going to tell me at all?'

'I… I thought I did already.'

'Don't bullshit me,' Jake said, raising his voice. The look on her face told him to stop and he suddenly became conscious of the girls sleeping upstairs. Quieter this time, he continued, 'I thought I told you I'd get us out of this mess.'

'She offered…'

'And if she'd offered to give birth to Maisie or Ellie for us, would you have said yes without consulting me?'

Elizabeth's face dropped, eyes narrowed. 'Why would you say that?'

Jake knew that he was out of line, but it was too late to go back now. He hoped the benefit of hindsight would make his next words better.

'You heard me,' he said with an air of stubbornness he usually only exuded when he was in the interview room with a witness or an offender.

Maybe not.

'Don't you dare bring them into this. You see, *this* is part of the problem. You can't put your ego aside, can you? It hurts you – *pains* you – that my mum helped.'

'Because this was *my* problem to solve!' He slammed his hand down on the kitchen counter.

'Why? Who told you it was? Some sort of man-god who only speaks to egotistical men like you? Did he tell you to deal with this alone? Christ, you can be such a prick sometimes. My mum was trying to help. Accept it. It doesn't make you any less of a man; nor does it change my perception of you. In fact, if you'd have asked for help sooner, I would have probably respected you more.'

Probably…

Jake exhaled deeply and continued to stare at her. At those unrelenting, powerful eyes. At the woman who'd given birth to his two amazing children. At the woman who put up with all of his shit. The love of his life.

He had no right to be upset; Martha was just trying to help. It was nothing more than that. Nothing less. Jake looked down at his hand and pretended to play with a blemish on his skin. 'Would it be completely out of the question to get a hug?' he asked.

'Does that mean you admit you're wrong?'

'It does.'

He forced a smile. Elizabeth reciprocated, rounded the island and embraced him. Her body felt warm against his. Argument forgotten about. He wished he could spend more time with her, but the job didn't allow it. And it killed him every time he missed out on one of the girls' milestones. Like the time Ellie had rolled over, Maisie's first word, the first time she'd said daddy, the first time she'd introduced a friend to Elizabeth at nursery. They were all life-changing events that he'd missed, and he was never going to get a chance to see them again.

Before he knew it, they'd be grown up, moved out and living adult lives of their own. That was a thought that didn't bear thinking about.

Elizabeth pulled away, keeping her hands still wrapped around his neck.

'You didn't really mean it what you called me a prick, did you?' he asked. This time the smile came more naturally to him.

'That was one hundred per cent the truth. But you're *my* prick.'

Jake gave her a kiss on the lips and then another on the forehead. He snatched a look at his watch, realised he was running late and hurriedly gathered his things together. As he headed out of the door, he said: 'How about I treat us to a takeaway tonight, something to celebrate?'

'What're we celebrating?'

'Life. Family. Everything. And we're making some real advances at work. We should be finished with the case soon.'

It wasn't a total lie. He just didn't want her to know about what he was dealing with. For her own good. The two needed to remain separate, because when work started to interfere with his personal life, that was when the problems would begin.

CHAPTER 39

TOYS

Liam's body ached. His legs. Stomach. Arms. Chest. Neck. Even his head was pulsating with a gentle throb that sent the walls into a spin and his nausea into a frenzy. Yesterday's treatment had taken it out of him. But there was a silver lining, however – no matter how small. According to his doctors and the copious number of tests he'd endured as part of the treatment, he was responding well. The cancer in his lungs was gradually diminishing. But he didn't know how it was going to go. Some days were good. Some days were bad. Some days he felt happy to be alive, while others left him wanting to swallow a bullet. Instead of doing that, though, he'd found another way to kill himself. If the cancer didn't, alcohol would. It was a poison. Probably the worst he'd ever taken, and that was saying something because in his time he'd reached the end of the alphabet of drugs, and he'd learnt his ABCs from scratch. But alcohol was different. Worse, yes. But different. And different, in this particular instance, was good. It warmed him, it didn't completely derail his senses and it numbed some of the pain. But only if he consumed it in moderation.

Liam lumbered out of his seat, shuffled to the back of the room and opened the bottom drawer of his filing cabinet. Inside was a bottle of whiskey – Jim Beam, his favourite poison – and two burner phones. He loved the sweetness of it and the way it burnt his throat. The two phones were used for emergencies only. One of them was his discreet line for Drew – which he also used for everyone else – and the other was the one he used to communicate with The Cabal.

The sight of the burner he used for Drew gave him an idea. He kicked the drawer shut, filled his reusable plastic coffee cup with whiskey and put it in the top drawer of his desk. That would last him for the rest of the day. Just a little tipple every now and then to keep the levels up, sustain his mellowness.

He swirled the whiskey and held it against his lips, then drank. Delicious. Smooth. Neat.

The only thing it needed now was some delicately placed cubes of ice, and it would have been a perfect start to the morning.

Setting the lid on the cup, Liam reached for a pack of mints in his pocket, threw one into his mouth and chewed on it. As the menthol spread like wildfire around his mouth and throat, Liam moved to the office door and called out to Drew. He was the only one in the office at the moment, save for some of the other little jumped-up shits on his team who he didn't really care about. They kept themselves to themselves, and he let them. If they needed anything, they knew where his office was.

'Morning, fella.'

Liam grunted by way of response. 'Take a seat.'

Drew did as he was told, leaning back into his chair, arms spread wide on the two either side of him, one leg crossed over the other. Looking like he owned the fucking place.

'Have you had a chance to do what I asked?' Liam asked.

Drew dipped his head. 'I've got the comms all linked up to my laptop at home. I'll give you software and login details so you can listen as well.'

Following Liam's instructions, Drew had placed recording devices inside Garrison and

Jake's cars, just so that he could keep a watchful ear over both their movements and discussions. Somewhere there was a snake beneath the reeds, and Liam was intent on finding out who the fucker was. He was the mongoose, readying himself to let loose.

'Shit…' Drew said.

'What?'

'Garrison's car. He's getting his new one today.'

'Fuck. Already?'

Drew dipped his head again.

'Bug it as soon as he comes back. I don't want him getting away with anything.'

'What about Charlotte – do you want me to do hers too?'

Charlotte? Who the fuck was Charlotte? Maybe the cup of whiskey wouldn't last till the end of the day after all.

Liam stared at Drew blankly.

'You didn't hear? Erm… she's a DI. Grayson. From Bernie's. She's been rostered in to help us out with the case.'

Bernie's was the name given to Croydon's police station, a moniker that reflected its high-profile and prevalent drug taking during the eighties and nineties. The same way some people referred to Bow Green as Snow Bow. A lot had changed since those days; a lot of people had moved on. Drew, however, had never received the memo.

Liam breathed slowly as he absorbed Drew's words. Croydon. Jake's old stomping ground.

'I must have missed all those emails.' Liam shook his head. 'I bet this is Penrose's doing, jumped-up wanker. When does she start?'

'This morning. She'll probably be here soon.'

Liam looked down at his hands and played with his fingernails. His cuticles needed pushing back.

'Bug her car too. I want to hear everything she's saying. I'll do a background check on her. See what her credentials are.'

'Anything else?'

'Keep an eye out on Garrison as well. He's been showing his face a lot less recently. I don't like it.'

Drew stopped himself as he rose out of his chair and then slowly stood up. He looked like he was just finishing up a job interview. Nine times out ten, Liam wouldn't have given it to him.

'Something else?' Liam asked, fearing he already knew the answer.

'Any… any news on Matheson?'

There it was. There it fucking was. Henry Matheson again. Typical. *Single-minded prick.*

'No. Now go and find the old bastard.'

That cut the conversation off immediately. And as soon as the door was closed, Liam removed The Cabal's burner phone from the cabinet and dialled.

There was no answer.

Liam gripped the phone hard and held the bottom of it in his mouth. He clamped down on the buttons, his teeth breaking into the plastic, splintering some of the internal mechanisms of the device.

Liam let it fall from his mouth and removed his personal mobile.

If there was someone who would know what was going on, it would be Assistant Commissioner Richard Candy. The man had his finger in a lot of pies – the nature of the job. He was the type of career officer, nine times out of ten, who knew what was happening and when it was happening. He'd been that way ever since he'd joined the police, and that was one habit that was never going to die.

'Candy speaking.'

'It's Liam. What's this I hear about a DI from Croydon being called in to help with my investigation?'

'What's your question exactly?'

Liam and Candy had been friends for a long time. They'd started their careers at the same time, and plenty of back-scratching had taken place since then, but right now, Liam sensed the man was about to be a colossal cunt.

'Let's start with *why* shall we? Why's she joining us?'

'The investigation needs help.'

'That didn't answer my question.'

'It did. It's just not what you wanted to hear.'

Liam grabbed his computer mouse and squeezed like it was a stress ball. Through gritted teeth, he hissed, 'Don't fuck with me on this one, Richard. I swear to Christ.'

Candy said nothing. From experience, Liam knew his friend was letting him calm down, think about what he was saying and who he was saying it to. The power play between the two of them had begun. And there was always only one winner.

Once Liam's breathing was controlled, he continued, 'Who authorised it?'

'I did. On your behalf.'

Liam sighed, let go of the mouse.

'When does she leave?'

'As soon as the case is put to bed.'

'Who does she report to?'

'You. She's a part of your team. Treat her like it.' There was a pause – welcomed. 'Think of it as an extra incentive to get it done sooner rather than later.'

And there it was. Hard and obvious, like a slap in the face. Richard might not have noticed it, but he'd just given away the real reason she was there.

'You buckled that easy?' Liam began. 'I'm disappointed. One little fuck-up in a press conference, one little telling-off from a *lord,* and you lose your shit and get the next available officer to help us out.'

'You heard him, Liam. Penrose wants this swept away. The world's eyes are watching.'

'Sell-out.'

'Like I said, it's an incentive to solve the case quicker.'

'No need,' Liam said. 'We've already made a breakthrough. Yesterday. Our prime suspect killed himself. We're waiting on forensics now.'

'Then you can put your toys back in the pram.'

Liam hung up and threw the phone onto the table.

If only things were that simple. Richard Maddison. The suicide. Getting the investigation squared away as soon as he would have liked. The dynamic of the investigation had changed. They had an outsider. Someone who was no doubt not of the same ilk as Liam and Drew and Garrison and now Jake. Which meant she would question everything about

Richard Maddison's suicide and threaten to overturn all their hard work.

From here on they were going to have to be extra careful if they were going to carry on with their part of the plan. And Liam was going to have to do everything in his power to make sure she didn't discover the truth.

And that started with sending her back to the shithole she'd just come from.

CHAPTER 40

RULES

There were certain rules in the contract killing business. Some dos and don'ts.

The first rule was to never use any names. The second was to never discuss the job after it had been carried out. And the third was to take a deposit payment upfront and then settle the rest on completion of the contract.

They weren't hard and fast rules, but they were Georgiy's own.

And he'd broken every single one of them.

By now, Georgiy knew the name of the man he was about to meet and vice versa. DC Pete Garrison. A real arsehole of a man. Always had something to say, always had to voice his opinion. Like a backseat contract killer. As part of his agreement with The Cabal, it was his responsibility to report every minute detail of

Danny Cipriano's and Richard Maddison's deaths. That way The Cabal could plan and prepare for any fallout afterwards if necessary. Georgiy hadn't approved, but if he wanted his money, he was going to have to play ball. And that had led to the final rule being broken. For both hits, he hadn't received a single penny.

The location was the Warwick Reservoirs just a few miles north of Stratford and the Olympic Stadium. Garrison's choice. It was open, expansive and, to Georgiy's surprise, almost entirely deserted – save for a dog walker taking a Labrador out for a walk. A slight chill whipped along the roads, if they could be called that, and the early morning sun glistened on the dew on the gravel and grass. On the other side of a steep bank and thin line of trees was one of the reservoirs, a vast expanse of murky water. On the other side of that was a train line, distorting the quiet serenity of the place.

Georgiy was parked in the middle of a manmade pathway. He exited the car and leant against the bonnet, surveying his surroundings. He was wearing one of his favourite suits, and the blazer flapped about in the steady breeze. When it came to business, he liked to dress appropriately.

Far off in the distance were the towering skyscrapers of Canary Wharf, home to some of the country's biggest criminals. A few feet in front of him, a duck emerged from behind a bush, stopped and stared. Georgiy eyed the creature suspiciously.

Then he heard the sound of an engine piercing the stillness. Georgiy spun on the spot as Garrison pulled up behind him.

He checked his watch. 'You're late,' Georgiy said as he wandered across to Garrison's door. The duck followed.

'Sorry,' Garrison replied, stepping out. 'I was picking her up. What d'you think?'

The man pointed to the brand-new Jaguar. It had that new-car authenticity to it. The shine. The brand-new number plate. The perfectly untouched and unscathed windshield. The unblemished tyres and alloy rims. It was a beautiful piece of machinery, Georgiy conceded, but it wasn't what he'd come to see.

'Who's your little friend?' Garrison asked, pointing to the duck that had followed Georgiy. 'Reckon he suspects some fowl play?'

'What?'

'Never mind.'

'You have money?'

'In the boot.'

Garrison rounded the back of the car and opened the boot.

'Remember what we said. Keep a low profile.'

'Don't tell me how to do job.'

'We don't want anyone catching wind of this or seeing this.'

Georgiy looked around him. 'You choose somewhere in open for exchange… Stupid.'

'There's always method to the madness.'

Garrison reached inside the boot and produced two large black gym bags, unbranded and inconspicuous.

'Everything?' Georgiy asked as he took the bags from the policeman.

'It's all there. Five hundred grand. Half a million. More money than I'll ever see in my life.'

'Then I know where to go if some missing.'

The comment incited a smirk from Garrison, and as he closed the boot, he wiped his forehead with the back of his sleeve.

'The Cabal was very impressed with your disposal of Maddison, by the way.'

'Oh?'

'I thought you should know.'

Georgiy accepted the compliment, deciding there was no need to tell him that Richard Maddison had been almost dead already, gasping for air and clinging to what remained of his life when they'd found him. There was no need to tell him that Nigel had made a mess of the crime scene as he tried to drown Richard before the rapid blood loss could steal his soul from the planet; no need to tell him that it was the easiest money they'd ever earned.

'I was very impressed too,' Garrison continued. 'You know, if my wife ever gets too much and I need to get rid of her, you'll be the first name that comes to mind.'

Georgiy glanced at the duck. 'You can't afford me.'

Garrison chuckled, pointed his finger at Georgiy. 'I like you. You're funny.'

He moved back to the driver's side of the car and opened the door. 'Remember what I said. Keep yourselves quiet for a bit, all right.'

Georgiy turned his back on Garrison, headed to his car and threw the money into the rear seats. Before closing the door, he opened one of the bags, checked that the money was in there and that they hadn't been double-crossed, and then closed the door behind him.

As soon as Georgiy slotted the keys into the ignition, Garrison pulled up beside him with the passenger window down.

'I forgot to mention, but it's likely we'll need your services again soon.'

'How many?'

'One. Maybe two.'

'Details?'

Garrison smirked. 'I'll be in touch.'

CHAPTER 41

BROTHER

Liam had called a meeting early on in the morning where he'd welcomed Charlotte to the team – to which there had been an odd grunt and an even less enthused 'hello' from some of the team members – and then given them a brief on the actions of the day. Their main suspect in Danny Cipriano's murder was dead, suicide, but they still needed to inspect the events surrounding Richard Maddison's death to see if there was anything suspicious about it. Jake had breathed a heavy sigh of relief at that; it meant Liam had done a full one-eighty and was beginning to get paranoid about Charlotte potentially finding holes in their plan.

All Jake had to do was point her to them.

The Major Investigation Team were at their desks, typing away, inputting information into

HOLMES and the PNC, signing documents, stapling pages together, hole punching, answering the telephone, discussing particulars of the case. Everyone was busy. Except one person. Garrison. Jake hadn't seen the man all morning, and Drew was up and down to the toilet like he was beginning to develop a problem.

But right now, Drew was at his desk, burying himself in a coffee with his headphones plugged tightly in his ears. He seemed absorbed in his own little world, oblivious to everything that was going on around him.

Two down, one to go.

Jake slowly rotated his neck until he peered over his shoulder and looked into Liam's office. The blinds were closed and the door was shut, so Jake had it on good authority that he didn't want any visitors. Then he turned his attention back to his desk and scribbled a note on a Post-it. Tearing it off the pad, he rose from his chair and wandered over to Charlotte, who was sitting opposite him, hidden from view behind a large partition. She was in the middle of completing a document on her computer, her glasses perched on the edge of her nose.

As he walked past her, he surreptitiously placed the Post-it on her desk and wandered down to the toilets, found himself a cubicle and closed the door behind him. Counted in his head. Thirty seconds. Forty-five. A minute. A minute thirty. Two.

Just as he was about to leave, the door to the bathroom opened.

Shit. He held his hand on the handle, waiting for the person to leave. *Please use the cubicle. Please use the cubicle.*

The bloke didn't. Whoever it was.

Jake stood there waiting impatiently, tapping his foot on the floor as the other man seemed to take forever to drain his bladder into the urinal. After thirty long seconds, he finished, washed his hands and left.

'Finally,' Jake whispered under his breath. He yanked open the door and headed out of the men's. As he exited, he snapped his head left and right and made sure there was nobody coming from either direction.

He ducked into the women's toilets opposite, praying that only Charlotte was inside. The only time he'd ever intentionally set foot into a women's bathroom was when Elizabeth had needed rescuing on a night out after drinking too much and almost passing out with her head on the toilet seat.

Inside there were three cubicles in a row, with the sink opposite. Jake exhaled deeply. The cubicle on the far end was in use. He hoped it was Charlotte. He sauntered up to it, making sure his feet made as little sound as possible, and knocked on the door.

'Yeah?' came the response. He'd only heard her talk a couple of times, but he recognised her south London accent immediately.

'It's me,' he whispered.

The door burst open, and standing in the cramped space was Charlotte.

'Can—'

Just as he began to speak, the bathroom door opened. Panicked, he leapt into the cubicle with her, locking the door behind him. Jake held his breath and strained his ears. It was an intimate situation, and it gave him a good opportunity to inspect her features. She was slightly shorter than him – *just*. Her hair was pulled off her face and tied in a ponytail. She'd removed her glasses, revealing a set of golf-green eyes beneath the bright artificial lighting overhead. Their bodies were pressed up against one another in the confines of the cubicle like they were dancing at a wedding ceremony. Nice and slow. He hoped his breath didn't smell. He could feel her breasts against his chest, and his legs against hers, but it was too late to change position now.

Please be quick. Please be quick.

Finally, the occupant who'd just entered finished and was out of there.

As soon as Jake heard the door close, he panted and caught his breath.

'That was too close,' Charlotte said as she created some space between them.

'I'm sorry,' he said, 'but I need to speak with you.'

'And I needed to speak with you. But there are better places than this.'

'The sooner the better.' He paused a beat until his lungs were full. 'I know who you are. I know why you're here. But there are some things you need to understand. I can't be seen with you. In the office, I mean. They think I'm one of them. They're behind the Danny Cipriano killing – they know who did it and now they're covering it up. Some guy called The Farmer. Contract killer, I think. Richard Maddison was the scapegoat. They're making it look like a suicide.'

'You don't think it was?' She stared at him blankly, as though she were a robot computing everything he was telling her.

'I know it wasn't. They're gonna be treading on eggshells now you're here. They'll be doing things more by the book. They won't want you getting involved with their investigation too much. Which is exactly what you need to do. Force their hand.'

'How?'

'Blood on the walls and door in Maddison's bathroom. Mud on the rug too. One of the SOCOs should have gathered it as evidence. That's your starting point. If you raise that with Liam, it'll look like Maddison was murdered, and then Liam and the rest of them will be forced to do something else. That's when we need to get them.'

The brain was a funny thing. It had the ability to remember things – names, places, discussions, locations – but in Jake's mind, there was only one thing standing out for him. An image, flashing in his mind.

'There was something else as well. A note. Underneath Maddison's bedroom table. It could have been a suicide note. I forgot to pick it up or flag it. Hopefully one of the SOCOs has bagged it.'

Charlotte rolled up the arm of her blazer. 'I'm impressed, but we need to speak in different conditions.' She gazed around the cubicle. 'Somewhere a little less intimate, and somewhere a bit more public as well.'

'The pub,' Jake said. 'The Head of the House. It's where we usually go. If anyone asks, I'm welcoming you to the team.'

'It's a deal,' Charlotte said. 'Tonight.'

Just as Jake was about to open the door, she placed a hand on his arm.

'You need to be careful, Jake. Don't get yourself in too deep with these people. That's why I'm here. I'm trained in it. If they can have Michael Cipriano killed so easily, then think of what they can do to you.'

'Michael?' Jake asked, confused. 'It was Danny…'

Well, shit.

A thought popped into his head. One he didn't want, but he was grateful it had come sooner rather than later. Michael Cipriano. Not once throughout the investigation had Jake thought about him. Was the final Cipriano brother still alive or had he been killed off as well? How much information did he have about The Cabal? Or had he already spilled it and his name was next on the list?

Jake needed to speak with him before any of that happened.

CHAPTER 42

CONNECTED

Jake hadn't bothered to call ahead before he made the ninety-minute journey to Guildford. No point. He wanted to speak with her in person. Face to face. And if she knew he was coming, then she might get spooked and drop off the radar like she had yesterday.

Clouds swallowed the sky and a light patter of rain had started to fall on the south of England. He was sitting in his car outside Danika's house, gazing fervently at the bay window. Despite the rain, he saw movement.

Jake made a phone call. Danika picked up on the second ring.

'Tanner?' Her voice sounded wheezy, as if she had a cold. 'Is that you?'

'Yeah, it's me all right. You free to talk?'

'Erm… Yeah. What's up?'

'I need to speak with you privately.'

'How private?'

'Danny Cipriano private.'

A moment of silence.

'Yeah, that's not a problem. We can talk about it now if you'd like.'

Jake kept his eyes keenly planted on the house.

'No, it's OK. I'll come round.'

He hung up the phone and waited. Within a minute, the front door opened and Danika – looking flustered and panicked – hurried out of the house. She froze mid-step as her eyes fell on him, staring back at her. He rolled down the window.

'Get in.'

The sound of the passenger door closing echoed around the inside of the car and then disappeared, replaced by silence. Jake's hands felt clammy – a combination of anger and adrenaline and fear surging through his body. His chest rose and fell heavily, worsening by the second.

'Off somewhere?' he asked her.

'What's with all the cloak and dagger, Jake?' Danika asked, surprisingly bubbly and full of excitement, laughing it off like nothing was awry. But Jake saw right through it. She was nervous. And she had every right to be.

'I think you know, Dan.'

'What were you saying about Danny?'

'He's dead.'

She threw her hand to her mouth and let out a little gasp. 'Oh my God. I didn't—'

'Cut the shit, Danika.' Jake gripped the steering wheel until his knuckles whitened. 'I know everything. How you helped Bridger get him out of remand by convincing the CPS to throw the case and dismiss all the evidence. And I know you know something about who killed him.'

'Jake…' She placed a hand on his knee. Her eyes, and *face*, looked tired and weathered. 'I don't know who killed him. I promise.'

'But you admit to everything else?'

'It wasn't me. It was Bridger. He… he forced me into it. Bullied me.'

'You could have said no.'

'Still oblivious to your own ignorance, aren't you? I'm involved with some dangerous people now. I don't know who I can trust. I don't know where's safe to go, what's safe to do. They've ruined my life all because I agreed to get them in the WPS. But now they've got me, and I'm not going anywhere.'

'Why are you leaving the service?'

She ignored the question. 'These people will find out anything and everything about you.

They will uncover every lie you've ever told, every mistake you've ever made, everyone you've ever held dear – and they will use it all against you in order to get what they want. And there's never a chance to get out.'

'What did they have over you, Dan?'

She turned and looked ahead, out of the windscreen. As the time passed, tears began to form in her eyes. 'You don't know what it's like. When I lost my kids, it killed me inside. It still kills me a little bit more every day. And do you know what I used to the numb the pain? Alcohol and drugs.'

Jake's brow collapsed, but he didn't disrupt Danika's flow.

'A lot of them. But then Bridger found out. He told me that he needed a favour and, in exchange, he would keep his mouth shut. One of his stipulations was that I get medical help – he wanted me off the drugs and drink until everything was settled. He couldn't risk me getting wasted one night and talking about something I was supposed to keep a secret. He warned me what would happen. I handed in my notice because I couldn't do it anymore. Keeping up the façade of happy detective. I couldn't get the help I needed. I'm a risk. I'm a liability.'

'Are you using again?'

She wiped away a tear. 'I haven't felt pain in months, Jake. Forced myself not to. I will always live my life in fear.'

'Why didn't you tell me any of this, Dan? You could have come to me, trusted me—'

'You fucked off.' Danika's voice was laced with so much venom that he retreated a little. 'You transferred to Stratford and left me alone at Surrey, just so you could look like the star fucking pupil. You didn't know it but I needed you. I *still* need you. But it's too late. They're gonna come after me like they did Danny…'

'Danika…' Jake caught a lump in his throat and tried to swallow it down. He was unsuccessful. 'Tell me who you and Bridger were dealing with. Their names. What they look like. Who they are. I can help you.'

'I never saw any faces. I never knew any names. I only dealt with Elliot. I don't know anything about The Cabal, Jake. And I know that's why you really came here.'

'But you know everything about the brothers. You must have met with them, spoken to them. Did they not tell you anything?'

'That's what got Danny killed.'

'What about Michael? Where's he? I need to speak to him.'

'No.'

'Does Bridger know where he is?'

She shook her head. 'He kept his hands clean of it all. Wanted nothing to do with it.'

'Then tell me. Help me so we can help him. If Danny knew things, then so will he. We can help put this to rest.'

'Who's we?'

Jake paused, swallowing, and then licked his lips. He'd done it again.

'What have you done, Jake?'

'I've got a UC helping me from the DPS. I think this thing – this web of corruption – spreads far and wide. It's connected to my team in Stratford. We're working on Danny's murder now, but they're covering it up. And I need to make sure I can speak to Michael before anything happens to him. I just need you to tell me his address. That's it. That's all I ask.'

Danika slowly turned to face him, her eyes moistening again, pupils dilating. 'If I tell you, then you become implicated. And then when they find out, they'll find you. And then they'll do exactly the same to you as they've done to Danny.'

'Not with the DPS protecting me. I can stop —'

'Nobody can protect you.'

'At least let me try.'

Danika hesitated for what felt like an eternity. The silence was profound, and it felt like it was pulling Jake into the abyss with her.

'Michael's address. That's all I ask,' he insisted. 'You're the only one who knows it. You're the only person I could come to – the only person I could trust. You're the only person who can help Michael survive. I'm one of the good guys, remember? I can get to him first. I can protect him and keep him alive.'

Danika looked down at her lap and played with her fingers, then she rubbed the snot away from her nose and sniffed hard.

Reluctantly, she gave him the address.

CHAPTER 43

FLAIR

Garrison loved that particular new car smell. The fresh leather. The polished surfaces. The brand-new Jelly Bean air freshener that the sales team had given him as an extra gift for his 'services to the community' after he'd told them he was a police officer. *Pffft. Yeah right. Services to the community. Ain't that the half of it.* In his lifetime, he'd only ever bought three cars, and each one had excited him more than the last. It was a bit like a drug, an extreme hit of dopamine as he sat behind the wheel of his latest toy. But the real high came when he drove them for the first time. They were his babies – until they stopped performing to the best of their abilities – that was when the drug was used up and he needed a new fix.

His latest fix was a brand-new Jaguar XKR Coupe. Fresh off the production line – five-litre petrol engine, 503 BHP, 0–60 mph in 4.6 seconds. Beast of a car – the fastest thing he'd ever owned. And, at just a tipple over seventy grand, it was the most expensive thing he'd ever owned as well. Thanks to the help of a little disposable income courtesy of Danny and Richard's deaths. Their loss was his gain. He needed to squeeze it back into the economy somehow. And if that was by lining the pockets of a big corporation, then so be it. He was happy. The salesman who got his commission was happy. The CEO was happy. The taxman was happy. Even the head-turning mongrels on their way to work were happy.

The only person that wasn't happy, he supposed, was the person about to get in the seat beside him.

Garrison had called the meeting as soon as he'd finished with the Russian. He was stationed outside the BBC News headquarters in Shepherd's Bush, parked up on the side of the road opposite the building's entrance. He turned his head and saw Tanya Smile wandering towards him, struggling to walk properly in her high heels. She was dressed in a dark blue suit that clapped and waved in the wind, revealing a red nylon interior in the blazer and a skirt that was tight around her legs. Her hair bounced and bobbed gently as she walked, making it look as though it wasn't moving at all. She came to a stop by the zebra crossing, looked both ways and then jumped into the car as soon as the coast was clear.

Garrison pulled away before giving her the chance to put her seat belt on, delighting in the smell of her perfume, which accentuated the rest of the aromas in the car, adding to the dopamine hits racing about his brain. They drove in silence for five minutes towards a multi-storey car park in North London where he climbed to the top of the structure and reversed into a spot tucked away in the corner. The car park was poorly lit, save for the struggling early morning light that crept in through two giant holes in the sides of the building. They were in the perfect hiding spot, giving Garrison complete autonomy over the occupants, including Tanya.

'What's this about, Pete? Does Liam know I'm here?' she asked.

'Your boyfriend doesn't know a thing. I'm surprised he's spoken to you since you went live with Danny's information yesterday.'

There was a pause. 'He hasn't. I've tried but he's not picking up.'

'Giving you the tough love act, eh?'

'We had a good thing going. If you fuck it up for us then I'll never forgive you.'

Garrison placed his nails in his mouth. 'You've got me quaking in my boots.'

'I did exactly as you asked. And now I'm the one getting backlash.'

'Not my problem. So long as you continue to do exactly as I instruct and don't start showing any sign of deviating from the plan, everything's fine. We can make sure your job is safe.' Garrison placed his hand on the steering wheel and turned to face her. 'But when it comes to your life, I can't make the same guarantees.'

Tanya's lips parted and she shifted closer to the door.

'Don't do anything stupid,' he said as he locked the car from his driver-side panel.

'Please… Why am I here?'

Garrison loved hearing women beg. Made him feel almighty and powerful – that they would do whatever he wanted at the snap of a finger.

'I know you're the reporter Danny Cipriano spoke to in witness protection. I know you're the one he told all those dirty little secrets to. I just want to know exactly *what* he told you.'

Tanya inched away from him. He hoped she could see the menace in his face; he was making no effort to hide it.

'Please… What are you going to do to me?'

He had something in mind – lots of things in fact. But one stuck out to him. Something he'd wanted to do for a long time.

'That depends on how much you tell me.' Garrison moved his hand to his groin. Tanya noticed the movement.

'I… He… he… he didn't tell me anything. He knew that he'd be killed if he said anything. But you guys went and did it anyway. He wouldn't tell me any other names than the ones I already knew. I told him I knew about Liam… You… Drew. He only knew Liam by name but had recognised both you and Drew.'

'How did you meet him?'

'Through a police officer. She was in charge of getting him into the witness protection scheme. I'd done my research and approached DS Bridger, but he told me he had nothing to do with any of it. He'd passed that buck onto another officer – DC Danika Oblak, Surrey Police. She's the only one in the country outside of the witness protection team who knows both Michael and Danny's locations.'

Good little Isaac. The man had told the truth.

'This next question is very important, Tanya. And I need you to answer it truthfully... Did you, or are you going to, meet up with Michael?'

Tanya shook her head violently. Small wisps of hair slapped her across the face yet her gaze remained fixed on his.

'Danika wouldn't tell me his address. She said she wanted to wait and see what happened to Danny. Now she probably knows... I can't imagine she'd give it away easily.'

'We'd better hope you're right.' Garrison paused and turned his attention to the dashboard, lost in the beauty of the engineering and the rainbow colours of the dials. 'You know, usually, this is the time where I would either pull out a gun on you or have you followed and killed before you're able to call your boyfriend and tell him what's going on.'

Tanya let out a little gasp and opened her mouth to speak, but nothing but air came out.

'But this is a brand-new car, and I don't want to ruin it on its first day. Nor do I want to expend such resources on killing you through the appropriate channels, when there are bigger fish to fry, as they say.' He faced her and then raised his hand. She flinched, but then as his hand moved closer to her face, she froze. He stroked her soft warm skin and caressed her hair. 'I'm sure we can come to some other arrangement. A little secret between us.'

Garrison groped his groin again. This time he was certain she'd seen it and understood exactly what he meant.

'No. I won't. Liam…'

'Liam doesn't need to know. Our little secret.'

'I can't.'

Using his free hand, Garrison reached in the side panel of the car and pulled out a Glock 17. 'Like I said,' he continued as he set the gun on his lap, 'we can come to an arrangement. I don't want to have to use this, but I will if you force me to. Now, do we have a deal?'

Tanya's eyes glistened. Garrison admired and respected her. She was a tenacious journalist, always doing the best to seek out a story and report every excruciating detail. But she'd got involved with some of the wrong people – through no fault but her own – and now she was going to have to suffer the consequences of it.

'How?' she asked.

'I think you know how.'

Garrison placed the weapon back where it came from, unzipped his trousers and pulled them down to his ankles. The air-conditioned air tingled his testicles. He hadn't bothered to shave – in fact, he hadn't bothered to shave in years; his wife hadn't touched them in over ten – so she was going to have to make do with it. He gave her a nod and then, closing her eyes, Tanya leant over into his lap. It had been a long time since he'd last had his dick sucked, and for a moment he wasn't sure if he'd be able to get it up, but as soon as Tanya touched it, he was rock hard. A sensation he hadn't felt in a long time washed over him. He tilted his head back against the headrest and settled himself in. The best start to his new car's life he could have hoped for.

As Tanya set to work, he reached across and grabbed his phone from the dashboard. While placing one hand on her head, to keep her pinned down, he made a call.

'Yes?'

'Michael Cipriano. DC Danika Oblak. You have to get through her to get to him. But keep her alive until he's been taken care of. I'll leave the logistics and flair up to you.'

CHAPTER 44

ETERNITY

The house was somewhere in North Ockendon, a small town just on the outskirts of the M25. Situated in a cul-de-sac called Fen Lane, the building was the fourth out of five. All the houses were evenly separated from one another and looked as though they'd been built by the same bloke. Almost identical, but not nearly as identical as some of the new builds that were cropping up everywhere nowadays.

Jake parked at the bottom of Fen Lane and wandered the rest of the way on foot. He stopped at the front door and knocked. Less than ten seconds later, a figure appeared. He was dressed in a gilet, his hair slicked back, and he wore a couple of rings on his fingers, with a Rolex sparkling in the light. To Jake, he had an air about him that suggested he was an Essex millionaire – living out the luxuries of a purely material existence – rather than an officer left in charge of an informant's safety.

'You, Jake?'

Jake nodded.

'One of Garrison's boys?'

He hesitated. For a split second, he almost told the man no. But then he remembered where he was and who he was supposed to be.

'Yeah,' he replied. 'One of Pete's guys. Can I come in?'

The man seemed flustered, his behaviour slightly erratic, jumpy, like he was nervous. Or on something. Perhaps it was the confirmation that he was one of Garrison's men. But why did he ask about Garrison? *I thought it was Liam in charge of all this.*

The interior of the house was bleak. There was no colour in the walls nor flooring, and very few windows, save for a skylight at the top of the landing that illuminated the property. A flight of stairs was immediately in front of him that circled to the top. To his right was an open-plan living room. To his left a bathroom and, beyond, a dining room.

'I'm Isaac by the way,' the witness protection officer said. He held out his hand nervously; it felt moist as Jake took it. 'Just in case Garrison asks who you dealt with.'

Jake nodded, unsure what to say. The less time he spent pretending to be someone he wasn't, the better.

'Where is he?'

'Oh. Yes. Michael. Sorry. I forgot! H-He's upstairs in the office. Playing *Grand Theft Auto*.'

Jake followed Isaac up the steps. As they climbed higher, the sound of Michael shouting and yelling at the television, and the sound of heavy machine-gun fire and explosions grew.

Isaac entered the room without knocking.

'Micky, you got a visitor.'

'Who?'

Michael was already on his feet when Jake entered and baulked at the man's appearance. It was like he was staring at a new man. His hair was long, wavy, and shaggy, pulled off his face and slicked behind his ears. He'd grown a beard, which was as dark as his hair but not as full; there were patches around his jawline and the chin was sprinkled with specs of grey. His eyes looked deep and hollow, darkened by bags that underlined them like words on a page. His muscle mass had seriously depleted, and what had once been a thick body with thick shoulders and even thicker arms had been reduced to... normal. Probably less than normal. It was frightening.

Michael Cipriano was the middle brother. And the biggest of the three of them. It was often cited that, during their heists, The Crimsons would use him to act as a deterrent to anyone trying to be a hero.

'The fuck's this prick doing here?' Michael hissed.

'Good to see you too, old friend.'

Jake turned to Isaac before Michael had a chance to launch another verbal assault on him. 'Could you leave us? I need to speak with him in private.'

'Of course.' Isaac dipped his head. 'I'll be outside in the car. Call me when you're done.'

With that, Isaac left. As he disappeared and descended the steps, Jake and Michael locked onto one another. Even though Michael looked as though he was weakened and nutritionally deprived, Jake was almost certain that he would still be able to beat him up. Despite the couple of inches that separated them, Jake was certain all it would take was one right hook from Michael Cipriano and he'd be out cold on the floor.

'How you keeping?' Jake asked in a vain attempt to warm the frosty mood.

It didn't work.

'The fuck d'you think you're doing here?'

Jake swallowed before continuing. 'I suppose... I suppose you heard about your brother.'

'Half the world knows.' Michael moved over to the sofa, fell onto it and picked up his controller.

'How'd you find out?' Jake asked as he hovered in front of the corner of the television screen.

'The same way as the rest of the population. The news.'

'Nobody from the police told you?'

Michael turned his attention away from the video game. 'I think you already know the answer to that question. Good riddance, if you ask me. He was already dead in my eyes. Worthless piece of shit. Probably deserved it.'

'Do you wanna know why he died?'

'Go on then.'

'Because he started talking to someone he shouldn't have. The Cabal and the rest of them had him killed.'

'Never could shut his mouth. That was Danny's problem. Always was. Especially when he fucking told everything to that bitch Louise.' Michael shook his head in derision. 'So why're you here? I doubt it's 'cause you wanted to tell me about my brother.'

'I'm here to protect you.'

Michael scoffed and shook his head. 'You ain't gonna be able to make that happen.'

'Why not?'

'Because you just told me what they done to Danny. They can easily do the same to me.'

'Not if I can stop it,' Jake said, stepping closer to the centre of the television screen so that he had Michael's full attention.

'You ain't gonna be able to stop it. Even bigger and better people than you have tried and failed.'

'I need information,' Jake said bluntly.

'What?'

'I need to know everything,' Jake said, realising that it was a long shot as he spoke. 'Names of the people you worked for. Places. Dates. Events. Times. All the details. From the very beginning to now.'

'What makes you think I'm gonna do that? I ain't dumb. And they ain't either. As soon as I tell you, they'll find out and they'll kill me. Just the same way they done Danny.'

Jake stepped directly in front of the television and moved closer to Michael. Michael paused the game and set the controller on the coffee table.

'I can help you. I can protect you. Trust me,' he said.

'Why would I do that? You're the one who fucking put me in this situation in the first place.'

'Things have changed. *I've* changed.'

Michael eased into the sofa and rested one foot on the other knee. 'You've joined the dark side? After all this time?'

'So long as the people that matter believe that, yes.'

'The great Jake Tanner; bent. Never thought I'd hear those words.'

Jake sighed. Michael was blowing things out of proportion, and he didn't want that.

'Can you help me or not?'

'I wish I could, fella, but I never knew any names. I never knew any faces. Places, dates, times – all the juicy little details you want. I don't know any of them. I mean, we were propositioned back in the early days. A bent cop scouted us and signed us on. We called him Desmond. Used him for our next few heists in exchange for a cut of the takings. They took fifty per cent while we split the other fifty between us.'

'Do you know who it was you dealt with?'

Michael shook his head. 'I never knew his real name. Always dealt with Freddy, and then Danny after Freddy got nicked.'

'So Freddy knows?' Jake asked, his pulse racing. A glimmer of hope, perhaps?

'Yeah, but you ain't getting it outta him. Ever. These people are smart, man. I mean, they're cops for fuck's sake. Some of the most dangerous people I know. They know everything about you. And if they don't, they'll find it. And as soon as they found out Freddy had a kid… Man, they've been holding little Sammy hostage ever since. That's why Freddy ain't saying a word to no one. So long as he still gets to see his son – thanks to you, I hear – he's staying *schtum*.'

Jake sighed and looked at an empty beer can on the floor. The one person who knew the potential identity of The Cabal was the same person he'd helped put in jail. And now he wasn't saying a word to anyone. Jake's own tenacity and hard work had been responsible for shooting himself in the foot.

'Is there anyone else?'

'Yeah. The same bent cops you're pretending to work for. But bear in mind, right, that if they find out what you're doing to them, they'll fucking kill you. All bent cops are the same – they only wanna look out for themselves, and they ain't afraid to hurt you if it comes down to it. The only reason I'm alive still is because I don't know nothing, and I intend to keep it that way.'

'So you're not going to help? You're going to live the rest of your life in the witness protection scheme, hiding.'

'Hey,' Michael said, holding his hands in the air in mock surrender, 'it's an easy life. And the easier the better.'

'What if they come for you?'

'They have no reason to…' Michael hesitated for a moment. Then he leapt off the sofa and lunged at Jake. 'I don't fucking believe it. You cunt. You set me up?'

'Wh-What are you t-talking about?'

'They're gonna find out you've been here, and they're gonna assume I've done the same thing my brother done. They're gonna fucking come for me, aren't they? That prick Isaac ain't afraid to grass on no one.'

Jake didn't like to admit it, but he had just bargained with Michael's life.

'I told you, I'm working for them. If they ask what I'm doing here, I'll tell them I was making sure you stay quiet, that you don't tell anyone else anything. They'll believe it.'

'Nah, I don't like this. I don't fucking trust you as far as I can throw you.'

'Let me help. Danika – the same woman who sent me here – can help you. We can move you to a different location. Somewhere they'll never find you.'

'I ain't running. I've done enough of that in my time. Fuck that. I ain't doing it again. Nah, you need to leave. You need to get outta here before Isaac starts to get suspicious.'

Michael grabbed Jake by the blazer and hefted him out of the room, carried him down the stairs and to the front door.

'I swear to fucking God,' Michael continued, 'if anything happens to me, I'm cursing you and your family for the rest of eternity.'

CHAPTER 45

CONVERSATIONS

Liam's office was submerged in darkness. The blinds were pulled, and he only had the light coming from his laptop screen to illuminate the room. He was on a mission – and had been for the past hour – burying himself into Charlotte Grayson's life. Something still wasn't sitting right with him. Sure, Assistant Commissioner Richard Candy had told him that she'd been sent in from Croydon to assist with the investigation just to appease Oliver Penrose, but what if that wasn't the case? What if she was working in the upper echelons of The Cabal's organisation and had been sent in to report back? Worse, what if she was working for the DPS or the IPCC?

He didn't know, but he was going to have to satisfy his paranoia. No matter how long it took.

And so far: nothing.

Everything about her checked out. All her documentation was above board and had been filed officially. Her record was immaculate. She was a good detective and had been her entire career. Been in the service for nearly ten years. Seen and done a lot. Achieved the promotion to DI only a few months ago. Hard worker, go-getter. All the other adjectives. Received high-praise from the commissioner and there was even a request to transfer to Greater Manchester Police, like she was part of a Premier League football team.

It was all too good to be true.

But there was still something amiss – a fly in the ointment niggling at the back of Liam's mind.

All he needed was the proper access to it. To follow the paper trail, to find the signatures of who'd signed off on it. And he was going to.

Liam loaded his emails. There were several hundred unread messages sitting in his inbox – some of them important, most of them requiring his attention and all of them a waste of his time. He entered Charlotte's name into the search bar of his email filter, then hit return and waited. The operating system hesitated while it churned out the responses.

At the top was the latest email. Time-stamped in the early hours of that morning, presumably when the decision had been made to notify him of her arrival.

Bingo.

The mail was filled with the usual formal bullshit. Hope you're keeping well, etc. What a waste of time. Just say what you've got to say and be done with it, he thought.

His eyes scanned the text, taking nothing away from it. What he really wanted was the attachment – where he would find the signatories to Charlotte's appointment.

There it was, sitting at the bottom of the email chain.

He opened the attachment and read. After a few seconds of absorbing the information, he had the name, rank and department of the person from Croydon Station who had authorised everything.

'DCS Phillipa Marston,' the woman said after he'd located her contact details and dialled. She spoke with a thick Yorkshire accent.

'This is DCI Liam Greene, from Bow Green.' Liam had no intention of sticking with formalities and pleasantries. Just say what you've got to say and be done with it. 'I had a question regarding DI Charlotte Grayson if that's all right… You have a few minutes?'

'Er, yes… Course. One second.' Marston disappeared for a moment and then returned. 'Is there an issue, Liam?'

'No, not at all. I just wanted to clarify a few things.'

'OK. Sure.'

Liam grabbed a pen and scribbled nonsense on a piece of paper while keeping his eyes trained on the screen. 'Were you the one who authorised the transfer?'

'Yes.'

'Have you ever dealt with DI Grayson before?'

'Oh, yes. For several months. She's been a part of the team ever since I got her. Fantastic inspector.'

'And where did the request originate? Are you able to tell me that?'

Marston hesitated for a moment. 'As far as I'm aware, it came from outside of the service. I think there was an external request that somebody be sent to your team to assist with an ongoing investigation.'

'Do you know who made the request?'

'I… I… I'm sorry, Liam. I don't know whether it's my place to say.'

'It's all right. As I'm sure you can appreciate – considering you're in charge of your own team as well – when someone puts in a request to bring someone in because they don't think you're doing a good enough job, that can be a bit of a kick in the teeth. Wouldn't you agree?'

There was no hesitation in her response. 'Completely.'

'So, would you mind sharing that information with me? You don't have to give me names…'

'I'll be honest with you, Liam. I don't remember, and I don't think it's in my best interest to either. There's… It was all a little suspicious if you ask me. I know that the LOCOG were involved, but I think there was something else going on too. I felt under a lot of pressure to second DI Grayson to you for the foreseeable future. I'm sorry I can't give you any more details.'

'No,' Liam said, wearing a smile on his face. 'You've been more than helpful.'

Liam hung up and placed the phone on the table delicately. He reached for his drink and swallowed two large mouthfuls, the alcohol stinging his throat. It was settled – his questions answered. The whole thing smelt of The Cabal. The secrecy, the pressure, the scapegoat of Oliver Penrose and the LOCOG. The Cabal, through their unending tentacles of persuasion, was trying to undermine him at every turn. Had been since—

A knock came at the office door. Liam screwed the lid on his cup frantically and moved it out of sight.

'It's open,' he called, grabbing a pile of forms that were missing his signature and pretending to sign them.

'Sorry to interrupt, guv,' Charlotte said as she entered, 'but there was something I wanted to discuss with you.'

'Oh?'

'It's regarding Maddison, sir.'

'Oh?'

In her hand she held a folder. She strode across the office and passed it to him. As he took it, the chills on his back started multiplying.

'Some of the forensic analysis came back from Maddison's flat. There's a match between the cement used to kill Danny Cipriano and the cement found on Maddison's clothes. But there's something else.'

'Oh?'

'Footprints and fingerprints different to Maddison's were found at the crime scene.'

Fuck.

'The fingerprints were found on the walls and door frame. There's no way Maddison could have killed himself and then reached that far.'

Fuck fuck fuck.

'I don't think Maddison killed himself, guv. I think we should turn this into a murder investigation.'

Fuck fuck fuck fuck fuck.

Liam stared her blankly, his mind devoid of any thought. In a few very brief sentences, she'd done several things. All of which made him sick with fear. First, she'd proved to him that she was straight, and the estimation that he'd made about her being bent moments ago was wrong. Second, she'd single-handedly re-opened their case and sent them back to square one. It was meant to be an easy one, open and closed. And now it looked like it was going to be open for a lot longer. Third, she'd just made her future very uncertain.

'Excellent work,' Liam lied. 'Perhaps a slight oversight from some of the team, but I suppose that's why you're here.' He smiled at her facetiously. 'I want you to focus your efforts on this please. I'll get some of the others to help you out too.'

Charlotte nodded, thanked him and then left. Liam stared at the door long after it was shut. *Fuck fuck fuck fuck fuck.* If he was going to keep

Charlotte away from anything she shouldn't be seeing, a solution was required fast. And it was his job to come up with one.

Liam grabbed his drink, downed the rest of the whiskey and then slammed the cup down. He needed another. But not yet.

He pulled out his burner phone and called Drew.

'Ah, guv,' Drew answered. 'I was just about to call you.'

'We've got a problem. Charlotte's turned Maddison's suicide into a murder investigation.'

'Shit.'

'I need you to work on it and come up with a solution with me on how to throw her off the scent.'

'I'll do it when I'm back,' Drew said.

Liam clambered out of his chair, ignored the aching joints in his knees and moved over to the window that looked out onto the street.

'And… what about… Garrison?'

There was a pause.

'I don't think you're gonna like it.'

'Tell me.'

'I followed him to the BBC headquarters. He picked up Tanya and took her to a multi-storey. I don't know what they were talking about, but at the end of their conversation she… she…'

'Spit it out.'

'She went down on him.'

Liam's body turned cold.

'Guv…? Guv…? Guv?'

'Come back to the station. Work on this thing for me. Leave Garrison and Tanya to me. This has gone too far now.'

CHAPTER 46

SEISMOGRAPH

There was always a certain electricity, a certain excitement, in the air whenever they received their next hit. The furore usually came from Vitaly or Tatiana or, even more infrequently, Nigel. But it was always Georgiy's job to stifle it before it got too heavy. Excitement led to adrenaline; adrenaline led to eagerness; eagerness led to mistakes. And in this business, mistakes were unacceptable.

The rules on this one were simple. A three-part process.

And they were already onto step one.

Georgiy and Vitaly were outside Danika Oblak's semi-detached house. Vitaly had managed to find the address with ease using various police databases that Garrison and The Cabal had given them access to, and it had taken them a little over an hour to get there. Georgiy had driven, Vitaly riding shotgun, while Nigel and Tatiana sat patiently back in the nightclub, waiting for their call, ready to begin the second phase of the hit.

They both exited the car and wandered up to the front door, surveying the area around them. In the distance, at the other end of the road, was a small Asian man wearing headphones, walking in the other direction. His chicken legs moved so fast they became a blur. Georgiy dismissed him as a potential threat instantly.

At the house, Georgiy pressed the doorbell. The sound of the television playing loudly echoed on the other side.

There was no answer. They rang again, this time holding the doorbell down until it became a monotonous, unending sound.

Eventually, the front door opened.

'DC Oblak?' Georgiy asked, trying his best to hide his accent. 'May we come in?'

Georgiy and Vitaly entered without giving Danika any time to respond. Georgiy moved into the living room while Vitaly stood guard at the door, cutting off her exit.

'You guys have caught me at a really bad time. What's this about?' Danika asked, rubbing her nose and wiping her mouth. She sniffled hard, and a faint smell of weed wafted through the air.

Georgiy reached inside his pocket and produced a forged Metropolitan Police warrant card. It was one of the many forms of identity The Magnate, their contact in that profession, had made for them all. Whatever they needed, he could get.

'We're from the witness protection scheme,' Georgiy continued, speaking slowly. 'We have credible threat to Michael Cipriano's life. We need everything you have on Michael and his whereabouts.'

'What?' Danika asked, sniffing hard again. Her face looked pale and dark circles sat beneath her eyes. Her jumper slipped off her shoulder and she rubbed her nose with the back of her sleeve.

'We need all the documents you have. We need to destroy all the evidence of his whereabouts.'

'I don't understand.'

'His life is in danger. We need destroy evidence of his address to protect him.'

Danika shook her head. 'I don't have any documents. I've never had any documents.'

'Then where?'

'It's all in my head.'

'And...'

'And what?' Danika asked.

'What is the address?'

Danika rubbed her finger over her lips and let out a long breath. 'It's in North Ockendon. Fen Lane. Number sixty-seven.'

Georgiy committed the address to memory, then nodded. 'Perfect. You have wrong address. No need to worry.'

'What... I don't... I don't understand...' Danika's eyelids dropped and bounced up and down like a seismograph during an earthquake. She faltered and her legs gave way. She regained balance and composure by clinging to the wall.

'Everything OK?' Georgiy asked as he reached out a hand to her.

'I'm fine. Fine. Nothing to worry about,' she said. A white sheen covered her face, accentuated by the light coming in through the bay windows. 'I just need to sit down. I'm not... I'm not feeling well.'

Georgiy carried her over to the sofa. There, he saw the small bag of weed on the coffee table, two thin white lines and a syringe.

'V!' Georgiy called.

Within an instant, Vitaly was standing in the door frame, his thick body touching either side of it.

'Help me.'

Vitaly grabbed Danika's feet and together they lowered her dead weight onto the sofa. By now her eyes were glazed over and her body was rigid. Georgiy felt for a pulse. Found one. Weak, but enough to convince him she was alive. If she was overdosing, she'd be dead by now.

'What we do?' Vitaly asked.

'I go North Ockendon. You stay. Watch her. If she wake, you follow. Make sure she not call anyone. Understand?'

Vitaly nodded.

'We need her alive. For now. But watch every move.'

'I understand.'

Georgiy crouched down by the table and inspected the contents. Resting on the surface was a mountain of white powder that had fallen out of a plastic bag and spread across the wood. Beside it was the thing that caught his interest. A syringe. Whether it had been used or not, he couldn't say for certain, but that didn't mean it wouldn't be.

'How you get Michael?' Vitaly asked, distracting his attention away from the drugs.

Georgiy stretched his legs. 'I have an idea.' He reached inside his pocket, produced his phone and called Tatiana as he moved out of the living room. 'Tat, it's me. We have Michael address. I have plan. Listen carefully.'

CHAPTER 47

GOOD EGG

Jake was sitting inside his car, unaware of how much time had passed since Michael had chucked him out of the house. He'd been trying to piece together everything Michael had told him. Which wasn't a lot. And for a brief moment, he even thought about driving down to HMP Winchester and speaking with Freddy but decided against it almost immediately. In the past few months, Jake had tried to make contact – just to keep the semblance of a relationship alive between them – but Freddy hadn't responded. Perhaps Michael had been right – perhaps Freddy was staying quiet for fear of any harm coming to his son. Jake didn't blame him. He would have done the same.

Just as he was about to switch on the ignition, a liveried police car pulled into the cul-de-sac and sped past him.

'What the…?' Jake mouthed as he watched it whizz by.

The tyres kissed the asphalt as the vehicle skidded to a halt, and two uniformed officers alighted, charging towards the front door. Jake unclipped his seat belt and twisted in his seat to get a better look.

The two officers, both male, both dressed in uniform, pounded on the door. A few seconds later he saw Isaac. This time the man looked more flustered, like he'd just been caught with his trousers down. The uniformed officers barged past Isaac and stormed into the house. Less than thirty seconds later, they reappeared, grappling Michael in front of them with his arms behind his back. They shoved him into the back of their car, jumped in and then sped off down the road, blitzing past Jake. As they did so, Jake and Michael's eyes met. There was a look of defeat and fear in Michael's.

Something wasn't right.

A knock came on the window that startled Jake. It was Isaac.

'What's going on?' Jake asked as he wound down the window a fraction.

'They've nicked him.'

'Why?'

'Said they've received reports that he's broken the conditions of his protection.'

'Where?'

Isaac stared at him blankly. 'I don't know. Please don't tell Garrison…'

Jake turned the key, buckled his seat belt and gave chase, leaving the witness protection officer in his wake. He swerved into the oncoming traffic, overtaking cars as fast he could, his foot glued to the accelerator. The liveried police car was nearly half a mile ahead of him, making good progress south. It made a sharp left turn at a junction; Jake followed. Within seconds they were in the middle of nowhere. Just their cars on narrow lanes, surrounded by large fields and farms for miles either side, every now and then the flat skyline disrupted by a tree or two. It didn't take long for Jake to catch up with the police car from a safe distance. The only problem was, they were the only cars on the road. He was too obvious, but there was nothing he could do about that; he was just grateful to be in an unmarked car. Making sure Michael was safe was his top priority, but right now he didn't have a clue how to achieve that. His body was running on a dose of adrenaline combined with the fear of what lay ahead.

The police car made another turn and entered another stretch of road that seemed exactly the same as the other. No, there was a slight difference: the road was raised, and on the right-hand side was a ditch running along the length of the tarmac.

In the distance, a black van came in the other direction. As the opposing car drew rapidly nearer and nearer to the police car – a hundred feet, fifty, twenty, ten – the van swerved in front of it. The police car, reacting quickly, darted to the side of the road and vaulted into a ditch a few feet below. The sound of the crash was horrifying, like a gun had been fired inside Jake's car.

But the black van wasn't finished. It spun out of control, veering onto the side of the road, but as the driver corrected its trajectory and swerved into the middle of the tarmac, the van headed straight towards Jake.

He had a split-second decision to make: collide with the van and die, or swerve into the ditch and survive.

The answer was simple.

He yanked a hard right on the steering wheel, narrowly missing the van charging towards him, ripped through a bush on the road and skidded down the slope into the ditch. He stomped on the brakes, but the traction they picked up on the grass and earth was useless. The incline was moderate, and his body tilted to the side. Tensing, he tried balancing the weight of the car into the centre.

Eventually, he reached the bottom of the ditch, both hands glued to the steering wheel, his foot stuck to the brakes. The car stalled, but he didn't care. There were bigger things to worry about. Like whether he'd shit himself in the process, or whether his arse was clenched so tight that he could make a diamond up there. Fortunately, the answer was neither. Instead, he stared directly through the windshield, paralysed, panting.

Then he screamed – no words, just noise.

It wasn't until he heard a sharp noise that he came back to reality. He shook his head violently and then jumped out of the car, scrambling towards the damaged police vehicle. Running alongside the ditch was a row of bushes and small trees, kept in line by a fence. From his position, it looked as though a couple of thick arms had pierced the windscreen of the overturned police car. In the accident, the bonnet had impaled itself in the mound of earth and the vehicle had rolled on its roof so that it was now running parallel with the road. Smoke and steam billowed from the front of the vehicle and quickly filled the air with a rancid burning smell.

Jake knew he didn't have much time. Preservation of life was his main focus.

He rushed over to the front of the vehicle to find it was filled with debris and foliage. A single branch, as thick as a lamp post, had plunged into the driver's stomach. Thick globules of blood dribbled from the man's mouth as he dangled upside down, stuck in place. Meanwhile, the officer next to him was plastered on the dashboard like a rag doll. Showered in glass, limbs broken and twisted in various places. The sight made Jake want to vomit. He tried for a pulse on both men but soon realised his efforts were worthless.

Next, he tried the rear of the car. In the force of the collision, Michael's passenger door had opened and buckled.

As Jake approached, he heard a deep groaning sound.

'Michael! Michael! Michael!' Jake whispered frantically. 'Are you there? Are you all right?'

He peered inside the car and saw Michael hanging upside down, his body kept in place by the seat belt. His hands were loose – they'd come free in the collision – and blood gushed from his head and ran down his arm. Jake climbed inside, unhooked him from his seat and lowered Michael to the ground.

'It's me, Michael. Everything's going to be all right. Help's on the way!'

Jake hefted Michael from the wreckage and dragged him onto a small bank at the side of the road. The man's body was heavy, and Jake felt his muscles shake under the pressure.

Michael was messed up. In a bad way. Not only was his face covered in blood, but his nose was broken, half his teeth were missing and his arm was clutching his stomach as if he were clinging on to his life.

'I'm going to get you help,' Jake said, trying to console him.

As he stood up to leave, Jake heard Michael whisper something.

'What?' he asked.

'No.'

'Speak louder.'

Michael curled his finger in the air and gestured for Jake to join his side.

'Listen,' Michael said. His voice was raspy, and he choked on his blood after every syllable. 'Listen. No names. Never any names.'

At first, Jake didn't understand what Michael was trying to say, but then, as he realised, his attention focused on Michael's lips.

'No names. Yes. I get it,' Jake said. 'What else?'

'But... I remember...'

'What?'

'The guy... The one who found us... I heard him once... something he said... a lot... a phrase...'

Yes, yes, yes.

'He always... used to call me...'

Jake leant closer.

'He called me a... good egg. I was... a good egg.'

| PART 4 |

CHAPTER 48

SITUATION

Jake's pulse pounded hard, the rhythm of his heart flexing the skin on his neck pervading every other noise in the area. *Dumfdumfdumfdumf*. His breathing was panicked, and his body trembled with the rapid onset of adrenaline. Or was it shock? He was alone, in the middle of a country lane, holding Michael Cipriano's lifeless head in his lap. Torrents of blood continued to dribble from Michael's temple and neck – the extent of his injuries worse than Jake had anticipated – and it quickly soiled Jake's trousers, forming a red petal on his leg.

He tried to piece together what had happened. The black van, coming towards them in the opposite lane, then swerving into the police car, sending it over the mound of earth into the ditch; the driver of the van, features and identity hidden behind the reflection of the sun on the windscreen. In the time it had taken for Jake to crawl out of his car, the van had since disappeared and the fields were now filled with silence, save for the wind rustling the bushes behind him and the sound of petrol dripping inside the police car.

I was… a good egg.

Michael's final words echoed and bounced through the chambers of Jake's mind. There was no doubt who he'd been talking about. But what did it mean exactly? Was Liam just the one who'd scouted The Crimsons in the first place? Or was he The Cabal, organising all these hits? Jake didn't want to believe it. Sure, he knew that Liam had his darker side – he'd made that apparent in the past few days – but he'd never believed his friend was capable of murder. Of organising someone's brutal and merciless death.

First Danny. Now Michael.

Who next? And when?

A noise distracted him – the sound of car tyres skidding on tarmac and screeching to a halt. Car doors slamming. Voices shouting.

Jake snapped his neck round and looked at the row of bushes behind him. Instinct washed over him and told him to run. Fight or flight.

And he wasn't willing to gamble with his life. There was no way it could be the police – he hadn't called them, and he hadn't seen anyone in the vicinity who could have made the call.

Someone was coming back to finish the job.

Jake let go of Michael's head in as dignified a way as he could manage, scrambled up the bank on the opposite side of the road and then jumped over the hedges, tearing through the twigs and thorns and nettles. He landed awkwardly on his leg and then rolled onto mud. Once he'd righted himself, ignoring the stinging in his arms, he peered through the gap he'd created in the foliage.

Two figures were standing at the top of the bank opposite him, peering down at the overturned police vehicle. Their faces were hidden behind black masks and in their hands they each held sub-machine guns.

At the sight of them, Jake struggled for another breath; his brain communicated to his lungs that it was a bad idea. The air remained silent as they cast their gaze around the area.

One of the figures started down the mound. The other grabbed their shoulder and yanked them back before they were two steps in.

'What you doing?' the voice behind the mask asked. Jake noted it sounded Russian. Female.

'We've got to check on him. We need to make sure he's dead,' the other voice replied. This one was markedly British. Essex. A complete contrast to the other.

Jake watched the British attacker slowly turn, raise his gun and train it in Jake's direction. He panicked and lay flat on the grass, shielded his ears with his hands and closed his eyes, water seeping through his clothes, sending chills through his chest.

'Wait!' the Russian said. 'Stop. Don't shoot. Make look like mistake, remember. No shoot.'

Jake breathed a heavy sigh of relief as he heard those words. But it wasn't over yet – not until he heard the sound of a car door closing and the car leaving.

'What about the other car?' the Brit asked.

Jake's ears perked up.

'I'll check it.'

Fuck.

The female hurried down the bank, skipped over kicked-up tufts of grass and raced towards Jake's car. She kept the gun close against her chest and peered into the vehicle.

'Empty!' she called back.

'Where've they gone?' the Brit replied.

'I don't know. Run, maybe. You see anyone?'

'Check through the hedges.'

Fuck fuck fuck.

Jake was trapped. Nowhere to go. Nowhere to run. Nowhere to hide. And they were coming for him. *She* was coming for him.

He heard her footsteps approaching softly, winding her way through the bushes. And then he saw her.

A tall figure all in black. Head to toe. No identifiable features, save her accent. She was much taller than he anticipated. In her hands she held her firearm, pointed at him. As soon as she caught sight of him, she froze and lowered the gun, her eyes – hidden behind the letterbox of her mask – narrowing. Jake rolled on the grass, hand over his mouth to stifle his heavy breathing, panicking as he studied the gun.

Toe to toe with death, he cowered into a ball, something he wouldn't be afraid to admit. Images of Elizabeth, Maisie and Ellie flashed in his mind like a strobe light. Each one replaced by a new one almost instantly. How would they cope without him? How would they get by without their daddy to look after them, protect them?

'You found anything?' the Brit asked from the other side of the bushes.

The Russian remained frozen. She placed her finger on her lips and called back, 'Nothing. There's nobody here.'

And then she ducked through the foliage and returned to the other side, almost as quickly as she'd come. Gone. He'd been spared. She'd let him live. But there was no time to be grateful or ponder on why; the Brit was advancing towards Michael. Keeping himself flat on the grass, now doused in a layer of his own sweat, Jake peered through the branches and watched the man come to a stop by Michael.

The man knelt by Michael's side and checked for a pulse.

'He's still alive!'

What? Had Jake left him there alive? He'd been certain the final Cipriano brother was dead.

Then a muffled sound disturbed Jake. The masked attacker was punching and beating and kicking Michael in the head and the rest of his body. He kept this up for the next two minutes – with his fists and feet and the butt of his gun – until Michael was finally dead.

After he'd finished, the man hurried back to the top of the bank, and then the two of them disappeared out of sight.

As soon as they were gone, Jake rolled onto his back, panting. He'd stopped watching after the first few punches, and he'd plunged his fingers in his ears, but it hadn't stopped him from hearing every punch land on Michael's defenceless body.

No time to think. No time to lie there.

The sound of car doors closing and an engine starting kicked Jake into action. Rolling onto his front, he propelled himself off the ground, vaulted the bush and hurried back to his car. He couldn't bring himself to look at Michael as he passed him. Seeing his bloodied and beaten face out the corner of his eye was enough.

By the time Jake reached his car, the attackers were already heading left, about half a mile ahead. He jumped into his car and slammed his foot on the accelerator. Clumps of mud and grass kicked up as the tyres fought for grip. Eventually, they found it, and the car mounted the bank, breached into the road and gave chase.

As he roared along the tarmac, Jake tried Danika's mobile. If something had happened to Michael, then it was possible something had happened to her too.

No answer.

'Bollocks.'

Next, he tried Charlotte.

'Jake?' Charlotte asked, almost uncertain whether it was him.

'Urgent assistance required! I repeat, urgent assistance required. Michael Cipriano has just been killed,' he said between frantic breaths.

'What?'

'In pursuit now. Two suspects carrying firearms. Black Transit van.' The vehicle was in sight, and Jake squinted for a better view of the registration number. 'Vehicle reg Alpha-Bravo-six-five, X-ray-Yankee-Zulu.'

'Please repeat.'

'Ahh, fuck!' Jake smacked the steering wheel. 'It's a fake. Repeat: the registration is fake!'

'Where are you?' Charlotte asked. 'I'm getting you some backup.'

Jake glanced at the satnav and said, 'Heading south on Grove Barns.'

'ARVs will be there shortly.'

Jake didn't respond; he was too focused. In the time he'd spent talking to Charlotte, the attackers had managed to distance themselves from him by another half a mile.

They tore down the country lane, swerving in and out of what sparse traffic there was. He followed them for another mile until they eventually came to a stop outside an abandoned farming factory. The structure was monumental – double the height of Jake's home, and about ten times as wide, like an old airfreight hangar.

Jake pulled the car to the side of the road several hundred feet away, concealed behind an oversized bush that dotted the landscape. It was twenty feet tall and twenty feet wide, just large enough to conceal him and the car. The factory was at the cross point in a junction, and there was nothing else around him.

Jake felt exposed, out in the open, a sitting duck.

But so were they. They were going nowhere. Cornered. The only problem was, there was one of him, and at least two of them. Keeping his eyes focused on the factory, Jake grabbed for his phone and called Charlotte again.

'Charlotte… it's me…' As he stared out at the warehouse, two vehicles exited from either side, split up left and right, and quickly disappeared out of sight.

'Jake! Jake! What is it?'

'Abort,' Jake said. 'Call it off. Get rid of them. We don't need them.'

'What's going on, Jake?'

'I need you. Just bear with me, all right. Whatever happens, make sure you come down here.'

Jake hung up the phone, returned to his address book and dialled. The call was answered almost immediately.

'Liam… we've got a situation I thought you should know about.'

CHAPTER 49

PHRASES

Liam wanted to throw the phone at the wall. He wanted to throw it at the window, at the desk, at the computer. Fuck it, he wanted to throw it at everything.

It was all beginning to spiral out of control. Michael Cipriano was dead. And it was now going to be *his* responsibility to tidy the mess up. Just like with Danny, Richard and all the other cover-ups before them. He was going to have to come to the rescue like he always did. Wearing the cape and tight spandex.

The Rover to the rescue.

He let out a little groan. If there was one thing that was certain, it was that Jake was beginning to turn into a little rat. Tanner's presence at Michael's abduction and murder concerned him. And what concerned him even more was the threat that Jake now posed. Had he and Michael met up? How much had Michael disclosed to Jake? How much had Michael shared with Jake before he died?

Liam had had direct dealings with Michael in the past. They'd met on several occasions after he'd originally recruited The Crimsons, and Michael had clearly seen Liam's face. That in itself was too much of a risk for him. The past was coming back to haunt him like a dirty secret. He'd been compromised, and he was vulnerable.

Action had to be taken against Jake. And fast.

Liam slid out from beneath his desk, scooted over to the safe hidden within the filing cabinet, unlocked it and stared inside. Sitting at the bottom of the metal box was a dense roll of £20 notes wrapped tightly in elastic bands. Ten grand, left over from the last job The Cabal had given him as part of their agreement on The Crimsons' last hit. He'd kept it there for safekeeping, or as a get-out-of-jail-free card. And where better place to hide the proceeds of his corrupt activities than the exact place nobody would think to look?

Liam scooped the money into his hand and pocketed it, then exited his office. MIT was thin on the ground: the group of admin workers at the back were busy on their computers, shoulders hunched, eyes inches from the screen. Nearest to him were Drew and Charlotte, working almost in the same manner.

Liam wandered over to Jake's desk with purpose, pulled out Jake's chair and nodded at Charlotte as he sat down. There, he waited, just in case Charlotte rose from her chair and peered across the partition.

Slowly, once he deemed it safe enough, he pulled the money out of his pocket and placed it on his lap, concealed beneath his palm.

'Drew!' Liam shouted, taking Drew by surprise.

'Yes, guv?' Drew asked with a slight hint of fear in his voice. Then his eyes fell on the wad of money.

'How are we coming along?' Liam asked, acting casual. 'What's the latest on Maddison's death?'

'Well, sir, it's... We...' Drew's gaze was darting between the money and his computer screen. Irrational. And if he didn't sort it out soon, it would draw unwanted attention to them both. 'I had a look at Maddison's psychological profile from when he was in prison for the sexual assault. He was considered a suicide risk, and he was supposed to be kept under close scrutiny both inside prison and out...'

Liam eyed Jake's top drawer. He reached for it, hooked his finger under the handle and slowly – and as silently as he could manage – pulled it open.

Drew continued, oblivious. 'While he was inside, he underwent several counselling sessions with the therapist to abate his suicidal thoughts.'

'But how does that fit in with what DI Grayson is suggesting?'

Liam planted the wad of money on top of the ten grand that Drew had already given Jake and scribbled a note on a strip of paper.

Drew cleared his throat. 'It doesn't, guv. Richard Maddison was a suicide risk.'

Liam removed his phone, opened the camera and took a few photographs of the money inside the drawer. He said, 'But there's evidence found in the forensic report that suggests there was someone else in the house at the time of his death. Have you not already had these discussions with DI Grayson?'

At the second mention of her name, DI Grayson leapt out of her chair and rounded the side of her desk. She stood in the aisle between Liam and Drew with her arms folded, watching over them both.

'Well, yeah…' Drew began, flustered. 'But there's something else I meant to tell you.'

'Will it make me happy?' Liam asked, raising an eyebrow.

'Yes, guv.' Drew wiped his nose and sniffed hard, giving Liam a nod.

'Great. Then I wanna hear it.'

The three of them had a variety of coded phrases that they used to communicate in open conversations when others could be listening. There was seldom a need for them, but they always worked effectively when there was.

'It occurred to me that it would be almost impossible for Maddison to abduct Danny out of witness protection, take him to the construction site and kill him alone,' Drew began. 'He would have needed an accomplice, someone who could have helped him. Someone with higher criminal connections who could make that sort of thing happen. That's what I've been looking into. While Richard Maddison was in prison, he became close friends with a particular inmate of interest who's got connections with organised crime. I think they may have plotted to kill Danny Cipriano together.'

'Does it check out?'

Phrase number two.

'Yes, guv.'

'Chances of success?'

And there was number three – the final test to make sure this was a 'Go Ahead'.

'A hundred, I'm certain.'

'I like those odds. Who is it?'

Drew paused. 'Jermaine Gordon.'

Liam froze. He couldn't believe it; it was genius. Jermaine fucking Gordon. The man was a big-time player in the East End drug-trafficking world, one of the city's kingpins, second only to Henry Matheson, and together they owned over ninety-five per cent of the drugs coming in, and going out, of Stratford and West Ham – and the surrounding postcodes. Liam had only just managed to get his foot in the door – with the shipment and distribution side of things – with Henry, but the dealer had refused him further privileges on the grounds that he was too straight for a bent copper. But now Liam had an opportunity. A way in. With Jermaine Gordon off the streets and locked up for the murders of Danny Cipriano and Richard Maddison, there was no way Henry could decline his help. One less competitor meant a lot more trade for him. And a lot more money. For both of them.

'Do it,' Liam replied after a thoughtful silence. 'Build the evidence against him, prove it was him and then bring him in.'

Before Drew was able to answer, Liam pretended his phone had gone off. He answered the imaginary call.

'This is DCI Greene,' he said and then paused for a while. 'OK. Right… We're on our way, Tanner. Sit tight.'

As soon as he hung up, he jumped out of his seat and started towards the exit.

'What is it, guv?' Charlotte asked.

Liam spun on the spot. 'Michael Cipriano's just been murdered in a hit and run. Drew – we'll see you there. Charlotte – you're coming with me. We've got some catching up to do.'

CHAPTER 50

WALLET

Jake drummed his fingers on the steering wheel in time with the imaginary beat in his head, stopped, then massaged the sides of the wheel with his hands. He was traumatised. Worse, he was in fucking shock. He'd almost been run off the road, caught and killed, and watched a man die all within the space of an hour. He wanted to think of the silver lining – the fact that he'd been spared – but couldn't. Instead, images of Michael's body appeared in his mind, this time stained in indelible ink. The blood. The pale skin. The despair in his face as his eyes closed for the last time.

As he replayed the thumping sounds of the man beating Michael to death in his head, he felt the onset of a panic attack. With a vengeance. His heart rate increased. His breathing. His pulse. His skin became clammy. His vision became blurred; tunnelled. The car's walls were closing in on him, ready to crush him and his windpipe.

Frantically, Jake scrambled for the key, twisted it in the ignition and rolled down the windows, allowing a torrent of cold air to flood inside. He gasped heavily, in through the nose, out through the mouth, until his breathing had slowed and returned to some semblance of normality.

That had been close. Too close.

But not close enough for you to save Michael.

Jake grabbed his phone and dialled Charlotte's number. It rang several times, but there was no answer.

Frustrated, he tried again, this time bouncing his leg up and down in the footwell.

Still no answer. He was beginning to have a better relationship with her voicemail than her. Jake ceded defeat and squeezed the phone in his hand. There was evidence inside the factory, a lot of it, just sitting there, waiting to be found. And it needed to be found by *him*, rather than the bent forensics and emergency responders Liam would deploy as soon as they arrived.

There was only one problem standing in the way: he needed a warrant. Approval.

Something. Anything that could permit him to search the factory.

Jake made the decision for himself. He couldn't afford to wait around, let the attackers return and drive the vehicle away. He couldn't afford to wait for Liam and Drew and Garrison to arrive, let them seal off the factory and allow them to destroy pieces of vital evidence.

Jake opened the door and grabbed a pair of disposable gloves, the three remaining evidence bags he had left, an evidence log and an attendance log from the boot. He donned the gloves and then jogged towards the building, eyes darting left and right, lest anyone was approaching from a distance.

As he approached, the smell of manure and farm dirt assaulted his senses. Almost as large as Bow Green, the structure was made of steel and corrugated iron. There were two main entrances – a large shutter door at the front and another on the side of the building. Jake rounded the side and came to a stop at a small door. It opened with a creak. He held his breath. Then he paused and listened intently as the sound echoed around the vast expanse of space.

Seconds later, he crossed the threshold. The smell of manure was even stronger inside; it smacked him in the face and made him want to vomit, and a flurry of wind rushed past his ankles. There was an ominous feel to the place, like he'd entered a haunted house.

Sitting in the middle of the factory was the van that had been used to run Michael off the road. Either side of it were two sets of black tyre marks. In the corner was an overturned chair – probably used for some form of torture, Jake thought – and, beside it, the stains and marks of machinery that had been there for decades.

Opening the evidence bag, Jake approached the van, pulled open the driver's door and peered inside. He placed one hand on the seat to steady himself, and then searched the inside. In the middle of the armrest between driver and passenger, something caught Jake's eye. A wallet. He picked it up and leafed through the cards, stumbling upon the driver's licence. Danny Cipriano's face was glaring straight back at him. Though the name was different – Harry Winston.

He pocketed the wallet inside the evidence bag, then moved to the rear of the van. His fingers dipped beneath the groove of the handle and pulled. He tensed as he prepared himself for what he might see. Another dead body? Another crime scene? A murder weapon?

The boot lifted, and Jake's heart sank – there was nothing inside.

Cautious of the time, and aware that the rest of his team were rapidly closing in on him, he quickly removed the cotton bud from the bottom of the evidence bag, swabbed the floor of the van and returned it to its vial. He repeated the process for the driver's seat and steering wheel.

Then he tidied up.

He stuck a white label to each of the evidence bags – in the centre, folded either side – and wrote his name, warrant number, and the date and time. Whoever had abducted and killed Danny Cipriano had been driving this van. And whoever had killed Danny was responsible for Michael's death also. And he hoped the findings were enough to identify The Farmer and the rest of his associates.

Shortly after, Jake clutched the evidence bags in his grip and returned to his car.

CHAPTER 51

UNCOMFORTABLE SILENCES

Liam was brimming with questions as he sat beside Charlotte, driving east on the A13 towards Southend-on-Sea. Up until this point, their contact with one another had been minimal. On purpose, but now he wanted to change that. The car journey to North Ockendon was long enough for him to get to know her and find out what her real purpose was. He'd read her personnel file from back to front and committed it all to memory. Everything. Her birthday, the year she'd started in the service, the number of professional development reviews she'd had, the disagreements with her seniors, her operations and successes. He'd even confirmed her transfer with DCS Marston, but he still wasn't convinced.

At first, he'd believed she'd been sent in by The Cabal to highlight his ineptitude and either make him learn from it or to simply appease Oliver Penrose and the LOCOG – and, it was clear to him, that if it were the latter, only The Cabal had the connections to do it while keeping it under the radar. But when Charlotte had advised him about the bloodstains and footprints at Richard Maddison's suicide, he'd known instantly that he was wrong about her. She hadn't been sent in by The Cabal or the LOCOG.

She was here for a different purpose.

She was a bad egg.

'Please accept my apologies for not having introduced myself to you properly earlier,' he said, breaking the deadlock that had befallen them since the beginning of their journey. 'It's been a busy, stressful time.'

Charlotte stared out of the window at the trees streaming past, avoiding his gaze. 'I understand how it is.'

'How you finding it so far?'

She turned to him and flashed a smile. 'Interesting.'

'How so?'

'Because this is a complex case, more so than any I've ever worked on. We don't really get these sorts of things down in Croydon – at least, not as much. And it doesn't look like we're any closer to solving it.'

'That's the nature of the work. We don't get any easy wins. They're not handed to us. If they were, you'd be a DCS and I'd be the commander.'

'I know,' she said. 'It's just that, at Berin House, a case is opened and closed within a day or two, sometimes a couple. It's insane. Our guys are phenomenal at what they do, and—'

'You saying my team's not good enough?'

'No… Not at all. Your team are fantastic. I didn't mean to offend you.'

Liam chuckled. 'They can take it. They're adults.'

'What I meant was… What separates us from the rest of the boroughs in the force is our *methods*.'

'Methods?'

'How familiar are you with Occam's razor?'

'"Two explanations for everything and the one that requires the least guesswork is the one that's most likely correct" – that one?'

'Not far off,' Charlotte replied with a facetious smile.

'What's that got to do with anything?'

She shuffled herself on the leather seat so that her body was angled slightly towards him. 'When someone's murdered, there are two possibilities. The person who did it, and the person who didn't do it – Occam's razor, part one. But when you begin adding multiple suspects to the question. Three. Four. Five. Six… that's when things get tricky, and that's when it's more difficult to control, sustain and narrow down the correct explanation. You following?'

Liam took a moment to respond. 'I think so.'

'I mean, take Danny Cipriano's murder, for example. Who were the suspects? Richard Maddison to begin with. Perfect. We've got him, our main suspect. Should be easy. But now he's dead—'

'And you're the one who suggested to us that he'd been murdered rather than his death being ruled a suicide.'

Charlotte cleared her throat and continued, ignoring what he'd said. 'But now you're throwing Jermaine Gordon into the mix. One person again. One culprit. One suspect. If you start digging deeper and finding more names to add to that suspect list, that's when things become a little more complicated, if you see what I mean.'

'So you're saying that you lot over at Berin House like to arrest the first suspect so you can put the case to bed?'

Liam's suspicions were aroused. She was talking about something he reckoned she knew nothing about. If she really believed what she was saying, then she wouldn't have been the one to raise the suspicions about Richard Maddison's death. She would have just put it to rest. Like any good bent copper would have done.

'The way we like to do it,' she continued, 'is instead of finding ways to prove someone did it, we find the evidence that proves they did it.'

Liam contemplated for a second. 'And... when you say *finding* the evidence, you mean...?'

She shrugged nonchalantly. 'Sometimes the evidence has its own way of turning up conveniently when you least expect it – know what I mean?'

He did know what she meant, but he wasn't about to admit that to her.

'I'm sorry, Charlotte,' he said, reaching up to 95mph as they neared Rainham on the outskirts of the city. 'I don't know how you guys like to work over there, but we do things a little differently on this side of the river.'

'You sure?'

'Positive,' he lied.

She turned away from him, and as she looked out of the window again, she whispered to herself, 'S'not what I've heard.'

If she had any intention of him hearing it, she didn't show it. And if she didn't mean for him to hear it, then she'd just made the biggest mistake possible.

For the rest of the journey, Liam sat in comfortable silence – and hoped it was the complete opposite for Charlotte.

CHAPTER 52

TORTOISE, MEET HARE

Jake had been sitting in his car for the past hour, and in that time he'd seen nobody. Not even a tractor or a horse rider. Not even a cyclist – or road vermin as Martha, his mother-in-law, called them, much to his disgust.

While he was waiting, he'd managed to calm himself down, reduce his heart rate, think rationally, and clean the majority of Michael Cipriano's blood from his hands and face, although some remnants remained. His mind was still unable to shirk the thoughts of Liam and The Crimsons working together. In recent months, he and Liam had grown closer. They'd spent more time together outside of work – drinking beers, catching up with everyone else in the office, going on coffee runs together… Jake had even invited Liam over for a meal.

They'd bonded and Jake had allowed Liam near his children. He remembered it clearly… high-fiving Maisie, playing with her hair, asking how her day was.

But worst of all was the fact he and Elizabeth had named Ellie after Liam's mother. Now she would serve as a constant reminder of his betrayal and deviousness. The thought made him shiver.

A set of lights flashed in his rear-view mirror.

Garrison. In his brand-new car.

'All right?' Jake asked, getting out of his vehicle as Garrison pulled up in front of him.

'All right. What happened here then?'

Jake filled him in.

'Bloody hell,' Garrison replied. 'Have you got yourself checked out? You hurt?'

'No, no, I'm fine. Where's everyone else?'

'Er, I… er…' Garrison stuttered. 'I think they said something about stopping at the crime scene quickly, notifying Essex Police that there might be a slight conflict of interest. I said I'd come to meet you here, make sure you're all right.' Garrison twisted and nodded in the direction of the large structure behind Jake. 'You checked it out yet?'

'Been waiting for you.'

'Is that so I can be your muscle?'

'You mean the man who's old enough to be my dad?'

Garrison pointed a finger at Jake. 'You'd better watch your mouth!' He slapped Jake on the shoulder playfully. 'Just kidding! I'll let that shit slide this once, but if you say it again, I will have to hurt you. And just because I'm old, don't think I won't – or *can't*.'

Jake chuckled nervously. His attention was distracted by the sound of another vehicle approaching.

It was Drew. Rolling down the window, coming to a stop beside them both, he asked, 'What's all this about then?'

'Michael Cipriano's dead,' Jake replied.

Drew pursed his lips and nodded. 'Tricky one.' His eyes wandered to Garrison's car. 'This the new motor, Pete?'

'Isn't she a beauty?'

'Shame you don't pick your women like that, mate.'

Garrison shot Drew the middle finger and slapped him on the back of the head.

Jake observed them both for a moment. How immature they were being, defiant. Like petulant children, just waiting to be told off. One of the country's most prolific robbers had just been killed and they weren't phased by it at all. Of course they aren't, Jake soon realised.

They had nothing to worry about. They knew that they'd be able to cover it up and take care of it. Easy.

'You feeling all right, mate?' Drew asked him.

'Not particularly. Just watched a man die in front of me. But you know – I'll get over it.'

He wouldn't. The night terrors would be worse now. The sheets of white snow that he saw nearly every night would be covered with a new addition: Michael Cipriano's blood.

A few minutes later, Liam and Charlotte arrived.

'Jesus, what the hell happened to you?' Liam asked.

'I tried to save Michael Cipriano's life. Didn't have much luck evidently.' Jake said it with malice in his voice.

'We're gonna have to get you cleaned up. Don't want people in the office thinking you're a daredevil.'

Jake nodded and chuckled reluctantly. 'I've got a change of clothes back at the office.'

'Run us through what happened,' Liam said.

This was the part Jake had been dreading. If he told them all the real reason he'd met Michael, they'd suss him out and uncover the truth instantly. Fortunately, time had been on his side and he'd been able to spend those precious minutes coming up with a lie.

'I thought it would be a good idea to check up on Michael. See if he knew anything about Maddison, see if there was anything he could tell us about him and Danny.' Jake's eyes flickered to Charlotte before returning to Liam. 'I remember seeing somewhere that Danny and Richard had had dealings with Jermaine Gordon in the past, so I thought I'd see if Michael could shed some light on it.'

'And did he?'

Jake shook his head. 'He wouldn't tell me anything.'

'Then what happened. Why are you here?'

'I was just about to leave when a couple of uniformed officers picked him up. They rushed in and threw him into the back of their car. I thought it was odd, so I decided to follow them and then they were run off the road. The uniforms were killed instantly, but Michael was alive. I tried to save him, but then some guys came down and beat him to death,' Jake finished. He breathed heavily, hoping they believed every word. What he hadn't realised was that, because Charlotte was there, he needed to make everything look above board – like it was a fresh case and there was no history behind any of it.

'And you followed the attackers here?' Liam asked.

Jake sighed in relief. 'Yes, guv.'

'How many of them did you say?'

'Two.'

'And you couldn't identify them?'

'No. They were wearing black face masks.'

Drew folded his arms across his chest. 'It's highly possible this is Jermaine Gordon again, guv. Sending some of his boys to finish off the entire Cipriano family in Richard's memory.'

'Don't discount that thought, Drew. Very possible indeed,' Liam responded.

After he'd finished feeding Drew's ego, he turned his attention back to Jake. 'You seen anyone come in or out of the warehouse since you've been here?'

Jake shook his head. 'The attackers left in separate vehicles and headed in opposite directions. But the black van they travelled in's still inside the factory.'

Liam's gaze moved from Jake over to the building. He said, 'I think… maybe they've left it there for a reason, right. Which means they'll be coming back. Instead of storming the place with firearms teams and the forensic team, I think we should set up surveillance on this place. Wait for them to return.'

'And if they don't come back?' Garrison asked. 'What do we do then?'

'Give it twenty-four hours. If they don't come back for it, we'll investigate the van. Search it for evidence. The risks are bigger if we investigate the warehouse now. Which is why we should leave it. Play the long game. The tortoise beats the hare, remember?'

Liam clapped his hands; the sound echoed off the structure in the distance and bounced back to the group.

'Drew,' Liam began again. 'I want you to stay here while I get it all approved. You're on first watch. Someone else will swap with you later on.'

CHAPTER 53

CHOP–CHOP!

Liam called an immediate meeting in the briefing room as soon as they returned from the factory. The whole team had turned out – nearly fifteen of them sat in the room, paying attention. The majority of the ranks in the office were detective constables, with the addition of a few sergeants, leaving Charlotte as the most senior officer in there after Liam. But it raised the question of why Liam had called them all in. He never usually did – or, at least, infrequently. The rest of the team were the foot soldiers who picked up all the stuff that filtered down from the chain of command. It was Liam's preferred method of working, and it was the reason the team was a revolving door of new faces.

'Thank you all for being here,' Liam began. 'I thought it would be worth calling this meeting as I need to check up on where we are with things, so I can re-evaluate and refocus your priorities if necessary. This case seems to be getting slightly out of hand at the moment, and I need to rein it in. For those of you who don't know, Michael Cipriano has just been killed. We're going to be working closely with Essex Police on this, but there will be *some* things that we can do – and the majority of you will be doing that.'

Liam scanned the room, silently selecting the members of the team he was referring to with a curt nod. Jake was grateful he wasn't one of them.

'But for now, run me through what we know.'

The room fell silent. Nobody wanted to be the first to answer. Jake was certain it was partly due to the fact that almost everyone in the team was afraid of Liam in one way or another, as if he had something against them and they didn't want to speak at all for fear of reprisal.

Jake chose to go first.

'Danny Cipriano, dead. Buried alive in cement. Construction site worker, Richard Maddison, main suspect. Motive – Danny Cipriano put him in jail. Evidence found in Maddison's flat implicated him in the murder, but he couldn't have been working alone. He needed someone else, at least.'

Jake paused to gauge Liam's reaction; his boss gave him a gentle nod to continue. 'Enter Jermaine Gordon, renowned drug kingpin from East London. Also a convicted murderer. Has a history with Richard Maddison from when they shared jail time. And now we've got Michael Cipriano dead.'

'You're missing one important fact here, Jake,' Charlotte said. 'DNA samples were found at Richard Maddison's address, suggesting that he could have been murdered and his death made to look like a suicide. DS Richmond and I have been looking into it.'

'And where are we up to with that, Charlotte?' Liam asked.

'Still waiting on the results, guv.'

Liam nodded. 'Right now we need to look at the possibility that this is a revenge killing. Richard and Jermaine set out to kill Danny Cipriano. We have CCTV footage and mobile phone data locating Richard at Jermaine's estate the same night that Drew interviewed him as a witness. It's very possible that they argued about something – perhaps Richard threatened to come clean to us and then left. As we know, Richard suffered from mental health issues, so he could have become paranoid. Jermaine couldn't have that, so he had him silenced for good.'

As soon as he said it, silence invaded the room and wrapped itself around them while everyone absorbed what was being said. Even though Jake knew it was all a load of bullshit, he had to admit that it was convincing. Between the four of them – Liam, Drew, himself and Garrison – they'd made it look like a solid case against Richard Maddison and now Jermaine Gordon. If he didn't know any better, he would have believed it.

'But how does Michael's death fit into all of this, guv?' a confident voice from the back called.

Liam pushed himself off the edge of the table and wiggled his finger around in the air.

'I'm glad you asked, DC Cotton. That's precisely what we need to focus on now, with the help of Essex Police. We need to find a link between Michael's, Richard's and Danny's deaths. But first, we need to know everything about his movements and activities since he's been in the witness protection scheme.' Liam hesitated a moment, then looked at the ground. 'Meanwhile, Garrison, I'd like you to pick up where Drew left off with looking into Jermaine Gordon.'

'Is that the same Jermaine Gordon that's just been tried and acquitted for a double homicide?' another voice called from the back.

Liam nodded. 'The very same.'

'How'd he get away with that one?' Jake asked, his curiosity suddenly getting the better of him.

'It all comes down to who you know and how much money you have,' Liam explained. 'And in this particular example, our suspect – one of the biggest drug dealers in the whole of East London – happens to know the equally formidable and infamous lawyer Rupert Haversham and has a shit tonne of money to be able to afford him.'

'Are we not risking the same thing here?'

'Which is why we need to make the evidence watertight.' Liam shot a small sideways glance at Garrison. 'And I mean it. Water. Tight. Pete, like I said, you're in charge of that part of the investigation. As for DC Tanner and DI Grayson, DC Garrison will delegate tasks to you.'

Charlotte raised her hand. 'Forgive me, sir… and no offence to DC Garrison or anything, but how does that work? Shouldn't I be the one to manage the investigation as Deputy SIO? I'm a senior rank.'

'Granted. But in this particular case, Garrison has more experience. He's been dealing with Jermaine Gordon and people of his ilk since way before you were born. Garrison has the experience, and in my view, that trumps all, regardless of what epaulette – and chip – you wear on your shoulder.'

Charlotte opened her mouth to speak but was instantly cut off.

'The longer we sit around here, the less time we have to find evidence. Chop-chop!'

Liam clapped his hands, adjourning the meeting. Everybody rose from their seats and started towards the door.

'Wait!' Charlotte said, calling everyone back into the room. In her hand, she held her phone aloft. The tiny screen illuminated her face. 'You're going to want to see this.'

'What is it?' Liam asked.

'The forensic report on Danny Cipriano's body's just come in. They found something on Danny amidst all the concrete.'

'What?' Liam asked, a hint of fear and uncertainty in his voice.

'They found DNA on the body and they've had a confirmed match. It belongs to a convicted criminal… Nigel Clayton.'

CHAPTER 54

CURVEBALLS

Jesus fucking Christ.

Just as he thought he was getting a grip on the investigation and keeping it on the track he wanted it on, he'd been thrown another curveball. How could Nigel Clayton have slipped up so stupidly? Liam knew the name from a long time ago. The man was a fraudster. A bent accountant who'd helped launder millions of pounds out of the country during the mid to late nineties, who'd been caught after one of his clients got arrested for drug dealing and subsequently threw him under the bus. And now it seemed he'd ditched the accounting and got himself involved with The Farmer.

But that wasn't the most important thing for him to focus on right now. He needed to deal with this before anyone else got a chance to blow it out of proportion. Jake. Charlotte. Garrison. The list was growing.

Before storming into his office, he'd ordered the team to focus the bulk of their efforts and resources on Jermaine Gordon and push Nigel Clayton to one side for now. It wouldn't take long for certain people in the office to realise that was wrong and start raising flags. He doubted he'd given himself much time to prepare, but it was time nonetheless.

Liam poured himself another glass of whiskey and downed it in one sitting. Something to take the edge off. Nothing like a little bit of Dutch courage in preparation for calling a Russian hitman.

He left the message about the funeral flowers, followed the same pattern and finally got through to him.

'What you want?'

'You have a problem,' Liam responded as he moved over to his window. The blinds were pulled, but the slats were half open.

'What?'

'Nigel's DNA has just been found on Danny Cipriano's body.'

There was a pause. A long one. And for a moment Liam wondered whether he'd lost the connection.

'You joke?' came the eventual, monotonous response.

'I wish, but this fucks things up for us all. You especially.'

'Yes.'

'Where is Nigel at the moment?'

'In hiding after he kill Michael Cipriano.'

The seed of an idea popped into his head.

'Who was there at Maddison's house?' he asked.

'What you talk about?'

'Maddison. I know you wanted it to look like a Russian suicide, but it didn't work. There was extra DNA evidence found on the walls and the carpet, George. Who from your team was there?'

'All of us.'

Thank God for that.

'Then I think we can make this work. It's not going to be easy. But you have to be on board with it.'

'You no give me orders.'

Liam chuckled at the audacity and confidence the man had. 'You don't understand. I'm not asking, I'm telling. You forget that we own you. You're our bitch. And we can call upon you any time we want. Now you either agree to it, or you wait for us to come and arrest Nigel – and yourselves – for the murders.'

'I can't. He my accountant.'

'You can find another one. All it takes is for this information to go to the wrong person, and they'll investigate you and find you.'

'How his details on system? Thought they deleted when he leave prison?'

'I wish that were the case, mate. They're on there for life, and they'll soon be connected to these deaths. I don't want to do it this way, but I have no choice. He's made a mistake. More importantly, he's let you down. He needs to be punished for that. And what will our mutual employer say when they find out that one of their most trusted contract killers has got a rotten apple amidst the ranks. I don't think it's going to be a happy ending, do you?' Liam hesitated as he waited for a response.

'What you need me to do?'

A smirk grew on Liam's face just as a car screeched to a halt outside his office window, narrowly avoiding a group of children failing to pay attention as they crossed the road.

'Let me make a few calls. I've got just the thing in mind.'

Liam hung up, and as soon as the call was disconnected, he reached inside the bottom drawer of the filing cabinet and called Drew on the burner phone.

Come on. Come on. Come on. Pick up.

Eventually, after what felt like an eternity, Drew did.

'Everything all right, guv?' he asked. 'My arse is killing me sitting here.'

'We've got a situation. Do you have your work laptop with you in the car?'

'You don't wanna know what sort of things I've got in the car,' Drew replied.

'Cut the crap and pay attention. Do you have it?'

'Yes.'

'Good. I need you to log on to every database that you can and find everything on Nigel Clayton. Rewrite the man's history.'

'Rewrite it to what, guv? I'll have to check my permissions are still the same.'

'Jermaine Gordon. Richard Maddison. That sort of thing. Make it suit our needs. And do it quick. I want it done before the rest of the team sink their teeth into Clayton. Understood?'

'Understood.'

Liam held his finger down on the red button until the phone turned off, then removed the battery and chucked both objects into the filing cabinet. He returned to his seat and eased into the leather. He needed a fix. Another drink. A cigarette. A joint. Something that would take the edge off a little more than the alcohol. Fuck it, alcohol would do for now.

He poured himself another drink – this time from a secret bottle of Captain Morgan's rum that he kept for emergency situations – and started drinking. The liquor wasn't his favourite, but it would suffice. He knew that, soon, he'd want more. And more. And some more after that.

He pulled the burner phone he'd used to call The Farmer from his pocket and placed it on the table, staring at it as though it were a gun he was considering using to end his life. In a way, the phone call he was about to make would have the same effect. If his plan went wrong then his days in MIT, and on earth, would be numbered.

Good, he thought. He didn't have that long left anyway if his body started to reject the treatment.

Like a true captain, it was his job to steer the ship to safety. And he was going to do just that. Commandeering the wheel, he reached for the phone and dialled.

'Yes…'

'Listen to me and listen very carefully. This plan will only work if you do exactly as I tell you. Understood?'

'Understood.'

'Right. Now here's what I want you to do…'

The seas were looking nice and calm from here on out.

CHAPTER 55

CONDUCT

The news that Nigel Clayton's DNA had been found on Danny Cipriano's body elated Jake. Liam's cover-up of the investigation was crumbling like one of Garrison's chocolate digestives. And, right now, he couldn't be more grateful for having Charlotte with him. If she'd arrived any later, then he feared it would have been too late. Richard Maddison's death would have been ruled a suicide, Michael's death would have been forgotten about and Nigel's DNA on Danny would have been thrown in the bin. Things were finally beginning to fall into place for them.

Soon he hoped to be able to have enough evidence to convict all three of his colleagues for their crimes. And the surprising part of it was, he felt no remorse. These people had once been his friends, but they were breaking procedure, the rules and the law. They were playing with people's lives for their own financial and personal gain. It was unforgivable, reprehensible, inexplicable and they deserved to be imprisoned.

Just after he'd adjourned the briefing, Liam had ordered them all to focus on the Jermaine Gordon side of the investigation while he disappeared off to his office to 'make some calls'. Neither Charlotte nor Jake had any intention of following his instruction.

After he'd changed into a fresh set of clothes that he kept in his locker, Jake loaded the databases he had access to and entered Nigel Clayton's name into the search bar.

The results were interesting.

Jake perused each one, his eyes falling heavily over the words and their meaning. According to the reports, Nigel Clayton had been arrested in the late nineties for money laundering, perverting the course of justice and fraud. He used to work for an infamous crime syndicate family called the Hampton Brothers, renowned for being one of London's largest and most violent gangs. He'd heard rumours that they ran the city – stretching from the council-estate kids who would deliver and sell their drugs for them, right up to the higher echelons of the

British government. Corruption was deeply rooted in Nigel's history, and there was never any mention of Jermaine Gordon. In fact, it was almost virtually impossible for Nigel to be acquainted with either Jermaine or Richard.

After being arrested for money laundering the Hampton Brothers' money, Nigel had rolled over and grassed on everyone in the family in a final act of betrayal. If he was going down, they all were. And, as a result, he was registered as an informant and subsequently entered into the witness protection scheme. It wasn't until the final member of the Hampton family died – and the threat to his life with it – that Nigel eventually became a free man again. Many of the charges against him were dropped and he was free to go.

Straight into the hands of The Cabal and The Farmer.

It was a miraculous indictment of the criminal justice system, but it had worked wonders for Nigel. He'd been playing the police and the criminals against one another and making everyone look foolish in the process.

To preserve the evidence while he could, Jake snapped photographs of the information on his phone, screenshots of them on the computer and then printed them out in the corner of the room beside Lindsay. Digital and physical copies. The hallmark of any good investigation. He compiled the resources in a folder from his desk and placed it in his backpack, the most secure place he could think to put it.

Just as he kicked his bag underneath his desk, Liam emerged from his office; he swayed a little, using the door frame for support.

'Jake…' he began, slightly mumbling and muttering his words. 'Charlotte… I'd like… I want you both to… to head down to the SOCO lab and find out what' – he hiccupped – 'the latest on Richard Maddison's DNA report is. See if… they've got anything. Pl-Please.'

Jake stared at his boss for a moment, incredulous that he was showing signs of intoxication. Sure, Liam had a lot going on – both in his personal and professional life – but if he wasn't in any fit state to continue or have any sense of decorum, then he should leave and come back once he was better. If all else failed with the criminal investigation he and Charlotte were piecing together against Liam, then at least there was one last resort: unprofessional conduct in the workplace.

The stupid fucker was drunk in the office.

'Of course, sir,' Charlotte said, taking Jake by surprise. 'We'll do it right away.'

CHAPTER 56

TRUST

They walked in silence to the annexed SOCO lab at the back of Bow Green. Just after they'd headed off, Charlotte had made a quick call to her handler, and by the time they arrived, she'd been granted access to the inner corridors of the building. As they entered through the revolving doors and made their way across the floor, they were accosted by a domineering yet nasally voice which sounded as though the owner had been a radio host or a sports commentator in a former life. And a good one, at that.

'Excuse me,' the voice said. 'Where are you going?'

'To speak with Sandy…' Jake said as he came to a stop. 'Need to discuss an investigation with her.'

'She's been popular recently.'

Jake ignored the man and headed towards the double doors at the back of the entrance. While he waited for Charlotte to scan her key card, the man's voice sounded, like a foghorn.

'You need to sign in… *please*.'

Jake rolled his eyes and then turned to face the man, who was clearly making them work for a happy life. Then he skulked across the carpet, leant against the desk and grabbed the pen attached to a small chain. Jake scribbled his name and passed the pen to Charlotte.

'Twice in one week?'

Jake's eyes darted towards the man. 'Excuse me?'

'Twice in one week.' The man pointed to another row on the sign-in sheet.

Jake bent down and peered closer at it. His name. Signed and dated.

'Funny, I don't remember you though. I'm usually good with faces.'

Chuckling awkwardly, Jake shrugged it off, waited until Charlotte had finished and then crossed the threshold into the SOCO lab. As soon as the door closed behind him, he ran his fingers through his hair.

'That wasn't you, was it?' Charlotte asked, keeping her distance on the other side of the corridor.

Jake shook his head. 'It wasn't.' He'd been forty miles away in Guildford at the exact same time. 'But I know who it was.'

'Who?'

'Drew.' Jake closed his eyes and imagined him waddling through the building, all cocksure and arrogant, forging Jake's details and flashing a smug grin as he realised he'd managed to get away with it. On too many occasions people had reminded Jake that they looked alike – similar hair, similar build, similar facial features. The only difference lay in their height and age – four inches and seven years respectively. At first, Jake had taken it as a compliment, thought it was a good thing. Now he realised it was far from it.

'You sure?' Charlotte asked as they came to a stop at the other end of the corridor.

He replied with a simple nod. 'It was right before we found Richard Maddison dead. He must've come in here to steal some evidence samples.'

'The evidence found in his bedroom was taken from here?'

'If I had to make an educated guess.'

'But—'

A SOCO who Jake recognised from the countless crime scenes he'd been to stepped into the hallway, cutting them off. Jake and

Charlotte nodded at her, and as soon as she was gone, they made their way up to the crime scene manager's office on the second floor.

Jake knocked on the door but chose not to wait for consent before entering.

Sandy was sitting behind her desk, her attention fixed on her computer monitor. With one hand on the mouse and the other on her lap, she slowly turned her head to face Jake and Charlotte, neither fazed nor shocked by their sudden appearance. In her line of work, nothing shocked her – not even the impossibility of a dead body coming to life.

'Jake…' Sandy said. She wore a pair of spectacles on the top of her nose. It was the first time Jake had noticed them. 'You're in my office.'

He cast a quick glance around him as if to make sure of the fact.

'Yes. Sorry to interrupt, but we need help.'

'Who's we?'

'DI Grayson and I.'

Charlotte reached forward and extended her hand. Sandy took it and both women locked their hands for longer than seemed necessary.

'I'm joining the team for a while,' Charlotte said.

'Pleasure to meet you.' Sandy turned to Jake. 'Now, what's this all about?'

'Richard Maddison's body. What's the latest? Guv wants to know.'

'We've submitted the evidence to forensics. It's up to them now.'

It was Charlotte's turn to speak. 'What about the fingerprint marks and the footprints – did you submit those? They're of particular significance to us. We need those back as soon as possible.'

'There're only so many hours in the day, DI Grayson.'

'I appreciate that. But we need to—'

'Thanks for your help, Sandy,' Jake said, deciding to cut her off. 'You'll let us know if anything changes though, right?'

'Wouldn't be doing my job otherwise.'

With that, Jake and Charlotte left. It wasn't the outcome they'd hoped for. In an ideal world, they would have had the evidence that proved there'd been a second party present at Richard Maddison's death. Maybe even a third.

'Sorry about her,' Jake said as they stepped into the stairwell. 'She's stressed and understaffed. You'll learn what she's really like soon enough.'

'You mean rude?'

Jake chuckled awkwardly. 'Yes and no. A lot of people rely on her.'

'Have you ever thought of her being a person of interest?'

Jake hadn't. In fact, he'd considered the opposite. To him she was a stand-up member of police staff, always present at crime scenes, always informative, always methodical and thoughtful in her processes and reports, always working silently in the background, slugging away, getting on with what she needed to. But now Charlotte had planted a seed of doubt in his mind. It was a tough lesson to learn, but at least he was learning it – that in this life, and in this job, he really couldn't trust anyone.

CHAPTER 57

JUST DESERTS

Liam knew nothing could be taken for granted in this business. Especially when there were so many people – it seemed – who were against him. But, to his surprise, Jake and Charlotte had followed his commands without hassle. No fuss, no kickbacks. They'd been good little dogs and left the office so Drew could get to work on updating Nigel Clayton's profile. And it made him wonder whether he was wrong about them. Whether he was wrong about Jake.

He didn't know.

All he did know was that the great tyrant of depression was knocking on the door, waiting for further entry into the darkest recesses of his mind. But before he let it in, he embraced the dizzying sensations he'd come to appreciate in recent years. The swimming walls. The dancing letters on the screen. The true calm before the storm.

He poured himself another two measures of Captain Morgan's. Somehow he'd nearly finished the entire bottle. It was enough to floor even the strongest of individuals, but not him. His liver had grown accustomed to it over the years and now treated alcohol like an old friend who frequently came to stay.

Liam hadn't wanted to start drinking. It had sort of just… happened. The catalyst had been his wife's passing. Sudden and unexpected. She'd been ripped away from him just like this investigation was being pulled from beneath his feet. It had been a dark time, and he'd relied on the bottle then just like he relied on it now. And the drugs. Oh, the drugs. Somehow he'd managed to power through it all while hiding his secret. And he soon became a poster boy for success, standing on the plinth of a hundred needles and a thousand bags of Class A, B and C drugs. But now he was near the top, and he was doing things he'd never thought he would. Things were happening that hadn't ever been on his radar when he first—

His personal mobile vibrated, shocking him back to reality. He picked up the device and squinted at the screen. It was a message from Drew.

CM

Call me. The instruction was simple. Liam swayed in his chair and reached across to the bottom of the cabinet. He fumbled the burner phone in his hands as he tried to assemble it. Once the battery was in, he switched it on, waited, waited, waited, waited, waited, and then called Drew.

'What's going on?' Drew asked almost immediately. 'I've been trying to call.'

'Off,' Liam replied. 'Switched off. Is it done?'

'It's done. Everything's been changed. Nigel Clayton now has a history with Jermaine Gordon, Richard Maddison and Danny Cipriano.'

'Perfect.'

'Anything else you need me to do?'

'Yes. But later.' He hiccupped again, and this time he made no effort to hide his slurred words. 'The Farmer will visit you. You just… follow his lead.'

Just as Drew was about to respond, Liam's personal mobile started ringing. It was Tanya. Fuck, he was going to need another drink. He hung up on Drew without saying anything and placed the phone on the table, swapping it for his personal one.

Then he reached for his drink and swallowed a few mouthfuls before answering. Some more Dutch courage.

'Hey, you,' she said flirtatiously.

Liam grunted.

'Everything all right?'

Liam grunted again.

'Can you talk?'

'Not to you,' he said, finding that the words came clearer to him and that he enunciated them properly.

'What's that supposed to mean?' Tanya asked.

'I know everything, all right? So you can cut the shit.'

'What shit? Liam, what are you talking about?'

'Don't act dumb. Bitch. I saw you getting into the car with Pete. I saw you going to the multi-storey. I saw everything.' He paused a moment, more to catch his breath than anything else. 'Is that where you two go then, huh? Is that where you guys like to *fuck*, huh?'

Droplets of spittle flew from his mouth as he spoke.

'Liam...'

'How long's it been going on for?'

'You're drunk, Liam, aren't you? What have I said about this? You're being stupid. Please? I don't know what you think you saw, but I can explain it all. Honestly, I can. I would never lie to you. I would never do that to hurt you.'

There was a long pause. Liam deliberated whether to say anything or not. He decided on not.

'Tonight? Can I see you tonight?' Tanya asked.

'No. I'm *busy*.'

'Tomorrow?'

'Should be enough time for you to get one last shag in with Garrison.'

'Fuck you,' she hissed. 'You know I would never do any of this intentionally to hurt you. Please. Tomorrow. Usual place? Usual time?'

'Fine.'

'Please don't drink yourself dead. I can't let it happen to another man in my life.'

'Not my problem. Not my fault they say women go after men who remind them of their dad. *Daddy issues*.'

A long sigh echoed through the microphone in his ear. Did he feel guilty about his last comment? Yes. Was he going to apologise? No. She didn't deserve an apology. Not yet.

'Usual place, usual time, tomorrow,' he said before hanging up.

His and Tanya's relationship had been tumultuous from the start. It was frowned upon and seen as a conflict of interest for a high-ranking senior police officer to be fraternising and involving himself with a member of the press, so, at first, their relationship had been clandestine – exciting. Just sex. No strings. No commitments. No loyalties. No nothing. It was the exact thing he'd needed to help him mourn the loss of his wife. But as they'd spent more time with one another, and as they'd started talking, getting to know each other, that had changed without either of them intending it to. And the things that he'd missed from his wife had come flooding back in droves. The affection. The love. The adoration. The companionship. Someone to be with, talk with; someone to hold. And now she was about to throw it all away for some cunt named Pete Garrison.

A smile grew on Liam's face.

He couldn't wait for tonight.

That man was finally going to get what he deserved.

CHAPTER 58

SCAPEGOAT

Jake hurried back to his desk, feeling as though all eyes in the office were watching him and Charlotte return from the lab together – like they'd just come back from a quick shag in the toilets. It was an innocuous task they'd carried out, but there was still something in his mind that told him to be cautious of everyone and everything around him. He'd given nobody else in the office any reason to suspect him of illicit activity, but it didn't help to be a little too paranoid.

Falling into his chair, Jake swung his legs under the desk and shimmied the mouse until the computer screen awoke from its nap. Just as he was about to log in, his mobile lit up. It was a notification from Candy Crush telling him that his lives for the day were ready. Beneath it was a missed call from an unknown number.

They'd left a voicemail.

Jake unlocked the device with his four-digit PIN – the day and month he and Elizabeth had got married; a number he would never forget – and listened to the voicemail.

'Hi, Detective Tanner… it's Hannah… Erm, Hannah Bryant. You gave me your details. I, erm, I hope it's OK to call you. I hope I'm not disturbing you from something. Oh, of course I am – you're probably really busy. But, anyway… I, erm, I wondered… if you've had a chance to look into the thing we discussed? I'd, erm… I'd appreciate it if you could give me a call back.'

Shit. As soon as he heard her name, a pang of guilt knotted itself tightly in his stomach. For the past few days, he hadn't even devoted a morsel of his mental capacity towards finding the evidence that would implicate Drew. He could say that he'd been too preoccupied with everything else, but in reality, there was no excuse for it at all. This young woman had trusted *him* to get to the bottom of it and he hadn't. He'd allowed himself to become sidetracked when he should have focused at least some of his attention on Hannah. Maybe he was being hard on himself, but he didn't see it that way; it was part and parcel of the job, and if he couldn't manage several things at once, then what was he good for?

Jake stepped away from his desk and left the office. He made a left turn in the hallway and barged through a set of double doors beside the lift, entering into the building's only stairwell.

He tapped Hannah's number and called her back.

No answer.

He breathed a sigh of relief. Another easy way out, not having to deal with the guilt of explaining his malpractice to her over the phone.

The tone sounded in his ear and the voicemail started recording.

'Hi, Hannah. It's, er, DC Tanner. I was just… erm, returning your call. I wanted to apologise for the radio silence. I haven't forgotten about the investigation. As… as I'm sure you can appreciate, I'm having to do everything myself… so it can take… a while. I hope that helps? Call me if you need anything.'

Jake ended the call and hung his head low. What a shambles. He'd lied to her. Tried to defend his own actions. Even tried to make her feel guilty in the process. *I hope that helps. I hope that helps?* Of course it wouldn't fucking help.

Drew had destroyed a part of her. And there was no way he could make that any better.

You're a fraud.

Jake turned his back on the stairs, headed to the office and returned to his desk.

As the computer screen loaded, it opened on the same page that he'd left it on. Nigel Clayton's profile. Except now there were subtle differences, hidden throughout the document. Jake didn't notice it at first, but just as he was about to close down the application, a couple of the words on the screen jumped out at him.

Leaning closer to the monitor, Jake read through the passages again.

'I don't believe it,' he whispered to himself.

'What?' Charlotte asked over the partition between them.

'Come here. You need to see this.'

Charlotte rounded the desk and pulled Drew's chair over beside him.

Jake kept his voice low as he spoke. 'Nigel Clayton's profiles and reports on the PNC and HOLMES have changed.'

'Changed how?'

Jake pointed to the screen. 'As in, they've been rewritten. According to this, Nigel Clayton's now colluded and worked with Richard Maddison, Jermaine Gordon and

Danny Cipriano. Before there was never any mention of any of their names.'

Charlotte's eyes shifted behind her glasses and her lips moved as she read through the passages for herself. 'I don't believe it. They've falsified evidence to make Nigel Clayton a scapegoat.'

'But how? And who?'

Charlotte held a finger in his face, pulled out her phone and held it to her ear. Saying nothing, she climbed out of the seat and headed towards the women's bathrooms.

Five minutes later, she returned.

'Do I wanna know?' he asked, afraid that he already knew the answer.

'My team working on this case had a look at the back end of the PNC.'

'And…?'

Charlotte crouched beside his legs and supported herself on the desk's edge, then cleared her throat. 'In total, forty-two entries have been made to the entirety of Nigel Clayton's document on the PNC. In the last hour, six of them have been made by one person, and one person only.'

'Who?'

Charlotte tilted her head to the desk beside Jake's.

CHAPTER 59

PUB

Jake took his hands away from the keyboard and looked at the time. Somehow, it was seven o'clock, and it was pitch black outside. The office air conditioning continued to hum in the background, filtering the room with mild, clean air. Jake rose out of his seat and wandered up to the window. Outside, workers were rushing home. Some walking, some cycling, some driving. He emptied his mind of all thought and simply watched them whip past. In a way, he envied them. It was his job to make sure that they – and their families – were kept safe; to make sure that, if anything did happen to them, he would bring the person responsible to justice. But none of them knew what was going on in the *real* world, on the front line of duty. None of the people outside the window knew what he was going through in order to get the criminals off the streets.

Looking out of the window gave him a different perspective on things. Some days he'd rather be down there, going to a menial office job he despised so that he and his family could live a middle-class lifestyle. Other days he couldn't think of anything worse, and he cherished the opportunity to do what he did for a living. He wasn't jaded yet. And he didn't think he ever would be.

A door opened behind him. Jake twisted and saw Liam standing there, at the head of the room with his arms folded. Garrison had since returned to the office after another unexplained absence, and he'd spent the past half hour speaking excitedly about his new car. Meanwhile, the rest of the team had gone home, save for a couple of the civilian staff who were most likely looking for some extra brownie points. Now it was only the four of them – Jake, Charlotte, Liam, Garrison.

For a moment, nothing happened. Jake observed Liam – the minutiae of his facial and bodily movements – and concluded that he was still drunk. In fact, worse now than he'd been earlier, swaying a little from side to side with those bloodshot eyes that seemed to glaze over everything.

‘What’s n-new?’ Liam said, visibly trying his hardest not to slur his words.

‘Very little, guv,’ Garrison replied, leaning back in his chair and forcing a stack of biscuits into his mouth; a pile of crumbs quickly formed on his collar.

‘Actually,’ Charlotte said, lifting herself out of her chair. In her hand she held a folder. ‘I’ve got a few things I think will be of interest.’

‘Oh?’ Liam said. ‘I’d love to hear th-them.’

‘Poojah’s pathology report’s just come in for Richard Maddison.’

‘And?’

‘She found puncture marks in his arms – fresh ones – as well as what she believes to be traces of cocaine in his nose. That corroborates with his whereabouts the day before he died, according to the CCTV Drew found of him at Jermaine Gordon’s flat.’

‘Right…’

‘And there’s something else as well.’

‘Right…’ Liam echoed, proving it was the only word in his vocabulary that he could pronounce clearly while steaming drunk.

‘After looking into Nigel Clayton’s history on the PNC and HOLMES,’ Charlotte began, ‘it looks like they’ve all had dealings with one another. Richard. Jermaine. Nigel. Even Danny Cipriano. In the past, Jermaine has supplied to both Nigel and Richard since they all left prison.'

'So they're all in *cahoots* with one another?' Liam's voice reached a crescendo as he said the word.

'It would appear that way, guv.'

Liam used the wall for support. 'Well, I say that's all a load of splendid work you've done there, DI Grayson. In fact, the two of you' – he wagged his finger between Jake and Pete – 'need to get your shit together… Which reminds me… Garrison, you're up.'

'Up for what?'

'Swapping places with Drew. Poor little fucker's probably bored senseless out there on his own. Tell him that his shift's over for th-the day. I want you on night shift and I'll send someone down in the morning.' Liam's eyes fell on Jake. 'Tanner – it might be you.'

Jake swallowed hard and nodded. He'd been dreading that. He didn't want to be anywhere near that side of the investigation. He wanted to be inside the office with Charlotte instead – where he felt safe; where he could lean on her if needed.

Garrison lifted himself out of his chair and retrieved his car keys from his paper tray. 'Suppose I'd better put the new wheels to good use.'

'Don't forget your biscuits.'

Garrison gave a nod and a soft chuckle before leaving.

After the door shut, Liam turned to Jake and Charlotte.

'Get yourselves home, kids,' Liam said. 'Hopefully tomorrow we'll have something to celebrate.'

Seems like you've already found that something, Jake thought but decided to keep his mouth shut.

Saying nothing more, Liam kicked his office door goodbye like he usually did every day, and then stumbled out of the room. Silence, save for the sound of the civilian support staff working in the background, fell on Jake and Charlotte. They looked at one another and shrugged.

He checked his watch – 8 p.m.

It was time for the pub.

CHAPTER 60

BEAST

Drew's arse and legs were numb. He'd been sitting still for hours, playing games on his phone and doing the quick piece of work Liam had asked him to. It was a miracle he'd had his laptop with him, and that he was one of the few people who had access to the back end of PNC and HOLMES. For that, he hoped, Liam would hold him in some high esteem at least. Maybe even give him a bigger cut of the deal that he was working out with Henry Matheson.

Here's hoping.

For the last ten minutes, Drew had been staring at the warehouse in the distance. It was a complete waste of time him being there, but he knew it was necessary if they were to keep up appearances. It was all part of Liam's master plan. And that was what frightened him.

Typical Liam, Drew thought. Sending me in to do his dirty work.

Before he pondered it in any further, his mobile rang.

'Liam?' Drew answered.

'He's on his way. You remember the plan?'

'Yeah.'

'You remember what you have to do?'

'Yeah.'

'Good. He'll be there in a while. The Farmer's on his way too. Sit tight.'

Liam hung up. Drew placed the phone neatly on the seat beside him and ran his hands up and down the steering wheel in an attempt to staunch his nerves. It had no effect. He was going to need something stronger.

Drew leant across the car, reached into the glove box and pulled out an unopened packet of cigarettes and his half-empty bag of cocaine. Then he unbuckled his seat belt, shuffled forward on the seat and made a line using the remainder of what was left in the bag. Rolling the only note he had in his wallet into a tube and pressing it against his nose, he snorted the contents and allowed the chemicals to grapple with the nervous beast inside him.

Within seconds, they had tamed it.

Now he was ready.

CHAPTER 61

SEND

Two brilliant white lights cut through the terrain and shone in Drew's rear-view mirror, sending the hairs on the back of his neck on end. *He's here*.

Drew inhaled until his lungs were full. The rubber grip of the steering wheel felt hard and bruised his skin. He kept his eyes focused on the black silhouette that gradually approached him. A short while later, it idled past and pulled in front.

Garrison killed the engine and stepped out. Drew watched him keenly as he rolled down the window on the passenger side.

'You been waiting long?' Garrison asked, smiling facetiously.

'Piss off.'

'Can you blame me? I don't want to be here any more than you do.'

'I probably would've done the same. Especially on the night shift.'

'I think Liam's got it in for me,' Garrison said. He placed one elbow on the window frame and the other on the roof.

'How is he?' Drew asked, trying hard not to sniff and rub his nose. He needed to pretend to be sober. To *look* sober. When in reality the hit had been bigger than he'd expected and he could already feel himself beginning to lose control of his senses.

'Drunk.'

'Again?'

Garrison nodded. 'He disappeared for an hour earlier. No idea where he went. Now he can't stand up straight. Nor can the fucker talk in cogent sentences.'

'What a mess,' Drew said, shaking his head, even though he didn't mean it.

'Think the pressure's getting to him. Big time. All this stuff with Maddison and now Clayton… Only a matter of time until he breaks. Either that or The Cabal will get rid of him as soon as he realises Liam's a liability.'

Drew hesitated before he responded. 'Yeah,' he said, non-committal. The more he listened to the venom coming out of Garrison's mouth, the more he realised that what was about to happen was absolutely necessary. 'Liam'll be first to break. But then I reckon sooner or later, we'll all follow. And it won't be pretty when we do.'

'How long you reckon you got left in this game?' Garrison asked.

Drew blew a raspberry through his teeth as he considered a calculated response. 'Fuck knows, mate, if I'm honest. It all depends on this rape bullshit. If Tanner does as he's told and keeps it to himself, then everything should be all right. But if it keeps coming back – if she goes to the IPCC or something – then I'm done. It's taking it out of me, mate. Constantly worrying, making sure I've covered every track, making sure I haven't exposed myself, or you, or anyone else. It's fucking knackering. I've been so uptight for months now. I reckon if you shoved a clam up my arse, a pearl would come out within minutes. I haven't been able to jack off. I've not touched a pussy in months – I'm beginning to forget what one feels like. I'm pretty sure Suze has left me. She hasn't come home in months. Christ knows where she's fucked off to.'

Garrison laughed as though he genuinely found humour and enjoyment in Drew's pain.

'I've been there, mate,' he said. 'Trust me. We're going to have to take you to the strip club soon when this is all over, eh? Gotta make sure you spunk all your money on a different kind of crack.'

Drew's face dropped. 'How did you…?'

'I'm not a fucking idiot, mate. I was there for you when you first started. I knew the signs then, and I know the signs now. You need help with it?'

Drew closed his mouth and shook his head. 'I'm coming off it.'

'You better be. Otherwise, I'll have to intervene again. Just like last time. And if it's anything like that, you know you're not going to like it.'

That was true – he wouldn't. Ten years before, when Drew had first started snorting coke on the job, Garrison had become involved. To help combat the issue, Garrison had forced Drew to stay in Garrison's spare bedroom, so that he could keep a close eye on him. There, Garrison had locked him in and got him off the drugs, cold-turkey style. It was a drastic and brutal way of dealing with it, but it had been for the best. After all, Garrison had helped the rape allegation disappear, so Drew couldn't be angry. Much to his surprise, it had worked.

'Hey,' Drew said as he forced his mind away from all the good that his colleague had done him. He pointed at Garrison's car. 'How is it?'

'Pukka. Five-litre engine. Five hundred brake horsepower. Five G less than the asking price. This little beauty goes like a fucking rocket.'

'Let's have a look,' Drew said as he stepped out of the car and made his way to the Jag.

Garrison rounded the back of the car and hopped into the front. As Drew was about to join him, the nerves in his body trembled. It was time to do exactly as Liam had said. Distract him and keep him there for as long as possible until help arrived, because Liam was paranoid that, as soon as Drew left, Garrison would do the same.

He climbed into the passenger side and let the leather seat absorb his body. He didn't realise it, but he let out a little groan.

'Nice, eh?' Garrison asked.

Drew ignored him, reached into his blazer pocket and produced his new pack of cigarettes. Just as he was about to remove one, Garrison slapped the packet out of his hand, spilling the contents into the footwell and onto the gravel outside the car.

'The fuck you think you're doing? You can't smoke in here. No fucking way. I've only had it a few hours!'

Drew threw his hands in the air and then rushed to pick them all up. 'I'm sorry, Pete. I don't… I didn't…'

'Pick 'em up! All of them!'

Garrison leapt out of the car and hurried to Drew's side, throwing the door open wider, then bent down and started to scavenge through the gravel and dirt for the residual cigarettes. Once Drew had found all the ones that he could in the footwell, he clambered out of the car.

'Is that all of them?' Garrison asked.

Just as he said it, Drew fumbled a couple and dropped them to the ground. Garrison swore as he helped pick them up.

'Take them and get the fuck out of here,' he hissed and thrust them into Drew's chest.

'But, Pete… Come on, mate. It was just a joke!'

Garrison didn't want to hear it. He shoved past Drew, slammed the door shut and hurried back to the driver's side of the car.

'Go home, mate. Treat yourself to a wank, and maybe while you're there you can shove a couple of those up your arse too.' Garrison pointed at the mess of cigarettes in Drew's hand.

Drew didn't know what to say, so he headed back to the car, started the engine and drove away until Garrison's silhouette got smaller and smaller. As soon as he was out of sight, he pulled over and typed out a text message.

All yours.

He hit send. And waited.
A few minutes later, a black van drove by.

CHAPTER 62

LINGER

Jake had suggested The Head of the House – it was familiar, friendly and perfect for keeping up appearances. Charlotte had decided to leave before him, and he was under strict instructions to wait five minutes before doing the same, just in case they were followed. She was being cautious, and Jake decided to take a leaf out of her book.

He arrived at the pub ten minutes after he'd set off.

'All right,' he said, as he joined her by the entrance.

'Were you followed?'

'Not that I'm aware of.'

'You sure?'

'No. I'm not a spy.'

'But you've got common sense. You can tell when something doesn't seem right, and when someone might be following you?'

'I'm not stupid.'

'Good.'

Jake opened the door for her and allowed her to walk through first. She thanked him, and then they wandered up to the bar.

'All right, love?' Maggie, the bartender and owner, said. She had a piece of gum in her mouth and chewed horribly, making vulgar and revolting noises as she did, and revealing her teeth with each bite.

'Evening, Mags,' Jake said.

'You want your usual?'

'Oh, your *usual*?' Charlotte repeated, raising her eyebrow and giving him a disproving look.

Jake ignored her. 'Yes, please,' he said, and then turned to Charlotte. 'What do you want? I'm buying.'

'Vodka and Coke,' Charlotte replied without hesitation. Jake could hardly blame her. A stiff drink was exactly what they both needed. They'd been working themselves tirelessly, and they deserved a little reward.

Maggie disappeared around the corner, returned with two glasses and then began to pour the drinks. She set Jake's beer down on the counter first – bubbles rocketed to the top, while a dribble poured down the side. A few seconds later, she handed Charlotte her drink. 'I ain't seen your face round here.'

'She's just joined the team,' Jake replied.

'Well, I'm only here for a short while,' Charlotte corrected, taking the glass from the counter.

'This is our initiation,' Jake said.

'The others joining ya?'

'Sadly, they were all pre-booked.'

'Well, I hope you've got your thick skin on, love,' Maggie said to Charlotte. 'Some of them boys don't realise they're in the company of women sometimes. But you're all right with this one – he's one of the good ones. Shame he likes to drink piss though.'

Charlotte chuckled nervously. Jake took that as his cue to move the conversation along.

'What's the damage, Mags?'

Maggie held her hand in the air. 'This one's on me. Consider it a welcome to the team.'

Chuffed, Jake thanked her and ushered Charlotte to a seat round the corner of the bar, in the team's usual spot. The seating area was sparse, save for two men in paint-spotted overalls sitting quietly and nursing a pint each. Jake helped himself to a seat on the faux-leather cushion.

'I'm impressed,' Charlotte said as she joined him. 'First-name terms. Free drinks. I think she likes you. Do you charm all women like that?'

'Only if they offer me something for free in return,' Jake said and then instantly wished he hadn't.

Charlotte didn't seem to mind though; she laughed.

'It's good to get out of there – of work,' she said. 'It gets claustrophobic. Even though we're not there all the time, it feels like we are… If you know what I mean?'

'Sort of…' Jake said, taking a sip of his drink.

'Out here it feels like I can be myself, up to a point. But you never know when you're going to have to get back into undercover mode.'

'Must be difficult.'

'It is.'

'How much of the real you do we get to see?'

Charlotte took a large gulp. 'About ten per cent. I can't afford to get too comfortable. Otherwise people start to notice.'

'You seemed comfortable just now…'

'Excuse me?'

'With Liam. Feeding him that information. You were lapping it up as well.' Jake cleared his throat ready for his impression of Liam. '"Oh, Charlotte – I'm so impressed. Everyone else should be following your exceptionally high standard. You're going to be taking over my position soon!"'

Charlotte didn't see the funny side of it. 'You do realise I was doing my job, don't you? It's called getting him onside. Earlier in the day – before we got to your emergency call – I tried to pry information out of him. It didn't work, so now I'm—'

'Killing him with kindness?'

'Sort of. I'm telling him what he wants to hear. Men love that.'

Jake took another sip of his beer. 'It would just be nice to be kept in the loop with things.'

'You can't be, Jake. I can't. Not as much as you'd like. It would be too obvious for both of us, and then my cover would be blown. You'll just have to trust me to do my job. And I'll trust you to do yours.'

Jake paused a beat before moving the conversation along. 'How long have you been doing this UC gig for?'

'Long enough to know that I want a change.'

'What would you like to do instead?' Jake asked, hoping that she would lead the conversation away from work. At least for the time being. He wanted Charlotte to feel comfortable around him, for her to feel at ease, for her to feel like she could trust him. There was plenty of evening left to discuss work.

'I like horses,' Charlotte said.

'Horses…'

'You know, unicorns without the horns?'

'I'm familiar with the animal.'

'I grew up with them. My dad used to race and breed them. He was quite good at it actually.'

Jake nodded, absorbing everything she was telling him. 'Did you race?'

'I trained but was never good enough to become a jockey or compete.'

'I don't like horses,' Jake said. 'Never enjoyed being around them. I don't trust them.'

'Why?'

Jake shrugged. 'Just don't. They're too big.'

Charlotte burst into laughter, her eyes creasing. She slapped her hand on the table and placed her other hand on his playfully. Jake didn't feel comfortable with it being there, but he didn't do anything about it, even if her hand did linger for too long.

'You can't blame them for being the size they are,' she replied, her voice reaching a crescendo that disturbed others around them. It was an ugly laugh, but Jake didn't mind; he found it endearing.

'So how does a girl who tamed horses end up as an undercover police officer?'

Charlotte's laughter died down and she took another sip of her drink. 'Things happen in life. Plans change. It doesn't always work out the way you want it to.'

'How much of what you're telling me is true?'

'Jake, hun, it's my job to lie to people. It's one of the things I'm good at. I'll leave it up to you to decide how much you want to believe.' Charlotte finished off her drink, slammed it on the table heavily and asked, 'Now… fancy another?'

CHAPTER 63

PERFECT OPPORTUNITY

BBC Radio 2 was playing in Liam's car, though he paid it little attention. He was more focused on what was happening right in front of him than listening to the latest song from Linkin Park, his favourite band.

Jake. Charlotte. The Head of the House. Sitting together. Drinking. Touching. Flirting. More drinking.

It was all too perfect. All too fortunate. He was stationed in the car park immediately outside; after leaving Bow Green he'd decided to clear his head. He needed somewhere he could be alone, yet in the presence of other inebriated people – somewhere he could come to chill the fuck out or chat shit with strangers. Of course, there were some regulars whom he recognised – ones he'd give a nod to and have obligatory small talk with – but other than that, there appeared to be a fresh face almost every night. There was a certain anonymity to the pub and its patrons that he admired; it was his sanctuary, and if there was anything he could do to keep his mind off Garrison, he'd do it.

But now he felt like that had been taken away from him.

The song on the radio changed, startling Liam into action. He leant behind him and reached into the rear passenger footwell, fumbling for the digital camera he kept down there, stowed in a plastic carrier bag. It had twenty times optical zoom. Twenty megapixels – twenty times the clarity in the image. Twenty quid, from a keen seller who'd wanted to get rid of it. The man's urgency to dispense with the camera should have worried him, but it didn't. If it turned out that he was a paedophile or a child molester, and he'd used this particular camera to facilitate his preferred desires, then the solution was simple: destroy the camera and remove all trace of his ever having owned it. Nobody would think of a cop as a paedophile. Especially one with as immaculate a record as him.

He switched it on, opened the lens and zoomed in on Jake and Charlotte. They appeared to be enjoying themselves, engaging in friendly conversation. Perhaps a little too friendly.

By the looks of it, Jake had just said something funny as Charlotte reeled back in laughter. Liam waited for the camera to load, hoping he would be able to get a photograph in time.

Just as Charlotte was about to remove her hand from Jake's, Liam depressed the shutter, capturing the moment in a still image forever.

'Gotcha,' he whispered to himself.

That was all the evidence he needed. He didn't know when – or if – he'd need it, but it was there, and that was all that mattered.

Meanwhile, a plan that he hoped wouldn't be necessary started to form in the back of his mind.

CHAPTER 64

PUPPY–DOG EYES

Five minutes had gone by, and already he was bored. A part of him had considered leaving. He had no real reason to be there, so why was he? Because the other part of him was preoccupied with Drew. How they'd come a long way together. How he'd defended his inept colleague once before, and how he wasn't sure he could do it again. How Drew needed to be spoon-fed everything. How he had sucked up to Liam in recent months. How they'd both grown distant. How he himself was leaps and bounds ahead of both Liam and Drew in The Cabal's rankings – and whether he would be able to find it within himself to call The Farmer and organise a hit on one of them if the time came.

The answer was simple. Yes. He knew his mission, and he knew that he could.

A set of headlights appeared to the left of the warehouse. The car moved along the road and then made a right turn, heading towards Garrison.

He watched as whoever it was pulled up in front of him, killed the engine and exited the car.

'You're not who I was expecting,' Garrison said as Nigel Clayton opened the passenger door and slid in.

'I'm the only one that's available. The rest of them are hiding – waiting it out after what happened.' Nigel nodded to the warehouse he'd just driven past.

There was a long pause. Garrison used the time to inspect Nigel's face. There was something wrong about his presence, but he didn't know what. Garrison had been expecting one of The Farmer's team, but it was never Nigel Clayton; never the accountant.

'Why are you here?'

'The money. He… he asked me about the money. The Farmer. He wants it. It's a lot of money that we need to launder out of the country.'

'Out of the country?' Garrison asked.

A smirk flashed across Nigel's face but it didn't mask his frightened countenance. 'That's why I'm the best in the business.'

'Don't flatter yourself.'

'When is it coming?'

'I have it in the boot now.'

'Really?'

'No, 'course not fucking *really*. How stupid do you think I am? I thought you were intelligent?'

Nigel played with his fingers.

'When is it coming?' he repeated, looking out of the window.

'I'd rather speak with The Farmer about this,' Garrison replied.

'He's busy. That's why he sent me.'

Hmm. Something still wasn't sitting right with him.

'I can just call him.' Garrison reached inside his pocket, slowly at first to gauge Nigel's reaction, but when the accountant didn't react, Garrison pulled his hand out of his pocket. He continued to eye Nigel suspiciously. 'What's really going on, Clayton? Why are you really here?'

Nigel's head snapped towards him. 'Is it true?'

'Is what true?'

'The DNA. On Danny Cipriano's body.'

Garrison let out a long exhale, designed to make Nigel sweat that little bit more. 'You don't have to worry about it; it's being taken care of.'

'How?'

'You don't need to worry about that.'

'Yes, *I do*. I need to know. And what about Maddison's body? Is my DNA on that too?'

Garrison's brow furrowed. 'Why would it be? I thought he killed himself.'

Nigel scratched the back of his neck. He couldn't bring himself to meet Garrison's gaze. 'There was a scuffle. We came in just after he'd slit his wrists. But as soon as he recognised us, he tried to get out of the tub. I pinned him down and submerged him, but there was blood and mess everywhere. We cleaned up afterwards.'

Garrison couldn't believe what he was hearing. 'Thoroughly?'

Nigel looked up at him with puppy-dog eyes – which told Garrison everything he needed to know.

Just as he was about to make a phone call, another set of headlights appeared in his rear-view mirror. This time it was a van.

The vehicle skidded to a stop beside Garrison's car, and three figures leapt out, cloaked in black masks. In their hands they held weapons – a cricket bat, a baseball bat, a crowbar – and they swarmed the Jaguar, opening the passenger door first. Panicked, Garrison reacted quickly and started the engine, his hand flying to the automatic gearbox. But there was a problem. Force of habit dictated his next move: he thrust the gearstick into Drive, rather than Reverse.

And then his door opened. Out the corner of his eye, he saw Nigel's head roll from side to side like a rag doll as he was repeatedly struck by a cricket bat, and he knew that he was about to meet the same fate.

Standing beside him, with one hand on the door and the other holding a baseball bat, was a thick, heavyset, well-built man, masked behind a disguise of black. No other thought was permitted to enter Garrison's brain before the man brought the bat swinging down on his skull and knocked him into the unending world of unconsciousness.

CHAPTER 65

JUMP

Georgiy enjoyed wearing the black mask; it made him feel dangerous, threatening, invincible – as if nobody could touch him. The only downside was that, even on cold November nights like tonight, it still itched like a bitch. And it was only worsened by the sweat forming in the creases of his neck and his scalp – a by-product of his adrenaline.

Within seconds of their arrival, it was done. Nigel's car had been moved out the way and both men were unconscious and already in their positions. A thin trickle of blood ran down the side of Nigel's temple from where he'd hit the man too hard. He may have ruptured something inside the man's skull, but that didn't matter. It was something he'd deserved.

The accountant had made too many mistakes, and that alone was justification enough.

Vitaly slammed the door shut on the other side of Garrison's Jag.

'It is done,' he told Georgiy and rounded the back of the car.

'Get the brick.'

Tatiana was the one who followed the instruction; she returned a moment later holding a dense red brick in her hand.

'And the helmet?'

Tatiana chucked the brick to Vitaly before rushing to the back of the van. Vitaly caught it awkwardly, almost dropping it onto the top of the car. After he'd adjusted his grip on the brick, he rushed back to Garrison's side, placed the brick on the accelerator, closed the door and then returned.

Tatiana appeared in his peripheral vision and handed Vitaly the helmet. Then Vitaly exchanged the helmet for the black mask and, just like that, they were ready. It had only taken them a few minutes. Quiet. Clean. Calm. Efficient. Everything Georgiy wanted in a hit. Out of all their past ones, this had been the smoothest.

'Ready?' Georgiy asked Vitaly as the young man climbed into the back seat of the car. 'Remember instruction I tell you?'

Vitaly nodded. 'Do a right and then keep straight on.'

'When you dive?'

'Forty.'

'Good. What else?'

'Get van from warehouse and meet at number three.'

They shook hands before Georgiy slammed the door shut. Then he tapped on the roof, signalling to Georgiy that it was clear to begin.

The young man leant into the cockpit of the car and started the engine. At once, the brick revved the engine until it roared and disturbed the silence surrounding them. Inside the car, Vitaly slipped the gear into Drive.

The car leapt from its spot and sped down the road. As it reached the junction, it swung a right and disappeared out of sight, masked by the cover of darkness overhead. Georgiy squinted, searching for it. He followed what he thought was the outline of the car but turned out to be nothing other than his mind playing tricks on him.

The air fell silent as the distance between him and the car grew, save for the sounds of his heavy breathing. Less than twenty seconds later, the air was pierced by the gut-wrenching sound of a vehicle crashing and wrapping itself around an inanimate object.

Georgiy just hoped Vitaly had been able to jump out in time.

| PART 5 |

CHAPTER 66

BUSINESS PROPOSITION

Liam's skin prickled as he stepped out of his car and closed the door. Surrounding him from every angle was the sound of shouting, banging, crashing, playful laughter, television sets blasting repeats of daytime shows, and the heavy, repetitive din of house music. It was a cacophony of sound that intimidated him – would intimidate *anyone* – and he wasn't afraid to admit it.

As a rule, police officers weren't supposed to come here. Even the bent ones that had but a semblance of a relationship with the people who ran the estate. Liam included. But tonight was an extenuating circumstance. An opportunity had presented itself to him, and it was time to capitalise on it.

Every time he set foot on the Cosgrove housing estate in Stratford, Liam counted the minutes until he could escape. Everything about it scared him. Everything was dirtier here. The concrete. The buildings. The small patch of earth that was used as a football pitch. The basketball court beyond the grass. The garages and walls that were decorated in tasteless graffiti. The convenience store that had been broken into and ransacked and was now boarded up. Even the single, lonely orange street lamp situated in the centre of the square was scruffy. And, worst of all, was the smell – the stench of piss and alcohol lingered in the streets, drifting through the avenues and walkways on a tepid wind.

Liam sauntered across the square that was crowded by two dominating high-rise towers; one to the north and one to the south. His footsteps seemed to echo loudly around the estate. He was in plain clothes, but he was aware that even those who didn't already know who he was could work it out. Could work out *what* he was. Like they had some sort of sixth sense for spotting coppers a mile off.

Ahead of him, thirty yards away, was an underpass carved out of the bottom of the tower block. From within, a young boy wearing a hoodie and riding a bicycle emerged and approached Liam.

Liam paused where he was. Experience told him to. To follow the rules. Not to do anything stupid. Nobody would save him here; nobody would even hear him scream.

The young boy circled him a while, taunting him, eyeing him, until eventually, he slowed to a halt. 'Arms,' the boy instructed. He couldn't have been older than thirteen; his voice had just started to break.

Liam lifted his arms and the boy searched him, patting his pockets and legs, making sure he wasn't carrying any weapons.

Satisfied, the boy said, 'Shirt.'

Without needing to be told what he meant, Liam lifted his shirt, proving he wasn't wearing a wire.

'You're good,' the boy said, hopping onto his bike.

'Tell Henry I wanna speak to him.'

The boy shook his head. 'He ain't gon' like that… *pig*. You know what time it is?'

He didn't know precisely, but he was aware it was already gone three. Well past the kid's bedtime. And his.

'Just tell him, you little shit,' Liam snapped. 'It's important.'

'You better watch what you say in front of me, fam.' The boy, lightning quick, pulled out a flick knife from his pocket and held it at arm's length. The street lamp lit the three-inch blade orange, as though it were scalding hot.

Liam glanced at it and remained still. 'What's your name, kid?'

'Lewis,' the kid replied with pride and a quick snap of the chin.

'You know what I am, right?'

'That ain't mean shit when you step foot round 'ere… *pig*.'

Lewis spat on the floor by Liam's feet and set off on his bike, heading back through the underpass. While he waited, Liam observed his surroundings. The tower blocks were thirty storeys high, and there were several hundred people living there, most of them in run-down conditions. But not a select few. There was a hierarchy that not many people outside of the estate knew about. The dealers were naturally the wealthiest, occupying several flats at a time – mostly at the top, furthest from any rival gang members looking to start a turf war by making someone swallow a bullet. Then there were the runners, the 'youngers' – the young, apprentice-type kids who were no older than fifteen and didn't know any better – that would run the drugs around the streets, shipping them to the buyers. And, finally, there were the buyers – the desperate addicts begging for their next fix.

And then there was the one who supplied it to them all.

Henry Matheson.

Liam wondered which flat he was staying in. In the north building or the south? Before he could contemplate it any further, the boy returned, his brakes squealing as he skidded to a standstill.

'You caught him in a good mood. Follow me.'

Liam started off after the kid. They headed to the building on the other side of the basketball court, through the doors and up fourteen flights of stairs. There, the stench of alcohol and vomit ran up his nostrils, dived down his throat and settled in his stomach, making him want to vomit. As they came to a stop on the twentieth floor, Liam tried to force the smell from his mind. He needed to focus. There was a job to do and he needed his A game if he was going to be convincing in any way, shape or form.

Top form, Liam told himself. Top form.

The boy stopped outside a flat. There was no door number on it, but behind the door was the source of the heavy bass he'd heard from down in the square. After Lewis knocked, the music stopped and was followed by the sound of footsteps and a door chain being unlocked.

Henry Matheson was a beefy guy – his hair short, eyes deep in his head and his nose broken. He wore a gold chain around his neck and an even thicker one on his wrist. His complexion was fair and looked as though he maintained it well, which struck Liam as odd because he thought the last thing on a drug dealer's mind would be completing a skin routine every night. Henry was dressed in an Adidas tracksuit, with the trousers hanging halfway down his legs, and the unzipped jumper revealing a vest and a substantial amount of chest hair.

'This better be important. You didn't make an appointment.'

'You got business cards or something now then? A secretary I can call?' Liam hoped the light-hearted banter would make up for the disturbance.

It didn't.

Henry turned his back on Liam and disappeared into the flat. Liam took that as his cue to follow. The flat was dark, cold and stank of weed. It was a pleasant change from the piss and everything else he'd smelt on the way up. The air was filled with a dense mist originating from the smoke; Liam supposed it permeated through the walls and pores and molecules of everything that lived there.

He followed Henry into the living room at the end of the flat. The lights were off and the only source of light was the forty-inch television screen sitting on the floor on the left. Against each of the three remaining walls was a sofa. On them sat Henry and his dealers, all looking up at Liam with contempt, the flickering lights from the television dancing off their chains and earrings. As he panned the room, he noticed that, on either side of the television, two bodies were slumped on beanbags.

'They all right?' Liam pointed over to the two comatose girls.

'Let me worry about them,' Henry said, folding his arms. 'You just worry about making yourself heard in the next five minutes.'

With pleasure, he thought, stepping into the room. He saw a free space, large enough for him to sit on without coming into contact with anyone else, and sat on it.

'No, no. You don't get to sit,' Henry ordered, waving his finger at Liam to get up.

Rising to his feet in the middle of the room, Liam chuckled awkwardly and asked, 'How's business?'

Henry kissed his teeth. 'Fam, you come here at this time in the morning to talk about fucking accounting? You've just shaved off two minutes of your time. Get talking.'

Liam raised a defenceless hand in the air. Cut to the chase. Short, succinct, he told himself. 'What if I told you I could nearly double your income for you?'

Henry sat forward a little. 'I'd say you're chatting shit, but now you have my attention.'

'I'm sure you've heard about the Cipriano case? Famous robbers. Killed their mum with a spiked collar-bomb thing. Yeah? Those ones. Disgusting, I know. But one of the boys on my payroll did it. Offered him a large enough sum of money and he was happy to accept. Only problem now though is one of his boys has fucked up and managed to get his DNA on the body. Our person on the payroll in forensics didn't get a chance to discard it. Now we've got ourselves a situation—'

'One minute.'

Liam continued, regardless. 'We need someone to pin the murders on. And that's where you come in.'

At that, one of the dealers to Henry's left moved his hand to the arm of the chair, grabbed a gun from beneath a pillow and moved it slowly onto his knee, making very sure that Liam knew it existed and that it was pointed directly at him.

'What you talking about?' Henry asked.

'My original question. Business. It's going good, but it could be better, right?' Liam looked around the room as if he was actually expecting an answer. 'Your friend, Jermaine Gordon – how's he doing?'

'Still taking forty per cent of the market.'

'What if I got rid of him? My team can arrest Jermaine, plant some evidence on him that would make it look like he killed the brothers and then he's gone for a good ten to twenty years. With his record, he could even go down for longer. Frees up his share of the market.'

A moment of hesitation fell over the room. Liam felt like he was in court, being judged and assessed by a jury. Hopefully, the man with the gun wasn't his executioner.

'What's in it for you?'

Liam shrugged. 'A bigger cut than usual. Ten per cent.'

'Fuck off.'

'Ten per cent of your monthly takings. Think about it. You'll own one hundred per cent of the market. Ten per cent of that is negligible. And we'll keep letting you bring in the shipments, ship it around the city and stay out of any trouble.'

'Two per cent,' Henry countered.

'Eight.'

'Two.'

'Five.'

'Two.'

Liam opened his mouth to counter but stopped as he watched the man with the gun push it further up his leg. 'Fine. Two per cent. Usual delivery methods?'

'Yes.' Henry nodded. 'Is that everything?'

'Not yet. How long have I got left?'

'Ten seconds.'

'Good. One last thing – tell your boys to stop supplying to Drew. He's about to go off the rails if you keep giving him this shit.'

Henry leant forward, resting his elbows on his knees. 'I've got something I want you to have.' He turned to the man beside him and took the gun from the man's grasp, then placed it on the glass table in front of him.

'Wh—'

'Are you about to be ungrateful, Liam?'

Liam shook his head.

'Good boy. If your plan works and it all goes smoothly, then you're gonna have Jermaine's boys coming after you. And trust me, you ain't gonna want that. I don't usually offer protection to my clients, but as this is a special deal, and you're doing me a favour, it's the least I can do for you. All right?'

Liam nodded. He didn't know what to say. In fact, he was too afraid to say anything. A gun was pointing at him, and he didn't even want to think what sort of life it had had – how many lives it had claimed, how many bullets had travelled through its chamber, how many women it had widowed, children made fatherless.

'And what about Drew?' he asked, stalling for as much time as possible.

'You're just worried about him because you've not tasted the stuff for yourself in a while…' Henry reached behind him and produced a small bottle of Pepsi. He placed it on the table. 'You can use this. Try it and see what you think. Might help you forget that you're a dirty pig for a couple of hours. Like you used to. I remember it was your favourite. Go on. Time's up. Elijah can show you out.'

Without needing to be told twice, Liam grabbed the gun and Pepsi bottle, concealed them in his pocket and waistband, and left.

CHAPTER 67

DOUBLE

As soon as the front door closed, Henry sparked up a cigarette, inhaled the toxins into his lungs and kept them there until his breath couldn't hold any longer.

'Liam fucking Greene,' he said aloud, shaking his head amidst the cloud of smoke that hung in front of his face. 'Prick's getting too big for his boots. Nobody gets to dictate my business like that. Nobody.'

'What you gonna do, G?' Elijah asked.

'I already know what I'm gonna fuckin' do.' Keeping the cigarette in his mouth, Henry found his phone and pressed five on speed dial.

Silence descended on the room.

'Hello?' a voice answered.

'Rupert? It's me. Sorry to wake you like this.'

'It's fine. Perfectly fine.' A pause. 'Give me a moment; I'll get somewhere more private.'

Henry waited as Rupert shuffled around, opened a door and climbed down a set of squeaky stairs.

'What's up?' Rupert asked as he settled somewhere in his North London mansion.

'I've just had a meeting with a mutual friend of ours.'

'What have you done now?' Rupert asked. He spoke affluently. Even though they were in the same sort of business and earned similar sorts of money, they'd grown up on opposite ends of the societal spectrum.

'Nothing like that. It was Liam… Liam Greene. He came over to work out a deal. Just thought I'd let you know that he's planning on taking Jermaine off the streets in exchange for a cut of the take. He wants to pin a double murder on J.'

Rupert sighed through the phone. 'He's clearly not been keeping up with the times, has he?'

'His head's too far up his own arse to know it.'

'Or he's too focused on keeping The Cabal happy. What do you need me to do?'

'Keep Jermaine out of it all. I don't want anything jeopardising our new plans. Ignore anything Liam tells you. They've got nothing on J, and they'll struggle to make it stick, but I just thought you should be prepared to represent him when he needs you.'

'Consider it done. But I'm not charging my usual fee. I want more.'

'How much?'

'Double. Fifty grand.'

CHAPTER 68

DEVELOPMENT

Jake didn't remember coming home the night before. He and Charlotte had shared one too many drinks with each other. They'd spent hours discussing everything. Their lives. Their families. Jake's marriage and Charlotte's single life. Their interests, their desires, their hobbies. And then they'd moved on to the investigation. The progress they'd both made – how Charlotte had been working tirelessly in the background after hours. And then they'd discussed the effects that it was having on them. Jake had been upfront about the fact that, even though it felt like they were coming towards the end of the investigation, it still felt as though everything was only just beginning; that it was just the tip of the iceberg; that it was physically and mentally draining and he didn't know how much longer he could sustain it for; that it was putting an unprecedented strain on his and Elizabeth's marriage.

Charlotte had listened to him babble on with an understanding and sympathetic ear, but he supposed it was just out of politeness. Unfortunately, she was the only person he could talk to, and he appreciated her being there. Whether she liked it or not, she was more than just an undercover officer now; she was a friend.

'Morning,' he said as he entered the kitchen. Elizabeth was in the middle of making them each a cup of coffee.

'Morning,' she replied, avoiding his gaze. She finished pouring the water into the mug and stirred.

Jake walked up to her and gave her a kiss on the cheek, but she pulled away.

'Everything all right?' he asked.

'What d'you think?'

'I didn't wake you up when I came home, did I?' Jake asked, taking his coffee and finding a chair at the table.

'No.'

'What's the matter then?'

She threw the spoon into the sink then spun on the spot and scowled at him, the black bags under her eyes darkening, as if she were summoning the devil from inside her.

'We enjoyed our takeaway last night, thanks. Oh, *wait,* no we didn't – nobody fucking came home to bring us one.'

Regret assaulted Jake's body. Like a boxer, it punched him in the stomach repeatedly until he was consumed with guilt. Again. He'd let his family down. Again. And he hadn't even realised it. He'd made a promise to come home with a takeaway, and instead, he'd been at the pub with Charlotte. He was an awful husband. And an even worse father.

'Liz, I—'

'Save it.'

'I'm sorry. Let me make it up to you. But… maybe not today. I don't know when I'll be home.'

'I don't care. *We* don't care. Do what you want. The girls and I are going to the park for a couple of hours today. We're going to play on the swings for a bit, go on the seesaw, maybe even fly a kite. And then we're meeting Becky to go to the races.'

Jake took a sip of coffee and spat it back out; the contents were scalding hot and burnt his tongue.

'You're not going there to gamble, are you?'

Elizabeth took her coffee from the counter and sat at the opposite end of the table, as far away from him as possible. Amidst the mountains of paperwork and schoolbooks and folders, was their family laptop. He hadn't realised it, but the lid was open.

Elizabeth set her cup on the table and moved the trackpad.

'I didn't realise you had a problem with me gambling,' she said, defiant. As the computer screen loaded, she twisted the machine and showed it to Jake. 'Although you didn't seem to have a problem with it the other night.'

In front of him was the gambling site he'd visited a few nights ago, replete with all its bold, vibrant colours. *Shit*. He'd completely forgotten to log out and delete the browser history before taking Maisie to bed.

'I-I…' he stuttered. There was nothing he could say that would excuse what he'd done. 'I…'

'When you said you were going to find a solution to our problems, I didn't expect you to resort to this, Jake. You of all people know how much worse it can make everything.'

Jake dipped his head in embarrassment. He did know – all too well. When Jake was younger, his uncle, Adam, had tried to use his brother's position at Chelsea to gain insider knowledge for placing bets on their matches, both domestic and international. Ian had told him no, but Adam had quickly become addicted, and it wasn't long before he'd lost his house, marriage and kids. A few weeks after the divorce was finalised, his ex-wife had found him dangling from the ceiling after dropping the kids off for their weekend visit.

'I'm sorry,' Jake said, swallowing his guilt. 'But I didn't do anything. I just signed up.'

'What made you think signing up was a good idea?'

He shrugged. 'They had an offer on. Spend ten pounds you get ten pounds free.'

'We don't have ten quid that we can just throw away willy-nilly like that! And then there're all these taxi rides you're taking as well. What's going on, Jake? Where were you and who were you with last night? What else aren't you telling me? I swear to God, if I find anything else, I'm taking Maisie and Ellie, and we're going straight to my mum's.'

Maisie entered the kitchen, holding a teddy bear in her arms and rubbing her eyes.

'What are you doing awake already, sweetheart?' Jake asked, bending down to pick her up.

'You woke me,' Maisie replied, clutching the bear against her chest.

‘Where’s Ellie, Maisie?’ Elizabeth asked, rising to her feet.

‘Playing.’

Jake and Elizabeth looked at one another.

‘I’ll go.’ Elizabeth slipped off the chair, out of the kitchen and up the stairs.

Once she was gone, Jake turned his attention to his daughter. His beautiful, precious little daughter.

‘Did you sleep OK, darling?’

She nodded, her eyes still half closed. He moved over to the fridge and found her a juice. Unscrewing the lid, he said, ‘Don’t tell Mummy, OK?’

‘Secret.’

Jake chuckled. ‘That’s right. Our little secret.’ He hesitated as he heard the sound of footsteps descending the stairs. ‘Are you excited to go to the park today?’

Maisie’s eyes beamed and her tongue fell out of her mouth.

At that moment, Elizabeth returned, holding Ellie in her arms. She wore a stern expression on her face, and her cheeks were flushed. ‘Did you leave the gate open?’ she asked, even though the tone of her voice told him she already knew the answer.

He had. It had been an accident – a mindless, careless mistake, but he knew the consequences of what could have happened. And if Ellie – or even Maisie – had fallen down the stairs and injured themselves, he would never be able to forgive himself.

Before Jake could respond, his phone rang.

'Sorry it's early, fella, but we need you here. By the farm factory. ASAP. We've got a major development. It's Garrison. Something big's happened.'

Liam hung up, leaving the words to echo around Jake's mind. Farm factory. Garrison. What had happened to him?

'Sorry, hun,' he said, setting Maisie down on the floor. 'I've gotta go. I'll call you when I can, OK?'

As Jake leant in to give Elizabeth a kiss, she turned away and sighed a deep, frustrated breath.

CHAPTER 69

EMBASSY

Jake ordered the taxi to The Head of the House so he could pick up his car and drive down to North Ockendon from there. It was an extra leg in the journey, but it was better that he was late than arrive in a cab.

On the way, he tried not to think about all the possibilities of what could have happened to Garrison. There was no point dwelling on hypotheticals – not until he knew for certain what was going on.

As he approached the spot that had been chosen for their stakeouts, Jake eased his foot off the accelerator. Two thick lines, like runways, stretched from the gravel into the road, dust and stones kicked up behind them. Jake quickly glanced away from the bush and thought he saw a white stick – perhaps a pencil or a pen – on the other side of the road.

Paying it little heed, he continued driving, made a right turn at the junction and started down another long stretch of road. This time, at the end of it, before it curved round a bend, he saw a convoy of ambulances, fire engines and police vehicles, their lights flashing and dancing on the tarmac.

Jake pulled up to the police tape, showed his ID, signed in at the attendance log, donned a forensic suit and then ducked beneath the cordon.

Ahead of him, thirty yards away, surrounded by an army of road traffic police and the local crash investigation unit, was a car wrapped around a tree. Glass and debris lay everywhere, strewn across the strip of road. Jake recognised the car instantly as Garrison's new Jaguar and flinched – the sight bore too many significant similarities to Michael Cipriano's collision.

Already, Jake's suspicions and apprehensions were screaming at him.

He approached the wrecked car in disbelief and peered round the bend in the road. An ambulance crew were driving off in the other direction. To his left, Liam, Drew and Charlotte were hovering around the boot of the Jag.

'What the fuck happened here?' Jake asked, trying to dissociate himself from the personal aspect of what he was experiencing. He tried to forget that it was Garrison who'd been inside the car. That he was – and there was no doubt in Jake's mind – the subject of another corrupt and ruthless killing.

'Garrison,' Liam began. He sounded normal. Too normal. 'Garrison was involved in a collision in the early hours of the morning.'

'No shit, sir,' Jake said, staring at the wreckage in front of him. 'I can see that. He hit a fucking tree.'

He was trying to remain calm, but it wasn't working.

'Is he going to be OK?' Charlotte asked. She was standing beside Jake with her arms in her pockets, protecting herself from the bitter chill that swept across the asphalt.

'He's alive and breathing,' Liam replied. 'The paramedics are rushing him to hospital now. They've said there's no way of knowing what condition he'll be in when he wakes up…' A pause. '*If* he wakes up. The other person with him wasn't so lucky…'

'Who?' somebody asked. Jake didn't know who. He was too focused on Liam's moving lips to notice anything else.

'Nigel Clayton. The ID found in his wallet confirms it's him. Paramedics announced life extinct as soon as they arrived.'

Nigel Clayton. Nigel Clayton. Nigel Clayton. Jake repeated the name in his head in an unsuccessful attempt to clear his mind of every other thought. It didn't make sense. Why would Garrison be in a car with Nigel Clayton?

The answer struck him far later than it should have done.

'I can't believe this,' Drew said sheepishly, breaking Jake out of his stupor. There was no emotion in the man's voice – no sorrow, no empathy, no sympathy.

'I know it's tough,' Liam said. 'But Garrison'll pull through. He's a tough biscuit, our Pete. I just wish we'd found him sooner. Terrible accident. Poor guy – he's been trapped inside that car for hours.'

Jake squinted. 'Who found him?'

'I did,' Drew replied immediately, holding his hand in the air. 'I was coming over to do the morning shift at about six to relieve him of his duties when I realised he wasn't there. I called his mobile about fifteen times, but there was no answer. So I drove around the block and saw him like this. Glass everywhere. Blood everywhere, gushing from his face, his temple, his nose. He was still trapped inside the car when I found him. I think it was his legs. And one of his hands was trapped too. I tried to get him out but couldn't – the doors were locked. So then I called the fire service. It took them about twenty minutes to get here, and they've just spent the past hour trying to get him out of the car. It was horrible. I felt so helpless.'

Textbook. The over-explaining. Providing too much information. Giving the most complete story possible to try to overwhelm and prove their innocence. It was obvious Drew was lying.

'They must have been arguing or something inside the car,' Drew hypothesised, attempting to fill the silent void between them all. 'It looks like he lost control and careened off into the tree.'

Jake looked at the tarmac. 'How do you explain that? If he'd lost control, he would've swerved and applied his brakes. There's not a single skid mark in sight.'

Drew opened his mouth but was interrupted by Liam.

'People do funny things when they're face to face with life or death situations.'

'Wh…? How can you…? Are you…? I don't believe this.'

Liam raised his hands in the air in a sign of surrender. 'There's not much point arguing, Jake. Not when one of our own is in intensive care. But his being with Nigel Clayton raises more questions than it answers. I hate to say it, but we now need to treat Garrison as a suspect in this case. It's very possible that they were working with one another.'

Jake muttered something under his breath.

'Excuse me?' Liam took a step closer to Jake. 'I know you're emotional. I get it; I am too. But there's a time and place for it. Garrison was one of my closest friends – you don't think I'm feeling hurt? Fuck you. This hurts like nothing else I've ever experienced, and I'd love to have him here with us right now if we could, and I'd love for it not to be true. But it is, and there's nothing we can do about it.'

Jake moved closer to the car, turning his back on Liam, his mind trying to piece together the sequence of events that had led up to the accident. If they were both in Garrison's car, then where was Nigel's? He hadn't seen one on the way down. And how had this happened? He'd been in the car with Garrison in the past; the man was an accomplished driver – he'd never do anything as reckless as this. Why hadn't Garrison swerved? How had he lost control that badly?

A whole lot of questions, not a lot of answers. *Yet*.

Jake wandered round to the passenger side of the car and leant into the vehicle. While removing Nigel's body from the seat – so that he could be taken directly to the mortuary – the firefighters had been forced to rip away the door frame. In doing so they'd kicked away and removed a lot of the debris from the footwell and transferred it onto the asphalt. But not all of it.

It was an Embassy cigarette, as the helpful little script on it said – Drew's brand. Could he have been in the car at some point? Why?

'I want you to get back to the office,' Liam said, distracting him. 'You and Charlotte. Carry on what you're doing. Focus all your efforts on Jermaine Gordon. He's the only connection between all of these people right now.'

Liam turned to Drew. 'And I want *you* to bring him in. Take some uniforms with you as well, just in case.'

'On it,' Drew said, already starting towards his car.

Jake and Charlotte took it upon themselves to follow, each heading to their own vehicles. Jake jumped inside his and slammed the door behind him. Resting his head against the steering wheel, he closed his eyes. Over – he just wanted it to be over. But until then Liam and Drew would continue to ruin the reputation of the Metropolitan Police and get away with their deceit and corruption.

Jake waited until Drew and Charlotte had left the area before starting his engine. There was something he wanted to check out; something that had caught his eye earlier – and he needed to be alone.

Jake drove towards the farm factory, turned left at the junction and idled towards the stake-out point. He slowed to a halt beside it, making sure he was fully concealed by the overgrowth, and then stepped onto the tarmac. The sun was rising and the birds were beginning to sing, but still, the slight chill in the air remained. Perhaps it was nerves. Perhaps it was the fact that he was petrified at what he might see. Or perhaps it was because he felt like there was an unrelenting sensation of someone following him, watching him, observing his every move.

He crossed to the other side of the road, crouching low and gazing down at the ground, his eyes scanning the minutiae for any detail. And then something caught his eye. The same thing he'd seen before. It glimmered in the sun, licked with a layer of dew. Jake approached; his intrigue and curiosity and excitement building.

Hidden within the undergrowth was another Embassy cigarette.

'What the—?' he said to himself, cut off by his own bewilderment.

He crouched down and removed his phone, taking several photos of the cigarettes and chiding himself for using the last of his evidence bags the day before. He'd have to get more and come back before it disappeared.

And then he remembered what Liam had said only moments ago.

That it had all been an accident.

Jake was calling bullshit. He just needed to be able to prove it.

CHAPTER 70

SCANS

The warm smell of coffee welcomed Liam like an old friend and reminded him of what it had once been like to drink from the reusable coffee cup that was currently in his office. Good, was the answer, before the alcohol began to nullify the taste of it. He was in a local café, five minutes from the crash site – thirsty and in need of a drink. His head was spinning slightly from the night before, but more than anything he was hungry; he hadn't eaten anything in over fourteen hours, and he was beginning to shake.

The proprietor was busy working behind the counter, tending to another patron and seemingly managing the orders of everyone else in the shop. Liam waited in line and gazed up at the menu.

After a minute of waiting, the woman in front of him received her drink and left.

'Next, please.'

'Good morning,' Liam said cheerily. 'Could I have a double shot espresso and a croissant please?'

The owner smiled and asked, 'One of those days?'

'Now you mention it, make it a triple.'

'Coming right up.'

As he watched her make the coffee, Liam couldn't help but stare at her. She seemed oddly familiar – as though he knew her from a past life. In a way, she reminded him of Charlotte – the blonde hair and the gigantic glasses that swallowed her face and detracted from the size of her forehead. And then he quickly realised the longer he stared, the weirder he looked.

'Here you are,' she eventually said, placing the IKEA mug on the counter. 'I'll bring the croissant over to you shortly.'

Liam paid and found himself a seat by the window.

For a while, he sat there and thought about the clusterfuck he had to deal with. Danny. Michael. Richard. Nigel. Jermaine. Garrison. The accident. The hospital. The list was growing. The accident hadn't gone to plan. Garrison wasn't dead. Sure, there was a chance his friend wouldn't wake up. But there was too big a risk that he would. And what would happen then? Would he remember everything, or would he have suffered irreversible brain damage and memory loss? Liam hoped the latter. Garrison had rapidly become a problem that needed silencing, but right now, he was untouchable – in the back of an ambulance on the way to hospital with no way of knowing when anyone would be able to see him again.

There was nothing Liam could do except wait until Garrison woke up. Then he could silence him again. The dynamic of their relationship had changed and gone past the point of no return. With any luck, Garrison would take his secrets to the grave with him. Although, upon reflection, there was one secret Liam wanted access to most of all: the identity of The Cabal. It was clear to him that Garrison and The Cabal were close, had been in recent months, so it was possible he knew the person's true identity.

His phone rang, breaking him from his reverie. He sighed heavily before answering.

'I was just thinking about you.'

'Don't flatter me,' the voice said.

'Everything's done. It's sorted. Richard. Danny. Michael. We're even getting Jermaine soon. That should help everything you've got going on with Henry. I want my share now. A hundred K, just like we agreed.'

'You're not finished yet.'

'Yes, I am. Danny and Michael have both been taken care of. And I've even thrown Garrison into the mix too.'

'What do you mean… Garrison?' The Cabal asked. 'What have you done to Garrison?'

'Taken care of him too. He was becoming too much of a threat. He was nearing retirement – who knew what would spill out of his mouth once he was out of all this.'

There was a lengthy pause.

'You idiot. He never would have been out of it. He would have come crawling back.'

Of course you'd say that.

'You never had to work with him. He was becoming complacent. He'd given up. I couldn't afford for him to make mistakes. Don't forget I'm the leader of this team.'

The woman arrived and set a plate on the table. Her arrival startled Liam, and as he pulled the phone away from his face, he accidentally hung up.

'Here you are,' she said, smiling at him. He knew it was probably her customer service smile, but it turned him on.

'Thank you,' he said, smiling back at her. God, he needed sex. A release. Something.

As Liam picked up his phone again, it started ringing.

'Yes?' he answered, thinking it was The Cabal.

'Is this DCI Liam Greene?'

'Speaking?'

'Hi, this is Patricia, I'm calling from Thurrock Community Hospital, on behalf of our patient, Pete Garrison. I understand you told our paramedics to keep you informed on everything that's been going on with regards to Mr Garrison…'

'Yes,' he said, his voice filled with a mixture of trepidation and excitement.

'I'm just calling to let you know that he's undergoing surgery at the moment. His legs and ankles were badly injured in the collision.'

'Will he walk again?'

'It's difficult to say. We won't know the full extent of his injuries until we've finished surgery.'

'Is he going to wake up?'

There was a pause.

'I'm sorry, sir, but early scans of Mr Garrison's brain indicate that he may be in a coma.'

CHAPTER 71

MOST TO LOSE

Jake burst into the office and made a beeline for Charlotte, who was already typing away on her computer, holding the phone to her ear.

'I need to talk to you,' he said.

Charlotte looked up from her screen and gazed at him. She told the person on the phone that she'd call them back.

'What is it?'

Jake pulled a chair from beside her and leant in close. He kept his voice low so that it was almost a whisper. A part of him thought it would be wise to speak about it in private – outside, in the briefing room – but the other part of him didn't want to waste unnecessary time.

'Listen,' he began, 'something's not right about Garrison's collision.'

'I've been thinking the same.' She removed a sheet of paper from her pocket. 'When I was on the drive down, I called my supervisor and told him what the latest was. He's given me the green light for access to all call history and financial records.'

'For who?'

'Everyone in the team.'

Jake's heart stopped. 'Including me?'

Charlotte nodded.

Fuck. If she saw them and realised that he was in financial trouble, she would have no choice but to report it – worse, assume that he *was* secretly involved with all the corruption.

'How long will that take?'

'It's a shitty process. It takes a while. Hopefully, by tomorrow, we'll have everything. I've requested Liam's info as a priority.'

I hope I'm at the bottom of the pile.

'I definitely think he's hiding something,' Jake said, wanting desperately to change the subject. 'What happened to Garrison certainly wasn't an accident. There were no skid marks on the road, and…' Jake paused to look around him; there was no one in sight. 'I found a cigarette inside the passenger footwell of Garrison's Jag, and another on the floor by where he was parked up originally.'

She looked at him confused. 'And…?'

'They're Embassy – and Drew's the only one who smokes them. The others rip into him for it.'

'But we know that he was there before Garrison. They swapped shifts.'

'I know. I thought that too at first. But then I realised that Garrison got his new car yesterday. He's very precious about it. There's no way he would have let Drew smoke in there. And there's no way Drew would have left his cigarettes on the floor like that. He hates wasting them.'

Charlotte paused as she looked at the pen she was twirling in her fingers. 'I don't get it. What does this have to do with anything?'

Jake sighed briefly. 'I don't know. I'm still trying to work it out. But it puts Drew at the crime scene.'

'Like I said, we already know he was there. Is it possible Nigel Clayton smokes the same cigarettes?'

Jake placed a hand on the table. 'One thing I've come to learn in this job is that anything's possible. Please… I think it's something we should investigate.'

'Have you seized them as evidence?'

'I took photos. I didn't wanna contaminate them; I didn't have any evidence bags.'

Charlotte dipped her head and gave him a disappointed look, like she was his mother and he'd just broken a curfew for the first time. 'This morning we got the forensic report on Richard Maddison's body. I haven't had a chance to look through it yet. Read it over. Let me know if you find anything.' She reached for her car keys in her letter tray. 'I've got some evidence bags and gloves in my car. Where did you say you found the cigarette?'

'The bush where I watched the factory – on the other side of that. The vantage point. You can't miss it.'

'OK.'

'Can you check Pete's car as well? See if you can find the one in there.'

'Give me a couple of hours, and I'll be back with everything.'

'Be quick. If either of them has found the cigarettes and picked them up, then… I'm sorry… I should have retrieved them as evidence when I had the chance.'

'You of all people know better than to tamper with evidence. You did the right thing.'

Jake watched her leave the office, paranoia beginning to surge through his body. He envisaged the cigarette lying there on the asphalt, rolling gently on the ground as it was picked up and carried by the wind. Then he imagined Liam's car pulling up beside it, a foot stepping out, a hand picking it up. He closed his eyes and willed for that not to happen.

But there was nothing he could do about it now.

First, he needed to check the forensic report.

He swivelled round to his desk, logged into the computer and loaded his emails. The report flashed up on his screen and he began reading.

It didn't take him long to find what he was looking for.

The DNA found in the fingerprints on the wall matched Nigel Clayton's.

Which meant he was present at Danny Cipriano's murder.

Which meant he was present at Richard Maddison's suicide.

Which meant he was present at Pete Garrison's attempted murder.

Was he also the one who'd beaten Michael Cipriano to death? Accountant turned hitman?

The evidence suggested so. The only thing left to do now was find out who had the most to lose and hired the contract killer in the first place.

Fortunately, Michael Cipriano had already given him that information.

You're a good egg, Jake. You're a good egg.

CHAPTER 72

PRETEND

'He wants Haversham,' Drew told Liam bluntly on the phone. 'We can't let him. It'll ruin everything.'

Rupert Haversham was a man who needed no introduction. Over the past decade, his name had become synonymous with crime and the criminal justice systems. Working out of his small office in North London, many of the city's most prolific criminals – from all reaches of the spectrum – used his services to help them evade justice. The only problem was being able to afford him.

Liam sighed. 'You've done everything by the book, right? Told him his rights, signed him in, confiscated everything, made sure everything is as fucking perfect as it can be? We can't give that prick lawyer any reason to pull Jermaine out.'

'I think so...' Drew hesitated. 'You're making me doubt myself.'

'Doubting yourself for doing your own fucking job? Jesus. Leave it with me.'

Liam hung up before allowing Drew a response, and within a few seconds, the trilling tone sounded in his ears again.

'I was wondering when you might call,' Rupert Haversham said as he answered the phone. His voice was deep, authoritative and very commanding. It was no wonder he was successful in the courtroom. His voice had the power to intimidate and provoke even the most cocksure and confident of individuals.

'I suppose you've heard already?' Liam asked as he skulked to his car from the cafeteria.

'Are my services required?'

'Why else would I be calling?'

'Perhaps you fancied a chat. Who is it this time?'

'Jermaine Gordon.'

'What's he done now?'

'Committed triple murder. Potentially a fourth.'

'I'll believe it when I see the evidence.'

'You don't need to. I'll double it.'

'Double what?' Rupert asked, a slight intrigue growing in the man's voice.

'Whatever he's paying you. I'll double it.'

'I don't know what he's paying me yet. I haven't spoken with him.'

'Does it matter? Pluck a number out of the air and I'll double it. You just step away from the case, that's all. In fact, don't even step near the case – how does that sound?'

'I might be able to entertain the idea. Convince me.'

Liam sighed. 'What's your usual rate?'

'Well, that depends on the evidence presented against my client. If you've got a lot, then it costs more. If you've not got anything and it's purely coincidental, then it's still going to be costly because you've wasted my time. I'm in high demand.'

'As you insist on reminding me every time we speak,' Liam remarked.

'So… what evidence do you have?'

Liam swallowed. With the considerable lack of concrete evidence they had against Jermaine Gordon – there was none of his DNA on the bodies, nor was there anything connecting him to the crime *other* than his connections with Richard and Danny – then Liam knew there was no way he could convince Rupert to stand down. The man was too intelligent and tenacious for that.

Time to get creative.

'We found his DNA on Danny Cipriano's body. There were hair fibres as well as clothing fibres found that match Jermaine's. We've got so much of his DNA on the database, it was easy.'

'Is that all?'

'CCTV. Footage of him outside the Olympic Stadium construction site at the time of death. My guys are working on enhancing the imagery now.' Liam paused a beat. 'It's a lost cause. There's little for you to fight against.'

Rupert chuckled down the phone. It was soft and low. 'How long have you and I been working with one another?'

'I don't know – a few years.'

'Ten,' Rupert corrected. 'And in that time, I've watched you do some pretty dodgy things, Liam. I'm sure you know what I'm talking about. So what's to suggest you've not done the same things here with our old friend Jermaine Gordon, huh? I know how you work—'

'And I know how *you* work,' Liam interrupted, gripping the gearstick tightly. 'I doubt in the last ten years you've changed your philosophy on work, have you? Working for the highest bidder. Everyone in the country wants you, but not everyone can afford you. Like I said, I can. And I'll pay you double.'

'You have that sort of money to spare?'

'We've both been in this business for a long time, Rupert. You know I have. Are you taking it, or are you wasting my time?'

There was a long pause on the phone, filled with silence and the odd outburst of static noise.

And then: 'Fine. You've got yourself a deal. But it'll cost you a hundred grand. Transfer me the money by the end of the day, and I'll pretend I've never even heard of Jermaine Gordon.'

CHAPTER 73

TOILET BREAK

Jake had spent the last thirty minutes trying to make sense of it all, much to his dismay.

It was now confirmed that Nigel Clayton – the man who was now dead after being involved in a fatal car crash with Garrison – was present at both Danny Cipriano's and Richard Maddison's deaths. It was only a matter of time, he hoped, that it was confirmed he was also present at Michael Cipriano's murder to complete the hat-trick. Jake pondered for a moment as he recalled the event – how he'd been only a few feet away from somebody beating the life out Michael's body; how his heart had been in his throat as he listened to the sounds of Michael dying; how he'd cowered on the ground as he prepared himself to be seen and shot; how he'd been spared by the woman in black.

Nothing. There's nobody here.

She'd saved him. She'd let him live. But why? And who was she?

Jake turned his mind back to Richard Maddison's murder. To when Drew had called him and told him that a group of people had stormed into Maddison's house.

I'm outside Richard Maddison's flat waiting for him to come home, but I think The Farmer and his group have just broken into his house.

Danny Cipriano was murdered by a close associate of ours called The Farmer and his team.

At that moment, he noticed Drew returning to the office out of the corner of his eye, distracting him. The detective sergeant was hot and flustered, and looked mildly embarrassed, like he'd just been drink-slapped by a glass of wine. He turned his back to the wall and poured himself a cup of water from the fountain, avoiding eye contact as he sat down.

'Everything all right?' Jake asked.

'Yeah.'

'How'd it go?'

'How did what go?'

'Jermaine.'

'Oh. We're waiting to find his lawyer. He's requested Rupert Haversham.'

Jake nodded slowly, absorbing the name. It was a frequent occurrence in the office, almost as though Mr Haversham was a member of the team.

'Seems like half the city wants his services,' Jake said.

'There's a reason. He's good. I'd want him if I was in trouble.'

Of course you would, Jake thought, his mind conjuring images of Drew sitting behind a microphone, defending himself in court for raping Hannah Bryant.

'You reckon the evidence against him will stick?' Jake asked.

'Doesn't matter what I think. It matters what the CPS and twelve jurors think.' Drew smirked then turned his attention to his computer screen and grabbed a few documents from his letter tray. He began filling in the sheets, glancing up at the computer repeatedly as he completed the information.

'And what do you think twelve jurors will say about what happened to Pete?'

At the mention of Garrison's name, Drew stopped and snapped his neck towards Jake. 'What you talking about?' Before he afforded Jake a chance to respond, his head turned to Charlotte's desk. 'Where's *she* gone?'

'She had to pop out. Said something about going back to Garrison's incident and looking for evidence. I think she saw something in the bushes nearby and in the passenger seat.'

Drew's eyes shifted nervously and the colour drained from his cheeks. And that was when Jake knew he had the bastard.

Saying nothing as he shut off his computer screen, Drew slowly stepped out of his chair.

'Where you off to?' Jake asked, pushing himself away from his desk.

'Er… for a smoke… then going to – to the toilet.'

'Mind if I join you?'

'Fuck off, nonce.'

Jake puffed a small laugh out of his nostrils, then watched as Drew exited the office and turned left. By the time he reached the hallway, Drew was at the end of the corridor, angling his body to turn down another one. Jake raced after him down a flight of stairs. If he needed any indication that Drew was lying, this was it.

Shortly after they reached the station's entrance. Drew was twenty yards ahead of Jake, already holding his mobile to his ear.

As Drew approached the revolving doors, he froze and lowered the phone from his head.

Hannah Bryant had just climbed the steps to the building and was standing at the entrance.

They stood for a moment, staring at one another. Neither of them said anything, locked in a battle of unspoken and scathing words that had manifested themselves after years of silence and detestation.

'Hannah!' Jake said, feigning excitement to see her when in reality he was struck with bemusement. 'Thank you for coming in. I hope the notice wasn't too short?'

'No…' she said, unsure of herself. 'It was fine…'

'Journey OK?'

Out the corner of his eye, he noticed Drew's mouth had fallen open.

'It was fine thanks,' she replied, still unsure what he was up to.

'Good,' Jake responded. 'Well, if you wouldn't mind, DS Richmond, I'd like to speak to my witness for a moment. Didn't you have a toilet break you needed to take?'

CHAPTER 74

MISS B

'Why… why are you here, Hannah?' Jake asked, smiling awkwardly at her as they sat opposite one another in an interview room. 'Didn't you get my message?'

'I did. I'm sorry, Detective. I wanted to come down in person. I need to know what progress you've made on the case.' She looked down into her lap and played with her fingers. 'I'm sorry.'

Jake sniffed. 'Hannah… I'm sorry…'

'You've done nothing?'

'Hannah—'

'No!' she yelled, her demeanour and temper flipping on its head. 'I trusted you. You were the only one I could have trusted to do this for me, but you're just like the rest of them, aren't you!'

'Hannah – let me finish please.' Jake raised his hands in the air in an attempt to placate her. As soon as she quietened down, he continued. 'Things here have been so incredibly busy, they've taken up the majority of my time. I've been unable to—'

'Typical!' she shouted, rolling her eyes and leaning back in her chair, folding her arms.

'Not that it's any excuse, believe me. I want to help you, I really do. And I will be putting all my efforts into your case as soon as I can, but there's been a development and things may be a little trickier than originally planned.'

Hannah tilted forward slightly.

'DC Garrison – the man who was in charge of your case the first time round – was involved in a collision in the early hours of this morning. He's alive, but we don't yet know the extent of his injuries.'

'Good.'

'Excuse me?'

'Good,' she hissed, lacing the word with even more venom. 'He deserved it. Karma for fifteen years of suffering and pain that I've had to endure. I just hope DS Richmond's end is even worse. He deserves all he gets.'

'I'm sure you don't mean those things, Hannah.'

'I do. I can't wait till the day I find out he's dead. And do you know what I hope happens to him? I hope he suffers the same thing that happened to me. I hope they torture him. I hope they make him feel helpless. I hope they rape him to death and suck every last ounce of life from his soul.'

Jake opened his mouth and let it hang there, stunned, as he stared at her in disbelief. He couldn't believe what he was hearing. In fact, he didn't want to. She'd seemed so sweet and innocent. But Jake knew she wasn't. She couldn't be. What had happened to her was a terrifying ordeal, and it had shaped her life and behaviour and attitudes in ways he couldn't imagine. Without realising it, Drew had changed her life forever, and her reaction was a visceral product of the abuse and torment she suffered on a daily basis. Jake would never be able to understand the pain she went – and was going – through, and so, for that, he pretended he hadn't heard what she'd said. Even if it did mean that her name might be high on the list if anything did happen to Drew.

'Hannah, I promise you I will get to the bottom of this. I just need more time. But I can assure you they will face the consequences of their actions.'

Hannah shook her head. 'It's not good enough. The world needs to know what that man's done. How he's abused his power. How he should never be allowed to call himself a police officer ever again.'

'And I'm all for that. It's just going to take time. There are certain procedures we have to follow. It's a painstaking process, and trust me, it's just as infuriating for me as it is you.'

Hannah scoffed. 'Don't pretend like you can sympathise with me. You don't know the half of it. You don't know any of it. And you never will. You will never have to go through what I have.' She looked down at the table. 'Christ knows how many other people have.'

'Are you suggesting he's done this before? Did he ever mention having done it to other women?'

Hannah hesitated. 'Not that I can remember. I never thought to ask. He might have done. I'm sure he and DC Garrison had their own little gang going on.'

The hairs on Jake's skin prickled. If he could open an investigation into some other rape cases that had remained unsolved and forgotten about since Drew started in the force, then Jake might be able to build an even bigger case against him.

'What about any friends of yours at school? Did you have any friends that knew him or were offered the same kind of *help* from DS Richmond?' Jake was unsure of how to phrase it. He hoped he hadn't overstepped the mark with his word choice.

Hannah retreated into a state of reflection again. She ran her finger over her lips and then held it at the bottom of her nose.

'There was one girl. I never spoke to her properly. We were sort of friends, sort of not. We grew up on the same estate and went to the same school. Now that I think about it, I did see them together a couple of times. It's possible something might have happened to her too.'

'Can you remember her name?'

'Nancy.'

'Just a first name?'

'Unfortunately. Nancy B… Her surname began with B. Do you have access to school records and things like that?'

'We can do. What years were you there between?'

'Ninety-one and ninety-six.'

Jake pulled out his pocketbook and made a note of Nancy's name and the years he was looking for.

'And the name of the school?'

Hannah told him. Jake scribbled it down.

'Is there anything else you need to tell me? If I can find evidence against DS Richmond for this, then I might be able to look into Nancy.'

Hannah shook her head.

'Well, if you can think of anything, you have my number. Please, be patient. I'll do everything I can. But right now you need to leave DS Richmond to me.'

CHAPTER 75

LOBSTER

Drew struggled for breath. Fat fuck. He'd only sprinted across the car park to his car. What would he be like if he needed to outrun a car or The Farmer? An onslaught of adrenaline combined with fear pulsed its way through his body, shaking him. He fumbled in his pocket for his phone and, in his haste, dropped it into the footwell.

He was a mess.

Seeing Hannah Bryant had awoken a fear in him he'd suppressed for a long time – the feeling he'd had the first time Hannah had made rape allegations against him. And this time was no different. She was there for the same reason she had been fifteen years ago, he was sure of it. Except this time there was a slight change – Jake instead of Garrison. A straight cop instead of a bent one. It was then that Drew realised he'd been kidding himself into believing that Jake would keep his mouth shut, even with the money he'd attempted to bribe him with. No, Jake had continued the investigation into the rape, and he was getting closer to finding the evidence.

The evidence. There was none. Garrison had assured him that it was removed and taken care of. But Garrison had already proven that he couldn't be trusted. What if that was a lie as well? Shit. He wished he'd had a chance to find out before putting his colleague into a coma.

Drew reached down and grabbed the phone by his feet. He unlocked the device, found Liam's mobile number and dialled.

His chest heaved as he waited, his senses alert. His gaze darted left and right as he watched uniformed officers and police vehicles move past his windscreen.

'This better be important,' Liam said in Drew's ear. He'd half been paying attention, half focused on what was happening outside so he didn't register Liam's voice at first.

'It is. I… we… we've got an issue.'

'What?'

'Where are you?'

'Heading back to the station.'

'You need to turn around. Quickly.'

'Why?' Liam asked, unimpressed. Drew sensed the resentment in his voice.

'I fucked up. I made a mistake. I'm sorry.'

'What have you done?'

'I dropped some cigarettes in the car last night. In Garrison's car and on the tarmac by the bush.'

'Are you joking?'

'I wish I—'

'Fucking idiot!' Liam shouted. Drew heard his boss slam his hand on the steering wheel, brake hard and floor the accelerator. 'How can you be so stupid? You are inept. You are a fucking joke. If we get caught for any of this, I'm blaming you. This is all on you.'

'Liam, I'm sorry. I don't know… I… I panicked. I wasn't thinking straight.'

'Were you high?'

Drew paused and swallowed hard. 'You need to hurry. Charlotte's on her way down to the accident scene now. I think she knows about the cigarettes. You need to find them before she does.'

'Where'd you hear that?'

'Tanner,' Drew responded, glancing up at Bow Green – where Jake was now talking to Hannah Bryant. 'He said she'd left the office to go and check something out.'

'Son of a bitch. They're working together. You need to keep them apart. I'll take care of the cigarettes and you keep an eye on Jake. If he doesn't lay off, let me know. I'll find a way to make him listen.'

Drew hesitated. He steadied his breath until it returned to a natural rhythm. 'That's not everything either, guv,' he said, pinching the bridge of his nose.

'How much worse can it get?'

'I bumped into Hannah Bryant at the station. She's talking with Jake now.'

'About the rape?'

'Yeah.'

'But I thought you said Jake stepped off that? Thought that's what the bribe was for.'

'I did. He did. It was.'

'But he's still investigating?'

'Why else would she be here?'

'Jesus…'

'What if he finds out about the others?' Drew said accidentally, meaning to think it rather than say it aloud.

'Others? Thought you said it was just her.'

'I did. It was. But… there was another one.'

Another four.

Liam sighed. 'And what about her? Same situation?'

Drew nodded, even though Liam wasn't there to see it. 'Garrison was in control of it all.'

'Like we can trust anything that prick's ever done.'

'It's not exactly like we can fucking wake him up and ask him!'

They both fell silent. Drew's chest continued to heave, while Liam's car engine sounded in his ears.

'Give me some time,' Liam said. 'I need to think. But honestly, unless you can get rid of any and all evidence before Jake gets to it, there's nothing I can do.'

'Let me go after him,' Drew said. 'I can convince him to stop. If money won't work then I can get creative.'

'No. Don't go anywhere near him.'

'Why are you still defending him?'

'For reasons you won't understand. Just be grateful I'm still putting you before him.'

Drew gritted his teeth until his jaw ached. 'Fine. Princess Tanner will remain untouched.'

Drew clicked off, furious. Now the fear had been eaten and swallowed by fury and anger. He clenched his fist until his knuckles turned white and then repeatedly brought it down onto his thigh. *Thud. Thud. Thud. Thud.* Until the pain swelled in his knee and the muscles of his quadriceps turned numb. It was a softer alternative to beating the inside of the car door, or the steering wheel, or the dashboard, or a brick wall – but it still hurt as much.

For the next few minutes, he sat still and contemplated his options. The way he saw it, there were none. Liam wasn't going to help him. Like fuck he was; he'd just made that abundantly clear. And what if Tanner was close to the evidence – or already had it? His days as a police officer were numbered. And if he wasn't allowed to go after Tanner himself then what was he to do? If it wasn't Liam coming after him, then it sure as hell would be The Farmer and The Cabal, and Drew knew first-hand what these people were capable of – how easily they could dispose of someone like a piece of shit on a shoe. He couldn't defend himself against that. He wasn't about to become another of The Cabal's deadly statistics.

Drew reached across the passenger seat, unlocked the glove compartment and grabbed at the mobile phone.

A sticker on the back of the device read emergency use only.

He called the only number in the address book.

'Good afternoon, Clam Shell's restaurant,' the voice on the other end said. 'How may I help you?'

'I was wondering if I could book a table for one at seven o'clock?'

'For one?'

'Yes.'

'And would you like the lobster or salmon?'

'Lobster.'

'We've made a note of your reservation. Goodbye.'

The line went dead.

Drew took the phone away from his ear, slid open the case, pulled out the battery and removed the SIM card underneath. He snapped the SIM in two and burnt the golden chip with his lighter before returning to the office and throwing the remains in the bin.

CHAPTER 76

PAPER BILLS

Jake exited the interview room and headed towards the evidence lock-up unit in the basement of the SOCO lab. From memory, he recalled that according to the internal notes on Hannah's case, Garrison had accidentally misplaced the evidence and all the files on his desk. One night they were there; the next morning they weren't. Done and dusted. No further action required because Garrison was the one in charge of the investigation. All charges dropped. You're free to go. Simple.

But Jake didn't believe it at all.

Garrison was a workhorse. Despite his shortcomings, the man was methodical and thorough. Which meant that the evidence certainly did exist and that the paperwork lived and breathed somewhere, but was hidden –

somewhere he thought nobody would find it. Either that or it was in the most obvious place, the place nobody would think to look, brushed to one side, forgotten. Jake would never forgive himself if he didn't check there first.

After speaking with the same man behind the desk – who Jake now believed was a permanent fixture of the building – he slipped through the double doors, made a right turn into the stairwell and bounced down the stairs two at a time. Following their trip to Sandy's office the other day, the DPS had given him permission to get through certain doors that required particular levels of access. Right in front of him was one of them – on the other side were the evidence archives. Jake scanned his key card on the door and entered into the small square room. The first thing he noticed was the temperature – cold, the air still. No windows and no air-conditioning unit or air vents inside. Shelves ran along the perimeter of the walls at Jake's shoulder height, and underneath them was a row of filing cabinets interspersed around the room. Twelve in total, organised in crime category and date order.

Jake moved to the left of the room where he found the filing cabinet titled Rapes and Sexual Assaults. He pulled the top drawer open and sifted through the files, flicking through history until he found 1997.

Twenty cases in total. One of them was Hannah Bryant's.

'Gotcha!' Jake exclaimed as he pulled out the file.

He opened the thin manila folder and read through the contents as quickly as he could. The report was extensive and, in Jake's opinion, conclusive. It comprised a list of items given as evidence against the attacker – ones that had never surfaced again – with their corresponding evidence numbers. Things like saliva and semen deposits found on Hannah Bryant's clothes and hair. Bruises found on Hannah Bryant's body. DNA from her fingernails.

The evidence was there. Stark. As clear as day. Indisputable. And it had been discarded as though it was nothing. Jake couldn't believe what he was seeing. But he also couldn't believe how easy it had been to find. Like they'd been waiting for someone to stumble upon them. But there was a problem. Some of the contents were redacted – in particular the section of the report that stated who the DNA belonged to.

Garrison's middle finger.

Jake slammed the filing cabinet shut and left the evidence room with the folder firmly parked under his armpit. On the way back to the office, he made a quick call.

'Sandy?' Jake said as he climbed the stairs again.

'Is that Jake?'

'How did you know?'

'The inflection in your voice. Fortunately for you, you don't sound like the others. I'm sorry to hear about, Pete, by the way.'

'Yeah… So am I…'

'It's tragic,' Sandy added. When he didn't respond, she continued, 'What can I do for you?'

Jake stopped as he reached the third-floor landing. There was a small horizontal window that looked out upon the street. In the distance, there was a pelican crossing and he watched as someone crossed the road.

'Jake?'

'Evidence,' he said. 'I need some evidence. And the original forensic reports. Wondered if you still had it in storage somewhere.'

'What's it for?'

'CS/7163949/E.'

There was a moment's pause. 'Leave it with me. I'll pass it to Jemimah. She'll get back to you when she's got something.'

'Please,' Jake said and then hung up.

He placed the phone in his pocket, turned, and climbed the final few steps into the office. As he returned to his desk, Jake shuffled past Drew and placed the folder beside his mouse and keyboard.

'What was that about?' Drew asked.

Jake ignored the question as he scanned the desk for a black sleeve but couldn't find one.

'Jake? I'm talking to you. What did she have to say for herself?'

They locked eyes for a moment, and then Drew's flicked to the folder.

Jake shrugged. 'Why don't you just worry about your own problems.' As he said it, he pulled open his desk drawer. His breathing stopped as his eyes fell over what was in there: a wad of money. Paper bills stacked on paper bills. This time there was more than the chunk Drew had given him. And on top of it, a note.

Jake leant forward to read it, avoiding touching it – he didn't want to incriminate himself by getting his fingerprints on it.

Here's the money from the last drug shipment. More soon.

Jake sat back in his chair, squinting into the distance. Then he turned around. Faced Drew. 'Do you know anything about this?'

A smirk grew on Drew's face. He stood up and placed a hand on Jake's back.

'Why don't you just worry about your own problems, eh?'

CHAPTER 77

RECORDS

Jake felt like a snake was wrapping itself around his oesophagus as he watched Drew head off towards the kitchen. Somebody was playing games with him. Somebody was trying to frame him for something he didn't do. Somebody was trying to make it look like he'd done something illegal, corrupt, morally reprehensible.

The words on the note were testament to that.

But who? Drew? Liam? Garrison before his accident?

Jake's mobile rang, tearing him away from his thoughts.

He answered without checking the caller ID.

'It's me,' Charlotte said.

Jake blew out his cheeks. 'Where are you?'

'It's not looking good, Jake,' she said. She sounded out of breath, and in the background, Jake could hear birds singing.

'What's happened?' He slowly pushed the drawer shut with his foot.

'The cigarettes. They're not here. They've been moved.'

Jake clenched his fist and tensed his whole right arm. 'You think they got there before us?'

'It was either the person behind Garrison's accident… or Liam… or Drew.'

Jake watched his moving about in the kitchen. 'It wasn't Drew – he's been here all day. What about Liam? I've not seen him come back since this morning.'

'Do you even know where he is?'

'No idea.'

'We need to find him. He's the key that unlocks all of this, Jake.'

There was a brief shock of disturbance on the line, and Jake waited for Charlotte to continue.

'I'm going to speak with my handler – I'll request a search warrant for both Drew and Liam's vehicles and properties. They might have evidence in there connecting them all to this.'

Jake was about to speak, but she cut him off.

'I've also put in a request to trace and tap all of Liam and Drew's personal numbers. Their calls, their text messages – they'll soon be ours. We'll know what they're saying and who they're been saying it to,' Charlotte explained.

'Jermaine Gordon...' Jake whispered, thinking aloud. 'They're going to make it look like Jermaine Gordon is the one who ordered the hit on Garrison and Clayton. They're going to put absolutely everything on him.'

But why Jermaine? Jake asked himself. What was their interest in him? It can't have just been because he had a connection with Richard Maddison. There must be another angle, an ulterior motive. Amongst all the rubble, there was a clue that they needed to unearth, decipher, analyse, interpret.

'Listen,' Charlotte started, 'we'll get to the bottom of this. Trust me. We've got a team in the background working on it for us too. This is why they brought me in. But first I need you to find Liam. If he's been to pick up the cigarettes, I want you to wait for him and find them.'

CHAPTER 78

SELF-INCRIMINATION

The dashboard absorbed the heat from the beaming October sun like a sponge, warming the inside of the car. Pressed against the leather seat, his back was beginning to sweat, as were his neck, arms, legs and arse. It didn't help that the fear of being seen and having his cover blown worsened things.

It was past lunchtime and he was hungry. The espresso and croissant had done little to satisfy him, and he wanted another snack. But he couldn't afford to leave the area. He was in the perfect vantage point, hidden, discreet – stationed in the car park at the foot of Roundshaw Park, just east of South Croydon. The field was large, stretching across several acres of green, and it was surprisingly busy. The schools had broken up for the day, and all the mums and dads had decided to take their kids to the park for the afternoon. Some played on the swings and roundabout in the playground. Some played with a ball at their feet. Some skipped and hopped and jumped, while others sat on the grass and shovelled handfuls of it into their mouths.

But there was one family in particular that commanded Liam's attention. He'd followed them from their house in Croydon, watched them board a bus and driven behind them, keeping his distance at all times.

On the passenger seat beside him was the digital camera he'd used to snap the photographs of Charlotte and Jake at The Head of the House the night before.

Liam picked up the camera, switched it on and aimed it at the family.

Elizabeth Tanner was pushing a buggy while walking her eldest by her side. Maisie Tanner skipped along and smiled ebulliently, full of youth and a zest for life. Inside the buggy was Ellie Tanner, Jake's second daughter. Liam had been thrilled – ecstatic, even – to learn that they'd decided to name the child after his own mother. It was an honour, which made it even more of a shame that it had come to this. He liked Jake, Elizabeth, his family – they were loving, caring, welcoming people. But Jake had become a hiccup, and now they all needed to be dealt with in the same way.

We're going to pour water down this little problem's neck.

Eventually, Elizabeth and the girls found a seat on a nearby bench. The space was empty and Elizabeth was quick to occupy it all. She pushed the buggy along to the end of the bench, sat Maisie to her left beside the buggy and then herself on the other end. Then she reached down to the storage compartment and pulled out a bag, the contents of which made Liam's stomach grumble even louder.

For the next few minutes, he trained the camera on them as he watched them eat, snapping photos of them as they did. While he sat there, he tried not to think of Jake and how he had everything Liam had envisaged for himself: beautiful wife, beautiful children, beautiful home, beautiful life. He tried not to think of the fact that he'd never had children, never had the time to start a family with his wife, never had the *courage* to start one. It was his own fault really; only himself to blame.

Something up ahead distracted him, pulling him out of his thoughts.

Elizabeth had dropped something on the ground. It was her purse, and as she bent down to pick it up, a man wearing a black jumper with his hood pulled over his face and his back to Liam reached for it and handed it to her.

Quickly, Liam snapped a few images of the Good Samaritan returning her purse. A smirk grew on his lips.

He was at the perfect angle.

After the man had left, Liam opened the photo library on the device and scrolled through the photos. The small thumbnail clearly showed both Elizabeth and the Good Samaritan looking at one another, passing something between their hands.

From the photo, there was no knowing what had been exchanged.

From the photo, there was no knowing what their relationship was.

And that was exactly how Liam wanted it. He imagined the headlines: cop's wife caught in drug deal with kids in park.

All it would take now was for him to plant a piece of evidence inside the Tanner household, and then he could really crank things up a gear and make Jake wish he'd never started this campaign against him. For too long the man had ignored the warnings, and now it was time to deal with the fallout.

But first, before he did any of that, he would follow her for the rest of the day. Not just because she was nice to look at, but because he thought she might offer more opportunities to incriminate herself unknowingly. And he wanted to be there, ready to capture the moment when it happened.

CHAPTER 79

THE SOUND

The Farmer was a man of his word. If he was given a contract, he would see it through to the end – no matter how reluctant he might be to finish it off. It made good business sense. More dead bodies meant more money. More dead bodies meant more clients. More dead bodies meant more business.

But this next one was one he'd been looking forward to least.

Things were beginning to get out of hand. He'd originally only been contracted for one: Danny Cipriano. That was it. Nothing more, nothing less. But there had been too much collateral with Richard Maddison, Pete Garrison and Michael Cipriano thrown in as well. Too many. All in such a short space of time. And now he'd been forced to add his own team member into the mix. Nigel's death was unfortunate but vital. The man had been complacent, and if the contracts were going to keep coming in at the same rate they had been, then Georgiy couldn't allow any form of complacency.

His next appointment had come from above, direct from The Cabal.

The reasons are twofold, The Cabal had told him on the Kingdom of Empires messaging platform. *She knows too much. She's a liability. Second, you're doing this to hurt someone. Liam hasn't been doing his job. He's getting weak. Now you need to teach him and someone else an important lesson.*

The bounty on Danika Oblak's head had been placed at an extra hundred thousand pounds. The price of silence.

Georgiy cast his mind back to the day before. How she'd been as high as a kite, passed out on her own sofa, struggling to cope with the drugs coursing through her veins. A part of him hoped she'd overdosed, so he could earn the easiest hundred grand of his life. But he knew the reality of it was different; from the amount of drugs on the coffee table, she'd only be knocked out for a couple of hours. More than likely, she was alive.

For now.

Georgiy prepared himself by wrapping a pair of thick, black leather gloves over his hands. Leather was hot and sticky, but fingerprints could bleed through latex, and as he removed the Beretta M9 from beneath the passenger seat and placed it in the inside pocket of his leather jacket, he realised he didn't want any traceable markers pointing back to him. Inside his other pocket was a sound suppressor and a mask.

Pulling the face mask over his head, he opened the car door, swung his legs out and sauntered the short distance to the house, surveying his surroundings. There was nobody around.

Georgiy pressed the buzzer, listening intently for the sound of life.

It was there. The sound of coughing. Movement. The television playing in the background.

Footsteps approaching.

He wrapped his hand around the gun just as the front door opened.

Before Danika could react, Georgiy thrust the Beretta into her face and placed his finger to his lips.

'Nice and easy,' he said. 'You understand?'

Danika nodded, the whites of her eyes illuminating the rest of her face.

'In you go.' Georgiy pushed the nose of the gun harder against her skin, forcing her into the house.

Danika stepped backwards into the hallway, keeping her eyes locked on his. Behind him, Georgiy bolted the door shut.

Once they were in the living room, Georgiy ordered her to sit down on the sofa. He moved to the front windows, pulled the curtains shut and then muted the television.

'Are you here to kill me?' she asked.

'Is not personal,' Georgiy said, his fingers beginning to get sweaty beneath the leather. 'They pay me get rid people like you – people who know too much. They worried about *grassing*.' He struggled to say the final word. It was a new addition to his English vocabulary.

'Aren't *you* curious to know what I know?' Danika eased herself into the sofa, like she was making herself comfortable, already accepting of her fate. 'I could tell you things, you know. A lot of things.'

'Why I want that?'

Danika shrugged. 'Use it to your advantage. Help work your way to the top.'

'You bargain for life? You think I won't kill you?'

Danika shook her head. 'I've seen what's been going on in the news. I saw what you did to

Danny. And Michael. And Richard. And Garrison. I know there's no escape – I've known for a long time that something like this was going to happen. But you don't understand how fucking painful it is not being able to tell anyone about it. Now I don't have to live in fear of the consequence, because I can pass the burden on to you. Don't you want to find out where your money's coming from so you can get more of it?'

Georgiy didn't reply. He lowered the gun to his hip. The Cabal was a person of extreme secrecy and betrayal. And in his business, those were unfavourable characteristics. There would always be the concern in the back of his mind that The Cabal could, at any moment, hire another contract killer and place a bounty on his own head. He wanted to be prepared for if – and when – that day came.

A smile grew on Danika's face. She flashed a set of yellow and black teeth that hinted her drug and smoking addiction wasn't a recent affliction.

'Gotcha,' she said, winking at him. She reached across the sofa, grabbed her handbag and overturned it. A bottle of vodka spilled out onto the cushion, and a bag of weed landed beside it, along with a packet of Rizla, filters and tobacco. He watched intently as she rolled the weed and tobacco into a joint.

'You mind? I wanna be relaxed when you kill me.'

Georgiy shook his head, incredulous at was happening.

'You want some?' she asked, licking at the paper before rolling it tightly.

Georgiy shook his head again.

She grunted. 'I understand. You don't wanna get pulled over driving under the influence. That shit carries a max sentence of fourteen years.'

'What you think I'm here to do? I not here to chat.' Georgiy raised the gun and pointed it at her head again.

She pulled the joint away from her mouth and stared at him.

'You'd think I'd be scared, right? I wish I was; I really do. But I'm not. I came to terms with dying a long time ago. There are things in my life that I can never set straight, and I gave up trying an even longer time ago. All because of that cunt Jake Tanner. If he never caught the brothers in the first place, if he never put them in prison, then we wouldn't be in this situation, you wouldn't be holding a gun to my head and I wouldn't want you to pull the trigger. How different our lives could have been.'

Georgiy opened his mouth but struggled to say anything. This woman didn't deserve to die. She wasn't a criminal. She hadn't hurt anyone. Stolen from anyone. Murdered anyone. Raped anyone. Her only crime was having knowledge. Being in the wrong place at the wrong time. And now she was suffering for it. Judging by her frail body, it looked like she'd been suffering for a long time.

A bullet in her skull would only speed up the process.

Georgiy lowered the gun and started towards the living room door.

'Where are you going? You're going to leave me here… alone?'

'You've got your vodka.'

'One bottle isn't going to do too much.'

Georgiy froze in the door frame and looked down at the weapon in his hands. It was unregistered and the serial numbers had been scratched off. There was no DNA on it, no fingerprints, nothing. It was a ghost, just like him.

He removed the magazine from the weapon, decanted all the bullets bar one into the palm of his hand and then placed it on the arm of the chair.

'There,' he said. 'I leave up to you.'

Georgiy shut the door behind him.

He idled down the hallway, opened the front door and headed towards the van, keeping his head low. As he opened the driver's door, he heard the unmistakable sound of a gun firing from inside Danika Oblak's house.

His fingers wrapped around the sound suppressor in his pocket.

CHAPTER 80

MR MCNULTY

Drew had never felt so paranoid in his life and it was beginning to feel like it had all come at once. Thirty-three years' worth of life and paranoia and fear, all rolled into one. His leg drummed on the floor of his car and his eyes constantly bounced between the time on his dashboard and the empty multi-storey car park in front of him.

He was on the fourth level, parked in the usual spot. He just hoped that there had been no issues or delays with his reservation; the manner in which they communicated always meant it was a one-way stream. If anything had gone wrong, or if he'd somehow missed his slot, he wouldn't know until a few hours later, when his appointment was a no-show.

In the past, Drew had only ever needed to use their services once before.

It had been for a friend of his. A criminal. Convicted of multiple murders in a single gang-and-drug-related incident. Drew had been the one to help his friend evade capture then, and he'd never heard from him since. He supposed that was a good thing. If his friend could disappear, then he hoped he could too.

The sound of a car engine bouncing off the walls disturbed him. For a moment, he held his breath, for fear it was Jake or Charlotte or Liam or Hannah or someone else he'd managed to hurt in the past. But as he realised the number plate was false, he relaxed.

Keeping his body upright, he slid his left hand across to the passenger seat and wrapped his fingers around the flick knife he'd bought months ago as an extra source of protection. He hadn't needed to use it yet, and he hoped he wouldn't have to, but it made him feel safe knowing that he had it in his possession. It reminded him of all those stats that the press banged on about in an attempt to stop people carrying knives. That you're more likely to stab yourself than someone else. Bullshit. He was prepared to defend himself if it came to it, just like all others who carried one. The way he saw it, if you pull a knife out on someone, you intend to hurt them, and you most certainly know what you're doing. It's the ones who don't know what they're doing that get hurt, that become a part of the statistics. And Drew wasn't about to become another one of those.

The driver pulled the car to a stop. It was an old, sky-blue Ford Mondeo with blacked-out windows in the back and a suspension that had been lowered considerably. Whoever owned it was clearly still living in the late nineties.

The driver killed the engine. Drew tightened his fingers around the blade.

Keeping his head low, Drew exited and briskly walked over to the car. As he approached, the driver lowered the window. In the low light, Drew was able to discern the same features of the man he'd encountered last time. The broken nose. The grey hairs on his chin. The missing molar in his mouth.

'Didnae think ah'd be seeing yer face again,' the man said, his Scottish accent thick. The only name Drew had for him was his nickname: The Magnate. Other than that, details were kept scarce.

'It's been a while,' Drew replied as he loosened his grip on the blade in his pocket. 'Surprised you're still going.'

The Magnate grunted. 'Aye, get in the front.'

A little shocked, Drew shuffled round the back of the car and hopped in the passenger side. 'Tightening up security now, are ya?'

'Y'ken wha' they say – cannae be too careful nowadays.'

Without Drew realising it, the man reached into the side compartment of the door, pulled out a gun and pointed it at his chest.

'What? Why?' He'd always had a natural aversion to guns. They were too loud. Too deadly. Too dangerous. Too quick. Not to mention they were too fucking scary to deal with.

'Security.' The Magnate shrugged. 'People like tae think they can tak' things withoot paying for 'em. That's how ah lost this…' He pointed the nose of the gun at his tooth. 'Bastards nearly beat me tae death.'

'All over some documents?'

'People'll do anything tae get oot o' tha country nowadays. Cannae get oot o' this shithole fast enough. Cannae blame 'em really.' The Magnate turned the gun back on Drew. 'Yer pockets – empty 'em.'

Drew swallowed hard. 'Come on, man… is that necessary?'

'Empty 'em!'

Slowly, Drew put his right hand into his pocket and pulled the inside out. Then, he removed his left. At the sight of the small, concealed switchblade, The Magnate's expression remained impassive. Saying nothing, he reached across and snatched the weapon from Drew's grasp.

'Add that tae the collection. Dinnae try it next time, otherwise ah'll mak' sure this is loaded.' The Magnate wiggled the gun in front of Drew's face. 'You have the other thing ah asked for?'

'You didn't ask for it,' Drew said, reaching into his trouser pocket. 'You didn't tell me a price, so I assumed it was the same rate as before. It's not gone up, has it?'

Before the man had a chance to respond, Drew handed him a wad of money that he'd concealed in the inside pocket of his jacket. 'Fifty grand. It's all there. All yours,' he said. 'You're not going to count it, are you?'

The man said nothing and, still keeping the gun pointed at Drew's face, removed a brown envelope from the glove compartment and dropped it onto Drew's lap.

'Yer lobster, sir. Passport. Driving licence. Debit cards. Credit cards. National Insurance number. Twenty-thousand euros o' liquidated assets in an offshore account – all in tha' wee book.' The man removed the gun from Drew's face, slid it back into the door pocket and placed his hands on the steering wheel. 'We're done here. Tak' yer things and leave. Oh, and enjoy the rest o' yer life, Mr McNulty.'

CHAPTER 81

TOP BOY

Vitaly recalled what Tatiana had insisted on reminding him of, like he was a little child. Keep your head down. Don't look at anyone funny. Don't say anything to anyone. Don't even think about anyone. And, most importantly of all, don't do anything to draw attention to yourself.

His errand was simple, so why did they insist on making it so fucking hard?

Vitaly tucked his chin into his chest as he strode along the street, fighting his instinct to look at the short skirt that had just walked past him. A few feet later, he stopped by a red telephone box and turned left. In front of him was an off-licence, and to his right was the entrance to a multi-storey car park.

Keeping his head down, Vitaly entered the off-licence, bounded up to the cash register, grabbed a handful of the nearest pay-as-you-go SIMs from the revolving carousel beside him and slammed them onto the counter.

'Anything else?' the proprietor asked.

'Nah.'

The three of them were rapidly running out of SIM cards to use – especially when they were supposed to destroy them after each and every hit. But that hadn't quite gone to plan – not with the number of contracts they were receiving. They simply didn't have the time.

Emotions in the team were running high following Nigel Clayton's death. None of them spoke about it – they were all aware why it needed to happen – but it didn't make it hurt any less. But that was part of the problem. Nigel's death had hurt him a lot; a lot more than he thought it would. And it was all down to one thing: loyalty. In recent months, Nigel had been a close friend, a confidant – someone he could trust and turn to. And he'd been taught from the start by Georgiy that there were no loyalties in this business. He was beginning to learn why that was the case.

The cashier scanned through the SIM cards, took Vitaly's £50 note and slid the package across. Vitaly grunted by way of thanks as he decanted the SIMs into his jumper pocket. He turned his back on the man and left the shop, his wide shoulders barely fitting through the sliding doors. But as he exited the convenience store, he paused.

Two cars had just exited the multi-storey and were pulling out onto the road. The orange light from the street lamp illuminated the first driver's face. Vitaly recognised him instantly. He'd only spoken to him a few days before: The Magnate, the man who'd been responsible for forging all of their documents and making sure they all had new identities when they needed them, as part of their backup plan.

Then the second car pulled up to the junction. The driver's head was turned the other away, but as the car turned right, heading towards him, Vitaly chanced a closer look.

'I don't fucking believe it,' he whispered to himself in disbelief.

As the car drove past, both men stared at one another.

Vitaly removed his phone and dialled Liam Greene's number, which Georgiy had given to him as a precaution, a countermeasure, just in case.

'Hello?' Liam answered.

'It's Vitaly.'

'How'd you get this number?'

'Not important.'

By now the car had disappeared.

'What do you want?' Liam asked.

'There something you need know.'

'Is anyone in trouble?'

'You can say that.' Vitaly shrugged on his way back to the hideout. 'Ever hear of The Magnate?'

A brief pause. 'The document forger?'

'Yeah.'

'What about him?'

'He just come out of one his meetings.'

'Okay and…?'

'It was a meeting with your top boy… Drew.'

CHAPTER 82

FALLING

Liam let the phone fall from his grip. It clattered and clanged as it bounced beneath the car seat. He didn't care anymore. It was replaceable. Just like everything else in life. Just like Garrison. And just like Drew soon would be.

He'd had enough. Drew had crossed the line several miles back, but Liam had given him the benefit of the doubt time and time again. Time to change that. Drew was a good egg turned bad. The cheeky bastard was thinking of leaving the country and starting a new life abroad, all because he was afraid that the mistake he'd made fifteen years ago would come back to haunt him. Good. He deserved whatever came his way for that.

In a way, this worked in Liam's favour. He couldn't be seen having a rapist on the team as well as a bent cop. The press would have a field day. They were already beginning to harass him, calling with condolences for what had happened to Garrison – as was every other member of the Metropolitan Police Service – and it would only get worse if word got out that Garrison wasn't as stand-up as everyone thought he was.

Liam reached over to the glove compartment. The small light inside illuminated the items in there: the Glock that Henry Matheson had given him and the bottle of Pepsi.

He grabbed the bottle first. It had been a long time since he'd last held one of Henry's patented designs. The bottle was split into three sections, and each section was connected by a screw top. In the middle compartment, hidden behind the Pepsi label, was a bag of cocaine, while the top and bottom thirds were filled with soft drink, so that it looked like a generic consumer product – despite its more sinister and illicit purpose. It was a genius idea and was already proving to be a massive success in the market – one of the many reasons Liam wanted more involvement in it.

He unclipped his seat belt, shuffled forward on his seat and poured the powder onto the dashboard. Using his debit card, Liam shuffled the powder into a line. It emitted a delicate and thin strawberry aroma. He'd heard on the streets that Henry had recently started spraying his drugs with sweet-smelling chemicals because that induced bigger hits of dopamine and serotonin in the brain. But, more importantly, it made the drug more memorable so that its users would keep coming back for more.

Marketing at its finest.

Before he did anything, Liam checked the time. It was 7:30 p.m. He was supposed to be on a date in half an hour.

He made a call. The dialling tone rang in his ears.

'Hello?'

'Tanya, it's Liam.'

'Hey.'

'Can we take a rain check on dinner?'

'Seriously? You're blowing me off?'

'Are you in any position to argue?'

'I thought we were going to talk things through.'

'We are. I just want to put it back to ten o'clock. I'll pick you up from your place on my way home from work, all right?'

'I'm spending the night at yours, am I?'

'This night… next night… night after that… who's counting?'

If all went to plan, the drugs wouldn't be the only source of dopamine in his body.

'Don't be late,' she said before hanging up.

Paying little heed to her comment, he discarded the phone to one side, rolled a ten-pound note from his wallet into a straw, lodged it in his right nostril, pressed the other side closed with his finger and then leant forward to snort.

Three, two, one.

Blast off.

The chemicals rocketed up his nose, burning and abrading the cartilage and skin, giving him an instant hit. And then the Welcome Back party started. His skin tingled. His brain tingled. His muscles. His bones. His entire body.

Liam eased himself back into his seat, falling, falling, falling. He felt elated, alive, euphoric. As though nothing could stop him. As though he was invincible.

A sound in the distance distracted him and he sat bolt upright, alert. The time was 7:45 p.m. Fifteen minutes had gone by in a flash.

It was time to act.

Deciding that he still possessed all of his faculties, he set off for Drew's house.

CHAPTER 83

PAPER HOUSES

The rear patio door opened into a small utility room. Inside, a washing machine thrummed and rotated as it finished the final stages of its cycle, the smell of fabric conditioner and laundry detergent scenting the air.

As his body submitted itself to the cocaine, Liam slipped through the door at the end of the room and entered into the kitchen. The dining room table – if it could be called that – was nothing more than a circular lid approximately three feet across, resting on a four-foot-high plinth positioned right by his feet. The kitchen ran around the edge of the room, with a window looking out onto the garden. He turned his focus to Drew's cupboards and rooted through them; found a glass and poured himself water with some ice from the fridge.

After downing the first glass, he poured himself another and then grabbed a seat at the table.

It turned 8:15 p.m. and there was still no sign of Drew. He was getting tired, bored and restless waiting there. His heart rate was through the roof and he needed movement, excitement, something that would keep up with it.

A minute later, that changed.

The door that led into the hallway was directly ahead of him, and at the other end was the front door to the house. Liam tilted to the side to get a better look as he heard a key turn in the lock.

There he was, the man who had caused him so much stress and anxiety over the past few days, oblivious to Liam's presence. Drew closed the door behind him and started down the corridor. As he entered the kitchen, he switched the lights on. The room illuminated and blinded Liam. As his eyes adjusted to the bright light, he heard a scream.

'Fucking hell, mate,' Drew said, holding his chest. 'T'fuck you doing here?'

'Take a seat.' Liam pointed to the chair opposite him. 'You're a hard man to find.'

Pulling the chair from beneath the table, Drew replied, 'Sometimes that's the point.'

'Was that the point this time?'

'What's this about, Liam? You been drinking again?'

'I can't believe I've never set foot in here before.' Liam fanned his arms, spreading them across the breadth of the room. 'Quite a nice place you've got. You can tell a woman hasn't lived here for a while though. Or has she? I could never tell with you. You always were a secretive bastard, weren't you?'

'How long have you been here…?' There was an introduction of fear in Drew's voice.

Liam sniffed before continuing. 'I don't think you get it, do you?'

'Get what?'

Another sniff.

'That it's not all fucking hunky-dory anymore, Drew. That everything we've worked for in the past few years has gone to shit.'

'Yeah, but we know who's to blame for that, don't we?'

'Who?'

'Jake! Ever since he showed up, he just couldn't get with it, could he? Right from the beginning. Back to Bridger and The Crimsons. He had to stick his nose in and try to get to the bottom of it all. He still is!'

Liam shook his head. 'No… no…'

'You're being a cunt, Liam!' Drew slammed his palms on the table. 'You keep defending him when you know I'm right. He's poison to this department. He's wormed his way in, torn us apart and now look at us. Garrison – he's in the fucking hospital because of Jake.'

'Garrison is the reason Garrison is in the hospital. He put himself there. He went behind our backs for his own gain. He was doing all he could to get as close to The Cabal as possible, and don't kid yourself by thinking that wouldn't mean selling us out if it came to it.'

'But why? He kept saying he couldn't wait to get out of here. That he was done with it all.'

Liam continued to shake his head in disapproval. He lowered his hand into his pocket and wrapped his fingers around the hilt of the gun.

'You've not been a saint either,' he said.

'What's that supposed to mean?'

'You want a fucking list?'

'Only if you've got one.'

'Where do I begin?' Liam asked. 'Hannah Bryant, for starters. What you did to her should have been a sign to me that you're good for nothing in this business. That you're selfish. Conceited. An animal that only looks out for himself. You proved the same thing again tonight.'

'I'm starting to notice a pattern…' Drew replied, his voice surprisingly calm.

'Excuse me?' Liam pulled the weapon out of his jacket pocket and placed it on his knee. The movement was deft and out of sight.

'*You're* the poison of the group,' Drew began. 'You're the one making all these mistakes. Garrison and I were fine before you came along. And then you let that prick Tanner join the team. You're the one who should have noticed Jake's signals long ago, but you never did anything about it. You're the one who let Garrison's behaviour slip by for so long. And don't come at me with that Hannah bullshit – you're the one who kept me on the team despite knowing full well what I'd done.'

'Trust me,' Liam said, the conversation angering him, 'I wanted to send you on your way that night. Believe me. But Dennis persuaded me otherwise. We were good friends and I trusted him. He said you'd made a mistake… that I should give you the benefit of the doubt.'

Drew leant back in his chair, rested his elbow on the chair beside him and placed his leg on his knee.

'How much did you pay this time?' Liam asked, struggling to suppress a smile.

'What are you accusing me of now?'

'Scottish. Middle-aged. Overweight. Sweaty. Mick "The Magnate". But obviously, you knew that already, didn't you?'

'Why you asking then?'

'Because I wanna hear you say it.'

'Say wha…' Drew mouth fluttered open and closed as Liam raised the gun onto the table.

It was time to play.

'You know,' Liam began, licking his lips, 'someone once told me that what we do is like building paper houses. We – as a team, as a collective, as an army of bent coppers and criminals – work hard and risk our arses for the money we make, but if one of the sheets gets damp and ruins the integrity of the structure, then it needs to be taken care of. Garrison was a wet sheet. He's been taken care of. If he hadn't been then everything would have come crumbling to the ground.'

'Paper houses?'

'Paper houses.'

'Are you fucking kidding me? Come on, man. You're not making any sense.'

'I am if you think about it. But you don't think about things, do you? You don't think your actions through. Case in point: Hannah Bryant. You didn't think about what it would do to you and your reputation down the line.'

Drew opened his mouth but Liam silenced him with a wave of the gun. 'Another case in point: The Magnate. I'll ask again – what were you doing with him? Which part of the world is he helping you get to?'

'None of your business!'

Liam aimed the weapon at Drew. 'It is… so tell me.'

'Greece!'

'Greece?'

'I've got some family out there. Long time… I've… I've not seen them for a long time.'

'When do you fly?'

'Tomorrow.'

'And who were you going to tell all of your slippery secrets to?'

'Nobody. Honest. I swear. Liam, you've got to believe me!'

'I do. I do believe you. You won't tell anyone – I get that. I just need to make sure it stays that way.'

Liam raised the gun in the air, aimed it between Drew's eyebrows and pulled the trigger.

| PART 6 |

CHAPTER 84

ABODE

Blood and bits of brain matter splattered against the back wall, abseiling down the paint onto the skirting boards and tiled flooring. Drew's dead body slumped deeper into the chair, teetering over the edge on his left side, his arm dangling like an elephant's trunk. After the piercing ringing stopped in Liam's ears, he brushed himself down, tucked the weapon inside his breast pocket and slipped out of the house through the patio door, being careful not to step on Drew's body or any of the blood.

It was nearly ten, and he was nearly late for his date.

Liam strode towards his car, his footsteps on the stones of Drew's driveway disturbing the serenity of the street around him. He jumped in and snorted, bringing up phlegm from his throat and swirling it around his mouth. He leant out the window and spat a globule onto the pavement, which glistened in the artificial light from the street lamp. The effects of the drugs were beginning to wear off, as if the concentration and adrenaline that had come from shooting Drew had depleted the levels of cocaine in his blood.

More. He needed more.

Just a little bit. No biggie.

Liam reached for the plastic packet in the glove compartment, licked his finger and scraped what he could from the inside. Then he rubbed it into his gums frantically until the friction burnt. It wasn't much, but it was enough. A minor kick to bolster his alertness.

As he started the engine, it only just dawned on him what he'd done. He'd just killed a man with his own finger. Ended a life. Boom. Done. Just like that. Over. Finished. No more.

Good. It was deserved. Thoroughly.

But now there was no time to waste. He knew from his years' worth of experience that criminals always made the biggest mistakes immediately after committing the crime. They usually panicked as they tried to dispose of the body or cover it up, leaving a trail of breadcrumbs for the eager and slightly weathered detective working on the case to find them and arrest them. And Liam had no intention of becoming another statistic.

Tomorrow. He would sort it then. Tomorrow. Yes.

As for his focus right now, he wanted to have his cake and eat it.

Feeling an imaginary musical beat in his head as the drugs started to take over his body, Liam drummed away on the steering wheel and pulled away.

He was at Tanya Smile's house within ten minutes. She lived on the west side of Stratford, a few miles away from his own house. He was forced to drive slowly and conservatively. It would be no good now to get himself in a car accident. He was about to get laid.

Tanya's house was one of those posh, fancy ones that Liam had grown envious of. It was tall, marble white, and had two pillars by the front door at the top of a small flight of steps. To the left of the door was her living room. A dull yellow light escaped through the curtains, distorted by her shadow as she moved about the place.

Liam pulled over, bumped up on the kerb and texted her. Within a few seconds, she was out of the door and bounding towards him. She was wearing her black and white square-patterned blouse and a pair of black trousers and some sandals. Her hair had been cut short and was wavy.

'You're late,' she said, throwing her bag into the footwell.

'Nice,' he said. 'You look nice.'

The drive back to his block of flats was long and never-ending. As they arrived at Liam's building, he pulled into the car park and killed the engine.

'Welcome to my humble abode,' he said sarcastically.

CHAPTER 85

EMPTY

Jake's stomach wouldn't stop rumbling. This was only his second stake-out, and he hadn't anticipated how hungry he would get. In fact, he hadn't anticipated how long he would be forced to wait for Liam's return. The man had been a ghost all day. He wasn't with his friends, his family, or at any of his local hangouts. Jake had even made a visit to the pub and still had no luck finding him.

Until now.

Jake watched eagerly as Liam and the BBC News reporter Tanya Smile entered Liam's block of flats. He was sitting forty yards away, in the car park opposite the building, shadowed by an overhanging tree. In his hands he held one of Elizabeth's professional cameras, fitted with the lens he'd bought her after Ellie was born. It was the one she'd used at university to help her gain her first-class honours. He was under strict instructions not to damage it; if he did, he would have to replace it for her – which was an expense he certainly couldn't afford.

Jake pointed the lens at the two profiles, zoomed in and snapped.

'Gotcha,' he whispered to himself as he lowered the camera from his face. 'Now we know who's been selling our secrets to the hungry wolves.'

As soon as they disappeared out of sight, Jake leapt out of his vehicle and stealthily stalked across the car park, treading lightly and keeping his body low. Less than an hour earlier, Charlotte had given him the green light to gain access to Liam's and Drew's cars by whatever means necessary. Beside the boot of Liam's car, he put on a pair of disposable gloves, removed a set of pins and pick locks from his pocket and started to break in.

Beneath the latex, his fingers jemmied the lock until eventually it gave way and the handle opened. He was in, and it had taken him less time than expected; while he was waiting, he'd practised on his own boot, and in the low light it had taken him several minutes.

A small, red, incandescent light turned on inside the boot, illuminating its entire contents.

There he saw a Tesco bag for life, filled with bottles of sparkling water, a steering-wheel lock and an AA road map. Lurking beneath the map was the corner of another plastic bag. He lifted the map and revealed the two cigarettes he'd spotted earlier, placed inside two evidence bags. In the top corners of the bags were sticky labels. Each had been scored, signed and dated by Liam himself.

Jake stopped breathing momentarily as he pieced together what it all meant. Now it was confirmed that Drew and Liam had been complicit in Garrison's accident. The cigarettes were the evidence he and Charlotte needed. But why were they sealed in evidence bags and made to look as though they'd been found at the crime since to be exhibited as evidence in the case?

The answer didn't take long to form in Jake's mind.

It was an insurance package for Liam. Just in case he needed to use them against Drew. For whatever reason.

Jake shut the boot quietly, moved round to the front of the car, picked the lock and sat in the driver's seat. He gave a cursory glance over the contents of the middle section. There was nothing there except a half-drunk bottle of Pepsi and an empty sandwich bag. Deeming it clear, he leant over to the glove compartment. Before opening it, he swallowed, fearing what might be on the other side.

He opened it, then sighed heavily.

Empty.

Part of him was relieved, though the other part had hoped there would be something inside that they could use to pile the evidence against him. Maybe a weapon, or a packet of drugs, or a wad of cash; maybe even a burner phone that contained all of his illicit activity.

A sound in the distance distracted him – a twig falling to the ground or snapping underfoot. Frightened, his pulse raised, he shut the glove compartment, slipped out of the car and locked it again. Then he hurried back to his own car and made his way to the station.

CHAPTER 86

LONG NIGHT

Jake parked his car beneath a street lamp, out of fear that someone might tamper with it. Might place drugs or money in his car like they had his drawer, vandalise it or even steal it and then make it look like he'd been involved in Garrison's accident somehow. There was no knowing to what extent Liam and Drew would go. There was no knowing how far they were willing to push things.

He gazed up at the station building in front of him, the orange hue tinting his skin. All the lights inside Bow Green were on, although Jake knew there would only be a handful of people inside at this time of night. Bow Green was his second home. A place of refuge. Camaraderie. Friendships. Relationships. There were several fun and joyous memories that had taken place inside the four walls that comprised the Major Investigation Team. And there were also sad, distressing, soul-destroying times.

But, as with anything, the good always outweighed the bad.

Jake carried the evidence bags to MIT. The lights inside almost blinded him. Along the walls were large squares of darkness that gazed out at the street beneath. On the other side of them, the sporadic hum of cars passing the building sounded. Charlotte was the only body in the office. She was busy working at her desk, leafing through documents.

Jake waved. 'Evening.'

'Jake!' she said excitedly. 'I'm glad you're here.'

'You been working all this time?'

'Haven't taken a break,' Charlotte replied, immediately turning her attention back to her work. Beside her keyboard was a half-eaten chicken pasta salad from the Co-Op a few hundred yards from the station.

'What you got?' Jake asked as he approached her. He manoeuvred his way through the desks with the evidence bags in his hand.

'Lots. DNA report on the wallet you found in the warehouse, and the DNA on Michael Cipriano's body and clothes.'

'And?'

'Yours turned up, as was to be expected. But you were right: someone did beat him to death. Nigel Clayton. Again. His DNA was on both the wallet and Michael's body. Maybe he just doesn't wear gloves.'

'He's not a criminal like the others though. He was an accountant, a numbers person, not a hardened criminal who had an eye for being discreet.'

'What do you mean *others*?' Charlotte asked, swinging round on her chair to face him.

Jake pulled up a chair and sat beside her. 'Where's the black van that was left in the warehouse?'

'Gone. Nobody's found it.'

'So it was taken while either Drew or Garrison were on their shift. And Clayton's car was missing also.' Jake paused. 'I forgot to mention it, but when Michael died, there was someone else present. A woman. My head was all over the place; it completely slipped—'

'Are you sure?'

Of course he was sure. He hadn't been able to forget about her. Standing over him, gun in hand, finger on her lips...

There's nobody here...

'She let you go?' Charlotte asked after he'd finished explaining it to her. 'But why?'

Jake shrugged. The answer was beyond him.

'Did she know you were police?'

'Maybe. But it's not like I was wearing uniform or anything.'

Charlotte considered for a moment, grabbed her dinner and spooned a mouthful of pasta into her mouth. 'She might've thought you were a John Doe.' She paused to take another bite. 'Did you write down the reg number of the van after you entered the warehouse?'

Jake nodded and told her what it was.

'I'll run it through. See if it's been picked up since.'

'If it's the same one that they used to transport and kill Danny Cipriano in, then the plates'll be fake. But if you can find anything, I'll be impressed.'

'I've got a few tricks up my sleeve. A couple of people who might owe me a few favours.' Charlotte scribbled some more on the pad and then pointed to the evidence bags on the table. 'Is that what I think it is?'

Jake nodded slowly.

Charlotte reached for them, held them aloft and surveyed them. 'How'd you get them?'

'Liam's boot. He was in his flat. With Tanya Smile.'

Charlotte's eyes widened as she wiped her lips with the back of her hand. 'The BBC News reporter?'

'Unless she's got an identical twin.'

Charlotte said nothing, set the evidence bags down and grabbed her phone. The call had already connected by the time she placed it to her ear.

'Hello?' she said. 'It's me… We need emergency forensics to the office. Is Carl available…? Perfect. Send him down.'

Charlotte hung up, and, just like that, it was taken care of.

'What happens now then?'

'My handler's getting someone to collect the evidence. He'll run some tests on it and then we should see if there's any other DNA on it.'

'How long's that going to take?'

'With him… fingerprints'll take a couple of hours… anything else, a couple of days… minimum.'

Charlotte grabbed her mug of coffee and swirled it.

It was empty.

'I'll get you another one,' Jake said, taking the mug from her. 'I've got a feeling it's gonna be a long night.'

CHAPTER 87

ADDRESS

The hours seemed to drag by without any hint of sunrise climbing through the windows like a character from some Japanese horror film. Jake's eyes felt heavy and a tirade of yawns assaulted him. His body was drained of energy, and to keep himself awake, he strode around the office, forcing himself to stay active. And to stay awake.

He took stock of everything they knew about Liam, Danny Cipriano and everything in between. Danny Cipriano was murdered by The Farmer, a contract killer, and his conspirators. They'd abducted him from witness protection and buried him alive at the construction site. The DNA of Nigel Clayton, an accountant, was discovered at the crime scene. Done. Next up was Richard Maddison, the main suspect – in the eyes of Liam, Drew and Garrison. All bent. Richard was killed in his own flat by The Farmer and his conspirators. Again, Nigel's DNA was discovered at the scene. Then it was Michael Cipriano's turn to suffer the same fate as his brother. Except this time it was different: it was just two of them. Nigel Clayton and a female. Russian. Identity unknown. Had saved his life and spared him.

Who was she, and, more importantly, who was The Farmer?

The million-dollar question.

If they found out who The Farmer was, Jake was hopeful they'd uncover the identity of The Cabal.

Shortly after Charlotte had made the call to her handler, the scene of crime officer, Carl, had retrieved the cigarettes and taken them away to be investigated. Jake and Charlotte had then spent the next few hours conducting tasks that were usually carried out by a team of five or more. They started with Nigel, first checking to see whether he had any registered home addresses. They'd found one that he'd given before he went to prison but, after a quick check, Jake discovered the building had been knocked down and turned into a petrol station with an adjoining convenience store attached to it.

Dead end.

Jake spun on the spot and glanced over at Charlotte. Just as he was about to ask her something, her mobile started ringing.

'Yes?' she answered sleepily. 'I can talk. I'm still at the office with DC Tanner. What's up?'

There was a long pause in the conversation; Jake listened intently.

'Oh, that's perfect. Thank you so much… Yes. Of course. That's understood… Please send it across. I'll log in now.'

Charlotte hung up and placed the phone on the desk. She grabbed a pen and scribbled something on a piece of paper.

'What was that about?' Jake asked.

'We've got the call logs for Liam, Drew, Garrison and Clayton all in one go. My handler's sending them across now.'

'What about the live info from the phone towers? Is he getting that info?'

'He's on it. If they're stupid enough to get their DNA on the bodies, then they might be stupid enough to leave their phones on.'

A large grin grew on Jake's face, and he was unable to shift it until the email arrived in Charlotte's inbox. She printed two copies of the reports and handed one to him. On it was a long list of mobile numbers, dates, times and the duration of the call, side by side with a series of maps that showed the locations of the calls. So much data, such little time.

'Jake,' Charlotte began, 'bear in mind that these are calls that have been made by phones registered in their names in the last twelve months. If Liam, Drew or Garrison have done anything on unregistered numbers, then we won't have it. Unless we can find the phones they might have been using. Did you find any in Liam's car?'

Jake shook his head and then turned towards Liam's office. 'Bet there's a gold mine of answers in there,' he said.

'No, we can't.' Charlotte lifted her glasses onto her forehead and massaged her face, deep in thought.

'Course we can. What if I search the office for something to do with Danny's murder?' Jake asked. 'I go in there, find a phone and it starts ringing. That seems suspicious to me so I leave it. I wait for the call to finish and then inspect the phone.'

'Jake…'

He lifted himself out of his chair and edged towards Liam's office. It was unlocked.

The smell of alcohol lingered in the air – the kind that seeps through your pores; the kind that doesn't wash off after a shower the morning after the night before. Jake ignored it and made about the room, tentatively, cautiously. He couldn't shake the paranoia of feeling like he was being watched, monitored, or at any time Liam might knock on the door and ask him what the fuck he was doing. Composing himself, chiding himself for being stupid and thinking such things, Jake searched through Liam's drawers by his desk. Lifted everything out. Nothing. He left them and turned his attention to the filing cabinet in the corner of the room.

The top drawer was filled with paperwork and folders. As was the second. So, as he reached the bottom, Jake didn't hold out too much hope.

He placed his hand underneath the handle and pulled.

His breathing stopped as he recognised what was inside. A bottle of whiskey and a mobile phone.

'Oh, Liam,' he said. 'Liam, Liam, Liam.'

Jake called Charlotte into the room and she came bounding over.

'What is it?'

Jake showed her. 'A burner I reckon.'

'Don't touch it. Let me get some gloves and an evidence bag.' Charlotte exited and then reappeared a few moments later with an evidence bag and her hands clad in blue latex gloves. She reached inside the cabinet, removed the phone and took it back to her desk.

'This is adding to the already-long list of paperwork we need to fill out once this is all done,' Jake remarked.

A smirk grew on Charlotte's face. 'Paperwork is what makes this job what it is.'

'Think we're going to need to put your priorities straight.'

Charlotte placed the phone on her desk, turned it on and scrolled through the most recent calls. Jake grabbed the printouts and set them beside the phone. They spent the next couple of minutes cross-referencing the numbers in the address book and the numbers in the log.

Shortly after, they had a hit. Several.

Jake ran his finger along the row on the sheet.

'It's a landline number. Mobile phone accessory shop. Elm Road,' Jake said after looking at the corresponding location on the map.

'Perfect for money laundering,' she replied. 'Let's check it out. I'll pack this up, you call SO19. Get the AFOs in. These are people who have access to firearms. I don't want to leave anything to chance.'

CHAPTER 88

LEAVING BEHIND

Blue flashing lights illuminated the street, marauding their way into buildings and windows and people's private lives. Jake and Charlotte were the first to arrive and waited for the remaining officers to attend the scene. The location they'd uncovered was a mobile phone accessory shop on Elm Road, just west of Bow Green. It was small, quaint and, for the most part, inconspicuous – save for the vibrant green facia that adorned the door and the walls. The front of the building housed glass windows, and the displays were complete with mobile phones, refurbished laptops and games consoles, as well as row upon row of every conceivable type of mobile accessory – cases, chargers, screen protectors, selfie sticks. The works.

An armed response vehicle pulled up beside them. Five men clad in black clothing and protective gear, armed with SIGs erupted from the van and approached the building quietly. Four of them spread either side of the entrance, while one of them hurried towards the door – deftly and silently. He bent down beside the lock and forced it open. As soon it was, the armed officers screamed, 'Armed police! Come out with your hands on your head!'

It wasn't the criminal's chance they deserved, but it was one they got. When there was no response, it was time to send in the police dog. Bounding out the back of a dog van was a German Shepherd dressed in its own bodysuit. Attached to a lead still, it raced towards the front door. As soon as they were within a few feet of the entrance, the handler let the dog off and it ripped into the building, tearing its way through the lobby and into the back rooms. Within seconds, its deep and powerful barks disappeared and became muffled, almost silent.

Less than a minute later, the hound returned, panting, exasperated, tongue dangling from its mouth, dripping saliva.

Next, it was the armed officer's turn to enter the property. Once the dog was back with its handler, the officers flooded in – weapons raised, faces concealed, screaming the same two words that managed to prickle the hairs on the back of Jake's neck every time he heard them. Armed. Police.

Jake cast his gaze left and right, observing the length of the street. Within minutes, on the outskirts of the perimeter that had been set up by the uniformed officers, residents from the surrounding homes had allowed their curiosity to get the better of them. Most were wrapped in their dressing gowns. Some graced everyone around them with a view of their shirtless chests, despite the nip in the air. Others were fully clothed, hugging themselves for warmth.

Jake paid them little heed.

Two minutes later, the five armed officers returned, holding their weapons in both hands still. None of them seemed out of breath, and none of them seemed fazed by the adrenaline surging around their body.

Charlotte and Jake approached them.

'What you got?' Jake asked.

'Empty,' one said. Jake assumed him to be the senior officer. 'Nobody's in there.'

'Any signs of life at all?'

The officer shook his head. 'Everything's been shipped out. Whoever was in there has done a full sweep.'

Jake kicked the pavement beneath him.

'Very well,' Charlotte said, hiding the frustration in her voice. She turned to Jake. 'Let's get forensics in. They might have left something behind. And, if they have, we'll be onto them.'

CHAPTER 89

RECORDINGS

The soft light of morning, tinted a shade of blue by the low-hanging clouds, filtered in through Liam's bedroom windows, rousing him. He was a light sleeper – always had been. His mind was too active – bordering on the paranoid – and he always struggled to sleep. Even the slightest disturbance would wake him. And the drugs hadn't helped either.

Tanya was lying beside him, her body radiating warmth through her soft and delicate skin. Last night it had taken her an entire two minutes to explain herself and defend her actions before he eventually forgave her. It wasn't her fault at all; that onus lay with Garrison – and the man was exactly where he deserved to be.

And then it had taken them another two minutes to make up.

Twice.

Tanya was wrapped beneath his duvet, snuggled up to her ears, facing away from him. Liam shuffled closer to her body, linking his arms around her. He pulled her gently into his chest and squeezed.

'Morning,' she said, keeping perfectly still.

'Sorry. I didn't mean to wake you.'

'It's all right. I needed to wake up soon anyway.'

'Sleep OK?'

'Perfect. You?'

'Even better.' He kissed the back of her neck. She wore her bra still, and his hand ran up and down her back before it fumbled the catch and released it.

'Not now,' she said, turning onto her back. 'Sorry.'

'I just need something to get me in the mood for work.'

'We could talk about that instead. You didn't say much about it last night.'

Liam propped himself up on his elbows. 'And who's to blame for that?'

Tanya rolled over and faced him, flashing that grin he adored.

'But in all seriousness,' she continued, breaking him from his thoughts. 'We need to talk about it. You don't seem to be coping well. I've never seen you so cagey and tense.'

'It's all up the fucking spout. You're about the only person I can trust at the moment, surprisingly.'

'How so?'

He hadn't told her about Drew. And he'd only been brief on the details surrounding Garrison's accident. He didn't want her to know how much of an involvement he had, afraid of what she might think of him. Afraid that she might suffocate their relationship and cut off its air supply, the same way Danny Cipriano had died.

'Garrison went behind my back with you and the Cipriano murders. He was trying to cover them up when I was trying to solve them. And I think Drew might have been responsible for what happened to him. He's got this rape allegation he's trying to defend and he's getting paranoid. Garrison's the only one who knows what happened. And I think he might have tried to silence him.'

'But what's that got to do with you?'

Liam paused. 'Because Drew knows I'm onto him. He knows I know about it all. He's paranoid.'

'Are you sure *you're* not just being paranoid? These people have been your friends for years now. I can't imagine they would betray your trust like that.'

You and me both.

He shrugged. 'I suppose you're right.'

'Of course I am. I'm a woman. We're always the voice of reason and logic. I know enough about you to know that you assume the worst about all situations.'

'It's called being—' Liam stopped, his mind wandering. 'Wait, what did you just say?'

'That I know enough about you—'

'Before that.'

'That of course I was right – I'm a woman…'

'Yes, but no. You mentioned about being the voice of reason.'

Tanya lifted herself onto her elbows, pulling the duvet up to her chest as she did. 'I don't see the significance.'

Liam looked away from her, then his eyes fell onto her lap. 'What other woman is the voice of reason?' he whispered to himself.

'Your mum?' Tanya answered, uncertain.

Without saying anything, Liam leapt off the bed, raced through the hallway and into the living room. The remnants of the previous night's Chinese takeaway sat on the open-plan kitchen counter – and there, on Liam's dining room table, was his laptop. He retrieved it and returned to the bedroom.

'What's going on?' Tanya asked. She looked a little frightened.

Liam ignored her and opened the computer, his mind working on autopilot. The home screen loaded, and he launched a piece of software on his desktop. It was the audio software Drew had installed for him after he'd placed the bugs in his targets' cars. On the home page was a list of devices the software was currently tracking. Beside it was the time and date of the last recording and the location. Liam clicked on the top result, pressed the space bar and listened. The timestamp dated it yesterday lunchtime.

At first there was the sound of background static noise. Then the voices began.

'Guv?' Charlotte's voice said, loud and clear.

'Liam, what is—' Tanya interrupted, but he silenced her with a wave of his hand.

'This is proof that I'm not going insane,' he replied.

Liam blanked her and returned his attention to the audio recording.

'I'm OK. We've just had another incident. DC Pete Garrison. Road traffic collision apparently. Looks dodgy to me.'

'What do you need?'

'Phone and financial records of DCI Liam Greene and DS Drew Richmond.'

'Anything else?'

'Search warrants for their home addresses and vehicles.'

'Leave it with me. Anything else?'

'No, sir.'

'Are we near to a breakthrough?'

'Yes, sir. It's imminent. DC Tanner and I will have Liam and the contract killers in custody very soon.'

'Good.'

There was a brief pause and for a moment Liam wondered whether the conversation had finished.

Then the man on the other end continued. 'How are things? Your health, well-being?'

'Fine.'

'Missing the family?'

'I'll be all right.'

'You sure?'

'Yeah. I've got her ashes, some photos. Work is helping take my mind off it all.'

'I'm sure,' the voice said. 'But if you need anything, just let me know. I'll get those documents over to you as soon as I can.'

'Cheers, guv. Appreciate it.'

The line went dead and the recording stopped shortly afterwards.

Liam stared into the pixels of the screen until his eyes became fuzzy and accustomed to the harsh brightness. He instantly felt physically sick, like he wouldn't make it to the bathroom, and his carpet would have a new indelible stain on it.

'Liam?' A distant voice called to him. 'Liam?'

It was Tanya.

'Liam!' she said, this time touching him.

He startled back to reality and snapped his head towards her.

'What was that all about?'

'It's… it's my… I fucking knew it!' Anger swelled inside of him like a rising tide inside a cave, and he needed somewhere to release it. 'Those fucking… snakes…' He screamed, filling the room with a deep roar.

'You're scaring me, Liam,' Tanya replied. 'Calm down. Please. What's going on? Talk to me.'

Liam kept his distance. He'd never hit a woman in his life, but that didn't mean he wouldn't. Not if she got too close. He hadn't felt this much rage in a long time, and his knuckles had never recovered properly since then – neither had the man's face he'd bashed into oblivion.

'My team. Jake. The new one, Charlotte. They're coming after me for Danny's and

Michael's murders – and now Garrison's incident. I bet they're working with Drew. I bet they have been all this time.'

'Why? Why would they be coming after you? Is it true?'

'No! Of course it isn't true. I had nothing to do with any of them. They're looking for someone to blame it on.'

'Is it going to come back to me?' Tanya asked. She slid her legs off the side of the bed, clasped her bra together and pulled on a top that had been thrown to the floor before the sex began.

'What?' Liam snapped.

'Is it going to come back to me? The phone calls. The call logs. Are they going to realise we're working together?'

Liam shook his head in disbelief. 'You really think that's what I'm worried about right now?'

'No, but *I* am. *I've* got a career to look after too. It's not all about your sodding life, Liam.'

Liam ignored her. He hurried to his wardrobe, grabbed a white shirt and started pulling it on.

'Where are you going?' Tanya asked. It was beginning to feel like they were having a couple's argument. The kind where he was in the wrong, and he was running away from his responsibility of talking it through with her.

He chose not to answer.

She rounded the bed and approached him. His adrenaline was running and his pulse bounding. She touched him on the arm, and, to his surprise, the anger inside his body dissipated slightly. 'I've never seen you like this. You're scaring me. I don't like it.'

'I'm going to Tanner's house. I need to have a word with his wife. Speak with his family for a bit.'

'Why?'

'There are some things I think his wife deserves to know. No doubt they've got the call logs already. Jake is the only one who can stop this from going any further. I'm sorry, Tanya, but I've got to go and finish this.'

CHAPTER 90

NINETY-NINE PER CENT

Jake's head hit the table – hard. It was nearing six o'clock in the morning, and he hadn't slept a wink. His body was almost running on empty, and it wasn't something a full English breakfast or copious amounts of coffee could fix. He needed sleep, and he needed it now.

He and Charlotte had returned to the office immediately after their failed raid on the mobile phone shop, dejected and a little defeated.

Their options were running low. And Jake couldn't help feel like they were rapidly running out of time too. They didn't know who they were looking for; nor did they know where to look for them. The final piece of the puzzle wasn't fitting into place. For all they knew, The Farmer and his associates could have left the country by now.

It was something that didn't bear thinking about. It would do no good to assume the worst.

'Coffee?' Charlotte asked, her head peering like a jack-in-the-box over the partition that separated their desks.

Jake paused while the cogs in his brain slowly began to rotate. 'If I have any more,' he said, 'I won't have anything else left in my stomach. It's running straight through me.'

Charlotte paused and gave a disapproving look. 'Disgusting.'

Jake chuckled. 'Sorry. Sometimes I forget where I am.'

Charlotte smiled and disappeared into the kitchen. As she started to boil the kettle, the office doors opened and Lindsay Gray entered. She carried a laptop bag in one hand and a cup of coffee in the other. She had a set of white headphones buried deep in her ears. As soon as she noticed Jake, she pulled them out and wandered over to his desk.

'Morning!' she said vibrantly. 'Didn't think I'd see you here this early.'

'We've been here all night. Are you usually here at this time?'

'Every morning. This place isn't going to run itself, you know.' Lindsay took a sip of her drink and paused. 'Is it just you and Charlotte?'

'Yeah. She's out back.'

'Still trying to get somewhere with this Cipriano case?'

Jake scoffed. 'And the rest, Lindsay. It's never-ending.'

'You guys close, or…?'

'Closer than we have been,' Jake said, making sure not to share any particulars. Not because he didn't trust her, but because Charlotte had instructed him not to discuss it with anyone. He appreciated Lindsay's effort at making small talk nonetheless.

'I'm sure you'll get to the bottom of it.'

Lindsay placed her hand on his back, resting it there. 'I heard about what happened to Garrison,' she said, glancing over at Pete's desk. 'It's devastating. Truly.'

'We're going to find the cause of it, don't worry.'

'Have you heard anything since it happened?'

'What do you mean?'

'I mean, have you heard the latest? He's in a coma. They don't think he'll ever wake up.'

Jake's pulse slowed. 'How do you know?' He felt slightly offended that someone outside his team knew that information before he did.

'I'm here all day every day, almost. I hear the gossip. It must have been while you were out. I think Liam told everyone. Apparently, Garrison put him down as an emergency contact.'

Jake stared up at her, devoid of any emotion and sentiment. Before he could think of anything to say, Charlotte returned.

'I'll leave you two to it,' Lindsay said. 'You both look really busy.'

Just as Jake's thoughts began to turn towards Garrison in his hospital bed, his phone rang. He glanced at the caller ID, recognised who it was, and stepped away.

'Hello?' he said, keeping his voice low.

'DC Tanner?' a bored, robotic voice asked. 'It's Jemimah; I'm calling from the lab. I'm calling regarding the document you requested the original, unaltered files for? Case number CS/7163949/E.'

'And?'

'I decided to run the evidence through on the case again. We still had it locked up somewhere. A new report's being sent to your email now.'

Jake thanked Jemimah, told her he owed her one, hung up, and then checked his email.

'What's going on?' Charlotte asked as he returned to his desk.

'I'm waiting for a—'

His phone chimed. He read the email, his palms clamming up as his eyes scanned the document.

'I don't believe it,' he whispered, a knot forming at the pit of his stomach.

'What is it?'

'Hannah Bryant. The engineer witness at Danny's burial site. One of the reasons you're here. Well, a few years ago, while he was still a PC, Drew raped her, but the case was brushed to one side and thrown away. This is the file confirming Drew as the suspect, and pointing the finger at him with ninety-nine per cent accuracy.'

'Jesus,' Charlotte replied, stunned.

'I have to go. There's somewhere I need to be.'

'Where?'

Jake started towards the exit, stopped and turned to face her. 'I need to see an old friend.'

CHAPTER 91

CONSOLATION

Jake Tanner lived on a quaint, narrow street. Cars were parked on either side of the road, leaving a gap large enough for one stream of traffic. Giant oak trees were interspersed evenly along the pavement like the holes in a belt, casting large, ominous shadows over the houses.

Liam was seated inside his car with the window rolled down, stationed directly outside Jake's house. He rubbed his hands up and down the steering wheel, preparing himself. He had a speech in his head, a plan, a sequence he wanted their conversation to follow. He'd rehearsed it several times on the way down. But the reality was, life wasn't a play: it didn't go exactly how you wanted it to. So far, the past few days had been a testament to that. Liam hoped this next conversation would be different.

He picked up his camera from the passenger seat, exited the car and made his way to Jake's front door. Sounds of a child screaming echoed from the other side. He knocked.

Within seconds, the door opened and he was greeted by a flustered-looking Elizabeth. She was in her pyjamas and her hair was a mess, yet she still looked elegant and beautiful – the crush that he had on her definitely wasn't abating. And he thought it never would.

'Liam! Are you all right? What're you doing here?' she asked, wrapping herself up in her dressing gown.

Liam said nothing. It didn't take long for her to begin thinking the worst.

'Oh my God.' She threw her hand to her mouth. 'Jake? Is it… Is he… Is everything all right?'

'Can I come in?'

Elizabeth wailed, her voice carrying up and down the corridor. Her eyes welled and her cheeks turned red.

'Mummy!' came a voice from within the house. 'Who is it?'

At that moment, Maisie Tanner entered the corridor, holding a bottle of water in her hand.

'This is one of Daddy's friends, sweetie,' Elizabeth said as Maisie hurried towards her. When she reached her leg, Elizabeth bent down and picked her up.

'Can I come in?' Liam repeated.

'Yes. Yes… Yes, please come in.' She stepped to the side and allowed him through.

Liam breathed a sigh of relief. One of the hardest parts was out of the way.

He stopped by the entrance, indicated at his shoes and asked, 'Shall I?'

'No. Please keep them on. Go into the kitchen. You're scaring me, Liam. Is everything all right?'

He waited until he was in the kitchen before responding. 'Jake's perfectly fine,' he said, coming to a stop beside Ellie in her high chair. He stroked her cheek and ruffled her brown hair. 'He's not in any danger.'

'Are you sure?' Elizabeth asked. She set Maisie down on the kitchen counter. 'He didn't come home last night. But he texted a while ago to say he was still at work. Has anything happened to him?'

'No,' he said. 'He's perfectly safe. But I just wanted to pop by because…' He hesitated for effect. 'This isn't easy for me to say, Elizabeth…'

'What? What is it?'

'There's something you need to know about Jake.'

'Tell me.'

Liam let go of Ellie's hair. 'How have you two been recently?'

'Fine. Why?' Elizabeth replied, instantly getting her back up.

'At work, he's mentioned a couple of times that you two have been struggling... financially.'

'He did *what*?'

'He's only told me. Nobody else in the office knows. I think he was quite ashamed of it. But he said that he'd been looking into methods of trying to pay off some of your debts.'

'Yeah,' Elizabeth said sharply. 'I found him looking at gambling sites the other night.'

Liam pursed his lips and shook his head. 'I'm not talking about gambling sites, Elizabeth. The other day I found something in his drawer.' He paused. 'A large sum of money. I think there was about ten thousand in there. Maybe more.'

He took out his phone, scrolled to the photo he'd taken of the money and showed it to her. 'I questioned him on it, but he didn't tell me where he got it from. I think... I'm worried he might be doing something dodgy. Something he shouldn't be. There's a lot of corruption in our job. They're lured in by the money. Most of it's just turning a blind eye to drug deals and things like that. But I wanted to make sure you knew about it before I took it further – higher up the chain.'

'You can't!' Elizabeth snapped, struggling to tear her eyes away from the photo.

'I have to, Elizabeth. This is a professional conduct matter. He's broken several regulations, not to mention the law.'

Elizabeth took a step back, bashing into the kitchen counter behind her. Her fingers began trembling as the shock set in. That was the first couple of jabs. Now it was time for the right hook. The finisher.

'There's something else as well.'

'More?'

'Unfortunately.' He paused again, building the suspense. 'Has Jake ever mentioned Charlotte's name to you before?'

Elizabeth shook her head, her eyes wide with fear.

'She's new to our team,' he continued. 'She's been with us for a few months now. Just over half a year. They spend a lot of time in the office together. Going for lunches. Coffees. Chatting. Laughing. Giggling. At first, I didn't think anything of it, but then… the other night…' He cleared his throat as he picked up the camera. 'The other night I saw them together in the pub.

I had my camera in my car and… I'll let you scroll through them.'

Liam nudged the camera towards Elizabeth. At first, she didn't touch it – simply glared at it, as if willing it to self-destruct with her mind. But then, as the tears started to well in her eyes again, she took the camera and held it, her wrist shaking. Liam watched as she scrolled through the photos of Jake and Charlotte at The Head of the House. Before leaving the flat, he'd placed all the relevant images on a new memory card and slotted it in the device. The last image was the money shot – the shot that he'd been fortunate enough to capture.

'Oh my God,' Elizabeth said as she clicked to the final image. She set the camera down and wiped away her tears. Maisie, who was still perched on the edge of the counter, asked what was wrong. Elizabeth didn't reply.

'I'm sorry, Liz,' Liam said after a while. 'I haven't shown these images to anyone else, but I thought you should know. I'll leave this here for you.' Liam tapped on the device and then made to leave.

As he opened the door, he stopped on the half turn. 'I know it's not much of a consolation,' he added, 'but I want you to know that I'm always here for you if you need me.'

Liam opened the door, stepped into the street and started towards his car, a smile growing on his face. It was done. Dusted. Everything Jake held dear to him was about to come crumbling down. And Liam was going to be there when it happened.

As he climbed into the car, his mobile rang. 'Yes?' he answered.

'You've got an issue. You need to get down to Drew's house now.'

His smile didn't last long.

CHAPTER 92

TALK

Drew's car was still parked on the driveway of his detached house in Chigwell and didn't look as though it had moved at all; in the night, there had been light rainfall, and there was a clear patch of pavement beneath Drew's car. It was just after eight, and there was no excuse for Drew to be late for work, even if the lazy son of a bitch was nursing a hangover or something.

Jake bent his knees and peered through the letterbox. Morning light from the kitchen flooded into the hallway, illuminating the solid wood flooring and the bottom of the staircase. Jake squinted, hoping it would give him a better view.

Something caught his attention. An obstruction in the door frame. A leg and a dangling arm.

Fuck sake. He's wasted.

Jake tried knocking on the door until his knuckles hurt, but it was no use. Drew didn't stir.

'Oi!' he yelled through the letterbox. 'Drew! Wake up – it's Jake!'

Still nothing.

Jake sighed heavily and moved round the side of the house, searching for an entry point. He found it in the form of a small side gate that led to the garden. It was ajar. Jake had only been to Drew's house on two previous occasions – to celebrate Drew's fifteenth anniversary in the service, and for a premature Christmas team outing. On both instances, there'd been no mention of Drew's wife; nor had there been any sign of her. And, also on both instances, Drew had instructed them to enter the property round the side. So it didn't strike him as odd that the gate was ajar. Perhaps a minor mistake, a lapse in judgment. The alcohol making Drew forget.

Jake ambled along the side of the house, made a left turn and stopped by the utility room. He slowly opened the door, his suspicions growing the nearer he got. The hinges squeaked and screamed at him as he teased the door wider.

'Drew?'

Silence.

'Drew?'

Still nothing.

Jake crossed the threshold into the property and tensed, preparing for something – or someone – to jump out at him covered in blood, rabid. He'd been watching too many late-night films while the girls were asleep.

The utility room was empty, but the smell of washing detergent and conditioner lingered in the air. There was a full load in the washing machine, presumably left over from the night before. Jake walked to the end of the room and made a right turn.

Then he froze.

On the wall was a spray of blood, crimson droplets running down the paint. Some had coagulated and dried and were beginning to crust over in the morning sun, while the puddle on the floor was thick and a darker shade of red.

'Drew…' Jake's voice was nothing but a whisper.

The sight in front of him made him want to be sick. A large hole had been blown out of Drew's bloody, disfigured head, and there were bits of bone and brain matter running down the back of his neck and into his blazer. His hair was matted and dampened by the blood.

Jake retched. He opened his mouth to breathe, but it only aggravated the sensation.

He threw his hand to his mouth and sprinted out of the house. Feeling disorientated and nauseous, he staggered into the door frame of the utility room and froze solid as he stared out of the doorway. Somebody was blocking his way. His heart leapt into his mouth, and he swallowed the mouthful of vomit that had risen through his throat.

'You're not going anywhere just yet, Jake,' Liam said, pointing a gun at him. 'We need to talk.'

CHAPTER 93

THE CONFESSION

Jake's throat tightened; he was petrified. Looking directly at the man who had put one colleague in a coma and shot another in the head in cold blood.

This is it. This is how I'm going to die.

Jake spoke, hoping he didn't sound as nervous as he felt. 'What... what're you doing here, Liam?'

'I've come to return this.' Liam wiggled the Glock 17 in the air.

'Is that what you used to kill Drew?'

'He used it on himself.'

'Don't lie to me. Just tell me the truth. Is that what you used to kill Drew with?'

'Yes,' Liam said defiantly, like he didn't care about the ramifications of his actions. 'Drew was becoming a problem for us all.'

'A problem for who?'

'For me. Georgiy. Our mutual employer—'

'What are you talking about, Liam. Who's Georgiy? Who's your mutual employer?'

Liam ignored the question. 'Drew was a burden, and I was fed up cleaning his mess. Now the only thing I have to clean up is his *actual* mess.' Liam pointed to the pool of dense blood that had formed by the skirting board.

'I can't let you do that. I can't let you do anything else. You've hurt too many people.' Jake reached into his pocket, pulled out his phone and started to call Charlotte.

Liam waggled the gun. 'Please don't do that. I said we need to talk.' He sighed. 'I have a confession to make, Jake.'

Jake kept the phone pressed against his ear. On the other end, Charlotte answered. Confused by the silence, she called his name.

'Then let's talk,' Jake said, using his thumb to turn down the volume of Charlotte's voice.

Liam reached out his other hand. 'Give me the phone.'

'I'm not going to do that, Liam.'

'How much more is it going to take for you to do as I say, Jake? Give me the phone.'

In his ear, Jake heard Charlotte instruct him that she understood he was under distress, that she was going to help him. With all the Queen's horses and all the Queen's men.

That was all he needed to hear.

'OK, OK,' Jake said, lowering the device from his face. 'Fine. You can have it. It's all yours.'

Jake disconnected the call and lobbed it to Liam. The phone was suspended for what felt like an abnormally long moment, but eventually, Liam caught it, threw it to the ground and stamped on it. Glass smashed and scattered across the tiled flooring.

'You'll be able to buy a new one no doubt… with the special delivery I left in your drawer.'

'That was you?'

'Nothing like a little bit of blackmail. You know, I *really* wanted to believe that you were onside. When Drew told me, I was overjoyed. Ecstatic even. But then I realised that was never going to happen. You were never going to turn bent. So I had to make it look like you were. All it will take is a tip-off to the DPS and they'll have you for corruption, money laundering, handling stolen goods, misconduct in a public office and anything else they can chuck at you.'

'You would never have been able to make it stick,' Jake protested.

'Of course I would. When you add it to the fact that you're in debt, that you're struggling financially and that your details have been on the Dark Web – I could have made *anything* stick. And if that wasn't the cherry on the cake, then this was.' Liam reached into his pocket and produced his mobile. He unlocked the device, loaded an image and showed it to Jake.

Jake stepped forward for a better look. He froze as soon as he realised what he was looking at. It was an image of his family – Elizabeth and the girls in the park, sitting on a bench. Relaxing. Enjoying themselves.

Liam swiped to the next image. This time it was of a man and Elizabeth frozen together, exchanging something.

'What is this?' Jake asked.

'Nothing alarming,' Liam began. 'I was watching them yesterday, and Elizabeth dropped something. This man helped her pick it up. Entirely innocuous. But to someone who doesn't know the context… this looks like a drug deal of some description. Or maybe she's a sex worker taking a payment from her next client. Imagine that: a police officer deep in debt, using proceeds from organised crime not to pay off the debt but to fuel his wife's drug habit. Ouch. It doesn't make for good reading, does it? And I'm sure my friends in the media could make it look even worse than it really is. People will believe anything they read nowadays.'

Jake's chest rose and fell heavily, his body seething with anger. Liam was a much more malignant, manipulative and calculating individual than Jake had even imagined – and ever given him credit for.

'I went to see her this morning as well, your gorgeous wife. She really is beautiful. I still can't work out how you've managed to pull that one out of the bag,' Liam said. 'No one can.'

'What did you do?' Jake asked through gritted teeth.

'Just showed her a couple of photos. Told her about the money in your drawer. She was wondering where you got to the other night – when you were really late, having drinks with Charlotte…'

At the mention of Charlotte's name, Jake's lips parted.

'Yeah, I know about that,' Liam continued. 'I was there. I was going to have a couple of drinks, treat myself. But when I saw you two, I realised you'd given me an even bigger treat. Although, I don't think Elizabeth appreciated seeing the photos I managed to get of you both. Charlotte's quite *hands-on,* isn't she? Very touchy-feely. Why did you have to get her involved, Jake? I never thought you had it in you to roll over and grass on your mates. Who's she working for? The DPS? The IPCC? We looked out for you. Took you in. You don't know how many times we saved you. Somebody wanted you dead. Somebody still does. You're alive because of *me*.'

Liam hesitated a moment to catch his breath. 'I didn't stay around long enough to find out what Elizabeth thought of it all. But she's still got the photos as evidence, so I expect she'll be staring at them all day, plotting some sort of revenge, working out what she's going to do with the kids, her belongings. Who knows? She might be packing her bags as we speak. But that's conjecture. I mean, she's your wife. You know her better than anyone.'

Jake's mind raced with myriad thoughts. He didn't know where to begin. He should have been thinking about his wife and the damage Liam had done to their relationship. But he wasn't – couldn't. Not when there were bigger questions that needed answering.

'Who wants me dead?'

'The Cabal,' Liam replied. 'You've heard that name by now. In fact, I know you have.'

Jake looked at Liam, stunned. 'I thought *you* were The Cabal.'

Liam chuckled. 'What gave you that impression?'

'Michael Cipriano. He said the only person he ever knew, the only one who dealt with him and The Crimsons used to call him a good egg. I thought...'

'Afraid not, kid. I just helped form The Crimsons. I was the one who discovered them... on behalf of The Cabal. Made them who they were, helped them evade justice for so long. But as for The Cabal... it's bigger than you can imagine. And, by the way, they still want your head.'

'Why?'

'Because we want you to back the fuck off and let us carry on with what we're doing. There are a lot of things going on behind the scenes that you don't know about. Lots of facets to this organisation. We've got a lot of money still left to make in this business and The Cabal doesn't want it ruined by you.'

'How have you saved me then?'

'Aren't you listening? The Cabal wanted you dead. I said no.'

'Did he want Garrison and Drew dead too?'

'Garrison and Drew were different,' Liam replied. 'They'd spent years fucking things up. It only reached a head after Danny died.'

'How?'

'Garrison was getting too big for his boots. Going behind my back. Telling The Cabal about every cock-up I made. I think he wanted some extra brownie points before he retired.'

'So you tried to kill him?'

Liam held his hands up in mock surrender. 'I had nothing to do with that. I didn't touch any of it. I just orchestrated it. Drew and Georgiy simply followed my orders.'

'Who's Georgiy?'

No response.

'Is Georgiy The Farmer, Liam?'

Still no response. Jake tried a different angle. 'How did it happen?' he asked. 'What happened to Garrison?'

'There are only two people who can tell you that. One of 'em's dead on the other side of this wall.'

'And the other's Georgiy…'

'If you can find him. He has a habit of not wanting to be found.'

'He can't run forever.'

'The Cabal's been doing it ever since this whole thing started. Nobody knows who they are or where the fuck they are. Not even me. And you think Georgiy can't do the same?'

'You can tell me where he is,' Jake bargained.

'My head will be on a stick next if I do that.'

'Who else works for him? Where are they?'

Liam wiped his forehead free from sweat using the back of his sleeve. In that split second, while Liam's concentration was broken, Jake contemplated lunging at the man and detaining him, but by the time he'd decided upon it, Liam's focus was back on him.

Jake moved the conversation along. He wanted to find out all he could before Charlotte arrived. There was no knowing how much Liam would share in a police environment.

'What about Drew?' he asked. 'Why did he deserve to die?'

'Drew was a mistake, a wrong'un. He should've never been a part of this team. He should've never been a police officer. He couldn't do anything right. I know you found the cigarettes, and I know you found out about the rape allegation. And the bloody son of a bitch thought he could leave the country without me knowing, or thinking I wouldn't ever find out. He was a liability.'

'A liability you couldn't afford?'

'Precisely,' Liam said, dipping his head.

'And what about me? I've been the one to throw open your investigation the most – why haven't you killed me? Why haven't you tried to silence me like you did the others? Or have you finally come to do it now?'

Liam shook his head and, to Jake's surprise, lowered the weapon.

'It's complicated. I tried to get you out of this. In truth, I never wanted you to become involved in any of it. You're too young. Too naïve. You have too much promise; the rest of your career ahead of you. A family. None of us had that. And I didn't want you to ruin your life by following the same path as we did. In the long run, it wasn't worth it. It still isn't.'

'How can you say that when you've just planted evidence against me and told my wife I've been having an affair?'

'I don't want to kill you, Jake – only ruin your life like you've done mine. There are people I know in certain places who could have got the drugs and the money and the affair off your record and wiped it clean. They would have transferred you to another department in a different borough, perhaps, but you would have been allowed to stay in the Met. You would have been free of it all, up to point – so long as you said nothing and kept your mouth shut about everything you knew. It just meant you would be forced to live your life, and the rest of your career, in constant fear and paranoia. In fact, you still will, regardless. Now your name's become a target, The Cabal'll come for you and insist on making your life hell. If you let me go, then I might be able to protect you. But if you arrest me now, there's nothing I can do for you.'

Jake opened his mouth but he couldn't think of what to say.

'If you get rid of me, Jake…' Liam continued. 'If you get me off the team, I'm not gonna be there to defend and protect you. Remember that. They're ruthless, Jake – they don't care who you are, who you care about, who you love. It's a business, with each cog working as part of the machine, and at the end of the day, businesses can't have weak cogs, Jake. They simply can't.'

'Who is it, Liam? Who is The Cabal? You must know. Tell me and I can help you.'

'Like you've managed to help Bridger? Like you've managed to help Danika?'

Jake's expression dropped.

'Yeah,' Liam continued, 'I know about your conversations with them. I've got recordings of all the calls with them both, two more bent cops who you've dealt with closely in the past couple of years – just in case I needed more ammunition to add to the blackmail. And how is it going – getting them out of this corruption we're all a part of?'

'It's… I… What'll happen to them? They told me everything. They told me that you're always watching them, always listening, always following. They're frightened for their lives. When is it going to end for them?'

'Now,' Liam said bluntly, taking Jake aback. 'It's already ended. In more ways than one. They've served their purpose.'

Jake's mouth opened as he realised something. 'You killed them?'

Liam chose to ignore the question. 'Bridger is out of the equation for reasons you can't understand, I can't understand, nobody can understand. The Cabal *needs* Bridger. But the same doesn't apply to Danika. I can't guarantee she's safe. She was just a small cog, serving an important purpose. But now she's a dirty cog, messed up, someone who knows too much. Last time I checked, she was making new friends with Molly and Charlie, and some other friends called Jack. She's ruining her life at the end of the bottle, and it won't be long until she opens her filthy little mouth. But without me watching her, with me out of the picture, anything could happen to her. It could go two ways: she either tops herself, or she gets dragged back into this world as a dirty cog, which she will always be. And we know what happens to dirty cogs…'

'I can stop that from happening.'

'You don't get it, do you? It's all just paper houses. It's all part of the master plan. Everything's been calculated for. Including you.'

As soon as Liam finished, a sound erupted from behind him, followed by two armed officers clad in black vest jackets storming into the utility room.

'Armed police! Put your hands in the air!'

Liam flinched and, in that moment, dropped the gun to the floor. Before he had any time to react, it was too late. The armed officers were on him in a flash, throwing him to the floor and pinning him there, their knees resting on his back.

'Clear!' one of them cried as he finished placing handcuffs over Liam's wrists.

Next to appear in the utility room was Charlotte. She was also wearing a protective vest wrapped around her body.

'Jake, are you all right?' she asked, hurrying over to him. She stepped aside as the two armed officers carried Liam out of the house.

'I'm fine. Fine. I'm fine.'

'Come on, let's get you out of here.'

Jake turned to the kitchen door and pointed. 'Drew… what about Drew?'

'We'll get forensics in.'

Jake's body was in a state of shock. His muscles wouldn't move, and he didn't know where to look or what to think. Everything he'd just been told scared him – petrified him, even.

And there wasn't enough time for him to process it all.

'Where are we going now?' Jake asked absently, aware of the narrow patio ahead of him.

'Back to work.'

CHAPTER 94

LAUNDRY

'Where are we going?' Jake asked as he and Charlotte drove past Bow Green. It was the first time he'd spoken since entering the car. Out of choice, he'd remained quiet. He knew she had a barrage of questions that she wanted to ask him, and he knew they were necessary for the investigation, but he just needed time and quiet to allow his mind to process everything.

'My HQ.'

'What do you mean?'

'Time for you to meet the rest of the team.'

Before he knew it, Charlotte pulled off the road and into an underground car park, somewhere in the north end of London. The air down there was chilly, much colder than the air outside, and as he climbed out of the car, his body shivered. Charlotte led him to a staircase, where they climbed four flights of stairs and eventually entered into an office space. The sign on the wall told him that it had recently been let. The inside of the office was almost a carbon copy of MIT. There was an enclosed room to the right where the briefing room usually was, another smaller room on the left which would have been home to Liam's office, and the bulk of the floor space was occupied by nearly a dozen desks and computers, at least two personnel manning each.

'What is this place?' Jake asked as he scanned the surroundings, taking it all in. The men and women were dressed smartly, folders and tablets they held in their hands. The muted conversations. The furious typing. The distant sound of telephones ringing. For a moment he thought he'd entered into an alternate reality.

'Welcome to the home of Operation Jackknife…' Charlotte said as she strolled round the office.

Jake felt obliged to follow her.

'There are about fifty people working on this case right now. Everything they've been working on is here. Everything you've already given them. Everything we've managed to find ourselves.'

'But what about the call logs back at Bow Green?'

'They're in the car. I packed them already.'

'And Liam?'

'Headed towards Wembley police station. Think he's requested Rupert Haversham's services, but the solicitor's refused. We've got our investigators down there now working on him. They've taken control of the entirety of MIT. Nobody's allowed to do anything else until we say they can.'

'Like CIB back in the day.'

'Only better,' Charlotte replied.

And then a thought popped into his head. Rather, an image.

'The money,' he said to her.

'Excuse me?'

'Money. There's some in my drawer. Twenty grand. Ten from Drew, ten from Liam. They planted it there to make it look like I was bent. Just in case some of your guys find anything.'

Charlotte shot him a disapproving look that suggested she didn't believe it had been planted there, but in the end, she ceded, thanked him and told him that she would pass the message on. It was better to get it out in the open now rather than explain himself later. If only he'd done the same with certain aspects of his marriage. Directing his mind away from that, he took stock of what was happening around him, in awe of it all. At last, he felt proud of what he'd done. All these people were working on something he'd brought to their attention, working on something that wasn't completely preposterous and inconceivable.

This was all down to him.

'What now?' he asked.

'I think you and I need to have a chat.' Charlotte gestured for him to sit at a desk in the centre of the room that was in almost the exact same position as his desk in Bow Green. He wasn't sure whether it had been designed that way to inspire some sort of familiarity, or whether it was just fortuitous, but he liked it nonetheless.

As soon as they sat down, Charlotte's expression turned to resolve. 'What did Liam tell you, Jake? Did he confess? Did he kill Drew? Danny? Michael? Richard?'

'Only Drew. The killers of the rest of them are still out there. The people working with Nigel Clayton. The woman I saw in the ditch, and a man called Georgiy.'

'Did Liam say anything about him?'

Jake shook his head. 'Nothing. I just know his name's Georgiy.'

'Did he say anything else about who Georgiy might be working for, or with? Anything at all?'

'I wish he had. I didn't have enough time to get it out of him.'

'Rather that than he put a bullet in you though, eh?' Charlotte said with a smirk. Despite the severity of the situation, she still managed to find some humour in it all.

Jake tried but struggled.

Over her shoulder, a fresh-faced detective, dressed in a newly pressed designer-looking suit with not a hair out of place, approached Charlotte. He looked no older than nineteen, twenty at a push, yet he had the confidence of a detective who'd been in the service twenty years.

'Ma'am,' he said, handing her a set of folders.

Charlotte took them from him and removed the elastic band wrapped around it. 'Fancy giving me the TL-DR version?'

The young detective stood to attention, as though he'd had some form of military past. 'Certainly, ma'am. We've been unable to locate the black van that was used at Danny's and Michael Cipriano's murders.'

At the mention of the van, Jake's brow furrowed. 'Did you use the plates I gave you?'

The detective nodded. 'They were fake, as expected. Nothing's being picked up on CCTV either. But we've arrested the owner of Tyred Out Mechanics. Turns out he's been wanted for fraud for a long time. We suspect he's the one who made the number plates in the first place.'

Makes sense, Jake thought. It explained why the hooded woman had forced him to put the plates on; he was supplying them.

'What about Clayton's missing vehicle?' Charlotte asked.

'No luck there either,' the young officer said.

'Have you got any good news for me?'

The young man gave her a thumbs up. 'Memory stick, ma'am. It was found on Nigel Clayton's body when they lifted him out of the car wreckage.'

'And?' Jake asked.

'We're going through it now.'

Jake leapt out of his seat and followed the detective to another desk in the far corner of the room, with Charlotte in tow. The occupant of the desk was introduced as Steve – a man whose fuzzy black hair and sideburns looked like a badger's, and whose slightly bulging stomach belied the rest of his body, which suggested he was physically fit.

Jake and Charlotte joined the young detective behind Steve and watched his movements on the screen.

'It's packed with documents,' Steve said, his eyes moving rapidly across the screen.

'Any viruses?' Charlotte asked.

'Checked it twice. Clean. Only glitchy thing on there was a corrupted file. Other than that, we're free as a bird.'

Steve clicked the mouse and moved deeper into the USB memory stick. A list of seven folders appeared. Jake scanned the first two, and then his eyes fell on the bottom folder. Written in capital letters was: insurance package.

'That one.' Jake pointed at it. 'That's the one we want.'

Steve did as instructed. Inside the folder was a series of documents. Photographs. Microsoft Word files. Excel. PDFs. But most importantly – and the one that stuck out to Jake – there was an MP4 video file sitting at the bottom. After following Jake's instruction again, Steve played the video, raising the volume on the computer.

Immediately, Nigel Clayton's face occupied the screen. He was holding a phone or a video camera to his bedraggled, unkempt face and speaking into it.

'My name is Nigel Clayton,' he said, starting his monologue. 'But, chances are, if you've found this then you already know that. Depending on who you are, I'd imagine something bad has happened to me. Or, if it hasn't already, then it probably will. For a long time, I've been working with a group of Russian and Eastern European contract killers. Their names will be infamous and well known to any in law enforcement tasked with finding them. Not least the most influential in this group, the leader, who calls himself The Farmer. Real name, Georgiy Ivanov. The man's a narcissist, professional and there's no target too big.

'Next on the list we have Vitaly "The Lion" Antonov, but nobody calls him that. Big brute of a man. Dopey, young, learning the ropes with Georgiy at the helm. Only a matter of time until they either join forces permanently or go their separate ways, either amicably or not.

'And then, finally, we have Tatiana. Tatiana Malkovich. Honestly… I don't know what she's here for. She brings nothing to the table, but she's good with her feet and good with her tongue. I'm sure she's managed to wriggle herself out of a handful of difficult situations with Georgiy in the past. There's got to be some reason why she's still here.'

Nigel paused a second and stared into the camera lens. It was like he was looking right at Jake, blaming him for his death.

'The rest of the information you need on any of these individuals is in these files. Do with them what you will, but if you try to delete them, I have copies. And copies of copies. And so on.

'I'm making this because I fear for my life. For the past few years, I've been the group's accountant, helping them launder money into the economy via a series of successful businesses. But things have escalated. They've started asking me to join them on their contracts. I have no idea what I'm doing; I'm just an accountant. This isn't what I signed up for. And now I'm afraid that, if I leave, they'll kill me. I know too much. I've seen too much. I'm a problem for them. And I don't want that. So if anything does happen to me, I want this to be found, so that they can be caught. The truth will out.'

The video stopped, and Jake, Charlotte, Steve and the young detective with them were stunned into silence. And then a flurry of activity broke out. Charlotte leapt out of her chair and started to bark orders around the office, Steve removed the memory stick and hurried to the head of the room, the young detective disappeared down a corridor and dived into another room. Meanwhile, Jake sat there, devoid of any thought, staring at the black screen that had, moments ago, held Nigel Clayton's face. Jake didn't know why he couldn't move. Perhaps it was the shock of it. Perhaps it was the excitement that they finally had a lead. Or perhaps it was the realisation that he had been right all this time; Nigel had been a cog in The Cabal's machine, along with The Farmer and the others.

In the end, he determined it was all of them.

'I want all the information we have on each of these three individuals ASAP!' Charlotte ordered the officers scurrying around her. She was standing at the head of the office. There were windows either side of her, but immediately behind her was a projector screen, with Steve setting up the projector in front of her. The beam of light shone on half her face. 'I want somebody to check the rest of the files and let me know what's in them.'

Within minutes, it was done. The projector had been set up and was now showing the list of folders on the screen. Officers were around their desks, scanning through the information in the memory stick's files, absorbing it. And Jake watched in awe at the efficiency of it all.

'This must be what it's like in a well-oiled team,' Jake said to her as she hurried across to him.

'One of *my* teams,' she said, placing a hand on his forearm. 'Don't worry, I'm sure you'll get to experience what that's like soon enough.'

Just as Jake opened his mouth to respond, a voice cried from the other side of the office.

'Ma'am,' a female officer with short, vibrant red hair shouted. 'In here it says they've got three hideouts.'

'Where?'

'One for each kill.'

'Where?'

'A nightclub. A mobile phone shop. And a launderette.'

'In that order?

'Yes.'

'And the addresses?'

'All on this document.'

'Bring it up,' she said, and a second later, it was displayed on the projector.

Jake and Charlotte moved to the middle of the room, focusing their eyes on the pixelated text in front of them.

The nightclub. They'd had no idea about that. But they did the mobile phone shop – they'd been there the previous night and there had been no sign of The Farmer or his associates. But at least they were on the right track.

In that order... one, two, three in total... Danny... Richard... Michael...

'They're in the launderette,' Jake said aloud.

'We'll deploy tactical firearms units to the locations now.'

Charlotte moved across the room and grabbed a set of car keys. As she hurried back to

Jake, she called to someone in the office to email the street addresses to her pronto.

'Come on,' she said to him, jingling the keys in her hands, a pleasant smile on her face. 'Let's go find them, shall we?'

CHAPTER 95

FIVE MINUTES

'Are you sure you felt a pulse?' Tatiana asked from the other side of the room.

'Yes. You don't trust me?' Vitaly replied, standing in the doorway stubbornly with his arms folded. 'It was there. I'm certain.'

Word had got around to them that Pete Garrison was still alive, albeit in a coma, breathing through a tube in a hospital bed, attached to a machine. Bad news, in short. And it meant that they now needed a contingency plan. If, at any point, Garrison woke up, he'd come for them. And he'd be able to finish them off, especially with the information he had on them.

'Can we not get him first?' Georgiy asked as he clawed at the frayed fabric on the arm of the chaise sofa. 'We send Tat into hospital. Pull out plug.'

Tatiana shifted uncomfortably on the sofa opposite. The three of them were upstairs in the attached accommodation above the launderette, their third money laundering business. The constant, monotonous din of the washing machines they'd put on to keep up appearances echoed through the building and vibrated the floor and walls. By now, though, Georgiy had grown accustomed to it, and, oddly, it soothed him, helped him relax and clear his mind. He should have been angry, furious – at Vitaly for not killing Garrison. But he wasn't, because the options were simple: kill him or run.

'I don't like that idea,' Tatiana said, her eyes bouncing between Georgiy and Vitaly. 'It's too dangerous. They have cameras everywhere. I will be seen for sure.'

'Maybe we get Vitaly to do it. As sacrifice,' Georgiy said.

'Sacrifice. For what?'

'For not kill him in first place.' He leant forward and picked up the fluff that had fallen onto the floor and balled it in his hands. 'You make mistake. Mistakes not good. Nigel makes mistakes…'

He hoped Vitaly understood what he was talking about.

Vitaly's expression told him that he did. 'I… I won't make mistake again…'

Before any of them could respond, a mobile phone rang. It was the only item on the coffee table in the centre of the room, and it shook violently as the call came through, the small screen illuminating with an unknown number.

Georgiy inched forward slowly. He didn't recognise the number. Nor was he expecting any calls.

He reached for the device and answered, holding his breath.

'Get out,' came a deep voice. 'They're onto you. They know everything. Who you are, your names, dates of birth. Your hideouts. Everything. You have five minutes to pack everything and go, otherwise, armed officers are coming for you. *Get out*.'

CHAPTER 96

SQUARE ONE

The laundrette was stationed in the middle of a row of houses. As part of the decor, a large washing machine dangled a few feet above the shop floor, buried into the brick. It hung precariously on the building and looked like the smallest gust of wind would be strong enough to knock it onto the ground. It was a miracle it had ever been approved. The surrounding bricks were grey and decrepit, while the windows were made from wood, now riddled with rot. On first impression, the building appeared disused, and as though it had been that way for some time.

'Paper houses…' Jake whispered as he stared up at the building, not realising he'd said it loud enough for Charlotte to hear. They were inside her car, and a few hundred yards away was a blacked-out ARV, where five members of SO19, from the Metropolitan Police's tactical firearms team, were stationed.

'It all comes crumbling down now,' Charlotte replied.

The radio on the dashboard bleated. 'This is victor-bravo-four-one, checking comms, over.'

They listened intently.

'Victor-bravo-four-one, receiving you loud and clear, from OFC, we are state amber. Prepare for state red on my command.' Then, a few seconds later. 'All victor bravo units, state red, state red.'

At once, the rear doors of the van burst open, and a flurry of armed officers erupted from within, spilling onto the concrete in perfect formation and sprinting towards the launderette. The last thing Jake and Charlotte heard, before they disappeared inside the building, were the customary shouts of 'Armed police!'

Jake watched and waited for a few anxious moments, the tension palpable and thick inside the car. Silence filled the air as the officers' cries disappeared into the building with them, but it was soon replaced by the sound of their succinct and authoritative reports coming from the radio on the dashboard.

'Bottom floor – clear!'

'Top floor – clear!'

'Bedroom – clear!'

Jake sighed dejectedly. He didn't even need to be there with them to know that they'd lost Georgiy. The strategic firearms commander confirmed his suspicions a minute later.

'They've been tipped off,' Jake said to Charlotte as they exited the car and moved across to the launderette's entrance.

The scene of crime officers that Charlotte had requested were in the middle of setting up their stations inside the building, and uniformed officers were cordoning off the street. For the foreseeable future, the launderette was now their playground.

'How can you be sure?' Charlotte asked.

'I can't. But my intuition is telling me that they must have been. Can we get Steve or someone to find all the phones that pinged in this area over the last twelve hours and see where they are now?'

Charlotte shrugged, non-committal. 'He could, but it won't give us anything accurate.'

'It'll be enough.'

Jake and Charlotte found themselves a forensic oversuit each, complete with overshoes, hood, gloves and face mask. As soon as they were dressed, they wasted no time in hurrying into the launderette.

As Jake entered, surrounded by the washing machines and tumble driers and racks of clothes and the smell of laundry detergent, visceral, vivid images of Drew flashed into his mind, paralysing him. The blood. The brain matter. The bones. The body slumped to the side. Jake retched beneath the heat of the forensic suit.

'You good?' Charlotte asked, noticing his discomfort.

'Fine,' he lied, swallowing the bile back down. 'I'll just be glad when this is all over.'

From the look in her eyes, he could tell that she was thinking the exact same thing as him: *if* this was over any time soon.

After quickly scanning the launderette itself – and deciding there was nothing of significance or importance – they ran upstairs to what appeared to be living quarters. Completely abandoned. The landing was empty, the kitchen cupboards and fridge were devoid of any signs of life, as were the bathroom and the bedrooms. But it was the living room that intrigued Jake and Charlotte most.

On the left was a sofa, buried deep in the corner of the room, beside it a cabinet – empty. In the opposite corner was a television, on standby. And on the right-hand side of the room was another sofa, this one in the shape of an L.

Jake sniffed. Another aroma – aside from the scent of laundry detergent – pervaded the air. And Jake's senses.

'You smell that?' he asked.

'What?'

Jake hurried around the room, searching for the source of the smell. He found it, hidden behind the chaise sofa.

'Bleach,' he said as he held the supermarket branded bottle in the air.

Charlotte folded her arms across her chest, then rubbed her forehead with the back of her hand. 'I bet this place has never been so clean…'

'Brilliant,' he said, shooting daggers at the bleach bottle. 'Now we're back to square one… square fucking one.'

CHAPTER 97

WAIT

Jake slumped into the first chair he could find in the satellite office, dejected.

They'd raced back as soon as they'd checked over the property and realised there was nothing of any interest. At least, that they could see. The minuscule levels of detail were up to forensics now, who, with any luck, would be able to find something microscopic they could use as evidence against Georgiy or Vitaly or Tatiana.

But that wasn't much use to Jake and the team now. They still didn't know where Georgiy had run off to.

'What have we got, people?' Charlotte asked as she moved towards the head of the room. As she arrived, a figure stepped out from beneath the shadows and pulled her into the corner of the floor.

Jake watched her go and then tilted his head back in a half-hearted attempt to fit the final pieces of the puzzle in place.

Think, he told himself. Think think think.

And so he did, starting to run through the events and information he knew, focusing on the facts.

Danny Cipriano was dead. Killed in the middle of the night after being abducted from witness protection. Murder pinned on Richard Maddison, now deceased. Suicide, allegedly. Nigel Clayton confirmed as being there. Now also deceased. And then there was Garrison and Drew. Garrison had been working with Georgiy closely, pulling the strings. But he was now in a coma, so he was useless. As for Drew? Dead. Also useless.

It rapidly became apparent to Jake that the number of people who knew anything about The Farmer and his associates was low – almost none.

Except… there was *one* other.

Jake jumped out of his chair and hurried across to Charlotte, who had just finished speaking with the figure.

'Jake, perfect timing,' she said, gesturing to the man beside her. 'This is my handler. DCS Dremel.'

Jake shook the ginormous hand of the equally ginormous man; he was nearly twice the height of Jake and only marginally wider. His hair was fire-red, and he had the grip of someone who'd been a fireman in a former life – someone who'd spent a life hefting heavy objects.

'Pleasure to meet you, Jake,' Dremel said, bowing his head slightly. 'I've heard a great many things about you. The work you've done on this investigation has been a true test of your abilities.'

'Well, thanks…' Jake said, trying not to come off as obnoxious and rude. He just hated accepting praise. Always had. Always would.

'What did you want, Jake?' Charlotte asked.

'Isaac Dawes.'

'I need a little more than that.'

'The witness protection officer in charge of Danny and Michael Cipriano.'

'What about him?'

'He's in on it all.' Jake swallowed and kept his focus on Charlotte as he spoke. 'He handed Danny over to The Farmer on the night that he was killed, and he was there when I went to speak to Michael, moments before Michael was abducted and driven off the road.' Jake paused to catch his breath. 'He must know something about them… But… But…'

'What is it?' Charlotte asked. Her hand reached towards his but then she stopped herself.

'After Michael was shoved into the back of the police car, Isaac came running over to me…' Jake sighed and hung his head low. 'Frantic, afraid. But he didn't know anything about what was happening to Michael. It was all set up without him. So I don't know if he'll know where The Farmer is… but it's a start.'

Charlotte placed a hand on his shoulder. 'Don't beat yourself up. This is the kind of information we need. This is good.'

She paused and turned her attention to a DC who was working in the background. 'Isaac Dawes,' she told the officer. 'Witness protection scheme officer. Get him in custody. Let's see if he can tell us anything about The Farmer and Danny's and Michael's murders.'

The DC leapt out of his chair, grabbed his things and left the room.

As soon as he was gone, Charlotte turned her attention back to Jake.

'How's Liam doing?' Jake asked.

'Quiet,' Dremel responded. 'Not saying a word about anything to anyone. Is there anything else he might have told you that you've forgotten or can't remember?'

Jake wracked his brains, hating the feeling of being under some sort of time pressure to work it out.

'No,' he said eventually. 'I've told you everything.'

'Is there anything else about Drew's murder that seems odd or strange to you?' Dremel asked, pulling Jake's mind out of The Farmer investigation and dropping him into Drew's murder.

He didn't appreciate it, but as he thought about it, the more it made sense.

Maybe, just maybe, the two of them could be connected somehow.

'Yes,' he replied. 'There is.' Before he gave Dremel a chance to reply, he launched a barrage of questions at Charlotte. 'Are we tracking the mobile numbers on the call logs we got from Liam's and Drew's mobiles?'

'Yes.'

'How are we getting along? Any numbers that are on the move?'

She shook her head. 'A lot of them have been disconnected and are no longer active according to the service providers.'

Jake nodded, his mind free-falling down a mountain of ideas. 'What about Drew's mobile number… has anyone tracked that? Did anyone trace his whereabouts last night before he died?'

'What significance does that have? Liam murdered him in his home,' Dremel added, weighing in on the conversation.

'One minute, sir.' Jake waved his finger in the air. His mind was working overtime and he needed to say his piece first. 'It didn't strike me before, but now it's beginning to make some sense. Liam said that Drew was a liability, a lost cause. That he'd taken the piss too many times before, and that he'd gone too far this time round. At first, I thought it was about the rape investigation against Hannah Bryant, but it wasn't. Liam mentioned something about Drew trying to get out of the country. And he was with us all of yesterday afternoon in the station, so the only time he would have been able to do it was in the evening, shortly before he was killed.'

Jake hesitated a moment as he waited for Charlotte and Dremel to catch up. 'So Liam must have found out, travelled to his house, waited for him and killed him. I was outside Liam's house the whole night, and I didn't see him once until *after* he'd killed Drew. Someone must have tipped him off.'

'Who?'

'I don't know. But Drew must have had himself an insurance package of his own. He couldn't leave the country with his current identity… he'd never be able to outrun it. He'd already seen what happened to Garrison – he was afraid the same thing would happen to him.'

'So he potentially had a contact sort him out a new identity, new details…' Charlotte said, her eyes widening as they quickly got on the same wavelength.

'Exactly… and he must have met up with them in the afternoon. Someone saw him, who then tipped off Liam, and then he went home to his death.'

Charlotte skipped past him and paced towards Steve in the centre of the room. She spoke hurriedly with him and then waved Jake over.

'Steve already had a quick look,' Charlotte explained as he loaded up software on his computer.

A map of Stratford appeared on the screen, complete with road markings, railway lines, places of interest and traffic lights. Three large circles, representing local telecommunications pylons, appeared in the top, right and left. In the epicentre of where the three overlapped was a small dot. Steve pointed to it.

'That's roughly where Drew's phone pinged on the local transmitters.'

'How accurate?'

'Given there are a lot more phone towers in the area than in the middle of nowhere, the area's roughly a half mile wide.'

'Brilliant,' Jake said.

Now they had the location, they homed in on sourcing Drew's whereabouts on the night he'd died using the CCTV in the area. It took them forty-five minutes to find him, and forty-five seconds to realise who the contact was.

On the screen, they watched Drew's car pull out of a multi-storey car park behind another one. The first car made a left turn at the junction, while Drew turned right. The CCTV footage was filmed from such an angle that they saw the entrance to the multi-storey, as well as the convenience store beside it. And, more importantly, the Russian contract killer standing in front of it.

'Contact the owner,' Jake said, speaking to no one, yet hoping someone would follow his orders. 'Request the CCTV footage from inside the shop; find out what he purchased.'

Someone, somewhere in the office was put to the task. They came back with the results half an hour later.

'Six SIM cards,' said the officer who'd been sent to check. 'Vodafone. All unregistered, pay as you go.'

'And…' Jake said impatiently. He'd been forced to wait an infuriatingly long time.

'Putting a trace on them all now, assuming they're live.'

'How long's that going to take?'

The officer checked her watch. 'Maybe an hour.'

Jake puffed out a lot of air and paced about the room. There was nothing left for him to do now except wait.

CHAPTER 98

MISTAKE

Georgiy didn't like to live with regrets. Regrets implied mistakes. Mistakes implied weak character. Weak character implied failure.

And yet, here he was, sitting in a safe house in the middle of nowhere, a living, breathing, walking failure.

It was a mistake to bring Nigel into the business.

It was a mistake to trust Vitaly again.

It was a mistake to get close to Tatiana.

It was a mistake to think he could build a group of contract killers.

'How long we have to be here?' Vitaly asked as he paced across the dining room.

'Until we know is safe…' Georgiy replied. His eyes fell on Tatiana, who was leaning against the dinner table, playing with her fingers.

Georgiy pulled himself away from the window and sat beside her. 'How you say you find this place?'

They were in Tatiana's hideout, an abandoned detached house just on the outskirts of the Hatfield Forest in Hertfordshire, east of the M11. Surrounded by a picket fence that was their only form of protection, they were isolated. It was the place she'd told them about moments before they'd been forced to leave the launderette. Initially, she'd been shy on the details, but now they were alone and in the security of the property, it was time for her to explain herself.

'I told you…' Tatiana said, a lump catching in her throat. 'Nigel helped me set it up. He told me… if I ever needed an escape, an insurance package, this should be it.'

'Insurance package?'

'You know… if something ever happened. If I ever needed to *get away*. If something happened to you guys.'

Georgiy looked deeply into her cavernous dark eyes, which seemed to consume all light that fell into them. He'd loved those eyes once, shared secrets with them, trusted them. But now, there was nothing. They were innocuous, inanimate objects. As was she.

Regardless of how much she told him, he took it all with a pinch of salt. For a few months now they'd been close. In fact, more than close. Lovers. They'd shared everything with one another, and he'd allowed her into his mind – an alien sensation he'd only just had the courage to allow her. But she'd lied to him, betrayed him, kept secrets from him.

He was determined to find out whether this was the only one.

'How long you have place?' he asked.

She broke eye contact and played with her hands again. 'A couple of months.'

'And you not tell me.'

'Clayton told me not to.'

As she said it, there was a slight change in her voice. At first, Georgiy didn't recognise it, but it sounded like there was a break in her accent, a falter in her speech.

'You wouldn't lie, would you?'

'No! Of course not!' She placed a hand on his knee. 'You know I wouldn't.'

There it was again. The break in her voice. The dropping accent. A thin English tone breaking through.

Georgiy placated her with a smile and then stood, returning to the window. He cast his gaze out onto the blackness before him, save for the dull glow of the moon breaking through the veil of clouds that hung over the countryside. He cast his mind back to the moment he'd found Tatiana. How they'd bumped into one another in the train station as he was on his way to a target. How she'd been on the same carriage as him. How they'd caught each other's eyes. How he'd known then, straight away, that she wasn't what she seemed.

Tatiana had been hired to kill him. There was an aggrieved former customer who he'd let down, and they'd sent Tatiana to finish him off. But, after some gentle persuasion with his mouth – both in and out of the bedroom – she'd ignored the hit and decided to join forces with him. Their relationship had started there, and it had never really ended.

Until now.

He was beginning to feel like everything she'd ever told him was a lie. He'd allowed himself to be blinded by a feeling he'd sworn he would never succumb to.

Her voice. Her accent. It was fake. Not Ukrainian like she claimed it to be. It was British, English. And she was an undercover agent.

Tatiana – if that was her real name – rose from the chair, its legs scraping against the stone tiles, and moved out of the room. Georgiy's gaze followed her. As soon as she was out of the room, he bounded across the kitchen and grabbed Vitaly's arm, tugging at his sleeve.

'Give gun, now.'

'Why?'

Vitaly took too long. Georgiy reached for the man's armpit and yanked the Glock free from his shoulder holster. Using his free hand, Georgiy stifled his cousin, who'd just opened his mouth to protest, then followed Tatiana into the living room.

He found her with her back turned to him, staring out of the bay windows, hands in front of her.

'What you do?' he asked as he entered, gripping the weapon, keeping it concealed. For now. 'Who you work for?'

Tatiana didn't answer.

'Who you work for?'

Still nothing.

'I know you undercover. Who you work for? The Cabal?'

Nothing.

'The Cabal make you work against me?'

Tatiana turned to face him. In her hand, she held a mobile phone. From his position, he saw that a call had connected. He didn't know who it was to, but he didn't need to.

Tatiana had just called in backup. They were closing in around him. And, situated in the middle of nowhere, there was no way out.

Georgiy raised the gun in the air, aimed the muzzle between those once-perfect eyes of hers and pulled the trigger.

CHAPTER 99

LAWYER

For half an hour, Jake and Charlotte, along with the operational firearms commander and his team, consisting of ten men, had been lying flat on a damp mound of earth in the middle of nowhere, attentively watching the desolate and abandoned house, water seeping through their clothing.

Steve, back at the satellite office, had been tracking the mobile numbers purchased by Vitaly at the convenience store the other night. And the number – only one of them was on for now, while another dropped in and out of service – had led them there.

Jake could see them through the windows of the house. Moving, talking. Through his binoculars, they looked anxious, agitated, like they knew they were being followed. Like they knew the rope was tightening around their necks.

Jake recognised Vitaly from the CCTV footage. He was a broad man, barely older than himself, with black hair that was beginning to grey on the sides. All the stress of killing people, Jake wondered.

Vitaly was standing by the window, gazing out at the surroundings. Jake and the rest of the team relaxed in the knowledge that they were barely visible in the pitch black. Thick, fathomless clouds loomed overhead, gradually diminishing the stars and moon from view; their cars were hidden half a mile down the road, and none of them wore reflective clothing. Besides, if it came to a shootout, Jake was just grateful that they had some of the Met and Hertfordshire Police's best firearms officers with them.

Sitting at the table, in a muted discussion, were Georgiy and Tatiana. Georgiy was sitting with his back to Jake. He zoomed in on Tatiana's face. He didn't know why, but she looked afraid, pensive – almost as if she was being held there against her will.

A second later, feedback sounded on the radio between him and Charlotte. It was quiet, barely audible.

‘All units report…’ came the static voice of the operational firearms commander, the officer in charge of making sure the strategy was in place.

‘Victor-five – in position.’

‘Victor-one – confirmed.’

‘Victor-two – in position.’

‘Victor-three – eyes on.’

‘Confirmed. All units in position.’

Adrenaline surged through Jake’s body as he heard those words, dominating the chill that was beginning to settle into his stomach and thighs. A light rain – the drizzly kind that seems to linger in the air as though it’s part of the atmosphere – had started the moment they arrived and was showing no signs of abating. Surrounding them was silence, save for the sound of his own breath, the gentle rustle of the blades of grass moving as the wind carried them, and the rain. He turned his attention back to the binoculars. Soon, he told himself. Soon, this’ll all be over.

Except for The Cabal, his raison d’être – the entire purpose of his career in the police, he’d decided.

As Jake pressed the binoculars against his face, he noticed something was wrong. Tatiana was out of her seat, heading into the other room, and then Georgiy was accosting Vitaly, reaching inside his pocket, pulling out…

It was a gun. A Glock.

Georgiy concealed the weapon against his leg and followed Tatiana into the living room. Her chest was illuminated, a bright shade of blue coming from her mobile, her face wracked with nerves.

'Something's happening,' Jake said, clawing for Charlotte along the grass. 'He's… he's got a gun.'

Jake couldn't tear his eyes from the action yet he needed to find the radio to alert the officers. Discarding the binoculars momentarily, he ran his hands through the blades of grass either side of him – the way he did through Elizabeth's hair when she was sat in front of him while they were watching the TV – but he couldn't find it.

'Charlotte! Charlotte!' he whispered. She was on her front, peering through her binoculars still, transfixed. 'Charlotte, where's the—?'

A single gunshot boomed, echoing through the house and around the undulating hills of the countryside.

Before Jake had time to acknowledge what had happened, two more rounds were fired. Three. Four. Followed by the devastating sound of petrified screams and the splintering noise of glass smashing.

Panicked, disorientated by the piercing sounds reverberating around his skull and knocking out his equilibrium, Jake fumbled for the binoculars again. He was just quick enough to see Tatiana standing there at the window, surrounded by the armed officers. Beyond her, Georgiy was being thrown to the coffee table in the middle of the room, his face pinned down onto the wood. To the left of Tatiana, by the entrance to the kitchen, was Vitaly, slumped, a streak of blood above him, staining the white door.

Jake blinked as he tried to work out what had happened. How could Vitaly die if he hadn't been the one holding the gun?

And then he remembered. Just as he'd lowered the binoculars, he'd seen Vitaly heading for the kitchen, out of the corner of his eye. He must have tried to get his weapon back from Georgiy – perhaps there had been a scuffle – and then the armed officers had shot the man with the gun. But he'd have to wait for the final report.

As Jake let out a sigh of relief, static came over the radio. He lowered the binoculars and looked at the communications device in Charlotte's hand. She was climbing to her feet and speaking into the microphone.

'House safe and secure. One fatality. Two in custody.'

Charlotte acknowledged receipt of the transmission and turned to Jake as she lowered the microphone to her side.

'It's over, Jake,' she said, touching his arm and wiping an insect away from his shoulder. 'You've done it.'

Jake wasn't convinced. Sure, he'd uncovered one aspect of The Cabal's corruption within the police, but he was beginning to get the impression that Liam, Drew, Garrison, The Farmer, Bridger, Michael, Danny… they were all just very small cogs in a very large machine.

It was up to Jake to break it.

A minute later, Jake and Charlotte were standing by the police van that had been brought in to transport the offenders back to the station. It hadn't taken long for the rest of the police force to arrive – the emergency responders who were in the middle of helping set up the cordon, and the forensics squad who were in the middle of donning their protective gear just as the firearms team returned with Tatiana and Georgiy locked tightly in their grips.

'Get off me!' the woman screamed, wriggling, her arms pinned behind her back. 'You don't know who you're dealing with.'

A firearms officer hefted the woman into the back of the police van and threw her onto the seat. A few feet behind her was Georgiy. He seemed more reserved, more relaxed, as though he was already beginning to figure out an escape plan in his head. Jake hoped that wasn't the case.

'Lawyer. I want lawyer,' said Georgiy.

Jake smirked. 'Let me guess... Rupert Haversham?'

CHAPTER 100

NAMES

The four of them were finally seated around the table in the interview room at Loughton police station, on the inside track of the M25. Jake, Charlotte, Georgiy, and Rupert. Four hours had elapsed since Georgiy and Tatiana had been arrested, and the majority of that time had been spent trying to find Rupert Haversham. But now that they were all there, Jake was relieved they could finally begin.

He got the formalities out of the way as quickly as possible. They were well into the early hours of the morning by now, he still hadn't slept, and it didn't look like they'd be finishing any time soon – they'd be lucky if they could submit to the Crown Prosecution Service by the end of the day.

'Tell me, Georgiy,' Jake started, 'what do you know about Danny and Michael Cipriano?'

'No comment.'

'And what's your relationship with Pete Garrison?'

'No comment.'

'Drew Richmond?'

'No comment.'

'Liam Greene.'

'No comment.'

'Do you know anyone at all?'

'No comment.'

'Were you hired to kill any of these individuals?'

'No comment.'

'Right.'

Jake turned to Charlotte. This was going to be harder than he'd originally thought. It was clear to see Haversham's tactic of staying silent was working out. Both he and Charlotte had allowed him some time to speak with Georgiy before the interview – they were forced to do everything to the letter of the law when it came to Rupert; the man's reputation preceded him, and he was able to find the smallest of gaps in the truth, the smallest of holes in the procedure that may have been overlooked.

'Georgiy...' Charlotte began. 'We have evidence of phone calls made to and from your mobile by a non-registered number that was being used by DCI Liam Greene. We also have the recordings of these calls. We've also traced the unregistered mobile number that you've been using, and it puts you in the exact location of Danny Cipriano's and Richard Maddison's deaths. What do you have to say about that?'

'No comment.'

'Will you be answering any of our questions today?' Jake asked.

'He is answering them,' Rupert interjected. 'He's just not giving you the answers you want to hear.'

Jake offered a forced grin to Haversham. 'Right. Fine. I think that concludes everything for now.'

Jake reached across the table to terminate the interview, but then he hovered his finger over the button. An idea had popped into his mind. 'I was… I was wondering whether you would be able to answer me this. Does the name The Cabal ring any bells to you?'

Georgiy reacted the way Jake had expected: obstinate, defiant, the same way he'd reacted to all the other names. But it was really Rupert's expression Jake was looking for. The man might have been a highly successful criminal defence lawyer with an ability to lie his way through court, but he wasn't a very good poker player.

And that told Jake everything he needed to know.

Jake terminated the interview and stood up to leave.

'Thank you both for your time.' He nodded at Haversham and then turned his attention to Georgiy. 'I'm sure we'll be back again very soon.'

They left the interview room in silence. As soon as the door closed behind him, Jake clenched his fist and smacked it against the wall in a flurry of anger.

'What're you doing?' Charlotte asked.

'It's a waste of time. I don't think he's gonna tell us anything.'

'At least he's on the other side of that wall instead of being out there where he can hurt someone else.'

Jake shrugged. 'Try to put whatever positive spin on it you want. We're still no closer to finding out who The Cabal is.'

'We'll get there. Trust me, we'll get there.'

'How?'

Charlotte looked up and down the corridor, opened the door nearest to them and pushed him inside. They were in the men's toilets, and before she spoke, Charlotte checked all of the cubicles. Once she deemed that they were the only ones in there, she spoke.

'I've been thinking recently.'

'Yeah?'

'My career. Maybe it's time to change. What do you say about me joining MIT? You're gonna need a pretty big rebuild. I've done some great things with the DPS, don't get me wrong. And I love the people I work with. But I can't do what I do there anymore. It's too taxing. It's too horrible. I like to think there are still some good guys left out there.'

'Does it not feel better to catch the bad ones?'

'Do you think so? I mean, here we are, having just arrested someone who's hired to kill people for money and another for being bent – and you're worried about the bigger scheme of things. Does it really feel that satisfying? There'll always be a bigger fish.'

'Paper houses,' Jake whispered. 'A few sheets have fallen but the house still stands. I'm gonna burn it to the ground. Until there's nothing left.'

The door opened and a uniformed officer entered. The man froze, stunned at the female presence in the men's bathroom. Before the door closed, Jake told him to get out. The man did, sharpish.

'Coffee?' Charlotte asked. 'My treat.'

'Kill for one,' Jake replied. 'I suppose maybe I could get used to having you around the office more often.'

'If that's going to be the case, then there's something else you should probably know.'

'What's that?'

'My real name. It's not Charlotte. It's Stephanie.'

CHAPTER 101

BLOOD MONEY

Later that day, at some point in the afternoon – he didn't know when; his internal body clock was completely off – Jake drove home in silence, preparing himself for what was about to come his way. Overthinking was an understatement. He wondered what Elizabeth was going to say when he returned. How much Liam had told her. How much she'd believed. How much she'd argued, and protested that Jake wasn't capable of having an affair, of doing any of the things Liam had accused him of.

A part of him wanted the drive to take longer, for him to be delayed in traffic, caught behind a tractor in the middle of the A222. Something that would delay the inevitable. But, sadly, there was nothing, and by the time he pulled up to his house, the journey had taken him just under an hour.

He killed the engine, grabbed his bag and then wandered up to the front door. He was welcomed by silence as he stepped inside. He felt like a stranger in his own home, breaking in to ransack the place.

'Hello?' he called, the walls absorbing his voice. 'Liz? Maisie? Ellie?'

Nothing.

'Anyone?'

He idled down the hallway, peered into the living room on his left, saw nobody was there, then continued through to the kitchen at the end of the hall. The kitchen had been cleaned, but there was no sign of a note or anything.

At that moment, Jake feared the worst.

Liam. The man had set foot in his house. He'd shown Elizabeth all those photos. But what if he'd sent in Georgiy shortly after? What if they'd abducted Elizabeth and the girls? Or worse, what if they'd killed them and left them somewhere?

Panicked by his imagination, he tried calling his wife's mobile. It rang and rang. Rang and rang.

He disconnected the call before it went through to voicemail and tried again.

Still no answer.

Jake paced clockwise around the centre island, clenching his fist in anger and fear. It was possible she just hadn't heard her phone, but he didn't believe that. And if she hadn't been taken, there was only one other option.

He moved to the fridge, grabbed Elizabeth's address book from the pile of papers beside it and found his mother-in-law's landline number. Martha and Alan Clarke were adamant at keeping their details private and making sure there was no digital copy of their phone number or address. Something about them being paranoid. A symptom of working for the government, Jake had always thought.

Either way, it was less than helpful in any situation.

Eventually, he found their number, punched it into his phone and dialled.

'Hello?' Martha answered.

'Martha – it's Jake. Is Liz there… please?'

There was a long pause, and in the background, he heard distant voices and whispers, answering the question for him.

He hung up the phone, rushed out of the door and jumped back into the car. Elizabeth's parents lived less than three miles away, in a stately Victorian home in Crystal Palace. The house was detached and was the only property in the street that had a swimming pool in the back garden, which looked onto the nearby golf course.

Jake arrived at their house ten minutes later and raced to the door.

Elizabeth opened it shortly after he knocked. Her hair was tied in a ponytail and her eyes and cheeks were circled red. She was wrapped inside a sky-blue cardigan and wore a pair of jeans. Despite looking distraught, she still managed to look beautiful.

'Liz…' he said, his voice weak.

'What do you want?'

'I want… I want to talk. Can we talk?'

'You can't come in.'

'That's fine. I don't want to.' He turned and pointed behind him. 'How about we sit in the car?'

'Give me your keys.'

'What?'

'Give me your keys.'

Jake looked down at his hand and rolled his car keys in his fingers.

'Of course. Anything.'

He unlocked the car over his shoulder then passed the keys to Elizabeth, who threw them into the house. She stepped outside and closed the door behind her. Jake had never seen her look so angry. He'd originally mistaken the red for upset. They walked to the car in silence, Jake mentally trying to prepare what he was going to say, how he was going to say it. But his mind was blank.

'I'm sorry,' he started after they'd got themselves comfortable. He turned to Elizabeth, but she gave him nothing back; she twisted and looked out of the window to avoid acknowledging him. 'I'm sorry for the past couple of days. The past couple of weeks. The past couple of months. I'm sorry for being a shitty husband. For never being there. I'm sorry for being at work so much and putting that in front of you and the girls, and I'm sorry for not solving this issue any sooner. In fact, I'm sorry for not solving it at all.' He took a deep breath. 'But whatever Liam showed you was a lie. All of it. The money in my drawer. The photos of Charlotte and me in the pub.'

'Oh, so that didn't happen then?' Elizabeth snapped her head round to face him. 'Liam's a master at Photoshop now, is he?'

'No,' Jake said, sighing. 'Yes, we did go for a drink. That was the reason I came home late. But it was nothing like that – nothing like that at all. We were talking about the case. She was new to the team – she'd just joined us and I wanted to welcome her in, keep up appearances.'

'What appearances? Make it look like you were being a good friend so nobody would realise you were fucking her?'

Liam had planted a deeply rooted seed in Elizabeth's head that would take some convincing to weed out.

'I promise you, Elizabeth Tanner, that it wasn't like that at all. Far from it. What did Liam tell you?'

'I'm not telling you that. Just so you can work out how to wriggle your way out of it. And I don't wanna hear excuses either.'

'They're not excuses. I fucked up; I understand that. Honestly, I do. But it's a lot more complicated than it seems.'

'Oh, I'm sure it is.' Elizabeth folded her arms and looked away.

This was useless. He was getting nowhere.

'You want me to tell you exactly what's been going on these past few days?'

'Aren't you worried Liam might tell you off for sharing that sort of information with me?' She said it with such disdain in her voice that it made him even angrier. He knew she was lashing out at him because she was mad, but that didn't make it hurt any less.

'Liam's been arrested.'

Elizabeth's gaze darted towards him again. 'What for?' There was a new emotion in her voice.

'Lots of things. Most notably, though, for killing Drew. Shot him in the head.'

Elizabeth gasped and threw her hand to her mouth. 'When?'

'Last night.'

'Last night? Oh my God. That man... he came... came into my house... *our* house!'

Jake placed his hand on her leg. She let it stay there.

'I know,' he said. 'It's OK. He's gone now. He won't be coming anywhere near you or the girls ever again. Did he do anything while he was in the house?'

Elizabeth shook her head. 'Just came in... said hello to the girls and... showed me the photos.'

'Do you still have them?'

Elizabeth nodded. 'He left the camera at ours.'

'OK. Did he do anything else? At any point was he in a room on his own?'

'No. I was with him at all times. I watched him leave as well. He didn't do anything he shouldn't have.'

Jake absorbed what she'd said, nodding and scratching the scar on the side of his face.

'What's going on, Jake? What's going to happen?'

She placed her hand in his. He squeezed it.

'Listen, it's complicated. The short of it is, for the last fifteen years between them, Liam, Drew and Garrison have all been corrupted by an external force somehow. Liam was responsible for recruiting The Crimsons all those years ago. Drew was in on it all, and he raped an innocent girl when he was younger. And they even hired contract killers to kill the Cipriano brothers. It's all been a bit hectic. Drew… dead. Liam… arrested. And Garrison… he's in a coma. Liam and Drew tried to get rid of him by staging a car accident. There's no knowing if he'll ever wake up. And, to top it all off, they were trying to make me look bent too.'

'How?'

'Those photos. The money they planted in my drawer. They even took photos of you and the girls in the park the other day. I'm sure there're other things they've done to try and make me look like one of them. Now I've got to find out what.'

Jake paused a beat to catch his breath. 'None of what Liam showed you is true. The photo of me and Charlotte – that happened, yes, I admit that. But not in the way you think it did. I went to the DPS about Liam and Drew and Garrison.

Charlotte is an undercover officer; her real name's Stephanie. We were working together to try to expose the three of them. But we were too late to save Drew and Garrison. That's all it was, Liz. There was nothing else to it. Nothing. You have to believe me.'

Elizabeth stared at him for a while longer. Her eyes shimmered with tears, but somehow she looked even more beautiful.

'I do. I believe you. I just… I don't know what to say,' she replied. 'Why didn't you tell me all of this was going on?'

'I didn't want to worry you. I didn't want you to think I was in any danger. I wanted to make sure that you knew nothing, just in case someone used you and the girls as leverage.'

'*Were* you in any danger?' Elizabeth asked, her eyebrow raised.

Jake thought of sitting on the other side of a hedge while Michael Cipriano was being beaten to death. Of his altercation with Liam. How he'd been staring down the other end of a gun in both instances.

'No,' he lied. 'I wasn't in any danger. I just wanted to make sure you and the kids were safe.'

'We are. We can leave them with my mum and dad for a while if you want…'

'That might be for the best. I suppose the silver lining in all of this is that I'm going to get paid a lot of overtime for the month.'

'I didn't tell you!' she said, slapping his arm excitably.

'What?'

'The money. The debt. My mum and dad. They've given it to us.'

Jake opened his mouth to protest but was instantly shut down by Elizabeth.

'I know you didn't want them to, but they offered. They don't think we're charity cases. They're just helping out. Just like they did last time.'

Jake breathed a deep sigh of exultation. He couldn't deny that he was upset about having to take the money from his in-laws. Again. Nor could he deny that he was upset about his family being in this position when he was only twenty-five. If they were struggling already, what was it going to be like in five years, ten, fifteen? It didn't seem fair on the girls. But taking the money from Martha and Alan – who had plenty of it – was the most ethical means of paying their debts in comparison to the other methods he'd considered – especially as it kept him far away from the money in his drawer. A part of him had been tempted to take it. But he'd known that would be a foolish decision. It was dirty, tainted. Blood money. It would be confiscated and he would face either imprisonment or dismissal, neither of which would be good for his family.

Because at the end of the day, they were all that mattered to him.

CHAPTER 102

CONTACT

A week later they were still in the thick of it, even with all the added help from Charlotte's DPS team. The number of tasks on Jake's to-do list was growing by the hour. He hadn't spoken to anyone – whether they were his friends, family or colleagues – properly in the past few days. He hadn't been able to discuss recent events with anyone to help him process them; he'd just been instructed to focus, focus, focus.

So when his phone rang, it was a welcome distraction.

'Hello?' he answered.

'Hello, pal.' It was DS Elliot Bridger, sounding more excitable than usual. 'You good?'

'As good as I can be…'

'You heard about Danika then?'

He had. And he wished he hadn't.

A few days after Liam and Georgiy had been arrested and processed and interviewed, Jake had received a call from DCI Pemberton saying that, after a patrol vehicle had been sent to Danika's house to check up on her, they'd found her dead on the sofa. Bottle of vodka and joint beside her. Shot in the head. Suicide.

Jake didn't believe a word of it.

'It's fucked,' he replied.

'This is why I told you to watch out for yourself, kid.'

'You too,' Jake replied. 'Get out of the country. Move on. Away from everything. Start a new life away from all this shit. You know more than Danika did.'

There was a pause.

'I can't, Jake. I appreciate your efforts and your advice, but I can't. It's not that simple. There are a lot more things going on than you realise—'

'So you lied to me?' Jake interrupted. 'It is true.'

'What is?'

'Liam told me you were immune in all this. He said you would always be safe for reasons I would never understand. What are they?'

'Jake, I don't know what you're talking about.'

'Why are you still lying to me, Bridger. After all this time, after all I've proven to you. What's going on?'

Bridger paused. 'Nothing. Honestly.'

Jake shrugged. He'd gone past the point of caring now. He had no fight left in him to try to convince Bridger to flee, to put himself first, to make sure he didn't suffer the same fate as Danika. He was done with it all.

'If you won't tell me, and if you won't help me, then I can't do this anymore. Now that this is over with Liam, we're going to have to sever our ties. This has brought too much angst and destruction to my career and my family.'

'You're the one who needs to get out, Jake,' Bridger said.

'Not when I have to fix everything here. Not when The Cabal is still out there and there's a ring of corrupt officers I need to catch.'

'If you're not careful, they'll come for you like they did Danika. Don't do that to yourself. Don't do that to your family.'

'Not if I get them first.'

Jake hung up and immediately blocked Bridger's number. If he was going to go through with what he'd just said, he needed to make sure he kept to his word.

And the first step was to cut off contact.

CHAPTER 103

BRIGHT

Thirty minutes later, it was home time. At least for Jake. Dremel had allowed him to get home to the wife and kids while the rest of the detectives continued working on Operation Jackknife. After what had been a surprisingly productive and happy day, all things considered, Elliot Bridger had put a noticeable downer on it.

But Jake was determined to make sure the rest of it went smoothly, and so he forced all thoughts of Bridger from his mind.

Outside the sky was covered with a blanket of black, stars beginning to break through the material like headlights bursting through the fog. Astronomy had never been an interest for Jake, but now and then he enjoyed gazing up, contemplating life beyond earth, beyond the universe, beyond anything – what lay out there; what it would be like to spend time in space.

Sometimes the thought scared him; sometimes it put things into perspective. That no matter how bad he had it – with Elizabeth, the girls, the job – it wasn't as bad as hurtling through space. His whole world felt like it was beginning to get back on track. And he couldn't wait to see what the future held.

Coming up was a short break. A two-day holiday from everything. Just him, Elizabeth and the girls, cutting themselves off from the rest of society in the middle of the Cotswolds. Sponsored by Martha and Alan, of course. Except this time Jake had been the first to accept the money to pay for it. He'd even put his differences aside and asked whether they'd like to join them, but Martha was unable to get time off work. They'd lucked out on that one, Jake thought. He hoped that, in the countryside, he'd be able to spend more time staring up at the sky, creating scenarios in his head, manufacturing lives and stories. Maybe even tell a few of them to the girls.

Something to look forward to.

And as he skipped his way across the car park, he realised there was something else to look forward to too. A takeaway. Chinese, his favourite. This time picked up by Elizabeth, given his previous history.

A smile grew on his face as he opened the car door and climbed into the seat. But as he got himself comfortable, he noticed something wasn't right. Something was off. It was only minor, minuscule, but something seemed out of place.

He sniffed the air and relaxed as he noted there was no overwhelming smell of perfume or body odour. And then he cast his eyes around the front and back. Everything was as it should be.

For a second he considered whether he'd imagined it. But that thought disappeared as soon as his eyes fell on the glove compartment. With his body tensing, his mind conjuring images of what he might find – a severed hand, a bomb, a gun – he reached across and opened it.

The reality of it was much, much worse.

Wrapped tightly in cling film was a large wad of money and another package of white powder. Drugs.

On the money was a note. Jake leant over and read it.

WE THANK YOU FOR YOUR SILENCE.

For some reason, the stars in the night sky

didn't seem so bright anymore.

EPILOGUE

DCI Liam Greene was charged with corruption, money laundering, perverting the course of justice, malfeasance in public office and murder. He was sentenced to fifty-three years in prison. He continues his cancer treatment.

The Farmer's assets were seized and he was sentenced to life imprisonment with no chance of parole. He's staying in HMP Belmarsh.

DC Pete Garrison remains in a coma. It is not known if he will wake up and what condition he will be in if he does.

A total of ten thousand hours were spent on Operation Jackknife. The investigation lasted three months, and there were no further arrests.

Elliot Bridger is alive and well. He is retired and lives in Surrey. He enjoys playing golf.

Vitaly was killed by the armed officers. Life was pronounced extinct at the crime scene.

Tatiana's real name was Theresa Appleton. It was later revealed that she was working undercover for MI5. She has since been deployed to a new operation.

Following DS Drew Richmond's death, Hannah Bryant started an initiative where five other women came forward, all claiming to have suffered sexual assault by Drew. He was publicly named as the rapist of all the women on the list.

Police were unable to locate Isaac Dawes, the officer in charge of Danny and Michael's witness protection. His whereabouts are currently unknown.

Jake, along with Stephanie, is looking forward to meeting the next additions to the team.

The identity of The Cabal remains unknown.

Enjoy *The Confession*? You can make a big difference.

Reviews are the most powerful tools in my arsenal when it comes to getting attention for my books. They act as the tipping point on the scales of indecision for future readers crossing my books.

So, if you enjoyed this book, and are interested in being one of my committed and loyal readers, then I would really grateful if you could leave a review. Why not spread the word, share the love? Even if you leave an honest review, it would still mean a lot. They take as long to write as it did to read this book!

Thank you.

Your Friendly Author,
Jack Probyn

ABOUT JACK PROBYN

Jack Probyn hasn't experienced the world. He's never even owned a pet. But he'd like to; there's still time. His twenty-two years on the planet have been spent in the United Kingdom, with a few excursions overseas – a particular favourite of his was Amsterdam. Or Norway. Both of which were lovely.

But what Jack lacks in life-experience, he more than makes up for in creative ingenuity. His Jake Tanner series is the birth child of a sinister and twisted mind, and a propensity to assume the worst will happen in even the most mediocre situation.

Finding himself pigeon-holed as a millennial, Jack decided to stick with the stereotype and do things his own way. After all, he felt entitled and he wanted to destroy industries.

Enter: writing.

The love of writing was rekindled in Jack's life when he (briefly) entered the corporate world, and the passion snowballed from there. No more will the millennial writer find himself working 9-5, indulging in the complexities of business life, or wearing a M&S suit.

He will take the world by storm with his pen (keyboard) and his ability to entertain and enthral readers.

Why not join him (and his future dog)?

Keep up to date with Jack at the following:
- Website: https://www.jackprobynbooks.com
- Facebook: https://www.facebook.co.uk/jackprobynbooks
- Twitter: https://twitter.com/jackprobynbooks
- Instagram: https://www.instagram.com/jackprobynauthor

Lightning Source UK Ltd.
Milton Keynes UK
UKHW010749191120
373689UK00004B/668

9 781912 628513